AN *Aster Bay* NOVEL

CLAIM TO *Fame*

CARA DION

Print ISBN: 979-8-9986457-0-9
Ebook ISBN: 979-8-9882826-9-3
Imprint: Independently published

First edition

Cover designed by Stephanie Anderson at Alt 19 Creative.

For Emily

Also by Cara Dion

Love Song Series
Irreplaceable

Indiscreet

Undeniable

Aster Bay Series
Whisking It All

Just For Show

First Comes Marriage

Claim to Fame

Visit my website to learn more and download free bonus content:

Content Warning

This books contains discussions of
eating disorders, fatphobia, and pregnancy.

Chapter One

"It has to be you."

Ethan Hart took a sip of his beer and considered the woman across the booth from him. AK Wild—Angie—was one of the most successful indie romance authors on the market. She also happened to be an old friend, so when she'd called him three years ago and asked for a favor, Ethan hadn't been able to say no.

He hadn't expected that favor to take on a life of its own.

"Why me?" he asked.

"Because you're Slade Hardcastle! You're *the* voice of all my books. Why should this one be any different?" He opened his mouth to speak, but she held up her finger. "Weren't you a dragon for Halloween in first grade?"

"No."

"I distinctly remember a cardboard dragon head with construction paper flames. You were born to play this part."

"I think that's a bit of stretch," he said rolling his eyes.

"Don't pretend you don't love it. I've had three author friends contact me this week alone trying to get in touch with you for projects."

"I turned those down," he said.

"I know. You're in demand, Ethan. And I demand you narrate this book."

Ethan glanced at the excerpt Angie had handed him.

I unfurl my wings so that she may look upon them. The heat of her fingers as they trace the membrane sears through me, heating my blood. I need to claim her, to make her mine. To mark her as the dragon duke's mate.

It was a departure from Angie's typical medieval romances, and he'd be lying if he said he wasn't intrigued by the challenge of voicing a dragon...

No one back in Aster Bay knew Ethan Hart moonlighted as Slade Hardcastle, spicy romance audiobook narrator. It was his secret, and he intended to keep it that way. But with each new book he narrated, the risk of someone finding out about his alter ego grew.

"C'mon. What's a few dragon shifter sex scenes between friends?" A slow grin spread over Angie's face. "Besides, who knew your talent for accents would be so useful outside of tormenting Mrs. Kemp during history class?"

Ethan threw his head back and laughed. "That was one time."

"I'll pay double your fee," Angie said.

"It's not about the money." Though the money was nice. Ethan had been setting aside all his earnings from the audiobooks in a college fund for his granddaughter, Julie.

"Then what's the problem?"

Ethan scraped his hand over his jaw. "It's just me at the vineyard now, Ang. I bought Mom and Dad out last year so they could move into some fancy independent living facility in Florida."

"That's great."

"It is. But the vineyard is their legacy, and they built that legacy on a wholesome image. Did you know my mom used to scoop ice cream in Sugar Grapes during the summers and that's how she met my dad?"

"I did. They used to tell that story to anyone who would listen. If I didn't write historicals, I'd work it into a book somehow," Angie said, leaning back in the booth.

"Everyone knows that story, and now Nuthatch Vineyard—a place built on the idea of family—has been taken over by a single guy in his forties."

"You can't honestly be telling me you're worried about sullying the family business with my smutty books?" Angie shot him a look that said he better think carefully about his answer.

"I love your smutty books. You know that."

"Then what are you trying to say?"

"I don't know." He ran his hand over the short hair at the back of his neck and sighed. "I guess I worry about what would happen if word got out."

"If people knew the guy who ran the small-town vineyard also narrated sexy audiobooks?"

"My parents will leave behind this amazing story, one I'm proud to tell to every person who comes through the vineyard. Someday it's going to be my daughter, my granddaughter, telling that story."

"And you're not sure if you want them to tell the story of you narrating dragon shifter pleasure Doms from the old toolshed."

"More or less."

Angie considered this as she took a sip of her wine. "I don't think your problem is the dragon shifters."

"No? Then what's my problem?" he asked, grinning around his beer.

"Maybe you really are afraid of people finding out about your British alter ego and it affecting the vineyard. There's a reason I write under a pen name, so I can't judge you for that. But you're full of secrets, Ethan Hart. I have to wonder, does anyone really know you?"

He didn't know what to say. Slade Hardcastle was a mystery man with a gritty voice and a British accent, an enigma in the audiobook world since he didn't have a social media presence and only narrated for one author. He was a figment of Ethan's imagination, a cardboard cutout to conceal his true identity.

But he was also defined by the scandalous words he read, just as Ethan had been defined for much of his life by the scandals of his youth. More than that, his teenage indiscretions had been the only thing anyone in Aster Bay associated with his family for years. While he didn't regret his decisions for a second, the last thing he wanted to do was have his private choices blow back on the people he loved...again. The last time Aster Bay sank its teeth into his private life, he'd lost everything. It was too big of a risk.

"Double your fee. Think about it."

"I'll think about it," he said, his voice inexplicably hoarse.

She tilted her head at him, the move so like the girl she'd been when they were kids growing up in their small Rhode Island town. "Why do you always want to meet here?"

"I don't—"

"Every time you come to Boston, you want to meet in the same hotel bar. There's a whole city out there, but it's always here."

Ethan pressed his lips together, narrowing his eyes at Angie and her too-shrewd stare. Her gaze flickered over him, and he knew she was taking in the exact same sight she'd seen each time he'd met her. The same craft beer, the same suit that always made him feel a little ridiculous, the same hotel bar with yet another Red Sox game playing on the television mounted on the wall.

"It's tradition," he finally said.

It was true. It was all part of the ritual. Talk a little business, pretend he didn't narrate the books as much for his own enjoyment as to help out an old friend, sip his beer and act like he gave a shit about the outcome of whatever game was on the screen, ignore the way his pulse jumped every time he heard heels clicking behind him on the parquet floors.

Because Angie wasn't the only person he came to Boston to see.

Three years.

Eight meetings.

And his heart still raced at the mere idea of seeing *her* again—Hannah, the *real* reason he was in Boston.

The first time had been an accident. Or fate, depending on how you looked at it. He'd been in town to meet Angie and discuss the very first audiobook he recorded for her. He hadn't intended to meet another woman—a woman who'd crawl under his skin like the heroines in the romances he narrated, entire clans of highlanders worshipping at their feet.

"You and your traditions," Angie said with a shake of her head. "Is that why Michael and I can never convince you to join us on Martha's Vineyard?"

Ethan smiled, some of the tension easing from their shoulders. "No, that's because your husband snores so loud it shakes the whole cottage. And Martha's Vineyard is overrated."

"I'm telling him you said that."

"About his snoring? Go ahead."

"No, about the Vineyard."

"Excuse me, sir," the bartender said, setting another beer in front of Ethan. "From the woman at the end of the bar." He tilted his head towards the woman in question and Ethan's heart hammered in his chest. How had he missed her coming in? "She said to give you this."

Ethan accepted the small envelope from the bartender, the kind of miniature stationery used to house gift cards and the notes that came with pricey floral arrangements. He lifted the flap to reveal a black plastic key card to a room in the hotel, the number 714 scrawled across the back of the envelope in a familiar hand.

Angie leaned around the bartender, trying to get a good look at the woman in question. But Ethan knew she wouldn't find her.

"Who's it from?" Angie asked, turning back to Ethan.

Ethan stood, buttoning his suit jacket and sliding the key card into his pocket. "A gentleman never kisses and tells."

Angie cackled.

At the end of the bar, Hannah slid off her stool. The tall brunette hid behind oversized sunglasses and a baseball cap, but he'd know the upturned end of her nose, the width of her hips, accentuated by her fitted pencil skirt, and the plush round of her backside anywhere. She disappeared into the hall without a second look in his direction and his blood rushed in his ears.

She was the real reason he kept coming back to this hotel bar. Uncomplicated, funny, sexy as hell. Best of all, no expectations, no obligations, no way to disappoint each other.

"When are you going to settle down?"

Ethan glanced back at Angie. He'd almost forgotten she was still there. "Now you sound like my mother."

"Come on, isn't that what your whole speech was about? Wanting the wholesome life—a wife, the picket fence, and two-point-five kids?"

"How do you have point five of a kid?"

"Don't change the subject."

Ethan sighed. "I don't know, Ang. Maybe."

What he didn't say was yes, of course, he wanted all that. He'd wanted it since he was sixteen and his high school girlfriend got pregnant—and then promptly refused to marry him. But now, staring down the barrel of forty-five, it was time for him to admit to himself that maybe he wasn't the kind of guy women settled down with. And if lately he wondered what it would be like, if he found his mind drifting to Hannah more than it should, well, that was hardly the point.

Angie grasped his forearm. "You'll think about the dragon shifters?"

He pulled a few bills from his wallet and dropped them on the table. "Send me the book. I'll do it."

Hannah was already in the elevator when he emerged from the bar into the hotel lobby, and he slid into the car just before the doors closed. Inside, she stood beside him as though they were any two people riding in an elevator together. As though they hadn't done this exact same dance eight times over the last three years.

"You grew a beard," she said, looking straight ahead at their reflection in the shiny metal of the elevator doors as they began to rise. "I like it."

He ran his hand over the scruff on his jaw. "You changed your hair." Last time he'd seen her it had been shorter, falling around her shoulders. Now it hung down to the middle of her back, the ends curled in a way he imagined had taken a long time to get just right. "Looks good."

"I'm glad you approve," she teased.

The elevator doors slid open on the seventh floor and she walked out ahead of him, shooting him a conspiratorial look over her shoulder. He let his eyes skate down the length of her body, taking time to appreciate the way her ass swayed as she walked. "Oh, I very much approve."

She tossed her head back and laughed, the sound washing over him as they moved through the maze of hallways leading to her room. At the door to room 714, she paused, reaching for her purse.

"You were meeting that same woman last time I saw you," Hannah said, her face turned down towards her purse so he couldn't catch her expression. "Should I be jealous?"

"Are you? Jealous?"

She didn't answer, but her shoulders stiffened. He shouldn't be so delighted by her response, but he couldn't help himself. He'd spent the six months since the last time they saw each other trying to convince himself he wasn't completely obsessed with this woman—after all, that was hardly part of the friends-with-benefits arrangement they had going. To think she felt even a fraction of the possessiveness towards him that he felt towards her was intoxicating.

Ethan moved behind her, coming close enough to smell the soft floral notes of her shampoo without actually touching her. He inhaled deeply, reveling in the familiar scent as it sparked a chain reaction of need through his body.

"She's just an old friend," he said.

Hannah nodded and continued to search through her purse, but her shoulders noticeably relaxed.

Removing the keycard from his pocket, he slid his arm around her side and held the card to the reader on the door. "Allow me."

She pushed open the door and turned to face him, taking hold of the lapels of his suit jacket and walking backwards as she led him into her hotel room. "Oh, believe me, I'll allow you to do a great many things before the night is over."

As the door closed behind them with a soft snick, she took off her sunglasses and hat, tossing them on the side table in the entryway. Ethan snaked his arm around her lower back, pulling her hips against his and kissing her. She tasted like the citrus seltzers she favored, and though he couldn't stand the stuff, mixed with the sweetness of her lips, her floral scent, and the plush give of her body against his, it was the best damn thing he'd tasted in months. She began to move away and he nipped at her lower lip, prompting her delighted giggle as she smoothed the lapels she'd held tightly in her fists only a moment before.

"I wasn't sure you'd come," she said, her eyes fixed on his chest.

Was he imagining things or did she seem like she'd been disappointed to think he might not make their rendezvous?

He tucked a piece of hair behind her ear, his fingers lingering on the soft curve of her cheek. "I wasn't sure either."

He'd debated not going, even though he'd read her text a thousand times between the moment it arrived on his phone and walking into the bar.

"What changed?"

What hadn't changed? His friends, one by one, had gotten married and moved on to lives that didn't revolve around their weekly trivia and board game nights. His daughter and his best friend had made him a grandfather last year. He was about to turn forty-five and what did he have to show for it? A thriving business, a secret life as an audiobook narrator of deliciously filthy romance novels, a family and friends he loved...and a bed he slept in alone.

Most of the time it didn't bother him, but lately he'd begun to wonder.

Maybe he'd become too emotionally invested in the romances he narrated. Or maybe...

"I wanted to see you."

From the lift of her eyebrow he could tell she thought it was a line. Ethan dropped his lips to her neck, sliding his kiss along the column of her throat, the curve of her clavicle. She tilted her head to give him better access as his lips drifted lower, through the valley between her breasts, and he got to his knees at her feet.

She sighed dreamily and dug her hands into his hair. "I'm glad you came."

He pressed a kiss to the swell of her belly through the silky fabric of her top, focusing on the softness of her skin as his fingers found the hem and slipped beneath to stroke the dip of her waist. "No one's come yet, sweetheart, but give me a minute and we'll change that."

She exhaled a soft laugh and ran a hand down the side of his face, stroking his beard. He turned his face up to her, watching the thoughts flit behind her eyes as she studied the scruff on his jaw. What he wouldn't give to know what she was thinking.

But that wasn't what they did, him and Hannah. They didn't talk about anything important, nothing worthy of talking about anyway. They teased and they bantered and they fucked until neither one of them had any space left for thoughts.

And then they said goodbye.

He didn't even know what she did for a living, or why she was in Boston. Just like she didn't know the answers to those questions about him. One night, three years ago, they'd both been in the same hotel bar, lonely and willing to take a chance on a one-night stand with a stranger. They'd only exchanged phone numbers because he insisted on her letting him know she'd gotten home okay the next day, even if he didn't know where home was.

He skated his hands down the backs of her legs, took a firm hold of her ankle and lifted, guiding her to step out of her high heels. She ran her fingers through his beard, through the hair at the back of his neck, as he dragged his hands back up over the curve of her calf, the length of her thigh. He never broke eye contact as he slid the zipper on her skirt down, the fabric falling into a pool at her feet.

Ethan pressed his lips to the line where the waistband of her panties cut across the softness of her belly, where her skin was marked with iridescent waves, smooth beneath his tongue. He hooked his fingers in the elastic waistband and left a sucking kiss low on her stomach. "Say yes, Han," he rumbled against her.

Her fingers tightened in his hair, guiding his lips lower. "Yes."

He hooked his hands around her thighs and urged her backwards until the backs of her legs hit the wingback chair in the corner of the room and she fell back onto its cushioned surface with a surprised laugh. Rising up on his knees, he captured her lips again, only stopping long enough to pull her top over her head. He skated his hands over her skin, soaking in the sight of Hannah reclined like a queen on her throne in her lacy bra and panty set.

"Ethan," she whined, gripping his hair again, guiding his face closer to where she wanted him.

He nipped at the soft inside of her thigh, loving the way she tensed at the sharp sting before relaxing deeper into the chair, her thighs falling open wider.

"Been thinking about this for weeks," he said, mostly to himself.

"This?"

"You," he corrected himself. He pulled her panties over her hips, down her legs, tossing them aside and hooking her legs over his shoulders as he settled between her thighs. With one finger, he stroked the length of her slit, a soft, reverent touch that had no place in their arrangement. "Are you as sweet as I remember?"

"Ethan—"

He licked a long, hot stripe up her center, pausing at the top to circle her clit with the tip of his tongue until it stiffened and grew plump against him.

"Better than I remember," he said before repeating the motion. A slow stroke followed by tight circles.

"Your beard," she gasped, her heels digging into his back.

Ethan hesitated, glancing up at her. "Say the word and I'll shave it off right now."

"Like hell you will." Her hips lifted towards his mouth. Impatient, needy, and so fucking gorgeous. "Do that again."

So he did. Again and again as her hips chased his tongue. He watched her over the mound of dark curls at the apex of her thighs, studied every catch in her breathing, every look of wonder passing over her face when he wrapped his lips around her clit and sucked. He watched as she tore down the cups of her bra, plumping and squeezing her breasts when he slid a finger inside her heat, a second, a third.

She rode his hand as he licked and sucked and teased her orgasm to the surface. And when she came, he watched the sparks dance across her skin, saw the pleasure take shape low in her belly and burst with a startled gasp and wave after wave of shaking bliss. He gripped her thigh with his free hand, pulling her tight against his mouth as he licked her through the haze of her climax, urging her to grind against him, to use him to heighten every last aftershock.

This he could do. He didn't know how to be both Slade Hardcastle and Ethan Hart, how to be someone's partner, how to make a woman want to stay, but this—making Hannah come so hard she forgot to breathe—*this* he could do.

"Ethan." Her voice broke through his swirling thoughts, her fingers tugging his face away from the heaven between her legs. She smiled indulgently at him, her thumb skating over the wetness clinging to his lower lip. He captured that thumb between his teeth, tugging gently. "Take me to bed."

He removed his clothing as she shed her bra and moved to the bed, sliding back until she rested against the headboard. Following her down, he watched with barely restrained need as she produced a condom from somewhere and slid the latex over his erection.

"I've been thinking about this for weeks too," she said as she pumped her hand over his length, slowly, like a promise.

"This?" he asked, punching his hips forward into her touch.

She bit back a smile. "You."

There was a sadness in her eyes that hadn't been there before. A softness he didn't recognize. He reached up and cupped her jaw, guiding her lips to his. Moving over her, he covered her body with his own, watched in awe as she guided the flared tip of his cock to her entrance, as she parted to make room for him, to let him inside. Hooking one of her legs with his elbow and opening her up further, he gave her more of his weight. Their kisses turned desperate as he worked himself within her, angling his hips the way he knew she liked, burying himself in her again and again as if he could stay there.

This time, her orgasm was slow to gather, but he didn't mind. He lost himself in the way she smiled at him, the soft moans and the breathy gasps, the feel of her stretching around him, the revelation that was being with her like this. For the next few hours, nothing mattered more than the gorgeous woman writhing beneath him as he hit the secret spot deep inside that made her shake.

"Come for me. Been waiting months to feel you come on my cock again."

She slid a hand between them until her fingers found her clit and he leaned back to watch as she stroked herself in time to his thrusts. He wanted to memorize it, to remember every goosebump, every shockwave rolling through her body, to be able to close his eyes and play back the sight of her touching herself as he fucked her.

"That's it," he purred as her inner muscles fluttered around him faster, tighter, warning of her impending release. "That's my girl. Let me feel it, sweetheart. Take what's yours."

She arched off the bed, her legs going stiff, toes pointing, as she clamped down around him, drawing his own orgasm from him as hers took hold. He fell forward, resting his forehead against her chest as he drove into her once, twice, then froze, electricity shooting down his spine as he filled the condom.

She smoothed the hair back from his forehead and he pressed his lips to her sternum.

"Missed you," he said.

His chest ached with the words he was holding back. How he hadn't been able to see another woman for the last year without wishing he was with her instead. How around six months ago, after the last time they'd gotten together, he'd stopped even trying. How many times he pulled up her number while he lay alone in his bed, wondering where she was, what she was doing. Wondering if he'd ever see her again.

"Missed you too," she said, and his heart swelled with foolish hope.

Once the condom was disposed of, he crawled back into bed beside her, gathering her against his chest. She snuggled down into him, her hips doing that happy little wiggle thing he was sure she didn't realize she did.

"I'm glad you came." He arched an eyebrow at her and she shoved at his chest playfully, rolling her eyes. "You know what I mean. I'm glad you came to Boston."

"Me too."

He pressed a kiss to her hair, smoothed his hands over her back, and for a moment, let himself imagine how it would be if she was his. If he didn't leave her each time wondering if he'd ever hear from her again, if he was an asshole for hoping he would—because hearing from Hannah meant she was still single. It meant she hadn't found her happily ever after yet. While he loved being the man she called whenever she was in town, she deserved the whole fairytale, not just whatever they were.

But what if they were more? What if he could give her the fairytale—if they could give it to each other?

They hardly knew each other but what he did know, he liked. And there was no denying they were compatible. Relationships had been built on less.

"Hey, Han," he said into the fading light of the hotel room, careful to keep her face tucked against his chest so she couldn't look at him for the next part. "What if we did this more often?"

"I'm not sure how much more often I'll be in Boston this year."

"No. I mean, what if we saw each other outside of this hotel? You could come to visit me and I could go see you. Fuck, I don't even know where you live. What if we—"

She pulled away and sat up beside him, her brow furrowed and her face serious. *Shit.* He knew that look. "Ethan—"

"Never mind." He scrubbed his hands over his face and sat up, swinging his legs over the side of the bed so his back was to her. *Way to ruin it.* "It was a stupid idea."

"My life is…complicated at the moment. I'm working through some things—"

"You don't have to explain. Really." He shot her what he hoped was a reassuring look over his shoulder. "Forget it."

Her hand closed over his shoulder, and he placed his hand on top of hers. "I know everyone says this, but I promise you I mean it: it's not you."

Ethan knew a brush off when he heard one. "It's fine, Han. I shouldn't have said anything." He forced his lips into the shape of a smile. "Blame it on the incredible sex."

"You're really alright?" she asked.

This was not how this night ended, with this trepidation in her touch. He might not be able to erase the gnarled knot of 'what if's in his chest, but he could make sure neither of them thought about anything of significance for the rest of the night. That was what these meetings were supposed to be about anyway—pleasure, a chance to lose themselves in each other, no obligation. No midlife crisis making him look like a desperate jerk who changed the rules.

He spun around and pinned her to the mattress, dragging his lips across her eyelids, her cheekbone, down the slope of her nose. "I'll be better after I make you come again."

He tugged her nipple between his teeth on his slow slide down her body, drawing a startled yelp from her.

"If you want to talk about—"

"Nothing to talk about." He parted her thighs, kissing along the crease where her leg met her hip. "Unless you want me to tell you all the things I plan to do to you before the night is through."

She shivered. "Yes, please."

And then he made it his mission to erase every last thought from both their minds.

Chapter Two

"I'm sorry, I'm sorry! I know I'm late."

Hannah burst into the small diner and darted over to the table in the corner where her friends were already chatting happily over mimosas. The flashes of the paparazzo's camera that had stalked her steps since she left her apartment was blissfully shut out thanks to the diner's "no photographers" policy.

"No baby today?" she asked Liv as she shrugged out of her jacket and took a seat at their usual table tucked in the back away from the large windows, though she could still see a photographer lingering on the sidewalk.

No doubt to take more unflattering photos of me when I leave.

"Daemon's on dad duty today," Liv said.

Liv and Daemon had met a few years back when they'd co-starred in a limited run of *Chess*. They'd been madly in love ever since, living a life Hannah could only dream of, complete with a cute townhouse and an even cuter pair of Broadway babies while they both still managed to keep performing. Hannah couldn't even keep a houseplant alive while maintaining her performance and audition schedule.

"How did the concert go?" Jennifer asked.

"It felt really good."

"Howard wasn't a total ass?" Liv asked. She'd had her own difficulties with the legendary director.

"No more than usual, and he said he might want me for another concert in the fall, but then he said something about waiting to see how the public reacts to the pro shot of *Bridget Jones' Musical* before they make a final decision, so who the hell knows," Hannah said.

Why did it seem like so much of her life was hinging on the release of a filmed version of the Broadway show she'd closed six months ago? How was a girl supposed to get on with her life when everyone around her was waiting to judge something from her past?

"Let him wait. He'll see how incredible you are and by then, he'll be competing with every other director in town to book you," Liv said.

"We'll see. I've been called in for the same parts so many times, I'm starting to think I'm stuck in a *Groundhog Day*-style loop," Hannah sighed.

"You'd be great in *Groundhog Day*," Jennifer said.

"They'll never cast me as Nancy," Hannah said. She had no illusions about the realities of being a plus sized woman on Broadway—though the fact a size twelve was considered plus size was some serious bullshit.

The server approached, dropping plates full of the most delicious smelling breakfast in front of each of them. "We ordered your usual," Liv said by way of explanation when the mushroom and Swiss omelet was placed in front of Hannah.

"Enough about short-sighted directors. How was Ethan?" Jennifer asked, shimmying her shoulders in excitement.

Hannah's face flamed red. "I never should have told you guys about him."

"Come on. I'm an old married woman now. Let me live vicariously through you," Liv said.

Hannah snorted. "Who are you kidding? You and Daemon probably still have more sex than I do, even with kids in the house."

Liv smirked and shrugged in a way that completely confirmed the accusation.

"Give up the details, Han. I haven't had sex in weeks," Jennifer complained. "Though those audiobooks you recommended have definitely been helping to take the edge off."

"Clearly you had a good time." Liv gestured vaguely to the spot at the edge of the neckline to Hannah's shirt where a bright red patch of beard burn was visible.

"Shit." Hannah tugged her shirt over to cover the offending mark.

Jennifer laughed and swiped a roasted potato from Hannah's plate, popping it into her mouth as though it didn't require a twenty-minute internal argument to decide to eat a starch. "God, I miss carbs," she groaned.

"We shouldn't even be talking about this in public," Hannah said, turning her plate so the potatoes were closer to Jennifer. "If someone overheard and word got back to Jackson and his team—"

"No one cares about your fake boyfriend's little publicity stunt," Jennifer said as Hannah shushed her.

"Someone cares," Liv said, gesturing towards the growing number of photographers lingering at the front window.

"It's only until after the release of the pro shot. We've managed to fool everyone for the last six months," she said, tilting her chin towards the paparazzi. "So I need you both to keep this to yourselves for the next few weeks. Then Jackson and I will issue a joint statement about an amicable split and we can get on with our lives."

"Does that mean you'll be going to the premiere with Jackson?" Liv asked.

"You should totally take Ethan," Jennifer said.

Hannah frowned and poked at her potatoes, willing the noise in her brain to calm enough to let her eat one. "Ethan doesn't even know I'm an actress. We don't really tell each other much of anything."

"Except 'harder' and 'faster,'" Jennifer said with a snort.

"Could you not?" Hannah hissed, glancing over her shoulder at the older couple at the next table who were a little too close for her friends' style of postmortem.

Jennifer stole another potato, gesturing with it still speared on the tines of her fork. "Shouldn't you be more relaxed? If some guy banged my brains out—"

"Jennifer!"

"—I sure as hell wouldn't still be strung this tight. Unless it wasn't as good as you remembered."

"It was better," Hannah sighed, squeezing her thighs together to feel the pulse of soreness there.

"Then what's the problem?" Liv asked.

"You mean aside from the fact that as far as the rest of the world is concerned, I'm in a relationship with Jackson Hayes? There's no problem." Her friends exchanged an incredulous look. "I'm not really supposed to be doing the casual sex thing," she whispered.

"Says who?" Jennifer asked.

"Says me." Hannah pushed her eggs around with her fork. "I haven't always made the best decisions about how to take care of my body. Putting a moratorium on casual sex is part of my recovery."

"But sex is more like self-care than self-destruction, at least the way you two did it," Jennifer said.

Liv considered for a moment. "Is it really casual sex if you bang the same guy in the same hotel every couple months? That's more of a sex tradition."

"Nothing casual about traditions," Jennifer chimed in.

"That's not how recovery works," Hannah reminded them.

Jennifer set her fork down and leaned towards Hannah, finally lowering her voice to an acceptable level. "Did you sleep with him to avoid binging?"

Hannah shook her head.

"To avoid eating?" Liv asked.

Another shake.

"Did you relapse in your recovery in any way while you were in Boston?" Jennifer asked.

"No."

It had been six months since her last binge—since closing night of *Bridget Jones' Musical* to be exact—after the intense restriction she'd imposed on herself during the run of the show. Six months of therapy and tiny milestones that put her on more solid footing every day, and yet… It all still felt so tenuous, like she was one misplaced bag of M&Ms away from relapsing into the depths of her eating disorder.

Or one night of casual sex.

But being with Ethan felt different. With him, she didn't feel out of control like she did in so many other situations. Instead she felt powerful, confident, capable, like somehow being with him didn't numb the feelings swirling inside her—it amplified them. There was no hiding from Ethan when he looked at her like he could see all the things she didn't say, and the truth was, she didn't want to hide from him. But if she was honest with herself, that kind of intensity scared her more than any calorie count.

"Don't be so hard on yourself. You deserve to have fun too. Even the sexy naked kind," Liv said.

"Especially the sexy naked kind," Jennifer added. "Audiobooks can only keep you warm for so long before you need the real thing, Han."

Heat crawled up Hannah's throat, her cheeks burning. "He wanted to see me again. Like for real. Like a date."

"I'm still not seeing the problem here," Liv said. "I thought you liked this guy."

"I do. But we don't even know each other."

"I don't think I'd say *that*. You know some things about each other," Jennifer said. At Hannah's glare, she continued, "Then get to know each other. That's what dating is for."

"It's too hard. It's a miracle he hasn't recognized me. Going to see him this weekend was careless enough as it is. If we'd been seen together... Until this thing with Jackson is over, I need to focus on auditioning and my recovery."

"That's what you've been saying for months. When are you allowed to focus on being happy?" Liv asked.

"I'll be happy when I book my next show."

"Will you?" Jennifer asked.

Hannah picked up her fork, despite the way her stomach gave a warning jolt in response to the mere idea of eating when she was this on edge. Eating was easier than looking too closely at the answer to that question, however.

She cut off a bite of her omelet with the side of her fork and popped it in her mouth before she could think too hard about it, forcing herself to chew, to swallow, to do it again. She refused to be defeated by a breakfast special. *Not today, Satan.*

"Where does Ethan live?" Liv asked, tapping away distractedly on her phone.

"Why?" Hannah asked.

"If the issue is that you don't know enough about him, then let's find out about him. We are millennial women with Instagram accounts. Give me his name and a rough idea of how old he is, and I'll find him within the hour," Liv promised.

"I highly doubt Ethan has an Instagram."

"But someone who knows him does," Jennifer said, swiping

another potato.

"Why don't you order your own home fries?" Hannah asked.

"I can't do that. I don't eat carbs," Jennifer said around the mouthful of potato.

"Oh, shit," Liv whispered, her eyes glued to her phone screen.

"What? Did your brother accidentally send his dirty texts to you instead of his wife again?" Jennifer asked.

"Worse." Liv lowered the phone, setting it on the table and sliding it towards Hannah. "Han…"

"What?" Hannah looked between her friends, her stomach sinking with dread at the concern in Liv's eyes as she reached for the phone. "What is it?"

There it was on *Superfan*'s homepage. Jackson Hayes kissing a woman in a bikini on a beach in Bora Bora. Her fake boyfriend with a tall blonde woman who looked like she hadn't eaten a potato in a decade.

Hannah clicked into the story, posted only an hour ago, to find a series of photographs. In one, Jackson gave the woman a piggyback ride in the waves. In another, he was practically on top of her, making out on an expensive looking lounge chair.

"What the fuck?" Jennifer snarled, leaning over Hannah's shoulder to get a better look.

Hannah slammed the phone face down on the table. "It's fine. It's not like we were actually together." When had her voice gotten so high?

"Yeah, but *they* don't know that," Jennifer said, pointing to the growing crowd of photographers outside the diner.

Someone opened the door and a flurry of flashes went off, her name called by at least ten different paparazzi as the unsuspecting patron tried to leave the restaurant.

This can't be happening.

"We had a deal," Hannah said, dazed. "We weren't supposed to break up until after the pro-shot premiered. It was *his* idea."

"Once a bad boy, always a bad boy," Jennifer said.

"But that's just it. He's not—" Hannah broke off at her friends' skeptical looks. "He's been famous since he was a teenager. He made stupid mistakes people make when they're young, but he did it in the spotlight."

"You aren't seriously defending him right now," Jennifer said. "Poor little rich boy. He was part of the biggest boy band of our generation."

"And the press ate him alive when he broke up the band." Hannah glanced at the phone. It was taunting her, even though it was face down. "I don't understand what happened. It was only a few more weeks. His publicist said it was working. Dating me was helping to win back good will from the band's fans."

"So much for that," Liv said, taking back her phone as Hannah's began ringing.

Hannah answered as Liv said, "Don't answer that."

"Hannah! This is Johnny Blue with Encores.com—"

She hung up and dropped her phone on the table as if it were hot. It immediately began ringing again.

"You need to call your manager," Jennifer said, silencing the ringing.

"It'll be fine," Hannah said, more to convince herself than anything, her voice a little too shrill to be calm. "No one could possibly care about this. I'm a nobody."

"You may be a nobody but Jackson Hayes is a capital S somebody," Liv said as she scrolled through the stories on her phone again. "They're saying he cheated on you with a Brazilian swimsuit model."

Hannah's stomach lurched and her mouth went dry. "Why would he do this?" she whispered. "I was *helping* him."

Liv reached across the table and took her hand. "You're going to have to ask him that. But right now, we need to figure out how to get you out of here."

Chapter Three

After slipping out the back door of the diner and semi-successfully dodging the press—there was a lone photographer at the corner smoking a cigarette who got a few shots off before they noticed him—Hannah insisted on going back to her apartment alone. She needed to call her manager and her parents and Jackson and—

But she didn't make it to her apartment. The cab pulled up in front of her building and was immediately swarmed by scandal-hungry paparazzi, the flash of their cameras blinding her as Liv and Jennifer tried to block the windows. Hannah ducked her head into her lap, folding her arms over her face, and forced herself to breathe. This was madness.

This is what you get for thinking you can lie and get away with it. There's a reason he was known as the 'bad boy.' Idiot.

She hardly heard Liv give the cab driver new instructions, directing him to drop Jennifer off at her apartment in Two Bridges before continuing on to Brooklyn. Hannah wanted to argue. There had been a mistake. These photographers didn't understand—she was just a Broadway actress. Broadway actresses didn't get hounded by the press.

Unless they're caught up in a cheating scandal with a former

boy band member about to launch a worldwide reunion tour.
  Shit.

As the cab slowed to a stop outside Liv and Daemon's Brooklyn townhouse, the front door swung upon, the imposing figure of Daemon Chase filling up the opening, though he looked decidedly less imposing with a toddler clinging to his leg and an infant strapped to his chest. He held the door open for them and swept his gaze over the busy street before shutting it behind them.

Liv lifted the baby out of the carrier her husband wore, cooing into the bundle's dark hair and chubby cheeks while Hannah followed behind, still too stunned to know what to do next. She'd tried to call Jackson from the cab but it had gone straight to voicemail. Her text messages were left unread.

Daemon pulled her into a side hug. "Are you alright?"

"I don't understand what's happening," she said for what felt like the hundredth time.

"I already talked to Micah. He's on his way," Daemon said.

Hannah and Daemon shared a manager. It was how she'd met Liv originally.

"This will blow over. I'm sure by tomorrow—" Liv stopped as Daemon shook his head, rolling his lips between his teeth. Hannah sank onto their couch, a squeaky stuffed duck protesting beneath her.

The doorbell rang and Daemon excused himself. "That'll be Micah."

Liv sat down next to Hannah, bouncing her youngest in her arms. "Are you alright?"

"I'm waiting for the anger to hit. I should be angry, right?"

But all she felt was numb. She'd trusted Jackson, fallen for his stories about cleaning up his reputation, tied her public image to his. It was the least she could do after he'd helped her pay for the expensive outpatient eating disorder treatment she'd needed, but now—

"I've been trying to get that little shit's publicist on the phone for the last twenty minutes," Micah said as he blew into the room.

"Shit!" Liv and Daemon's oldest, a bright-eyed toddler with curly dark brown hair, echoes, clapping happily.

Daemon scowled at his manager as he turned up the volume on the *Bluey* episode playing on the television in the corner.

"Sorry," Micah said. He paused to drop a kiss on Liv's cheek. "Hi, Liv. Hannah, have you heard from him?"

"He's not answering his phone," she said.

"Probably for the best. We need to distance you from this."

"How? Everyone thinks we're dating."

"You could make a statement. Tell the truth," Liv offered.

"That'll kick up another frenzy. Right now, at least, you look sympathetic. You're the victim."

"They're hounding me out of sympathy?" Hannah asked in disbelief.

"They want a photo of the devastated girlfriend to put on their covers. And in those stories, Jackson will be the bad guy, but if you admit you lied…" Micah shook his head.

"Right. Not an option." Hannah's gaze bounced between her friends and her manager. "So what do I do?"

Micah glanced uneasily at Daemon. "I think you just have to ride it out."

"No," Liv said. "They surrounded our cab outside her apartment building. She can't go back there when they're like this."

"It could be days before they settle down," Micah said.

"A week if there are more photos that haven't been released yet," Daemon added.

"A week?" Something at the back of her mind thrashed and flailed, trying to get her attention through the detached calm settling over her, but she couldn't give in to that now. If she did, she'd never stop panicking. She could panic later.

Micah pinched the bridge of his nose, his thumbs dragging over his closed eyes. "Daemon's right. And with the premiere only a few weeks away, there's a good chance Jackson's team will feed the fire to keep him in the press."

"You think he did this on purpose?" Hannah's entire body went cold, her toes turning to ice in her shoes. Daemon and Micah exchanged another one of those glances. "What? Tell *me*."

"I think you should stay here for a bit," Micah said. "Just until this dies down and it's safe for you to go back to your apartment."

"How long will that be?" Hannah asked.

"A couple days," Micah said.

"I'm sure they'll move on to something else by the end of the week," Liv said, though Hannah could hear the way the last word of the phrase turned up, the question she was posing to her husband, the only one of them who had been through this sort of thing before. Daemon rolled his lips through his teeth again, his eyes serious and stoic.

"You think it'll be longer?" Hannah asked him.

"No way to tell," Daemon said. "They'll move on faster, though, if they can't find you."

Hannah shook her head. Nothing about this made sense. That morning she'd had the usual handful of photographers who followed her from her apartment to the diner, the ones who were hoping Jackson would magically materialize by her side—he was the one they wanted a picture of. Not her.

The bundle in Liv's arms squawked and Daemon crossed the room in two steps, taking the baby from Liv's arms and pacifying her with his pinky finger, rocking her and whispering to her with a low rumble.

Hannah eyed the baby in Daemon's arms, the toddler

dancing in front of the television, the adoring look on her friend's face as Liv watched Daemon care for their child—it was beautiful. And she hated that it made her stomach twist with jealousy. She couldn't stay there for a week, watching their perfect love, their perfect family. She'd lose the feeble hold she had on her sanity.

"I can't just hide in Brooklyn. I have auditions this week." She turned to Micah, desperate for someone to say something that made sense, to tell her this had all been a mistake and she could go back to her life.

"You can submit a self-tape," Micah said. "Given the circumstances—" Micah's phone dinged and he dug it out of his pocket, his nostrils flaring as he read whatever message had just come through. He shared a look with Daemon.

"It'll be great, Han. Like a week-long sleepover," Liv said, ignoring the strange tension crackling between the men.

"Liv." The warning in Daemon's voice was so fiercely protective it made something inside Hannah crack, a bit of the flailing panic poking through.

"More photographs were just leaked," Micah said.

"How much worse can it get?" Hannah said.

"There's a second woman. Rumors of a third," Micah said matter-of-factly.

"Oh. So, three times as bad then."

The doorbell rang again, and Liv and Daemon shared a confused look. "Are you expecting anyone?" he asked her. Liv shook her head as Daemon handed her back the baby and stalked towards the front door. He glared through the window at the side of the door, then pulled a curtain closed over it, muttering to himself.

"You must have been followed," he said, returning to the living room. "There are photographers outside."

"Here?" Hannah stood up, but then realized there was

nowhere she could go, so she fell back onto the couch.

"We need to get you out of New York," Micah said. "Just until the premiere."

"I can go to my parents," Hannah said, swallowing down the panic and doing her best to block out the steady litany of Ben & Jerry's flavors buzzing in the back of her head, daring her to give in. If there was ever a time to stress eat, this was it, right?

"Your parents are in a major city," Micah said. "They'll find you there too."

"I—I—I don't have anywhere else to go," she said, fighting back the sudden tightness in her throat, the press of tears behind her eyes.

"I know a place," Daemon said, his eyes bouncing between Liv and Hannah. "My brother lives in a small town in Rhode Island. He and his wife—"

"You'll love them!" Liv turned to face Hannah more fully. "Jamie is a chef and his wife, Tessa, is a baker."

"Rhode Island," Hannah repeated, stunned.

Liv continued on as if she hadn't said anything. "It's the cutest town. Farmers' markets and beaches and town festivals. It's where Daemon and I got married. You'll love it."

"More importantly, the press aren't likely to look for you there."

"You want me to stay with your brother and sister-in-law, who I've never met, for two whole weeks?" Hannah shook her head. "I can't—"

Liv cut in, "They're good people. It'll be like a mini vacation."

By myself. Staying with people I don't know in a place I've never been while the paparazzi try to hunt me down. What kind of vacation is that?

"Unless you have a better idea…" Micah trailed off.

"No. This will blow over. I appreciate the offer, but they're not going to run me out of my own home. It will be fine."

It wasn't fine.

If she thought there as an intimidating number of cameras outside her apartment before, it was nothing compared to the mob waiting for her when she returned home from Liv and Daemon's. Thankfully, Micah had accompanied her, doing his best to shield her from the relentless press of the paparazzi as he helped her move between the taxi and her apartment's lobby. He tried, again, to convince her to leave town, but she insisted she was fine, despite the way her hands shook.

Alone in her apartment, she tried to pretend her life hadn't imploded at the hands of a self-centered former pop star. She'd thought they were friends. That they'd grown to understand each other during their months starring together on Broadway in *Bridget Jones' Musical*. Clearly, she'd been mistaken.

"Hannah, honey, what's going on? Are you alright?" Her mother's worry was somehow soothing, a familiar blanket she could wrap herself in even through the distance of a phone call. Her mother seemed no more flustered by the current media storm than she had when Hannah had sulked after being stood up for Homecoming sophomore year of high school. A gentle sort of concern always tinged with this-too-shall-pass practicality.

"I'm fine, Mom." She searched the cabinets of her apartment for a tea bag—any tea bag—as water boiled in the kettle on the stove. "It's all a misunderstanding."

"Hank! She says it's a misunderstanding!" her mother called to her father, forgetting, once again, to move the phone away from her mouth before she shouted into the other room. "Then you and Jackson are still together?" she asked.

Hannah hesitated. "No. We're not together."

Had never been together.

Would never be together.

She didn't say that part.

"Oh, well, that's a shame. Are you sure you're alright? There are so many photographs of you on the television."

"Why are you watching that?"

"How'd they get that one picture?" her father shouted in the background.

"What picture?" Hannah removed the tea kettle from the stove, pouring the steaming water over the tea bag at the bottom of her favorite mug, the one covered in illustrations from *Peter Rabbit*.

"Hank, shush," her mother scolded.

"What picture, Mom?"

"There was one photo on the TV that looked like you weren't expecting them to take it," her mom said.

"I wasn't expecting them to take any of the photos." There'd been the occasional photographer in the months since she and Jackson had debuted their fauxmance, but nothing like this. Nothing that interrupted her daily life.

It'll all blow over. By tomorrow, they'll move on to something else.

"There, I texted you a link. But really, honey, don't be too hard on yourself. No one photographs particularly well before they've put on their makeup."

"What are you talking about?" Hannah put her phone on speaker and opened the link her mother had sent.

Her screen filled with an image of herself, hair knotted in a messy bun on the top of her head, in an oversized Carnegie Mellon t-shirt and tiny black shorts. The same oversized t-shirt and tiny shorts she'd slept in the night before. This was a photo of her coming out of the bathroom that morning, the camera's flash reflecting off the mirror behind her.

"What the hell?" she said, taking the phone and moving across the apartment to the bathroom.

"What is it? Hannah?" her mother asked.

But Hannah couldn't answer. She was staring at the exact angle of the photograph in her hand and there was only one way that image could have been taken—from the fire escape outside her living room window.

Someone she didn't know had climbed her building's fire escape to take a photograph of her through the window. Someone had sold a photograph taken of her in her own apartment without her knowledge or consent.

Cold sluiced down her spine as she pulled the curtains closed, moving feverishly from one window to the next until she'd blocked out all the daylight.

"Hannah? What's going on? Are you okay?" her mom asked, her calm concern morphing into something more frantic.

But Hannah was not okay.

Her apartment was no longer safe.

"Mom, I have to go," she said, sinking onto the couch, still staring at the photograph, so unlike the sun-soaked images of the women in Bora Bora with Jackson. They didn't have cellulite on their thighs. She zoomed in on the image, blowing up the offending appendage until it took up the entire screen.

"Why don't you come home for a few days?" her mom asked. "We could get lunch at that little bistro you like on Main Street."

No, they could not get lunch at that little bistro, because the second Hannah showed up, the place would be overrun with photographers.

"I can't do that," she said. She set her phone on the coffee table and clasped her hands in her lap, as though that could stop them from shaking.

She couldn't stay in her apartment. And she couldn't go home to her parents. She couldn't go anywhere.

Where the hell was she supposed to go?

And why wasn't Jackson answering his phone? How could he do this to her?

Outside, a car horn blared and she startled, shrinking further away from the windows.

"Honey, we're worried about you. We're not sure you should be alone right now."

Because the photographers had taken a picture of her in her pajamas. Because there were already hundreds of comments with words like "cow" and "disgusting" filling the screen beneath her picture. Because this was exactly the kind of thing that would have sent her into a weeks-long binge/restrict cycle only a short time ago.

She forced a deep breath into her lungs and blew it back out the way her therapist had taught her.

"I won't be. I'm going to get out of the City for a while," she said.

"Oh, that's great. Hank, she's going to leave the City!" her mom shouted.

"I have to go now, Mom. I'll call you tomorrow."

She ended the call and slid onto the floor, ducking down behind the couch, as though that could protect her from the white noise slowly flooding her brain, the strange out-of-body sense overtaking her. She sent off a quick text to Liv.

Hannah: Alright. I'll go. How do I get to Rhode Island?

Then she curled into a ball on her living room floor, opening her audiobook app and letting the low, soothing voice of Slade Hardcastle wash over her.

From *The Lady's Knights* by AK Wild,
narrated by Slade Hardcastle

Lady Windtorn was unaccustomed to such attention. Her
handmaidens had tsked and tittered behind their hands at the
ample spread of their lady's backside. "Such a shame she is so
gluttonous," they'd say when they thought she could not hear.

But she had heard.

A lady should be petite," they'd say. "A lady should be docile."

But Lady Windtorn was done being docile, and she had
never been petite. If her alleged gluttony offended, then she
would make herself the most offensive. Then, at least, she would
not be forced to marry a man for the protection his name
offered despite his distaste for her. If her fiancé could bed a
serving girl the night of their betrothal ball without a care for
discretion, then she could make herself unmarriageable.

That is how Lady Windtorn found herself one night
the subject of the most enthusiastic affection she had ever
experienced. These were no handmaidens who had laid her out
on their refectory table, and her undressing had not been the
perfunctory work of someone paid to worry more about the
garments than their owner.

No, when Lady Windtorn lay back on the hard wood and
allowed herself to be admired, it was under the gaze of a throng

of knights. Sturdily built, war weary men who had no use for petite, docile creatures. Men who reveled in her softness, who devoted themselves wholly to her pleasure. Men who were happy to watch, to share, if it meant their lady was all the more satisfied for it. Men who followed the command of one alone, Sir Llewellyn, and he had made his command quite plain: they were to tend to their lady's every need.

Let them call me gluttonous, she thought as she took Sir Llewellyn between her thighs.

"You needn't fear, my lady," the towering knight said as he worked himself into her heat. "You are ours now. I will protect you."

Chapter Four

"Do you wear glasses?"

Ethan scanned the tiles in front of him. "No."

Baz, Gavin, and Jamie flipped down pieces on their own racks, the clacking of the plastic obnoxiously loud in the quiet of Ethan's living room. In the kitchen, Jo, Kyla, and Sabrina laughed at some joke he was sure he didn't want to hear.

"You're Dawson Leery!" Gavin shouted, pointing a finger at Ethan.

"Is that the blonde kid with the crying face?" Ethan asked.

"The one and only." Gavin turned his rack to show Ethan an image identical to his own.

"How the hell do you know the names of any of these people?" Ethan asked.

"Brodie loved that show," Gavin said.

"If he's Dawson, then you must be Dean from *Gilmore Girls*," Jamie said.

"You got me," Gavin conceded.

"So Baz is the blonde chick in leather pants?" Ethan asked.

"Buffy the Vampire Slayer," Baz said.

"Am I the only one who doesn't know any of these characters?" Ethan pushed his board away. When his friends were watching blondes in leather pants fight vampires, he'd been busy learning the names of the residents of Sesame Street. Give him a version of this game with Prairie Dawn and Grover and he'd clean house. "Who the hell brought this game anyway?"

"I did," Jo said, appearing in the doorway with Ethan's granddaughter, Julie, balanced on her hip. "It was supposed to be for girls' night."

"This isn't girls' night," Ethan grumbled.

Jo turned to Julie, dropping her voice as though she was about to say something very serious. "Your grandpa is extra grouchy today."

"Am not." Ethan took the squirming toddler from Jo's arms. "Don't listen to her, Jujube."

"Of course she listens to me. I'm her favorite babysitter," Jo said, pretending to be offended.

"And I am her grandfather."

"Yeah, but you're a hot grandpa, so it doesn't count."

Ethan nearly choked on his own saliva. "Excuse me?"

"Forty-five isn't even that old."

"I'm not forty-five." *For another two weeks.*

"Forty-six. Whatever."

"I'm forty-four," he corrected her.

"Even better." Jo bobbed her eyebrows suggestively at him.

Ethan rolled his eyes. Jo was a flirt, and she loved to push his buttons, but they both knew there was no chance in hell anything would ever happen between them. She was younger than his own daughter, for Christ's sake.

"Where is your mama?" Ethan asked Julie, as if she could answer.

"Mama!" Julie exclaimed, thrilled to repeat her favorite word. For an entire month everything had been "mama," including Ethan.

"Tessa's running late. Some kind of cupcake emergency," Jo

explained.

Kyla and Sabrina pushed past Jo into the living room. Baz immediately hooked his arm around Sabrina's waist and pulled her into his lap, nuzzling into her hair, and Gavin got up to hug Kyla from behind, his chin resting on top of her head. Ethan was happy for his friends, he really was, but he was also out-of-his-mind jealous. The cartoonish heart-eyes they got as soon as their wives entered a room didn't help.

"So, hot grandpa, tell us about your lady friend," Jo prompted as she took over his empty seat at the table and dug into the chips and queso.

"My what now?" Ethan asked, shooting a death glare at Baz and Gavin. He set Julie on her feet and let her toddle across the floor to the ever-growing cache of toys in the corner of his living room.

"Don't look at me," Baz said. "I have no interest in talking about your sex life."

"Was I not supposed to tell Jo?" Kyla asked, looking up at her husband.

"It's fine," Gavin assured her. "It's not like it was a secret."

"It wasn't up for discussion, either," Ethan barked.

"Wait, I thought you went to Boston for some kind of business thing," Jamie said. "It was a sex thing?"

"Come on. Spill. Ever since these two shacked up, there's no good gossip in this group anymore," Jo said, gesturing to Baz and Sabrina with a queso-laden chip. "Rumor has it, you have a sex buddy in Boston."

"Keep me out of your gossip," Ethan replied.

"Who is she?" Sabrina asked.

"I wouldn't mind knowing that myself," Jamie said, leaning back in his chair.

Ethan glared at him. "No one. Just a friend."

"Well, which is it? No one, or a friend?" Jo asked, her grin growing wider.

"More importantly, are you going to see her again?" Gavin asked.

"It's not like that."

"Her loss. You're a catch, even if you are a grandpa. And I'm not just saying that because we're friends. You're a silver fox in training." She gestured vaguely at his head. "Not enough silver yet."

"I'm in hell. I'm in actual hell."

"I'm here! I'm here!" Tessa said, pushing her way into the living room, a tray of cupcakes balanced in one hand. She set the cupcakes down on top of the scattered game pieces and bent to give Jamie a kiss. "What did I miss?"

"Nothing, princess," Jamie said.

"Hey, Dad. Welcome back." Tessa gave Ethan a quick hug. "How was Boston?"

"We were just about to hear all the details," Jo said with a smirk.

"No, you fucking weren't," Ethan said.

Tessa glanced around at their friends. "Is this a sex thing?" she asked, her nose wrinkling. "I can leave."

"It's not a—we're not talking about this!" Ethan said.

"But there *is* something to talk about," Gavin said.

"More like someone," Sabrina added.

"Definitely a sex thing," Jo laughed.

"You are a menace," Ethan said accusatorily.

"I think that's the nicest thing you've ever said to me." She took another bite of a chip, then got to her feet and gave Tessa a hug. "I gotta run. My shift at the bar starts in twenty minutes."

"Thanks for watching Julie this afternoon," Tessa said.

"Any time. I love that little squirt." She waved at the others. "See you all later." Then, with a wink, she said to Ethan, "Bye, foxy."

"Foxy?" Tessa asked once Jo had left. "Is something going on with you and Jo?"

"Definitely not."

"'Cause I thought I might be picking up on a vibe," Tessa said.

"No vibe. Not all of us like women young enough to be our kids."

"I think I should be offended by that," Gavin said.

"So the woman in Boston isn't significantly younger than you," Jamie said. He flipped a few tiles on his game board as if they were still playing.

Ethan scowled. "She's in her thirties. I don't—why are we still talking about this?" Ethan snapped, hating that he'd taken the bait and let any details about Hannah slip. He shouldn't have said anything to Gavin at all.

Tessa scooped up Julie and snuggled her close, ignoring the pudgy toddler hands tugging at her hair. "Then let's talk about something else. Did you ask him yet?" she asked Jamie.

"Ask me what?" Ethan glanced between his daughter and his friend suspiciously.

"No, I wanted to hear what he wanted first," Jamie said.

"I didn't want anything," Ethan replied.

"Your invitation was pretty cryptic," Gavin said.

"What's cryptic about 'come to game night'?" Ethan asked.

"It was the tone," Baz replied.

"It was a text. There is no tone."

"There was a tone," Jamie said.

"Are you all trying to fuck with me today?" Ethan demanded, a headache gathering behind his eyes.

Tessa's forehead scrunched and she sank into a seat next to Jamie, setting Julie down to explore the room again. "Dad, what's wrong?"

Ethan scraped a hand over his face and glanced around at his friends, his family, the people he trusted most in the world.

The people who were always there for them. What was he going to say? *You're all great but I'm jealous as hell you've found your partners and I haven't and it's starting to get to me?* Not likely.

"Nothing's wrong, T. What did you need to ask me?"

"You remember my brother Daemon," Jamie said, pausing for Ethan to nod in agreement. "He and Liv have a friend, another Broadway actress, who needs a place to lay low for a few weeks. Apparently, her boyfriend is someone famous—"

"Jackson Hayes," Tessa said to the women at the table, who each sucked in a breath, Kyla releasing a startled squeak.

"Who's Jackson Hayes?" Ethan asked.

"He's a member of Midnight Storm," Sabrina explained.

"I loved them!" Gavin said.

"I don't know Midnight Storm," Ethan said.

"Come on, yes, you do. Jackson and his brother—twins, right?—and a cousin. I don't think the other two guys are related." Gavin glanced around at his friends, but only the women seemed to know what he was talking about. "They were the biggest boy band for like a decade. Even Brodie used to listen to them. Do you guys really not know who they are?"

"Why do we care about Jackson Hayes?" Baz grumbled.

"Looks like he cheated on Daemon's friend and the press are hounding her. Following her everywhere," Jamie said.

"Some creep took a picture of her through her living room window," Tessa added.

"It's not safe for her to stay in New York right now," Jamie said.

"Poor girl," Kyla said.

"Daemon asked if she could come stay with me and Tessa for a little while, but you know Julie's not sleeping through the night again and our guest room is kind of an explosion of baby things." Jamie trailed off, looking at Ethan meaningfully. "I was hoping, since Tessa's old room is empty..."

"It would only be for a week and a half. Two tops," Tessa

said. "Just until the paparazzi frenzy dies down."

"You'd really be helping her out. And us," Jamie said.

Ethan dragged his hand through his hair, scratching at the back of his neck. He wasn't sure how good of a roommate he'd be, but at least playing host would give him a chance to take his mind off of Hannah. And if that distraction could also help out a friend in need, well, maybe that was a win-win situation he shouldn't turn down. "When does she get here?"

Tessa flew off her chair, wrapping her arms around Ethan and squeezing tightly. "Thank you, Dad. You're the best."

"What am I going to do? Turn her away? I'm not a monster," Ethan said.

"Just a recluse," Baz said.

Gavin smirked. "Unless you count the woman in Boston."

Chapter Five

It was colder than she'd expected. And grayer.

When Hannah had looked up the small town of Aster Bay, Rhode Island, it was all pictures of beaches and historic homes, charming shops and quaint cafes. Somehow she hadn't realized the town's tourism website wasn't necessarily the best representation of what to expect in New England in March. The constant barrage of phone calls and social media notifications had made it hard to think rationally.

Rain pelted the windshield of the car Micah had hired to drive her to Rhode Island as it navigated admittedly charming streets. They drove past those same shops, including a surprising number of adult-themed businesses—a sex toy shop, a lingerie store, and a boudoir photography studio all right there in the heart of the historic downtown. The calm voice of the GPS alerted her driver to an upcoming turn as the cheery sign for Nuthatch Vineyard with its hand painted, metallic gold grapevine came into view. Daemon's brother and sister-in-law had asked her to meet them there. Maybe they thought she could use a glass of wine after the last twenty-four hours. They wouldn't be wrong.

At the end of a long winding road that hardly looked wide

enough for two vehicles to pass at the same time, the farmhouse-style main building of the vineyard came into view. The sprawling grounds lined by tall pine trees looked even more lush and green in the spring downpour than they had on the vineyard's website. A faux grain silo on one side of the wood-shingled building stood out like a beacon on the horizon. The gravel of the driveway and parking lot crunched beneath the tires as the car pulled in alongside the half dozen others already there.

"Do you need help with your bag?" the driver asked.

"No, thank you." She did a last check of her hair in the rearview mirror, finger combing the frizzier bits. "It had to rain," she muttered as she climbed out of the car. Her heels immediately sank in the muddy gravel and she swung the purse over her head, shielding her hair from the worst of the rain.

The driver followed after her, opening the trunk and handing her the handle to her small rolling suitcase. She thanked him again, then jogged across the parking lot to the safety of the front door, dragging the bag through the puddles behind her.

At least there were no photographers.

The clack of her heels and whirr of the plastic suitcase wheels on the lobby's hardwood floor echoed in the cavernous space. At one side of the room, a spiral staircase with a shiny metal railing descended from the second floor beside French double doors of frosted glass. A wall of windows at the other end of the room overlooked the fields, rows of grapes with the bay in the distance. Oversized brown leather chairs were arranged in little seating areas throughout the space, a hallway disappearing off to the left, the walls lined with large black and white photographs: A young couple in front of the main building, the woman's pregnant belly cradled by both of their hands and the names Louise and Henry scrawled in pencil beneath the image. Another of a handsome young man, barefoot, holding up a bundle of grapes in the field above the words "Papa, 1952." A young girl, maybe two or three, proudly showing off a precarious stack of blocks: "Tessa's masterpiece."

"Hannah?"

She stiffened and turned to see a beautiful woman with dark hair and eyes watching her. *No camera.*

The woman pressed a hand to her chest. "I'm Tessa Chase. My husband Jamie is Daemon's brother."

Hannah breathed a sigh of relief and extended her hand. "It's nice to meet you. I'm Hannah Matthews. It's so kind of you and your husband to take me in like this."

"Can I get you anything? Glass of water or wine? Cupcake?" Tessa asked.

"No, thank you. I'm alright."

"I'm sorry Jamie's not here to greet you. There was a small mix up at his restaurant that he had to take care of."

"I hope everything's alright."

"It'll be fine. He got a large order of turnips and apparently the supplier brought him Gilfeather instead of Macomber."

"What's the difference?" Hannah asked.

"Haven't a clue. But Jamie is very particular about his produce." Tessa smiled, but it seemed hesitant. "And I'm afraid there's been a small change of plans."

"Oh?"

"We live in a very small cottage and our daughter doesn't like to sleep through the night," Tessa said with an uncomfortable chuckle.

Oh. I'm being sent away.

That was fast.

"Okay, sure," Hannah said, nodding as her mind unspooled. Why couldn't they have told her this before she drove four hours from New York? "It was a lot to ask. I'll see if my driver is still here and I—"

"No, no, I'm explaining this poorly. You can stay. We want

you to stay. You just won't be staying with us."

"Who will I be staying with then?" It was bad enough to stay with people she'd never met, but at least they were relatives of her friends. That almost made them her friends, through the transitive property or something.

"My father lives on the other side of the vineyard and has a lovely guest room. I should know—I've stayed there many times myself," Tessa said.

"Your father?"

"I promise he doesn't bite and you'll be perfectly safe. I'm sure Daemon and Liv would agree if you want to check in with them. Honestly, you staying with him would be doing *me* a favor because I wouldn't worry so much about whether or not he's feeding himself," Tessa said. "I know it's not what you were expecting, but I really think you'll have a much better time and sleep so much more soundly if you stay with him. I can take you back and introduce you before you decide."

Maybe this wouldn't be so bad. It wasn't what she'd planned, but it was only temporary. And her friends' parents had always loved her growing up. This would be like that. She shook out her hands, as if she could shake off the anxiety slowly simmering inside her.

It can't be worse than paparazzi climbing the fire escape.

Tessa led Hannah down the hallway past even more black and white family photos and glass doors offering glimpses of rooms filled with artfully displayed bottles of wine. At the end of the hall, the only solid wood door in the place stood slightly ajar. Tessa pushed it open, sauntering into the large office space. Like the lobby, it was decorated in dark hardwood and leather with an entire wall of windows overlooking the vineyard.

"Hey, T. When did you get here?"

Ethan's familiar voice crashed into Hannah, bringing her up short as her eyes caught a glimpse of the man in question through the partially open door. She froze where she stood in the hallway, drinking in the sight of him—strong forearms beneath the neatly rolled sleeves of his shirt, the beard she'd become intimately acquainted with only a few days before—

"Just now." Tessa gestured towards the doorway where Hannah stood. "It's alright. You can come in."

For a moment, Hannah considered turning around and running, begging Micah to send the car service back to pick her up, locking herself in her apartment and ignoring the photographers with their incessant phone calls and pounding on her door. She'd thank Daemon and Liv but tell them she couldn't do it. She couldn't stay here. Not when Ethan was standing right there looking at her like he'd seen a ghost—

But she didn't have anywhere else to go.

She took a deep breath and stepped into the office.

"Hannah?" Ethan's forehead creased, his brows drawing together, and he moved towards Hannah with alarming speed and a confused sort of half-smile. "What are you doing here?"

"You know each other?" Tessa asked.

His eyes flicked back towards Tessa, his lips pressed together. "We're acquainted."

"What are *you* doing here?" Hannah asked, the panic she'd barely contained stirring and stretching in her chest.

His eyes crinkled and his lips spread into a smile, disarming and questioning, and she wasn't sure if she should kiss him or run.

Run. Definitely run.

Or kiss him.

Maybe kiss him?

"I live here. This is my vineyard," Ethan said, looking at her like she should have known that crucial piece of information.

But how could she have known? She didn't know anything about Ethan.

Except that he can make you come five times in one night with his tongue alone.

"So you must be…"

"My father," Tessa said, filling in the end of Hannah's sentence.

No. This couldn't be happening. Tessa's father should be an old, decrepit man with thinning white hair and a cane. A frail senior citizen. Not Ethan. Not the man who knew how to make Hannah's eyes roll back in her head and her toes curl.

Oh, God, she shouldn't have had that breakfast burrito at the highway rest stop. She was going to be sick, right there in Ethan's office.

Tessa's eyes narrowed with concern. "Are you alright?"

Hannah tried to smile but it came out as more of a grimace.

"I'm going to get you a bottle of water." Tessa slipped past her, back out into the hallway, leaving Hannah and Ethan alone.

"If you're not here to see me, then what are you doing here?" Ethan asked.

"I'm—I'm here to see Tessa," she said. It was sort of true. Half true, at least. "You never told me you had a daughter."

"You never asked."

Ethan had a daughter. A stunning, full-on adult daughter who reappeared at that moment with a bottle of water.

"Look, Han, now's not really a good time," Ethan said. "We're expecting someone any minute."

Tessa glanced between them. "Dad—"

Ethan continued, "Why don't I call you later and we can get dinner and talk?"

"Ethan, I'm not—"

"I really am glad to see you," he said, squeezing her bicep, his fingers trailing down her forearm and brushing against her hand, leaving heat in its wake.

Tessa eyed Ethan warily. "How do you two know each other again?"

"We're good friends," Ethan said, his eyes crinkling as his smile widened. Something low in Hannah's belly clenched in response to that smile.

Not now.

"Dad, this is Daemon's friend, Hannah. The actress from New York we told you about," Tessa said slowly, as though she were explaining it to a child.

The confusion on Ethan's face contorted into a look of pain. Betrayal. "You? You're the one who's hiding out because her boyfriend cheated on her?"

Her mouth went dry and she forgot how to speak as his expression shifted, the mask of a man she didn't recognize replacing the openness and sparkle that had been in his eyes only moments before.

God, what must he think of me?

Ethan shook his head and spoke firmly, as though he could bend reality to his will. "No, there's been a mistake. You're not—I just saw you a few days ago. You— No." He stormed away from her, disappearing behind his desk and shuffling papers like he was going to find something to prove she didn't belong there.

"I should give you two a minute." Tessa inched towards the door, slipping through the opening and closing it behind herself with a soft snick.

"Ethan." He didn't look up. He just stood there, shaking his head and shifting through paperwork. "Will you please look at me?"

"You were in a relationship with someone else when we…" He trailed off, his voice gone cold.

She swallowed. "It's complicated."

"It's not, though, Hannah. Either you were someone else's girlfriend when you asked me to meet you in Boston last weekend or you weren't."

"Technically—"

"Don't do that shit. There is no gray area here. Did you use me to cheat on him, or didn't you?"

"No." She took a step forward, willing her voice not to shake. "I didn't. I wouldn't. Ethan, you and I—"

"But that's why you're here. Not to see *me*—" He broke off, pressing his lips together. "You're here because there's some scandal with your *boyfriend* and you need to hide from the press." She swallowed. Nodded. "Jesus, I almost feel bad for the fucker. He's getting dragged through the mud and you did the same thing."

"I *didn't*. Jackson and I—"

Ethan growled, a low rumbling sound of disapproval that did very inconvenient things to the parts of her struggling to remember it wasn't a sexy growl.

"We were never really together," she blurted. Ethan's brow furrowed deeper, his eyes narrowing to slits. "It was all a show for the media."

"Explain," he said, crossing his arms over his chest.

"Jackson was my co-star in a Broadway show, a musical adaptation of the Bridget Jones movies." A moment of surprise flickered across his face before he locked it back down, shuttering any emotion. "The show was filmed for a theatrical release. It's going to be the start of his big comeback moment, but he needed to clean up his image. He didn't want people to think of him as the 'heartbreaker' of Midnight Storm anymore. And the fans of the show were already speculating about us… So, we made an agreement that until the film released, we'd pretend to be a couple."

"Why would you do that?"

She hesitated. "Because he's a friend and he needed me."

Ethan seemed to consider this as he studied her face. "But you still called me last weekend. Why?"

She didn't have a good answer to his question. She'd been asking herself the same thing ever since she'd left him. It had been a stupid, risky move, but the idea of being in Boston—in *their* city—and not seeing Ethan had been untenable. "I wanted to see you."

"Weren't you afraid someone would see us together?"

"Hardly anyone ever recognizes me outside of the theatre district. At least, they didn't before yesterday."

"And your *boyfriend* didn't care you were fucking another man?"

She closed her eyes against the harshness of his tone, the bitterness dripping from each consonant and the cold look in his eyes. She'd never seen him like this and it made her want to rewind, go back and do this whole thing over, never get out of the car in the first place and keep driving until… *What? You have nowhere else to go.*

"He's not my boyfriend. He never was."

"He got closer to a relationship with you than I ever did."

"That's not true. I never slept with him."

"But you didn't hide him in a hotel room out of town either."

"I'm not the only one who was hiding," she shot back, anger seeping through her veins where her anxiety had been only moments before. "We both agreed. It was just supposed to be sex."

"I remember what we agreed," he seethed. "My mistake for thinking that after three fucking years it was time to admit—"

Her stupid heart fluttered in her chest, hope warring with her rapidly cooling anger. She didn't want to fight with him. She didn't want to push him away. "Admit what?"

"This is…a lot." A thousand emotions flashed over his face that she couldn't read, except the one coming through loud and clear: disappointment.

Her stomach twisted. "It's still me. I'm still the same person you've known for the last three years."

"That's the thing, though, isn't it, Han? We don't really know each other at all."

Jamie: Ethan, what's the deal with you and Daemon's friend?

Ethan: There's no deal.

Jamie: That's not what Tessa said.

Gavin: Ooo, ratted out by your own daughter. That's gotta sting.

Jamie: Tessa said you know each other.

Baz: That's not possible. Ethan doesn't know anyone outside of Aster Bay.

Ethan: Fuck you. You're more of a misanthrope than I am.

Baz: Yes, but I own it.

Gavin: How do you know her?

Ethan: It's a long story.
Ethan: And it doesn't matter. I said she could stay with me and I'm a man of my word.

Jamie: Tessa said she couldn't tell if you were gonna fight this woman or fuck her.

Ethan: She did not.

Jamie: Believe me, it hurt her to speculate about your dick as much as it's hurting you to hear it.

Baz: Which is it? Fuck or fight?

Gavin: Whatever happened to taking a woman to dinner first?

Jamie: Not a bad idea. You should invite her to trivia.

Ethan: No. She doesn't want to spend any more time with me than I want to spend with her.

Gavin: Uh oh. Grumpy Ethan has entered the chat.

Jamie: If this is going to be a problem, I can ask someone else to take her in.

Gavin: I'm sure my mom would be happy to.

Ethan: It's not a problem.

Baz: Because he's choosing fuck.

Ethan: I'm not choosing fuck.

Gavin: You can't choose fight!

Ethan: I'm not choosing either. She caught me off guard, that's all. Nothing is going to happen between us and I'm not going to fight with her so Tessa can't stop worrying.

Jamie: Then why can't you invite her to trivia?

Gavin: Oh! Maybe he's choosing flirt!

Baz: The precursor to fuck.

Ethan: I hate you all.

Chapter Six

There were daisies on the bedspread. Not just any daisies either. Pink and turquoise technicolor daisies stitched together in some elaborate pattern of fabric scraps. Someone had clearly spent a great deal of time putting together this particular Lisa Frank nightmare of a quilt.

There were daisies on the bedspread and Ethan could hardly look at her. Jackson still hadn't returned any of her calls, she was staying with a man who didn't trust her, and that morning *Superfan* had run an article comparing photos of the two women in the Bora Bora photos with a photo of Hannah in rehearsal for *Bridget Jones' Musical*, their beachy waves versus Hannah's messy ponytail, their bikini bodies compared to her upper arm jiggle.

Ethan pushed past Hannah into the guest room and swept the quilt off the bed, folding it with quick, efficient movements. "Sorry. Julie's been napping in here when she comes to visit. It's her favorite." He retrieved a plain pale blue quilt from a shelf in the closet, sliding the daisy bedspread into its place.

Hannah shoved her rising panic into a box in the corner of her mind. How many times could she do that before it refused to be tucked neatly away? Would it be like those science experiments kids did in elementary school where the baking soda and vinegar bubbled over, sliding down papier mâché volcano walls and spilling onto the floor?

"Who's Julie?" she asked, forcing her thoughts away from vinegar-scented explosions.

"My granddaughter." He spread the more subdued quilt on the bed and shot her a look, as though gauging her reaction. "Something else you didn't know about me."

"You're the youngest grandfather I've ever met." Hannah rolled her suitcase into the corner of the room and chanced a glance in his direction.

Why is this so awkward?

Because he doesn't trust you anymore.

"That's what happens when you have a kid while you're still in high school."

"High school?" She clamped her lips shut to prevent another outburst.

"Stephanie and I were sixteen when Tessa was born." Ethan gathered the stuffed animals from the top of the dresser until his arms were overflowing with plush creatures of every type and color.

A blue dinosaur made of some kind of fuzzy yarn fell to his feet and Hannah bent to retrieve it, handing it back to him. "That must have been hard."

"It was a long time ago." She held his eyes until he blew out a breath, shaking his head. "Yeah, it was hard."

She wanted to ask him so much more, to start the slow excavation of the mystery that was Ethan Hart, but he clearly didn't want to talk about it. At least, not with her.

And who's fault is that? You're the one who turned him down. You're the one who kept secrets.

She took a step back, giving him room to complete his tidying up as the stuffed animals were also deposited in the closet. She sat on the bed, stepping out of her heels and crossing one ankle over the opposite knee so she could massage her sore arches. Heels for a travel day had not been her best idea.

"Please tell Julie thank you for letting me take over her room for a few days," she said.

"It's good for her to learn to share. Girl's spoiled rotten," he said affectionately.

"I'm sure you had no part in that at all."

His eyes locked on the movement of her fingers over her foot and some of the coldness in his gaze melted away, replaced by something softer, something she couldn't quite define.

After a few moments, he looked away, clearing his throat. "Look, Hannah, while you're here, maybe it would be best if we pretended like there's no history between us."

She shouldn't have been disappointed, but she couldn't help the sinking feeling in her stomach. "If that's what you want."

"I think it'll be easier. For everyone."

She nodded. "Okay."

He looked away, scrubbing a hand over the back of his neck. "I'm meeting my friends for dinner in about a half hour. You—"

"I'll be fine."

"—are welcome to join us." He frowned, as though he thoroughly disapproved of her offer not to intrude on his dinner plans with his friends.

"That's alright. You don't have to do that. I'll just order a pizza."

"The Pizza Stone's closed this week. Every second week of March the owners go on vacation and shut down."

"Then I'll order from somewhere else."

"Or you could come to dinner with us. Unless you don't want to come."

"You're already doing so much for me. And what if there are photographers there?"

"In Aster Bay?" He snorted. "Not likely. Even if there were, I promised Daemon I'd look after you." He leaned against the wall opposite her, arching an eyebrow, like he was daring her to turn him down again.

Right. The only reason he was doing this was as a favor to their mutual friend.

"It's nothing fancy, if that's what you're worried about," he continued. "We get together every Monday night at a local bar and eat too much fried food, have a few drinks, and make complete asses of ourselves losing at bar trivia. If you come, we'll have enough people for two full teams. Double our chances of embarrassing ourselves."

"Double your chances of winning, you mean."

"We never win."

Hannah got to her feet, sliding back on her heels. "You've never had me on your team before."

His lip twitched. Not quite a smile, but she considered it a victory all the same. "We leave in fifteen minutes."

The bar was crowded for a Monday night. People in Aster Bay took their bar trivia very seriously, it seemed. Ethan's friends were already there when they arrived and he made quick work of introducing her to everyone. She was grateful to see Tessa at the table, her smile light and open as she invited Hannah to take a seat next to her.

On the other side of Tessa sat her husband, Jamie, who looked so much like his brother it was uncanny. Then came Gavin, with an open, curious smile and shaggy hair, and his wife, Kyla, a pretty blonde with a heart-shaped face. Next to Kyla was Sabrina, a tall redhead in a fitted dress, and her suit-wearing husband, Baz, who seemed to have a permanent scowl except when his eyes fell on his wife.

"Tonight's the night we win. I can feel it," Gavin said, grinning, as he grabbed another mozzarella stick from the platter in the center of the table.

Ethan hadn't been kidding about the fried food and Hannah had to take a moment to breathe, to remind herself there was no moral high ground for abstaining from foods that had been cooked in oil. Depriving herself of mozzarella sticks and Texmex eggrolls and some kind of buffalo chicken wonton thing that smelled amazing wasn't going to solve her problems.

Or make the press stop picking apart five-year-old photographs of her, sweaty from dance rehearsals.

And yet, the little voice in the back of her head—so much quieter now than it had been for the last decade and a half—still whispered that she shouldn't eat anything. She should down a glass of ice cold water before she took even a bite, suck on the lemon wedge that came with said water, slowly chew on the celery stick shoved to the edge of the platter. Then *Superfan* wouldn't be able to compare her cellulite against the swimsuit models' toned asses and concave thighs.

No. You do not have to starve to be in control. You can eat the buffalo chicken thing.

Hannah made a mental note to schedule a phone appointment with her therapist in the morning and carefully placed one of each appetizer on the plate in front of her. No one stared in shock at the fat girl daring to eat fried food. No one stood on their stool and shouted about her inability to control herself. No one even noticed. Despite nearly a year of being in recovery, she still marveled at the complete lack of attention others paid to her eating, as though they weren't all silently calculating the calorie count of every plate of food in sight.

Not that she did that anymore, but she'd done it often enough over the last fifteen years that sometimes the numbers flitted through her brain unbidden, especially in times of stress.

Like having every inch of her body analyzed in the media for people's entertainment.

Her therapist had assured her the constant internal chatter about food would stop in time, but Hannah found that hard to believe. Though her therapist had been right about the other things that stopped—the exhausting need to plan every meal, snack, and beverage in advance; the incessant staticky noise in her brain; the uncontrollable cravings for Oreos.

"Hannah?"

She looked up into the kind face of the tall redhead— *Sabrina, was it?*—who had clearly said her name more than once. Hannah set down her half-eaten wonton and folded her hands in her lap.

You are in control.

"I'm sorry, what did you say?"

"How are you liking Aster Bay so far?" Sabrina asked.

"This is all I've seen of it aside from the vineyard," Hannah answered, "but it looked beautiful on the drive in."

"You have to come with us tomorrow," Kyla, the blonde, said with a wide smile. "We're taking a painting class in the park. Girl's day out."

"That's so kind of you to offer, but I'm sure there are things I should be doing tomorrow other than intruding on your plans," Hannah said.

"Like what?" Ethan asked.

She opened her mouth but nothing came out. He was right. She didn't have anything to do. She'd left her entire life behind in New York. She could hide from the paparazzi at a painting class as easily as she could in Ethan's guest room. It's not like they were around every corner in Rhode Island like they'd been in New York.

"I should probably make some phone calls," she said lamely.

Tessa would hear no argument. "Whoever it is, call them after. I promise to get you back to Dad's after lunch. Jo is watching Julie until two o'clock and I intend to enjoy every last minute of my morning off."

"Besides, the park has surprisingly good cell reception," Sabrina added.

"That settles it. We'll pick you up at seven-thirty," Kyla said.

Hannah hesitated. These women were so kind, so welcoming. It wouldn't be the worst thing to have some friends while she was in town, especially with Ethan so on edge around her.

"I don't know how to paint," Hannah protested half-heartedly.

"That's why you take a class," Sabrina said.

At the front of the room, someone rang a bell and announced a three-minute warning until the start of the trivia competition.

"That's our cue," Tessa said, scooping up the platter from the middle of the table despite the men's protests. "Come on, ladies. Let's show them how it's done."

Tessa, Kyla, and Sabrina moved to an adjacent table, each digging into the platter with renewed interest.

Ethan leaned closer and dropped his voice so only she could hear. "You can play on our team if you'd rather, but Tessa will never let you live it down if you don't join them."

"Hannah!" Kyla called as if on cue, waving to Hannah with a mozzarella stick in her hand.

Ethan hung his head and laughed as Hannah's cheeks heated. "I guess I better..." She indicated the other table as she got to her feet.

"Get your cute butt over here!" Tessa added.

Hannah huffed out an embarrassed laugh, heat rushing to her cheeks. "Why is everyone obsessed with talking about my butt today?" she muttered, recalling the unflattering photo that had run on Encores.com earlier in the day.

"It's a good butt," Ethan said. Her eyes darted up to his, the embarrassed flush of her skin turning into something else entirely. His eyes scanned over her. "Great actually."

The words were flattering, but there was something beneath them, an acerbic edge undercutting the compliment.

"You might be the only one who thinks so," she said. "Well, you and your daughter, apparently."

Ethan's eyes traced her face, lingering on her lips for a fraction of a second too long, before the corner of his mouth quirked up, barely even a smile, but the edges of his eyes crinkled at the corner and she had to ball her hands into fists to keep from smoothing them with her fingers. She knew that smirk, and the deliciously filthy things that usually followed it. A tingle of anticipation danced across her skin.

In her bag, her phone rang, the obnoxious factory ringtone too loud in the overcrowded bar. She dug for the sound, finally retrieving the phone just in time to see Jackson's name flash across her screen before the ringing stopped. Ethan's eyes, glued to the screen in her hand, had gone cold again, his expression blank.

"I should—" She held up the phone lamely and ducked away from the table, slipping out the door and into the parking lot as she hit the button to call Jackson back.

"Hannah Banana!" His warm laughter filled her ears. "Have you seen this insanity?"

She leaned against the brick façade of the bar, resting her head back and tracing the path of an airplane as it streaked across the night sky. "Jackson, what did you do?"

"I know I fucked up," he said, his tone suddenly conciliatory despite the lingering laughter. "It was supposed to be a private beach. No photogs allowed. I didn't even know they'd gotten the shots until they showed up on the internet."

Something shattered in the background on the other end of

the phone, a chorus of laughter and teasing, Jackson's chuckle making it clear he was only half paying attention to their conversation.

"Where are you?"

"Crashing with a buddy in Mykonos. You'd love it here, Banana. The clubs are open all night. Best DJs in the world."

Hannah closed her eyes, sighing. "Should you really be clubbing right now?"

"Hell yeah, I should. You should be too. Gotta be business as usual until everyone moves on."

Because clubbing all night was business as usual for Jackson Hayes. Yet another reminder that the version of him she'd known while they were on Broadway together had only been a curated glimpse of his life.

"They surrounded my apartment building," she said. "They took pictures of me through my window. From my fire escape."

The background noise on the other end dimmed, as though he had stepped outside. "Yeah, I heard. I'm sorry about that, Hannah. I really am. Are you okay?"

"I'm fine." If she said it enough times, would it be true? "I left the City for a bit."

"Good idea. You should come to Mykonos!"

"Jackson, I can't—"

"We could have so much fun! We could even leak some photos for the press to throw them off the trail. What do you think? Want to put on a show?"

"Jackson, no," Hannah said, unable to hold back her exasperation. "I don't want to go to Mykonos. I don't want to plant even more lies in the press. I just want everything to go back to normal."

"It will," he insisted. "Hang in there with me for a little bit longer until the premiere."

"You're kidding. No one will believe we're still together.

They have photos of you with two other women."

"Three, actually," he said, and she could almost picture the abashed look, the 'aw shucks' boyishness that had kept him in his fans' good graces for all these years despite his reputation.

"We have to put out a statement. Micah thinks—"

"I know. He told my people all about what he thinks. What about what *we* think?"

She took a slow breath in through her nose and out through her mouth, watched as the airplane disappeared behind a bank of clouds. "I agree with him. I'm sorry, Jackson. I know I said I'd stick it out until the premiere, but this—" She broke off, swallowing the bile rising in her throat. "I'll pay you back for my treatment. It might take me some time, but—"

"I don't want your money, Banana." He sighed, the noise around him swelling again. "It's fine. I'll tell my people to work on a statement with your guy. We can say we broke up before I went to Bora Bora."

"Thank you."

"No sweat."

The line went dead and she allowed herself three more slow breaths before she went back inside. The trivia game was already underway, but when she re-entered the bar, her steps stuttered. Ethan Hart was staring at her, his blue eyes narrowed and cold, his jaw working, as though he'd stared at the door the entire time she'd been gone, willing her return. She met his gaze, searched his face, and, as she watched, all emotion slipped away again. Like he was wiping a chalkboard clean. How did he keep doing that?

She made her way across the bar, past him to the table with the other women who greeted her with a chorus of her name. But when she glanced back, he was still watching her.

Chapter Seven

"We are the champions!" Hannah sang more than a little off-key, her body swaying to the music in her head as Ethan unlocked the front door to his house.

"Only because Mrs. White and her friends weren't there tonight," he said.

"I told you I'd win."

"It was a lucky guess." He held the door open for her to go through ahead of him. Her hips swayed as she walked past, her eyes bright with laughter.

"We beat you by twelve points. That's a whole category, my friend." She adjusted the dollar-store tiara the girls had been presented with upon winning. It was clearly meant for a child and the plastic gem in the center bore the logo of last summer's blockbuster animated kids' movie, but she'd accepted it with a seriousness as if it were the real thing.

"Traitors, the whole bunch of you," he said, but there was no heat in it.

She laughed and stepped out of her heels. When she bent to pick them up, Ethan's gaze snagged on her ass, the fullness of it taunting him. Just as her laughter and the easy way she'd fallen in with his friends had been taunting him all evening. Just as that phone call and the way she'd gone pale at the sight of his name—*Jackson*—had been driving him slowly insane.

She turned, a question on her lips, and he looked away quickly. "Did you want something to drink?" he asked, heading towards the kitchen.

"Ethan Hart!" she gasped in mock offense. "Were you staring at my—"

"Nope." The tips of his ears grew hot, and he flung open the refrigerator door. She hadn't had much to drink at the bar, so he was confident she wasn't drunk, but she seemed far more relaxed than she'd been since she arrived in Aster Bay. "I've got hard cider, beer—"

"No more alcohol for me," she said, sliding onto a bar stool at his kitchen island. "I get cut off after two glasses."

"What happens after two glasses?"

"Uh uh," she said, shaking her head. "You can't trick me. My lips are sealed." She mimed zipping her lips, turning the lock, and throwing away the key, her hand knocking her tiara off in the process.

Okay, maybe she's a little drunk.

Now that he thought of it, he'd never seen her have more than one glass of wine, and she hadn't had much to eat at the bar either.

"How about something to eat? I think I have some leftover lasagna that's still good."

She leaned her chin on her hand and sighed dreamily. "We should have stopped for milkshakes. Small towns like this always have good milkshakes."

"What do you know about small towns, city girl?" he asked.

"I love small towns!" She wobbled on her stool, catching the end of the bar to steady herself. "When I was touring with *The Little Mermaid*, the girls and I would always find some small town not too far from the theater for our day off. There's always quirky shops and diners with the best milkshakes."

He reached for the milk and a jar of Tessa's homemade chocolate sauce, letting the refrigerator door close behind him. "Closest I've got is chocolate milk," he said, retrieving two glasses from the cabinet.

"I can't remember the last time I had chocolate milk."

"Do you like it?"

"Who doesn't like chocolate milk?" she scoffed. "If anything, I like it too much."

"No such thing." Something like disbelief flickered across her face. "I make a mean glass of chocolate milk."

"Oh yeah? What makes it so special?"

He repeated her lip-zipping gesture and she laughed, her head thrown back, hair dancing about her face. She was beautiful, and he liked her there, in his kitchen, with his friends.

She's not here for you. She's here to hide. She lied to you.

Did she? Or did she just not tell you everything?

He poured them each a glass of milk, spooning in the chocolate and stirring, the tinkling of the spoon against the glass the only sound in the room.

"When were you in *Little Mermaid*?" he asked.

"A few years ago. That's what I was doing in Boston the first time we…"

He watched her, waiting to see how she'd finish that sentence, and tried not to be disappointed when it became clear she wasn't going to. "What part did you play? The whiny one who collects forks?"

She threw her head back and laughed. "Ariel? No. They don't cast women who look like me to play Ariel."

"Why not?"

She shook her head, still chuckling to herself. "I was Ursula. The sea witch. They put this purple makeup on my—"

"Collar bone," he said as her fingers traced the spot in

question. "I remember."

Her eyes went wide, fingers falling away from her clavicle to rest on the countertop. At the time Ethan had wondered about the deep purple contouring. But it was another one of those things they hadn't talked about.

"If I remember correctly, there were purple streaks across the sheets in the morning."

What was he doing?

Watching the way her skin flushed pink, that's what.

She laughed. "You remember correctly. I still can't believe you were interested in me that night. I must have looked ridiculous."

"You looked beautiful. And only a little ridiculous. The Dockside makes a great milkshake. We can go for milkshakes tomorrow." He set a glass in front of her. "But that is the best chocolate milk you'll ever have."

She eyed the drink skeptically. "Looks like ordinary chocolate milk to me."

He raised an eyebrow in challenge and took a sip from his own glass, his eyes locked with hers the entire time. A blush crawled up her throat and his body hummed in recognition. He was fairly certain that if he kissed her, she'd let him. More than that, she'd kiss him back.

Stop. You're not supposed to be kissing her.

Why does she have to be so goddamn kissable?

He set his glass down on the counter and waited for her to drink. She rolled her eyes, the corners of her lips tugging up into a smile, and took a sip from her glass. "Oh my God." Her eyes fell closed. "Why is that so good?" she moaned, the sound going straight to his cock.

"It's Tessa's chocolate sauce. She adds espresso powder and I don't even know what else."

"You win. That is the best chocolate milk I've ever had."

He leaned his forearms on the counter between them so his eyes were level with hers. "What exactly do I win?"

The air between them hummed with the electricity of three years' worth of one-night stands, three years of meetings that ended with her writhing beneath him, screaming his name.

But that couldn't be the way things worked anymore, not when she was publicly involved with another man. Some boy band punk who had publicly humiliated her and left her to deal with the fall out. It was hard to maintain those boundaries when she was sitting in his kitchen, though, her bare feet dangling from the bar stool, her eyes hooded as they roamed his face.

"What do you want?" she asked.

Your thighs around my head. Your taste on my tongue.

Not helpful.

"What happens after two drinks?"

She blinked, the lust clearing from her expression as she processed his question. "After two drinks, I tend to make decisions that aren't very good for me."

"What kinds of decisions?"

She hesitated, then took another sip of her milk. Finally, "That information will cost you more than chocolate milk."

"Yeah? And what is it *you* want, sweetheart?" he asked, leaning closer and taking a sip of his own milk, watching her over the rim of his glass.

Her eyes dropped to his lips, and she got to her feet. "You have some chocolate…"

She swiped a stray bead of chocolate from the corner of his mouth with her thumb and he grabbed her wrist, holding her there for a moment, feeling her pulse jump beneath his fingers. He could kiss her. God, he wanted to.

He let her wrist fall from his hold and dug his hands into the pockets of his jeans, balling them into fists to keep himself from grabbing her again.

Like a freaking caveman. She came here to get away, to feel safe, and you're grabbing her like you have a right to.

Hannah held his gaze as she lifted her thumb to her own mouth, sucking it between her lips to lick the chocolate from her finger. Heat seared down his spine, gathering in his groin with a demanding pulse as he tracked the flick of her tongue, the scrape of her teeth, over the soft pad of her thumb.

"Ethan…"

He stumbled back a step, even though every part of him was screaming to get closer. He wanted to lift her onto the counter and kiss her until she remembered how good they were together, until all the tension in the lines of her forehead was replaced by the soft, languid expression of a woman who had been well pleasured.

After two drinks, I tend to make decisions that aren't very good for me.

He took a step back, dumping the rest of his milk down the sink so he wouldn't have to look at her while embarrassment clawed its way through his stomach. She was a guest in his home, a woman in need of sanctuary. And she'd already rejected him once, mere days ago. The sting of it still prickled at the back of his neck.

"You have a boyfriend," he said.

"It's not real," she whispered, as though that made it sting any less.

He leaned against the apron of the sink, crossing his arms over his chest. "Real enough."

Maybe it shouldn't have mattered to him, this fake relationship of hers, but he couldn't shake the sense there was more she wasn't telling him.

She took a step towards him. "No one would know."

Something cold and heavy congealed in the pit of his stomach, clinging to his bones and making everything feel wrong. He stared her down, stepping so close to her she had to tilt her head up to look at him. When he spoke again, his voice was darker, deeper than he'd intended. "I'd know. And I won't share you. Not even with a lie."

Her eyes went wide, darting between his like she was trying to puzzle something out. At last, he broke the connection, clearing the gravel from his voice and tilting his head down the hall. "There are towels in the hall closet. Help yourself to anything you need."

"Ethan—"

"Goodnight, Hannah."

He left her standing there in his kitchen, her cheap plastic tiara forgotten on the floor.

From *The Lady's Knights* by AK Wild,
narrated by Slade Hardcastle

Sir Llewellyn kept watch from the tallest rampart of the keep. Somewhere in one of the stone rooms below, with only the vicar and one of his knights as witness, Lady Windtorn was taking her wedding vows, not to that despicable oaf who had so misused her, but to Lord Havenbrook. A kind man. A gentle man. Misunderstood, seeking his own sort of refuge in the loveless marriage Lady Windtorn offered.

Still. It rankled.

Sir Llewellyn could offer her the protection of his body, his life and the lives of his men, but he could not stop the coming war. He could not secure the safety of her family. Only a union to a man such as Havenbrook could offer her those things. It mattered not that theirs would be a chaste marriage, a marriage in name only. It mattered only that in the eyes of the world, in the eyes of a god Sir Llewellyn wasn't even sure he believed in, she belonged to another.

He heard her footsteps approaching long before she knocked, the soft patter of her slippered feet on the ancient stone. He wanted to send her away, to reject the tender caress of her gloved hand on his chest, the softness in her eyes.

"It is done?" he asked.

"Aye."

He slid the glove from her hand, a pained noise rising in his chest at the sight of the gold and garnet ring on her finger. "You belong to another. All will know he owns a part of you I do not."

"It is a lie."

The pain in his chest curdled, calcified, drawing anger from his breast. Not at her. Never at her. Only at himself.

"Is it? I own you here," he said, roughly pressing their joined hands over her heart, even though the glint of her wedding ring mocked him still. "And here." A knee between her legs, backing her against the rough-hewn stone wall, the monster in him delighting in her startled gasp, the rise and fall of her bosom. "Tell me, my lady," he snarled, grinding his thigh against the heat at the apex of her thighs, "am I to trust that you lie only to them, and not to me?"

Chapter Eight

"Does this look like a tree to you?" Kyla squinted at her canvas, as though that would make the fuzzy brown and green paint smudges morph into something more closely resembling the tree their instructor was effortlessly painting.

"Sure," Tessa said, also squinting. She looked up at the tree under which the instructor had set up their easel. "Maybe you need more yellow?"

Kyla sighed. "Maybe I should stick to photography."

"It's impressionistic," Hannah said. "Or an abstract. You can definitely spin that into some kind of post-modern masterpiece."

"That's true," Sabrina added, etching deep grooves into the painted column of her tree trunk. "All the priciest galleries slap some kind of fancy label on a painting and it sells for double, even if it's random splotches. Not that your painting is random splotches!" she hastened to add.

Kyla laughed. "It absolutely is." She grinned, nudging Hannah's shoulder with her own. "But it's a post-modern impressionist interpretation of a tree. The vibes of a tree, really."

"They're excellent vibes," Hannah said.

Her own painting more resembled a kindergartener's drawing, all rudimentary shapes and blocks of color. Perhaps she could call it cubist and pretend it was intentional. Or she could ditch it in the dumpster by the parking lot when the class was over.

"So, Hannah, Tessa's too afraid to ask, but we're all dying to know how you know Ethan," Sabrina said.

"Oh, we've been friends for a while," Hannah hedged, suddenly very concerned with adding another layer of swirly leaf shapes to her tree.

"Really? Ethan hardly ever leaves Aster Bay. How did you meet?" Kyla asked.

"Umm we were staying at the same hotel. A few years ago. In Boston," she said. "We met in the hotel bar."

"Did he buy you a drink?" Sabrina asked.

Hannah could feel the blush heating her cheeks. "He did."

"And you've stayed in touch all this time?" Kyla sighed dreamily. "That's romantic."

"Oh, it's not—I mean, we're not—"

"Life is so funny. What are the odds you'd end up here now?" Kyla said, either genuinely confounded by the mysterious ways of the universe or teasing her.

But Hannah knew it wasn't a mystery—it was karma. She'd spent the better part of a year lying to everyone except Liv and Jennifer and now she was stuck living with a man who couldn't see past the lie.

All morning she'd swung between being supremely frustrated with his reaction—they didn't owe each other anything, and it's not like she'd actually lied to him since you can't lie to someone you don't talk to about anything of consequence—and feeling coated in shame and regret. It didn't really matter if she'd technically done nothing wrong. He felt like she'd lied to him, and that was enough to make her wish she could go back in time to their last meeting and say—

What? What would you say? Hi, Ethan, I'm fake dating a

*celebrity to help rehab his image—yes, that's a real thing—but we
should still bang?*

"It must be a relief to be staying with someone you know,"
Sabrina said. "I think I'd be freaked out about going to stay
with a stranger. No offense," she added to Tessa.

"None taken," Tessa assured her.

"Daemon and Liv are excellent judges of character and
good friends," Hannah said. "I trusted they weren't sending me
to stay with an axe murderer or anything."

"What she means is my brother-in-law is overly protective."
Tessa dropped her paint brush into the plastic cup of murky
water on her easel. "I give up. No more trees for me unless
they're piped in buttercream."

"Does that mean we can all give up now?" Kyla asked
hopefully.

"It is still so wild to me that Daemon Chase is your brother-
in-law. I must have watched the *Sound of Music* remake he was
in at least a dozen times just to see that man take his shirt off,"
Sabrina said, setting down her own paintbrush.

Tessa snorted. "Don't let Baz hear you say that."

Sabrina waved away Tessa's comment as they gathered their
things and made their way to the parking lot. "Sebastian knows.
He gets all grumpy whenever he hears the overture now."

"And speaking of celebrities," Tessa said turning to face
Hannah with a grin that could only spell trouble. "What's the
scoop on Jackson Hayes?"

Kyla flung her arm out, hitting Tessa lightly in the stomach.
"Tessa! Ixnay on the Acksonjay." She turned an apologetic smile
to Hannah. "You don't have to tell us anything. It's probably not
something you want to talk about."

It wasn't…and yet, she liked these women. She wanted to
be their friend, even if she was only in town for a short time.
And friends talked about their boyfriends, even the fake ones.

Maybe this would be good practice for telling the story their publicists had crafted.

"It's not as scandalous as the tabloids have made it out to be." *Unless you call pretending to date for almost a year scandalous.* "We met when we were in *Bridget Jones' Musical* on Broadway and hit it off right away, but we realized we were better off as friends. The split happened a while ago, we just hadn't announced it yet because we thought it would be better to wait until after the premiere."

It was the Cliff Notes version of the joint statement Micah had emailed her that morning. By tonight, it would be all over every news outlet that had carried the story of Jackson's cheating. At least, she hoped it would be.

"So he didn't cheat on you?" Sabrina asked carefully.

"Definitely not," Hannah said with a soft smile. "Jackson's a great guy. He's just not my guy."

Kyla leaned against her beat up Honda Civic. "Is Ethan your guy?"

"I'm—What?" Hannah stammered, her cheeks flaming.

Kyla glanced around their group. "You met in Boston a few years ago... You're the woman he saw in Boston last weekend, right?" She turned to her friends. "I'm not the only one who put that together, am I?"

"Jo is going to have a field day with this," Sabrina said.

"You and my dad…" Tessa trailed off, her nose wrinkling in barely contained disgust.

"I don't know what he told you—" Hannah began.

"Nothing. He didn't tell us anything," Kyla said reassuringly. "We wouldn't even know about it if he hadn't told Gavin who told me and then I kind of told them." She flashed an apologetic smile. "Oops."

Hannah sighed. "This is really awkward and I don't think Ethan would appreciate us talking about it."

"He definitely wouldn't," Tessa said. "And that's why we're not going to talk about it anymore, right, ladies? No more talking about my dad's sex thing." Hannah winced. "Sorry."

"Okay, but can you at least tell us why Ethan goes to Boston? He's always so twitchy about it. Unless he's only going to meet you?" Sabrina asked.

"I honestly don't know. The first time we met, he was already there, but I couldn't tell you why."

"He didn't tell you?" Kyla asked.

"I guess you didn't exactly spend all that much time talking," Sabrina said.

"Sabrina!" Tessa screeched.

Oh, God, the ground can open up and swallow me whole now, please and thank you.

Sabrina laughed. "What? Hannah's gorgeous, and Ethan oozes stern, daddy vibes—"

"And that's enough of that," Tessa said, clapping her hands. "Who's ready for lunch?"

"You look like hell." Baz walked into Ethan's office like it was his own, dropping a stack of files on the desk and taking a seat opposite Ethan. As if Ethan could focus on reconciling his finances today.

"It's Cheryl and Ricky's new rooster. It's getting harder and harder to be their neighbor."

Baz sucked his teeth and shook his head. "No, I don't think that's it."

"It wouldn't have something to do with the pretty brunette staying in your guest room, would it?" Gavin asked as he and Jamie joined them.

"What are you two doing here?" Ethan asked.

Jamie shrugged. "I'm here for moral support."

"How's Hannah?" Gavin sing-songed.

"You call this moral support?"

Jamie took a seat next to Baz. "You two seemed friendly enough last night."

Ethan scowled and flipped through the folders Baz had deposited in front of him.

"More than friendly," Baz added.

"Flirtatious even," Gavin said, grinning.

"She doesn't know anyone in the area. I didn't like the idea of her spending her first night in town alone. That's all," Ethan said.

"Oh, is that all?" Gavin's grin grew larger. "It didn't have anything to do with the fact you kept staring at her ass?"

"Did not."

"Yeah, you did." Baz took the folder from Ethan and flipped to the current year's income statement before handing it back. "But you weren't so grumpy about it last night."

"I'm not grumpy," he snapped.

"Definitely grumpy," Jamie said. "Something must have happened between last night and now."

Ethan looked away and tried to focus on the balance sheet in front of him, but the numbers blurred and dissolved on the page. He dropped the folder back on his desk and dug the heels of his hands into his eyes with a groan.

"The numbers are right," Baz said. "Double checked them myself this morning."

"It was nice to see you so relaxed last night. We haven't seen you like that in weeks." Jamie exchanged a glance with Gavin. "And we thought if the reason for that change was Hannah—"

"It's not."

"But if it *was*—"

"Nothing else can happen with me and Hannah."

Shit.

His friends' eyes widened and they exchanged another one of those glances that made Ethan want to put his fist through a wall.

"But something *did* happen?" Jamie asked.

Ethan sighed. He didn't suppose there was any point in denying it. "Hannah is the woman I spent time with in Boston."

Gavin leaned forward. "And by 'spent time,' you mean—"

"They fucked," Baz said.

"For Christ's sake," Ethan muttered. "We've known each other for years."

"*Years?* You've been seeing someone for years and didn't tell us?" Gavin asked, wounded.

"Not exactly." Ethan sighed. "We see each other a few times a year when we're both in Boston. That's it. Until she showed up here yesterday."

"Well, fuck," Baz said.

"Wait, I thought Hannah was in Aster Bay because her famous boyfriend cheated on her," Gavin said.

"I think we figured out why he's so grumpy," Jamie said, motioning to Ethan.

"I'm not grumpy!" Ethan forced himself to take a slow breath, but it didn't keep him from shooting daggers at his friends with his eyes.

"But they're not together now, right?" Gavin asked carefully. "I mean, she wouldn't have met with you in Boston if they were still together."

Ethan shook his head. He wasn't sure how much Hannah wanted everyone else to know about the terms of her relationship with Jackson Hayes, but he didn't want his friends to think she was a cheater, either. "No, they're not together."

"Okay!" Gavin leaned back in his chair as if that solved everything.

"Not okay. Hannah's made it very clear she has no interest in anything more than our previous arrangement."

"I'm pretty sure moving into your guest room is more," Gavin said, looking to his friends for agreement.

"That's just logistics," Ethan said.

Jamie leaned forward, bracing his elbows on his knees and clasping his hands. "Do *you* want more?"

Did he want more than a handful of nights a year of feeling like he hadn't missed his chance at love? Of course, he did. But dating was exhausting. Maybe that was why he'd asked Hannah to see him outside of their arrangement in the first place. He was tired—of trying to find his person, yes, but also of being alone.

It didn't matter. Anything with Hannah was out of the question. She had lied to him, even if she hadn't really been dating that slick boy band asshole. She still should have told him.

Like you told her about your life?

It was different. Her life was complicated in ways he couldn't even begin to imagine, and the last thing he wanted was a paparazzi spotlight shining in his direction.

"It might not be the worst thing she's here now," Gavin said. "It gives you both some time to figure out what you want from each other."

Ethan swallowed the bitter taste at the back of her throat. "I don't want anything from her. Did you miss the part about her being caught up in a media scandal?"

Baz shrugged and pointed at Gavin. "He married his son's ex." He flicked his hand towards Jamie next. "He got together with your daughter behind your back. My wife was supposed to be my sister-in-law. 'Famous ex-boyfriend' isn't so bad."

"Knock, knock!" Mrs. White's voice reverberated off the hardwood in the office as she and her friends pushed into his office. The four octogenarians had been Ethan, Baz, and Gavin's elementary school teachers. Now they settled for beating them at bar trivia every week.

"Nice jackets, Mrs. B," Gavin said to Mrs. Blumenthal, who had struck a pose to show off the hot pink bomber jackets they all wore, the words "Grandma Gang" embroidered across the back.

"Aren't you sweet," Mrs. Blumenthal said, grinning.

"Rumor has it your ladies wiped the floor with you at trivia last night," Mrs. Kemp said.

"I don't know that I'd say *that*," Jamie protested.

"What was it Mikey said?" Mrs. Greene asked Mrs. White. "That these boys didn't stand a chance?"

"It was only twelve points," Ethan said.

"That's a whole category," Mrs. Blumenthal said, barely containing her laughter.

"Did you all come down here to mock us?" Gavin asked.

"No, dear. As much fun as that does sound, we have some pressing business with Ethan," Mrs. White said.

"You do?" Ethan asked.

"We most certainly do! Who is the charming young lady staying with you?" Mrs. Blumenthal said. "Your mother didn't know anything about it."

"You told my mom?" Ethan groaned.

"I didn't realize I was telling her anything she didn't already know," Mrs. Blumenthal said.

"Wait, how do you even know about Hannah?" Jamie asked. "She only got in yesterday and you weren't at trivia last night."

Mrs. White scoffed. "One of these days you're going to learn, we know everything that happens in this town."

"Wait, do you know Midnight Storm?" Gavin asked, turning in his seat to better face the women. "They had that big hit about driving through a hurricane to take a girl on a date."

"That is definitely not advisable behavior," Mrs. Greene

said. "But, yes, I remember the song. The children in my class couldn't stop singing it all year," she said, shaking her head.

"Ha! I told you! Everyone knows Midnight Storm," Gavin said, turning back to his friends with a satisfied smirk.

"Don't change the subject," Mrs. Kemp said. "Who is the young woman in your guest room?"

"Her name is Hannah and she's just visiting. She needed a nice, *quiet* getaway," Ethan said pointedly.

"We should invite her to join us for book club," Mrs. Blumenthal said. "I bet she'd have lots of interesting things to say about this week's selection."

"You have a book club?" Baz asked.

"Of course, we do. Strictly romance novels," Mrs. Greene said.

"The filthier the better," Mrs. Kemp added with a wink.

"I bet you'd like this week's book, Ethan," Mrs. White said.

"I'm not sure I would," he said, the hair on the back of his neck prickling.

He should have known better. He should have sensed the old woman knew something. Hadn't she already said she knew everything that happened in Aster Bay? Not that he really believed it, except…well, maybe he believed it a little.

"It's a lovely medieval romance," Mrs. Kemp offered. "*The Lady's Knights.* That's 'knights' with a 'k,' you see—and there's more than one of them." She bobbed her white eyebrows suggestively and Ethan felt all the blood drain from his face.

"Not sure why you'd think I'd be interested in something like that," Ethan said carefully.

Mrs. White ran an assessing eye over him, like she could see right through him but was choosing to let him keep his secret for now. "My mistake," she said at last.

"We should host a book club meeting at this year's Reader Fest," Mrs. Blumenthal said.

"It's the least they could do to give us a space for a meeting since we're practically planning the whole thing," Mrs. Greene said.

"You're planning Reader Fest?" Gavin asked. "I thought the library was in charge of that event."

"Time to shake it up, don't you think?" Mrs. Kemp said.

"Tell your lady friend she has a standing invitation to join us," Mrs. White said.

He definitely wouldn't be doing that. "I definitely will."

"What was that about?" Jamie asked after the grandma gang had finally left.

Ethan shuffled the papers on his desk, avoiding his friend's eye. "I have no idea."

Chapter Nine

"Then I said to my Ricky, I said, 'Ricky, you get out of that tree!'" The woman broke off another piece of the giant chocolate chip cookie she held in its wax paper wrapping and handed it to the preschooler at her feet without missing a beat in her story. Hannah watched as the child accepted the treat with a chubby hand and a toothy smile. "I said, 'Jamie needs all your best Macomber turnips and he needs them now.' And wouldn't you know it, he didn't *have* any Macomber turnips and that's how Jamie got into this mess!"

Ethan shot a secret smile at Hannah. "Cheryl, have you met Hannah?"

"I don't believe I've had the pleasure," the woman said, dusting cookie crumbs off her fingers by brushing them against her pant leg before extending her hand to Hannah. "Cheryl DaSilva. My husband Ricky and I run the farm around the corner from Ethan's vineyard. We're practically neighbors."

"Oh, you're the one with the rooster," Hannah said as she shook Cheryl's hand.

Cheryl beamed. "Terrence."

"The rooster's name is Terrence?" Hannah asked.

"Terrence McFancyCock," Cheryl said seriously. "He's new.

Still settling in. Like you, I imagine?"

"Hannah's staying with me for a bit," Ethan supplied.

Cheryl's smile spread, her eyes bouncing between Ethan and Hannah where they sat in the diner booth as she handed another piece of cookie to her son. "Well, I just love that for you! About time, if you ask me," Cheryl said. "We've all be wondering how long it would take before you settled down."

"Oh, we're not—" Hannah said.

"Though, of course, I wouldn't have minded if you waited another few months. Then Ricky and I would have won in the pool."

"Excuse me?" Ethan said, his eyes narrowing at lightning speed.

"You know, the little wager some of us have going about when you'll finally meet your Mrs. Right. Don't tell me you didn't know about it? Mrs. Kemp mentions it in her weekly newsletter all the time."

Ethan scrubbed a hand over his face. "I don't really do email."

"There's a newsletter?" Hannah asked, glancing between Ethan and Cheryl.

"The Kemp Report," Cheryl said, nodding. "I think she has more subscribers than the local paper, last time I checked anyway."

"Of course she does," Ethan muttered.

"Mama," the little boy on the floor whined, tugging on Cheryl's shirt.

"Yes, sugar bear, we're going. It was so nice to meet you, Hannah. I'm sure I'll see you around." Cheryl took her son's hand and led him out of the diner in a whirlwind of hollered goodbyes and blown kisses to the woman wiping down the tables.

Hannah stared at Ethan in shock, not quite sure what exactly she should say in the aftermath of extravagantly named roosters and a town-wide bet on when Ethan would get married.

"Anyway, that was Cheryl," Ethan said, pulling his milkshake closer with a shake of his head and taking a long sip from the straw.

"She seems nice."

Ethan barked out a laugh that made Hannah smile despite herself. "She's very nice. Just like her husband and most of the people in this town, who have apparently been betting on my dating life."

"I guess we've both had our love lives put under a microscope recently." Hannah took a sip of her milkshake.

He frowned, stirring his milkshake with his straw. "How long do you think it will be before the press leave you alone?"

"I don't know. We're releasing a statement tomorrow that will probably fuel the fire for a bit, but hopefully it'll die down after that."

"A statement?" He glanced up at her, but quickly looked away again. She wished she knew what he was thinking.

"Mmhmm. Saying we broke up a few weeks ago, before the pictures were taken of him on vacation."

"So it doesn't look like he cheated on you," Ethan said.

"Exactly. If he didn't cheat, there's no story anymore. At least, that's what I'm hoping." She snagged a French fry off his plate and dragged it through her milkshake. The salt and sugar hit her tongue and she seriously regretted her choice to order a salad for dinner, but old habits die hard.

As if he could read her mind, Ethan pushed his plate closer to her. "And then you'll go back to New York?"

"Are you sick of me already?"

She'd meant it as a joke, but as the words landed between them, she realized how nervous she was to hear his answer, to be reassured he wasn't trying to figure out how quickly he could get her out of his house—out of his life.

Stupid. You were the one who turned him *down, remember?*

"No chance, Han," he said softly, nudging his plate even closer. "Don't like the idea of people saying shitty things about you, that's all."

It was her turn to laugh. "Ethan, the things the tabloids write aren't even the half of it."

"What does that mean?"

She shook her head. "Nothing. Let's forget about it. I don't want to think about the keyboard warriors right now."

"Hannah—"

"What should I do tomorrow while you're working? Tell me all the sights I should see."

He seemed to debate letting her deflect, his eyes roving over her face, before he finally leaned back in the booth, bringing his milkshake with him. "What are you interested in?"

"I don't know. Everything," she laughed. "I promised Tessa and the girls I wouldn't hit the shops without them, though. We're apparently having a girls' day out on Thursday."

"There's some good museums in town, a historic farm, some old mansions, that kind of thing. It's kind of cold for the beach but—"

"Museums sound great," she said. "Can I walk to them?"

He chuckled. "No, Han, you can't walk to them. We're a small town but we're not that small. You can take my truck." He arched an eyebrow, the corner of his lip lifting. "You do know how to drive, don't you, city girl?"

"Yes, I know how to drive!" She threw a wad of napkins at him across the table, laughing. She hadn't driven a car in at least five years, but he didn't need to know that. Driving was like riding a bicycle—it's not like she'd forgotten how.

He pressed his lips together to fight the smile as he fended off her napkin attack. "I'll draw you a map."

She rolled her eyes. "I have GPS on my phone, Ethan. If you can tell me what the museums are called, I'm sure I can find them."

They ate in silence, sneaking glances at each other between bites. Each time their eyes met, Ethan looked away, but Hannah didn't miss the way his eyes sparkled, his mouth curving into the smirk she saw so often in her dreams. His knee brushed against hers under the table, but neither of them moved away.

"So, what exactly does a vineyard owner do all day?" she asked, stealing another fry.

He shrugged one shoulder and set his burger down, wiping his hands on the napkin in his lap. "Mostly paperwork, to be honest."

"Scintillating." It was Ethan's turn to toss a napkin at her and she giggled as she caught it out of mid-air. "Did you always want to work in the wine business?"

"Didn't have much choice, really," he said. "Nuthatch has been in my family for three generations. My owning it one day was always the plan."

"I didn't ask about the plan. I asked if you always wanted to work there."

"Same thing."

"No, it's not."

He leaned back in the booth, his hands resting in his lap, and his knee still lightly pressed against hers. She wanted to focus on his words, but how could she be expected to pay attention to anything when she could feel the heat of his skin through his jeans?

"When I was six, I wanted to be a garbage man. I liked the idea of riding around on the back of the trucks." She crossed her forearms on the table, leaning forward with an encouraging tilt of her head. "Then, when I was ten or twelve, I wanted to be an engineer. Build bridges."

"And then?"

He cleared his throat and moved his knee away from her,

cold seeping through the thin fabric of her jeans. "And then when I was sixteen, I became a father, and it seemed like a pretty selfish thing to ignore the fact I had a built-in career that could easily support my family."

"Ethan—"

"What about you? Did you always want to be an actress?" He took a bite of his burger, chewing it slowly, his eyes focused on his food.

"Yeah," she said, sitting upright again and stabbing at her salad more aggressively than was necessary, spearing bits of lettuce and radicchio. "For as long as I can remember anyway. My mom says, when I was little, I used to stand on the front steps of our house and make up songs, sing to the passing cars and the birds." He looked at her then, his eyes focused on her with such intensity she thought he might be able to see the memory playing in her mind. She looked away, pushing sunflower seeds and shredded carrots around on her plate. "I almost became a nurse instead, though."

"Why's that?"

"My mom was a nurse. It's a good, stable job. And there aren't a lot of parts in professional theatre for women who look like me." She immediately regretted saying it.

"Look like you?" he repeated.

"Turns out I get squeamish at the sight of blood," she said quickly. "I changed my major before I'd even finished freshman year."

"What do you mean, women who look like you?" he asked.

She sighed, setting down her fork. "Women who aren't a size two. Women who aren't delicate or dainty or whatever."

He clenched his jaw, a low rumble of disapproval sounding in his throat.

"It's just the way it is," she said, picking up her milkshake. She brought the straw to her lips, then changed her mind, and set it down again. Ethan's eyes narrowed further. "It's part of the job."

"People criticizing your body is part of the job," he repeated as though it were the most unbelievable thing he'd ever heard. "You know, in other fields that's considered an HR violation."

"Welcome to show business," she said, flashing half-hearted jazz hands.

"Show business can fuck right off," he mumbled.

Her heart fluttered in her chest at the gruff protectiveness in his tone. After another few beats of eating in silence, he nudged her milkshake closer to her. "It's gonna melt."

She took a long sip, letting the cold liquid cool her rapidly heating blood.

"What was your favorite role?" he asked.

"Bridget in *Bridget Jones' Musical*."

She couldn't help but smile thinking about it, how surprised she'd been to get the call back, the absolute shock when she'd gotten the part. Not because she hadn't worked her ass off for it and nailed her audition, but because she'd started to think it might not happen for her. She might spend her entire career playing old women and witches, the occasional best friend, but never the romantic lead.

"Tell me about it," he said.

So she did. In a red vinyl booth in a diner in Rhode Island, she told him what it was like to stand on stage and feel free, in a part that didn't require her to squeeze herself into multiple layers of shapewear beneath her costume. She told him about the teenagers she'd meet at the stage door every night, girls in average sized bodies like her who said they saw in her the possibility of living out their own dreams, girls she wished she could spend the whole night talking to, encouraging, guiding them away from her own mistakes.

And when Ethan's knee slowly pressed against hers beneath

the linoleum tabletop again, she had a thought, fleeting and inconsequential, but so real she felt it in her bones—she'd sung for packed audiences, been picked apart and judged by thousands of people every night, and no one had ever seen her the way he did.

Ethan hit the side of his computer monitor with the palm of his hand. "Come on," he grunted.

"Dad? Are you in here?" Tessa's call from the lobby had Ethan on his feet and striding out of his office.

"I'm here. Everything alright? Where's Julie?" he asked as he nearly collided with Tessa in the hallway outside his office.

"Everything's fine. I came by to drop off some things for you and Hannah but I saw the light on over here." She lifted the stacked cardboard containers in her hands. "What are you doing in your office so late?"

Ethan took the containers from her, leading her back towards his office, the light spilling through the open door and casting shadows on the hallway.

"It's not that late."

"It's almost midnight."

Ethan set the containers on the edge of his desk and dragged his knuckles over his eyes. He'd been staring at the stupid computer screen for longer than he realized. "What are you doing out this late?"

"Julie finally went to sleep. I didn't get a chance to bring these things over earlier."

He gestured to the containers. "You didn't need to do that."

"We both know you don't cook. You barely grocery shop. I wanted to make sure you had some things—muffins, a loaf of bread, a quiche. Nothing fancy."

"Thanks, T. I appreciate it."

"I know you do."

"Next time, though, you call me and I'll come pick them up. You don't need to leave your house in the middle of the night for me."

She rolled her eyes. "Why are you working so late?"

"Not working. Just…checking on some things."

"Well, that's cryptic." Tessa rounded his desk, her eyes sweeping over his computer screen before they narrowed. "Are you Googling Hannah?"

"Trying to, but the stupid computer isn't working."

Tessa looked at him like he'd lost his mind. "You're not serious. You don't actually think this is how you Google something." She leaned closer to the screen and read off: "Google, plus sign, Hannah Matthews, plus sign, bad things?"

"Then what the hell am I supposed to do?" he said.

Tessa leaned forward, her fingers flying over the keys on his keyboard. "First of all, you don't need the plus signs. It's not the nineties anymore." He grunted, crossing his arms over his chest. "Second of all, it helps if you're using an actual browser window and not the search bar on your desktop. That one's for looking through your files and stuff, not finding things on the internet."

She straightened, crossing her own arms over her chest in a posture that mimicked his so perfectly it would have been funny if he wasn't feeling twelve kinds of foolish.

"And why are you looking up 'bad things' about Hannah? I thought you liked her."

"She said something at dinner tonight about people writing mean things about her online."

"And you wanted to read them because…"

"I don't know! Maybe I wanted to get a sense of what she's dealing with."

Tessa considered his answer for a minute before nodding and typing something into his computer again. "Be careful what you wish for, Dad."

With a final click, she stood upright and gestured for him to come take his seat in front of the monitor. The screen was filled with a list of articles with headlines like "Jackson Ditches the Dead Weight" and "Heartthrob Moves On; Plain Jane Girlfriend Devastated." He scrolled and the list went on, a never-ending stream of articles picking apart photos, entertainment 'experts' weighing in on their body language, so-called sources close to the couple offering their two cents about the inevitable demise of Hannah and Jackson's relationship.

"Jesus Christ," he said, clicking on the first headline. A photo of Hannah and Jackson at lunch in some New York City restaurant filled the screen, red circles drawn around Hannah's exposed upper arms, the profile of her chin, Jackson's hand holding his cell phone. The article beneath the photo called out what they claimed were signs the relationship had been on the rocks months earlier, starting with the ways Hannah had 'let herself go,' her alleged (but not visible) double chin their proof.

"Hannah probably wouldn't like you reading that," Tessa said.

"Then she shouldn't have told me about it. How do you leave a comment on this thing?"

"Dad—"

He jabbed a finger at the computer screen. "This dipshit—NotThatXtina97—is saying shit about Hannah that's not true. Someone needs to set the record straight."

"And that someone is you?"

"Look at this other loser—WannaFreakU—what the fuck kind of name is that? Mr. Freak—"

"Mr. Freak?"

"—thinks it's okay to comment on a woman's body on the internet. I bet he hasn't even seen a woman's body in real life."

"Dad, they're trolls. This is what they do. They go on the internet and they write shitty things in their own shitty little echo chambers. Do not feed the trolls."

"I'm not going to feed them, T, I'm going to rip them a new asshole."

Tessa leaned against his desk. "You like her."

"What?" He clicked aggressively on what he hoped was the 'reply' link, but instead an ad for Pure Sexxy Juice Enhancer filled his screen.

"You like Hannah." He glanced at his daughter, his jaw clenched so tightly he thought he might crack a tooth. "Come on, Dad. I already know she's the woman from Boston."

"How did you— I'm going to kill that husband of yours."

"Jamie didn't sell you out, don't worry. We try very hard not to talk about you as much as possible," she laughed. "It wasn't that difficult to put together. What I'm struggling to make sense of is why you're trying to act like she doesn't mean anything to you when you are so clearly into her."

"I am not," he grumbled.

"You couldn't stop staring at her ass the whole time we were at trivia."

"Fucking hell." He dragged his hand over his face, leaned back in his chair and looked up at Tessa, meeting her challenging stare with a scowl. "I thought you and I had an understanding: we don't talk about our love lives."

"So you admit there's something to talk about." Tessa grinned.

"It's complicated," he finally said.

"Why? Because of Jackson Hayes?" she asked. When she looked at him like that, all defiance and laughter mixed together, she looked so much like her mother it made him almost lose his breath. "She said it's been over for a while, long before you two had your little weekend getaway."

"She told you that?" Tessa shrugged, so he continued. "It's

not about Jackson. She lied to me."

Tessa's eyes went wide. "About what?"

"About all of it. About her relationship, and her job, and—all of it."

"Did she lie to you, or did she just not tell you?"

"Same thing."

"Did you tell her everything? Did you tell her you like her?" When he didn't answer, Tessa huffed out a half laugh. "Was that lying too?"

He deflated, the last of his bluster slipping from his shoulders. His daughter was right. He hadn't told Hannah anything about himself, not really, so what right did he have to expect she should have told him about her life? To punish her for holding things back?

Tessa tapped the tower of cardboard containers as she stood, moving towards the door. "Don't forget to put these in the refrigerator."

Alone again, he turned his attention back to WannaFreakU and the other trolls filling the comment section with their abhorrent views on Hannah's appearance. He wasn't sure what to do about the visceral longing filling his chest when he thought about her or the way his pulse had hammered in his throat when she'd pressed her knee against his beneath the diner table that evening, but he knew how to tell a patriarchal jerk to shut the fuck up.

Dear Mr. WannaFreakU, he typed.

From *The Lady's Knights* by AK Wild,
narrated by Slade Hardcastle

Sir Llewellyn watched from the edge of the forest outside the castle's walls as the rider drew nearer, a billowing cloak thrown over their form and shielding them from his view. The figure rode astride the great horse, their face in shadow, and his heart sank. She had sent someone in her stead, no doubt to tell him his lady would never come to him again. She was a married woman now, after all, even if he knew it to be unconsummated, a marriage in name only. A marriage nonetheless. A prison in its own way.

Bile rose in his throat.

The horse slowed a few feet from him and the rider threw back their hood, Lady Windtorn's long, raven-dark braid tumbling loose from the cloak. She smiled, the curve of her lips slicing through him sharper than any scythe or sword. He met her in two strides, lifting her from the horse and kissing her before her boot-laden feet ever touched the soft earth beneath them. He kissed to consume, to claim.

"I thought you would not come," he confessed when they pulled apart, gasping for breath.

"I will always come," she promised.

"Your husband may disagree," he spat.

"My husband is not here."

She caressed his cheek, the leather of her glove a cursed barrier between their skin he refused to tolerate. He tore the glove from her fingers, dropping it at their feet as he pressed her palm to his lips.

"I have made for us a refuge," he said as he trailed his lips along her jaw. "Our own kingdom, where none shall find us." He nipped at her ear with a wicked grin. "Save those you would like to join us, my lady."

"A world within worlds," she said, her limbs soft and pliant as he swept her into his arms, leading her and the horse deeper into the forest, towards the glowing torch light he'd left behind at the encampment.

"The one true world. Where your only duty is to yourself, to pleasure."

"And to you."

He shook his head. "Your pleasure is my own, my lady." He set her on her feet at the edge of the circle of canvas tents, each one guarded by one of his men, their mail glinting in the firelight. "As it is theirs."

Lady Windtorn scanned the circle of knights, men who had fought for her, loved her, who would gladly die for her, and her eyes brimmed with unshed tears. Sir Llewellyn bracketed an arm around her waist, pulling her snugly against his chest as she looked out at the men, at the world they'd built to give her respite from the weariness of her life. He ran his nose up the length of her neck and pressed a kiss behind her ear.

"Tell me, my lady, what is your pleasure?"

Chapter Ten

"I'm coming," Hannah mumbled into her pillow as her hand blindly searched for the source of the incessant ringing. Finally locating her cell phone, she glanced at the screen to confirm it wasn't yet another reporter hoping for a comment, and reluctantly answered. "Liv? Is everything alright?"

"Oh no, were you sleeping?" her friend asked over the sound of the *Sesame Street* theme song blaring in the background. "I'm sorry. My sense of time is all off. Sleep regression," she said.

"It's fine. What's going on?" Hannah dragged herself to a seated position, though her eyes were still barely open. Somewhere in the distance Terrence McFancyCock crowed… again. She wondered if there was any place in town that sold ear plugs. Or a rooster murdering kit.

"Can't I check in on my friend?"

Hannah's eyes opened. "Liv, seriously. You're freaking me out."

"How's your new roommate?" Liv asked in a sing-song way.

Hannah sighed. "I take it you talked to Jamie and Tessa."

Liv squealed, the sounds of Elmo and his friends growing more distant. "What are the freakin' odds? Is it amazing? Are you having the best sex of your life?"

"We're not doing that."

"Why not?" Hannah could practically hear her friend's pout through the phone.

"Because he wasn't exactly thrilled to find out I had a boyfriend," Hannah said, lowering her voice.

"Fake boyfriend. Come on, he can't really care about that."

"He did very much care about that."

"Okay, well now you don't have a fake boyfriend anymore, right? The statement is everywhere. Daemon got stopped on his way to the gym this morning by some guy from Encores. com looking for information about how to find you."

Hannah's stomach churned. "What did he say?"

"You know Daemon. He grunted and the guy backed off. You haven't had any issues where you are, right?"

"No, no issues."

Except I can't stop thinking about climbing Ethan like a tree.

"You sound tired. I'll let you go back to sleep and I'll see you at the premiere."

They said goodbye and Hannah let the phone drop. The premiere was in a little over a week and she had no idea what she was going to wear. She and Jennifer had planned to go shopping before her entire world imploded. Maybe she could convince Tessa, Kyla, and Sabrina to help her find something nearby on their girls' day.

Terrence crowed again. There was no use trying to go back to sleep, not with an agitated rooster terrorizing the neighborhood and the anxiety over finding formalwear that fit her hips beginning to gather behind her sternum. Resigned, she pulled herself from bed, tugging on the hem of her oversized sweatshirt as she gathered a change of clothes for the day. A hot shower always did wonders to calm her nerves, even if Ethan did have the largest bathroom mirror she'd ever seen in a private home.

She was so lost in thought about her need for a premiere outfit that she didn't even notice Ethan standing in the bathroom doorway until she'd nearly collided with his chest. He shot a hand out to grip her upper arm and steady her, holding her away from his bare chest, the swirl of dark brown hair between his pecs and the hard lines of his abdomen. He wore a towel slung low around his hips and her face heated as her eyes fixated on the loose knot keeping it in place.

"Sorry. Didn't know you'd be up so early," he said.

"I'm not usually. Liv called and—I'm sorry. I wasn't watching where I was going," she stammered.

She should take a step back, give them both space to breathe. But she didn't.

His lip quirked and she realized too late she'd left her panties on the top of her stack of clothing. With a sharp inhale, she pressed the stack to her chest, trapping the stupid sensible cotton briefs against her. His exhale almost sounded like a laugh and he cuffed the back of his neck, drops of water falling from his wet hair and sliding down his throat, over his chest.

"I was thinking, if you want, I could come with you today. Show you the sights."

Her eyes snapped to his, stupid, reckless hope fluttering in her chest. "I thought you had to work."

"They can live without me for one day."

Her stomach flipped, a strange sort of giddy anticipation bubbling through her, as though she were fifteen again and had just been asked on her first date. "If you're sure... That would be great."

He nodded once and moved past her, out of the bathroom and down the hallway, his chest brushing against her arm as he went past. Sparks burst along the place where they'd touched. She watched him go over her shoulder, his powerful thighs and ass moving beneath the towel as he made his way to his bedroom at the other end of the hall.

She was so fucked.

She shut herself in the bathroom, flipping the lock, and hurried out of her pajamas as the shower warmed. The small room was still humid from Ethan's shower and it smelled like him, like citrus and pine and *man*. The water hit her overheated skin and her eyes fell closed as she let the scent surround her, losing herself in the knowledge that only moments before he'd been in this same spot, naked.

Her hands skated over her breasts, plucking at the already hard tips before sliding down over her belly, her hips. *Just one orgasm, to take the edge off,* she told herself as her fingers found her clit. *Just one little orgasm.*

Had Ethan done the same? Did he stroke his cock in this very shower minutes before, needing to come too badly to care if she was in the next room?

The thought had her on edge faster than she expected. She pressed her forehead against the cold tile of the shower wall and circled her fingers faster as she pictured him, his cock hard and aching with the need to come, the way it would swell in his hand as he jerked himself, rough and fast the way he liked. How he would tilt his head back, the bob of his Adam's apple when he came, the way his abs would contract and his cock would lengthen, thicken. How he'd paint his stomach with his release. How badly she wanted him to empty himself inside her instead. She clamped her lips together to muffle her cry as she came, her head rolling against the tile.

It wasn't enough, not nearly, but it was the best she could manage with hands alone. She cursed herself for not thinking to pack a toy or two when she'd thrown together her luggage for this trip, but she hadn't planned on Ethan Hart.

She quickly finished her shower, dressing in a soft, floral sundress that accented her waist and skimmed over the flare of her hips. Ethan was in the kitchen when she was done, making coffee and looking slightly unsure of himself.

"How do you want it?" he asked. She froze, a thousand dirty thoughts flashing through her mind. Dammit, that orgasm hadn't scratched the itch at all. "Cream? Sugar?" he asked.

"Yes, to both," she said, shaking off the images of their time together last weekend, the filthy fantasies that had accompanied her in the shower.

He set a coffee cup on the counter and tilted his head towards a stool, inviting her to sit. She watched as he moved about the kitchen, gathering items from the refrigerator—a cardboard container of pastries, a jar of homemade jam, another container filled with mini quiches, a carton of strawberries. He set them all on the counter before taking a seat opposite her. They filled their plates in silence, but Hannah couldn't help stealing glances at him. First the knee under the table at the diner and now a full breakfast spread after flashing some serious man chest? She wasn't going to survive another week in his house.

"So, what did you have in mind for today?" Hannah asked as she helped herself to a mini quiche with zucchini slices arranged in a rose pattern in the center.

"There's the art museum at the university. And Aster Place is a historic house museum here in town, that could be fun," he offered.

She took a sip of her coffee, holding the warm mug between her hands as though it were some kind of shield, keeping space between them. "Sure. Those both sound good."

He took another bite of his Danish, his lips tugging into a frown. "What would you be doing if you were home?"

"Let's see, it's Wednesday, so I'd start my day with a yoga class, then do some vocal warmups, practice, maybe make a self-tape or two for any auditions." She spread butter on a carrot cake muffin as she continued. "Wednesday is albondigas soup day at the deli down the block, so that would be lunch, then maybe wander a few shops, bookstores, the quirkier the better." She took a bite of the muffin, moaning as the spices hit her palate. "Oh my God, that's good."

Ethan's eyes were locked on her mouth, his tongue sliding over his lower lip as he watched her eat. He was always doing that, as though the sight of her enjoying food was somehow attractive. She blushed at the thought.

After a moment, he blinked, looked down at his plate. "Tessa makes them. Brings me a box every week."

"That's nice of her."

"She thinks I can't cook for myself."

"Can you?"

He speared a mini quiche on the end of his fork and popped it into his mouth whole. "I manage."

"Meaning you know how to boil pasta?" she asked, arching an eyebrow at him.

"And make grilled cheese."

She laughed, shaking her head. "I can't believe your daughter and son-in-law are literal chefs and you can't make yourself a real dinner."

He frowned again and set down his fork. "Didn't much see the point in learning to cook when it's just for me."

She set down her own fork, reaching for him across the table. Her hand landed on his wrist, thumb dragging over his forearm. "Because nourishing yourself is important. And cooking for yourself is a small way to remind yourself that you matter. It can be incredibly healing."

His eyes held hers, a question forming in their depths she wasn't prepared to answer.

"You trying to fix me, Hannah?" he asked softly.

"Do you need fixing?"

He swept up their empty plates and carried them to the sink.

She got the sense he was taking longer than was necessary to rinse the plates and lay them in the sink. After a few moments, he turned to face her, leaning back against the counter. "I know where we should go today."

"Oh, Ethan, aren't you a doll to stop in today?" Mrs. Kemp smiled at Ethan and Hannah from behind the small antique table the museum used as its check in station. "Been a long time since I've seen you here."

"Probably since we came on that class field trip," Ethan said.

"No!" Mrs. Kemp cried, pressing a hand to her chest. "Ethan Hart, that was over thirty years ago!"

"Mrs. Kemp was my third-grade teacher," he explained to Hannah.

"And I clearly did not properly instill in you the value of our town's little museum," she tutted.

"What kind of museum is it?" Hannah asked.

"It's an everything museum!" Mrs. Kemp exclaimed. She pointed to the sign on the table. "The Museum of Everything. See?"

Ethan handed over a ten-dollar bill to cover their entrance fee then led Hannah through the doorway into the museum proper, Mrs. Kemp trailing behind them. The Museum of Everything was housed in a decommissioned elementary school on the edge of the Town Common, the wide hallways cluttered with a hodge podge of mismatched display cases and tables. Ethan kept his hand low on Hannah's back as he led her into one of Aster Bay's more eccentric cultural institutions, more to keep her close than anything.

After that moment outside the bathroom and their exchange

over breakfast, something had shaken loose in his chest, leaving him itchy and on edge in a way he didn't understand. But with his hand on her back, feeling her body shift beneath the thin fabric of her sundress, the itch subsided, soothed by the heat of her against his palm.

"Oh my God." Hannah spun in a circle, her eyes darting around the wide red-brick-and-linoleum hall, the fluorescent lights humming above them. She loosed an astonished laugh before turning back to him. "What is this place?"

He grinned, her delight releasing something in his chest he hadn't realized had been caged before. "Like Mrs. Kemp said, it's the Museum of Everything."

Mrs. Kemp stood in the center of the hall, holding court as she explained the story to Hannah. "It's in the town charter that Aster Bay maintain a museum of its history, but—as the story goes—no one could agree on what was considered worthy of being included. So, the town administrator threw up his hands and told the group of volunteers who keep this place running to do whatever they liked with it." She gestured to a small bronze plaque on the wall commemorating the official christening of the museum in the late 1960s under its current moniker. "Anything that any town resident deemed significant could be submitted for inclusion. But with no guiding criteria, everything that's ever been submitted has been accepted."

"You're kidding." Hannah moved closer to the first display: a collection of hats, ranging from a delicate pale pink pillbox hat with a gauzy lace veil to a garish yellow baseball hat embroidered with the town's name in a slanted script. "It's like the world's largest time capsule."

"It is," Ethan agreed.

"The volunteers, like myself, meticulously document every item donated to the museum. New acquisitions are published in the paper along with testimonials for the reason why someone thought they were important." Mrs. Kemp indicated the baseball hat. "That hat was worn by Lonnie O'Garrity on the day he led Aster Bay High to its first baseball championship." Next, she pointed to the pillbox hat. "And that one was worn by Mrs. Ethel Whitfield on the occasion of her third marriage to Mr. Josiah Whitfield. It was both her third marriage in general and her third marriage to him."

Hannah chuckled. "This might be the coolest museum I've ever seen."

Mrs. Kemp smiled. "I'm glad you think so, dear." She handed Ethan a fat stack of index cards held together with a metal ring through their upper left corners. "That will tell you anything you want to know about any of the items in the museum. Make sure you return it to the desk on your way out. Have fun, you two."

And then they were alone. Hannah moved between displays, excitedly pointing out items that caught her eye for Ethan to look up in the index cards: a wooden spoon Johnny Paulsen had whittled in Cub Scouts in the '80s; a pristine, child's-sized white gown worn by Harriet Fox when she was the first child to be baptized at the newly built St. Anthony's Church in 1912; a cracked China serving platter that had allegedly once been owned by George Aster himself. Ethan read off the stories, but he hardly registered them. He was too busy cataloging Hannah's reactions, the things that made her squeal with delight (a piano forte with a polished lid) and that made her recoil in repulsion (a taxidermied fox).

"What the hell is that?" she squeaked, spinning away from a display case and burying her face in his chest.

Ethan peeked over her shoulder at the shelves of ceramic clowns, each one flashing an unsettling, sinister smile. He chuckled, skating a hand down her spine. "Not a clown fan?"

"Hell no. Look at them."

He leaned forward slightly, cradling her head against him,

until he could read the label on the case. "Ceramic clown collection of Mrs. Winifred Penlow, long-time children's librarian. Donated by her children."

"Because her children knew those things were cursed."

"Cursed?"

"Possessed. Haunted. Whatever. Let's get away from them, please. I can feel them watching me."

He laughed again, guiding her away from the clown display. When they were out of sight, he gently lifted her face away from his chest. "All clear. You can open your eyes now."

She opened one eye, as though she didn't entirely believe him. "Thank you," she said, sheepishly.

"For saving you from the inanimate objects? Any time, Han."

They rounded a corner display of every sports trophy Aster Bay High had ever received and were met with a wall of yearbooks dating back to 1907. "Which one is yours?" Hannah asked, trailing her finger across the colorful leather spines.

Ethan reached around her and pulled a thick volume from the shelf, handing it to her. She arched an eyebrow at him in question, fingers poised to open the cover. "Go ahead," he said.

She flipped open the cover, skipping over the dedication and haphazard collages of dated fashion choices. "No way. Is that Baz?" she asked, pausing on a photo, but her attention was quickly drawn away. "Oh my God, look at you!" She jabbed her finger at his high school portrait, the floppy hair with the center part that had been so popular. "You had heartthrob hair."

He laughed. "It was the style."

She flipped a few more pages, stopping to laugh at Gavin's shoulder-length hair cut, until she got to the half pages designed by each graduating senior. Where his classmates had filled their half pages with collages of logos of their favorite bands, homecoming photos and snapshots of family pets, his stood in stark contrast. There were only two photos beneath his name. First, a photo of him, Baz, and Gavin as kindergarteners, standing triumphant in the treehouse in Gavin's backyard, juice boxes clutched in their six-year-old fists. Second, a department store family portrait of him, Stephanie, and one-year-old Tessa. It was the first time he'd seen that portrait in years.

Hannah ran her fingers over the photos, first the one of him and his friends as children, then the family portrait. "You look tired," she said.

"I was seventeen with a baby and a girlfriend who refused to talk about the future. I was exhausted."

"Are you two still friendly?" she asked.

"She passed a few years back," he said around the lump in his throat. His face was hot and his nose stung, as it did every time he said the words. He and Stephanie hadn't been together for over a decade at the time of her death, but it didn't make her loss any less painful. She would always be the mother of his child, a woman he had cared about deeply.

"I'm so sorry. Ethan, I had no idea."

"We hadn't been together in years. In fact, that photo was taken about twenty minutes before Steph told me she didn't want to marry me."

As soon as he said it, he regretted it. Not because he didn't want Hannah to know about his past, but because it didn't seem like the right place or time to unearth teenage traumas.

"You were just kids," she said.

"I wanted to protect her. Both of them," he said, unable to stop talking about it now that he'd started. "Steph's parents kicked her out when she got pregnant. It was the biggest scandal this town had seen in…a long time. I wanted to make it better. I fucked up her life and it was all anyone could talk about. She said it felt like everyone was staring at her, thinking about how we couldn't keep our pants on. I just wanted to fix it. But she wouldn't let me."

Hannah set down the yearbook and took his face in her hands. "You were teenagers and you made decisions, together, that gave you a beautiful daughter."

"She didn't want to stay here and I couldn't see how we could leave. But everyone was talking about us everywhere we went. I would have fixed it if she would have let me."

"Maybe she didn't want you to."

He pulled away from Hannah. It felt wrong to have another woman's hands on him while he talked about Steph, like he was betraying her memory or something.

"Ethan, I only meant—"

"You're right. She didn't want me to fix it. She didn't want *me*. She took my kid and left town, and it didn't matter that I wanted to be there for her, that I wanted to be the father Tessa deserved, because Steph couldn't handle being a town curiosity so she made those decisions for all of us."

He felt like he'd downed an entire pot of coffee, the strong stuff they brewed at those fancy coffee shops in Providence. He was jittery and too aware of every prickle on his skin but he also felt like he was teetering on the edge of a crash, a comedown so epic he could see it from a mile away but was powerless to stop it.

And he couldn't stop talking. Why couldn't he stop talking?

"So now you know." He crossed his arms over his chest and leaned away from her. "That's my sordid little story. I fucked up when I was sixteen and no matter what I did I couldn't put it right. I couldn't make us a family. I lost out on most of my daughter's childhood because I was always going to stay and Steph was always going to leave." He blew out a long breath, shaking his head. "Bet you're glad you let me tag along with you today."

"I am, actually." She stepped towards him again and wrapped her arms around his middle, pressing her cheek to his shoulder.

He tensed under her touch, but only for a moment, before he hugged her back, as though she could hold together the pieces of himself that were threatening to rip apart at the seams, the old doubts and fears bubbling to the surface. Hannah brushed her lips over his bicep and, as she did, some of his tension seeped away only to be replaced by a new kind of ache, a longing not for what might have been but for what could be.

For the first time in a long time, he let himself consider what it would be like to have what he wanted, not because it was the right thing or what someone expected of him or because it would fix anything, but because he wanted it.

He wanted *everything*.

With her.

Maybe this could be his second chance, one he hadn't dared to hope for. An opportunity to prove to himself—and the town —that he could do things right. He could love someone enough for them to choose him. He could have the picket fence and the kids and the life he'd forfeited when he was still a dumb kid.

Hannah lifted her head, her eyes studying his. "I want to know you, Ethan Hart. Even the messy, sordid parts."

Chapter Eleven

Hannah wasn't sure when Ethan had taken her hand in his, but she liked the feel of his rough palm against hers as they made their way from the Museum of Everything to Plot Twist, a used bookstore a few blocks away. As they walked, Ethan pointed out Tessa's bakery, Kyla's boudoir studio, and a large colonial home that handed out full-size candy bars on Halloween when he was a child. She collected each small piece of him, the glimpses of the life he'd led, as though they were precious gems, wrapped in her affection and tucked away for safekeeping.

The bookstore was nestled on a side street not far from the main downtown area of Aster Bay. Bookshelves stretched nearly to the ceiling with sliding ladders placed periodically throughout the too-narrow aisles. In the back corner of the store, a wisp of sheer fabric had been hung like a canopy over a half-height bookshelf stuffed with children's books, the floor beneath strewn with mismatched pillows and cushions. An elderly orange tabby cat prowled the aisles, casting disdainful glances at any customer who dared get too close.

"Is this quirky enough for you?" he asked as the cat passed, hissing at Ethan on his way by.

"This is perfect!" Hannah gushed, dropping his hand to run her fingers over a pretty hardcover with foil details.

"Ethan!" a tall man with a bushy beard of curly red and gray hair appeared around a row of bookshelves. He set down the stack of books he carried and clasped Ethan's hand in a firm shake. "How did Julie like those Sally the Dog books?"

"She loves them," he said, his eyes lighting up in a way that seemed to be reserved for his granddaughter. "Especially the one on the farm."

The tall man smiled. "If she likes farm books, I just got in a pop-up book she'll love."

Ethan started to follow him down an aisle, but hesitated, glancing back at Hannah. "Go," she said, shooing him away. "I can look by myself."

He nodded, sending her a soft, secret smile, before he followed the man to the children's area in the back corner. Hannah watched for a moment as the cat wove between their legs, flopping on the pile of cushions with an imperious glare at Ethan, and the bookseller began pulling books off the shelves. Her stomach swooped when Ethan opened the cover of one and threw his head back, laughing, then glanced back to find her, holding up the book to show her the giant pop-up cow face from across the shop.

She watched a moment longer, until Ethan was fully engrossed in the business of choosing new books for his granddaughter, before she wandered off in search of her favorite part of any bookstore: the romance section.

Hannah had always believed you could tell a lot about a bookstore by its romance section. Too few romances and the owners were literary elitists—or prudes. But Plot Twist's romance section was the stuff of dreams. An entire long aisle of shelves, lined on both sides with weathered paperbacks and sturdy hardcovers. There were Harlequins in a short, uniform line and larger contemporary romances with bright covers, historical romances with breathtaking paintings of the couples embracing inside the front cover and paranormal romances filled with werewolves and vampires. A treasure trove if she'd ever seen one.

Hannah trailed her fingers over the spines, plucking books from the shelf as she went, until at last she found a small selection of erotic historical romances by AK Wild. She'd only ever listened to Wild's books in audio, but faced with their painterly covers, the defiant heroines rendered in swirls of gold and red against medieval landscapes, she could hardly stop herself from buying a few.

She pulled her favorite, *The Lady's Knights*, from the shelf and flipped open the front cover, gasping when she saw the two-page image she'd only ever seen in fuzzy photos on the internet. A copy of *The Lady's Knights* with the stepback was hard to find—only a few thousand had been produced before the book had been redesigned—but there, in a little bookshop in Rhode Island, Hannah had found one, and it was even more beautiful than she'd imagined.

"What'd you find?" Ethan asked, coming up behind her, a stack of children's books under one arm.

She closed the cover of the book quickly to hide the scandalous scene in the stepback, though she wasn't exactly sure why. Ethan wasn't likely to judge her for reading romance, unlike some people she'd dated in the past, but she still wasn't sure she was ready for him to know about her love of kinky historicals.

"A romance novel," she said, tilting the cover towards him. "It's one of my favorites."

His eyes went wide, but only for a fraction of a second before they pulled low over his brow. He cleared his throat. "You've read it before?" he asked.

"Mmhmm. I've listened to the audiobook at least four times, but—"

Ethan dropped his stack of children's books, cursing under his breath, and bent down to gather them back up. He kept his eyes trained on the books on the floor. She knelt down beside him and helped gather the books, passing him a hardcover collection of Curious George stories. He mumbled his thanks but still didn't look at her.

"Are you going to be weird about this?"

"I'm not being weird," he said as he got to his feet.

She sighed. "You are. I didn't take you for one of those guys who can't handle a woman reading a romance novel."

"What?" His eyes flew to hers, but only for a moment before he looked away again. "I'm not."

"Then why won't you look at me?"

"I'm—" He paused, his nostrils flaring, and then deliberately turned to look her in the eye. "Didn't know you were an audiobook reader, that's all."

She rolled her eyes. "Don't tell me you think listening to audiobooks doesn't count as reading."

"Fuck no. Of course, it counts."

"Then what is this reaction?" She waved her hand in his direction.

"No reaction," he said, catching her hand in his. "Get the book."

"Not if you're going to be weird about it."

"Get the book, city girl," he repeated slowly, his voice low. And good lord, that tone did something to her.

"You should get one too," she said, inching closer to him.

"I've already read them."

"You've read *all* the books?" she teased.

His lips lifted in a smirk. "All of her books," he said, inclining his head towards the book in Hannah's hand.

"You've read AK Wild?" she asked in disbelief.

Ethan stepped closer, backing her up against the bookshelf behind her and leaning down until his lips ghosted over her ear. "Every one."

A shiver ran down her spine at the gravel in his tone, the heat of his breath on her throat. "Which one is your favorite?"

"That one," he answered, indicating *The Lady's Knights*.

Hannah scanned his face for any hint of a lie, but she knew better—Ethan didn't lie. His gaze fell to her lips, his presence crowding her against the bookshelf. He dropped her hand and wrapped an arm around her lower back, angling her hips towards him as he somehow moved closer.

"Get the book, Hannah."

She set the book down on a little side table and tilted her chin up towards him, her body practically begging for him to kiss her. "Maybe you'll read it with me later."

His brow furrowed for a moment, his eyes darting between her own. "Maybe."

Then his lips were on hers, soft but insistent, searching, seeking. As though this was their first kiss. In a way, she supposed, it was—their first kiss since they'd begun sharing parts of themselves with each other that couldn't be revealed by undressing. Their first kiss that wasn't about how many orgasms they could wring from each other before time ran out.

At least, she hoped that wasn't what they were doing this time.

Because she could no longer keep the Ethan she knew from Boston, the one who made her come harder than anyone had made her come before, separate from this new Ethan who picked out picture books for his granddaughter and couldn't cook himself dinner. And she was tired of pretending she wanted to.

He parted her lips with a sweep of his tongue, licking into her mouth, and she opened for him, lifting her hips to meet his. The books he'd been holding fell to the ground at their feet as he slid a hand into her hair, his knee slipping between her legs. She reached her arms around him to urge him closer. He kissed her senseless, his muscular thigh pressing deliciously against the desperate ache between her legs, and she ground against him, whimpering.

"I found a few more—woah," the bookseller cut off, turning away as he came upon them in the aisle.

Ethan and Hannah broke apart, panting. He dropped to his knees, sweeping up the pile of books as Hannah pressed a hand to her mouth, embarrassment mixing with the arousal still flooding her system.

"Sorry to interrupt," the bookseller chuckled. "Just thought you might be interested in this one for Julie."

Ethan grabbed the book, adding it to the stack. "Sorry, Mac."

The man shook his head, smiling. "No apology necessary. In fact, I think it's safe to say those authors would very much approve of what you two were getting up to," he said, indicating the shelf of romance novels.

Hannah groaned and buried her face in her hands.

"I think we're ready to check out," Ethan said, gesturing towards the register at the front of the store.

Hannah hung back as Ethan paid for the books, including *The Lady's Knights*, before following him out of the store into the too-bright sunshine. "I'm mortified," she said as soon as the door closed behind them. "I don't think I've been caught making out with someone like that since I was a teenager."

Ethan pressed his lips together in a—mostly failed—attempt to smother his laugh.

"It's not funny!"

That only made him laugh harder. And the harder he laughed, the more Hannah pouted, until he caught her around the waist and pressed another kiss to her lips, hard and fast.

"Come on. I believe soup was next on the agenda."

A few doors down from the bookstore was a tiny café with oversized window boxes and a cobblestone path leading from the sidewalk to the bright yellow front door. It looked like it had once been a rather narrow house, and the door was barely tall enough for Ethan to fit through without ducking. Inside, the room opened into a small waiting area with a pastry counter. One entire wall had been turned into a chalkboard with beautifully rendered chalk flowers and butterflies highlighting daily specials like The Marcy (a grilled chicken sandwich with pesto aioli) and The Nana (a Thanksgiving-style turkey sandwich on a house-made roll).

A short woman with a septum piercing and purple ombre hair fading to gray at the tips appeared behind the counter. "What can I get you folks?"

"Did Maria make her caldo verde today?" Ethan asked.

"You know it," the woman said.

"We'll take two bowls," he said.

The woman tapped their order into the register. "Anything else?"

Ethan looked to Hannah expectantly. Her eyes had fixed on a plate of magic bars in the pastry case, the curls of coconut on top seeming to beckon her closer. She scanned the offerings, assessing the lemon squares and shortbread cookies the way her therapist had taught her to. She could have any of them— all of them, really, if she wanted to. The point was to make an intentional choice, a decision about what she wanted, not what her off-kilter sense of stability was whispering for her to have.

Did she want anything else?

"Hannah?" Ethan asked.

"I'll take a magic bar," she said, an unexpected burst of pride blooming in her chest and making her stand up straighter.

"Make that two," Ethan said, oblivious to the years of mental gymnastics that had gone into Hannah's ability to place that simple order.

"That'll be right up," the woman said, handing Ethan a small plastic zebra figurine.

"What's that for?" Hannah asked as he led her to the outdoor seating area.

He held up the zebra. "It's their own way of signaling to the servers which table is which. Some restaurants use numbers. This place uses plastic zoo animals."

Hannah shook her head. "And they say city people are weird. Small towns are wild."

Ethan barked out a laugh and took her hand again, guiding her to a black metal dining set at the edge of the covered patio, away from the couple with the three dogs at their feet. Once they were seated, the zebra prominently placed in the center of the table next to the bottles of ketchup and malt vinegar, Ethan asked, "Have you always lived in a city?"

"For the most part. I grew up in Philadelphia, but I couldn't wait to move to New York."

He scrunched up his nose. "Why?"

"I always wanted to be involved with making live theatre, so I'm sure that was part of it. There are only so many cities where a girl can make a living in live theater."

"There's live theater all over. We have a few professional companies across the state."

"But there's only one Broadway," she countered.

He seemed to consider this for a moment. "Was it just about Broadway?"

Hannah shrugged. "Mostly. I mean, there is something magical about being able to order take out at any hour of the day or night, and there's always something to do. You never have to be bored."

"Being bored can be a good thing sometimes. How else do

you hear yourself think?"

Hannah adjusted the placement of the zebra, moving it slightly closer to the malt vinegar, as she considered this. "I guess you don't," she said at last. "That might have been part of the appeal."

He looked like he wanted to ask more, and she knew she would tell him. Anything he asked. He'd laid himself bare to her in the museum and she was surprised to find she was ready to do the same. Eager, even, to have him understand this part of her, the part so few people knew.

"Oh my God! Are you her?"

Hannah whipped around to find the source of the high-pitched voice. Ethan was already on his feet, moving between Hannah and the dark-haired young woman, her phone held out in front of her.

"You are, aren't you?" she continued. "Jackson Hayes' ex-girlfriend!"

"She has a name," Ethan growled.

"Ethan! Why didn't you tell me you knew Jackson Hayes' ex-girlfriend?"

Hannah winced at the rapid-fire electronic shutter sound of the woman's phone and turned away, hoping she would get the hint and leave her alone. Why had she allowed herself to get so comfortable that she forgot someone here might recognize her? She'd been so preoccupied with escaping the paparazzi, she hadn't paused to consider there might be other people—regular, everyday people who consumed celebrity gossip like candy—who would want to catch her off guard and take her picture.

"Tisha," Ethan said with the kind of calm that contradicted the tense set of his jaw and the stiffness in his shoulders, "we're having a low-key lunch, yeah?"

"Totally," Tisha said to Ethan over the sound of a few more

photos being taken. "I can't believe we have a real-life celebrity in Aster Bay. Cool shit like this never happens here."

"What are you talking about? They filmed a whole reality show here," Ethan said.

Tisha rolled her eyes. "With *Gavin*. That hardly counts." She leaned around Ethan to get a better look at Hannah. "You are so much prettier than your picture."

"Thank you?" Was that a compliment? Hannah wasn't sure.

Tisha barreled ahead, pushing past Ethan and approaching the table. Hannah recoiled against the wall of the building behind her, but Tisha didn't seem to notice. "What was it like to date a member of Midnight Storm? You have to tell me everything!"

"She doesn't actually," Ethan said, catching Tisha by the upper arm and turning her around, using her own momentum to lead her off the covered patio and back out to the sidewalk, out of earshot.

Hannah watched as Ethan delivered what appeared to be a very stern lecture, at least from what she could tell without being able to hear him. Tisha, pouting and rolling her eyes the whole time, tapped busily at her phone before flipping the screen around to show Ethan and stomping off down the street with one last hopeful glance over her shoulder at Hannah.

When Ethan returned to the table, he looked like he might crack a tooth from how hard he was clenching his teeth. "Sorry about that. She won't bother you again."

Hannah nodded, the adrenaline coursing through her system making her feel nauseous and suddenly lightheaded. She focused on the zebra, sliding it back towards the ketchup and letting her fingers play with its tiny plastic legs.

"She deleted the pictures," he continued. "All of them."

"Thank you," she whispered.

Ethan reached for her hand, but she pulled away, dropping

her hand in her lap and looking around, like another would-be paparazzo might pop out of the bushes at the edge of the patio at any second. His nostrils flared again, but he let his hand fall to the tabletop, his fingers drumming restlessly on the metal.

A server appeared, some teenager with a stained apron tied around their waist below a faded t-shirt for a band they had probably never actually listened to. They set bowls of steaming soup in front of Hannah and Ethan, placed a plate with two magic bars on the table, and whisked away the plastic zebra.

Ethan sighed, scrubbing a hand over his mouth, and reached for his spoon. "Eat, before it gets cold."

She hardly tasted a bite.

Chapter Twelve

Hannah retreated to the guest room as soon as they'd gotten home, but she'd started pulling away from Ethan the second Tisha had shown up, taking pictures of Hannah like it was a totally normal thing to do to a stranger. It didn't matter that he'd gotten Tisha to delete them. The damage had already been done. Hannah hardly spoke a word through the rest of their lunch, and on the drive home, she couldn't have gotten any further from him if she tried, curling herself up against the passenger side door of his truck, her arms wrapped around herself as she stared out the window.

He knew it wasn't about him—it was about that asshole, Jackson Hayes, and the fucking photographers, and even Tisha White with her lack of personal boundaries. But knowing that didn't make it any easier. Earlier, in the Museum, and again in Plot Twist, it had felt like they were turning a corner. Like they were actually understanding each other. Like maybe they could be more to each other than the occasional weekend hookup.

Ethan finished unloading the dishwasher, closing the lid a little harder than necessary, and braced his hands on the counter, hanging his head. He'd told her things—about himself, about his past—and it has been *nice*, goddammit. He'd wanted to tell her more, and have her tell him things in return.

But she didn't.

Well, she sort of did.

She told you she's afraid of clowns and she doesn't like to be alone with her thoughts. Nothing substantial. Nothing real.

The muffled sound of her moving around in her bedroom floated down the hall and he fought the urge to go to her, to demand she tell him something—anything—that might prove she was as mixed up about him as he was about her. But he couldn't do that, at least, not when she'd just had her privacy invaded in such spectacular fashion.

He also couldn't stay in the house, straining to hear any sound coming through her closed door and waiting for her to come out. If she wanted space, he could give her space. A little space would do him good, as well.

Ethan rapped his knuckles against the door to Hannah's bedroom. "Hey, Han, I'm going to work for a bit. Text if you need anything."

"Okay. I'll be fine," she called back through the door.

He hesitated for a moment, then turned on his heel and left.

The shed on the property line between the vineyard and Ethan's yard once housed rakes and weed whackers and other tools the grounds crew used to keep the Nuthatch property looking its best. But as the vineyard acquired more riding lawn mowers and giant snow blowers, their needs had outgrown the shed and Ethan had a new, modern barn built closer to the vineyard's main building to house the equipment they needed. Ethan dug out the key to the padlock holding the old shed closed and quickly undid the lock, slipping inside.

From the outside, the small outbuilding looked abandoned, the windows covered and the paint fading. But inside it was an audiobook narrator's dream. All four walls were covered with heavy soundproofing panels to keep the ambient noise of the vineyard and nearby street from bleeding in while also keeping his narration from seeping out. A high-backed, leather desk chair and simple farmhouse table took up most of the floor space. His custom-built desktop computer with the extra-large monitor that allowed him to have multiple windows open at once occupied the desk. His microphone was mounted on the wall, and a pair of over-the-ear headphones hung from the metal arm of the microphone stand. He barely knew how to use the pricey equipment; another narrator friend of Angie's had helped him pick it out and taught him the basics. After he recorded the files, he sent them off to the production team that edited everything together.

Ethan sank into the chair and cued up the audio for the scene he'd been recording before Hannah arrived. *The Dragon Duke* was a departure from his typical projects, but he loved all of AK Wild's—Angie's—books. More than that, he liked narrating for her. He liked becoming Slade Hardcastle, a man with a smooth British accent who spoke aloud the dirtiest fantasies he'd ever seen written in black and white.

Hannah listens to your books.

His cock kicked behind his zipper at the idea of her listening to some of the scenes he had recorded. Had she touched herself to his voice?

She doesn't know it's you.

He couldn't decide if he liked that fact or hated it.

It didn't matter. He had a job to do.

Ethan put the headphones on and hit play. His own voice in a low, aristocratic British accent filled his ears.

"You will submit to me, mea dulcis, on your knees, on your back. Any way I desire you. Every way. You will know what it is to be mated to the dragon duke, to surrender your body and heart to my keeping. And when you have done that, little one, oh how I shall reward you."

Ethan paused the recording and dug the heels of his hands into his eyes. Maybe this wasn't such a good idea, because now all he could think about was Hannah on her knees, Hannah with her plush mouth and her soft curves and the tight clench of her body around his. Hannah, opening herself to him in every way possible, and all the ways he could reward her for that gift.

All day he'd been thinking about finishing what they started in the bookstore. He pulled off his headphones and closed out the recording software with one hand as he worked the fly of his jeans open with the other. He was already hard and leaking at the thought of her, at the memory of sliding between her thighs and feeling her come apart beneath him. As he took himself in hand, stroking roughly, he let himself imagine, just for a moment, what it would be like to have Hannah for real— not passing moments in hotel rooms, but all of her.

I want to know you, Ethan Hart. Even the messy, sordid parts.

Her words came back to him like a punch to the chest and his hand moved faster. What would it be like to be known like that, to peel himself open for her and have her do the same? What would it take for Hannah to surrender not just her body, but her heart as well?

The images came faster now: Hannah against a bookshelf grinding against his thigh. Hannah spread out before him in the hotel room, waiting for him to taste her. The scrape of her nails along his back as he pistoned into her. The quivering in her thighs when he found the right angle. The way she cried out his name when she came.

Hannah listening to his audiobook, her fingers working her clit, but this time, knowing it was his voice.

He wanted hazy Sunday mornings spent in bed and rainy afternoons wrapped in each other's arms. He wanted to be the man who made her come, to help her see how goddamn gorgeous she was, to fill her with his release and fall asleep still inside her.

He came with her name on his lips and visions of Hannah reaching for him in the night, trusting him, choosing him. As the orgasm receded and he hastily cleaned himself up, he tried to hold on to that vision of a life he'd been afraid to want for so long, one he thought he'd already missed out on. His eyes fell on the open script on his screen. *Body and heart... oh how I shall reward you.*

Hannah may not trust him with her heart—not yet at least—but she'd never had any trouble trusting him with her body. Maybe it was time to remind her, to give her a taste of how sweet surrender could be.

"There are no new pictures of you online," Micah said for the third time at least. Even through the phone, Hannah could sense his growing impatience. "It was probably just a Storm Chaser."

"Jackson hates when they call his fans that," she said without thinking.

"I don't really give a damn what Jackson hates right now," Micah said. "The premiere is in a week. Keep laying low until then. No one knows you're in Rhode Island, I promise."

"You're right. I'm sure you're right."

"I've made you a reservation at a hotel near the theater for the premiere," he continued.

"Why? I'll just stay—" She broke off, remembering the photograph snapped through her living room window. "Right. A hotel it is."

"You'll need a date to walk the carpet with you and play nice with Jackson, to show you've both moved on but are still friendly."

Hannah glanced across the mall food court to where Tessa, Kyla, and Sabrina sat finishing their lunch. Kyla tried to wave her over. They'd taken her to the mall in Providence to help her find a dress and so far, all she'd done was talk on her phone, but Hannah held up a finger and turned her back on the group as she spoke to Micah. "I guess I could ask Leonard if he wants to go together," she said, referring to another member of the *Bridget Jones' Musical* cast.

"Leonard is bringing his husband," Micah replied. "It's their first appearance since the wedding."

"Of course," Hannah said, "I forgot."

"And bringing a gay man as your date doesn't exactly send the message you've moved on. You need someone the press can reasonably assume you might be dating."

Someone like Ethan.

Micah continued, "I can make a few calls, see if any of my other clients—"

"No. I'll find someone," Hannah said. She didn't need to add the humiliation of her manager calling in his other clients to take her to her own premiere. She'd had enough fake dates to last her a lifetime, thank you very much.

Micah promised to send over the details of her hotel reservation before they hung up. By the time Hannah rejoined the other women at their table by the taco stand, they were deep in a debate about whether the bourbon chicken from the Chinese place in the food court was superior to the fried chicken and waffle bites from the soul food place next to it.

"Hannah! We need your vote," Sabrina said, pushing a plate covered with miniature samples from every vendor in the food court towards her. "Chicken and waffles or bourbon chicken?"

Hannah eyed the plate, her fork poised and at the ready. Finally she speared a thin, rolled tortilla, bright yellow cheese oozing from the seam, and bit off an end. "Neither. Buffalo chicken taquito."

"A last-minute entry," Tessa said, grinning.

"Never count out the buffalo chicken," Hannah said, finishing off the taquito.

"Everything alright?" Kyla asked, tilting her head towards the little alcove where Hannah had retreated to take Micah's call.

"Great," she said, stabbing something that looked like a mini corn dog. "Who's ready to help me find a dress?"

"Not just any dress," Sabrina said. "*The* dress."

"The one that will make Jackson Hayes rethink his life choices," Tessa said.

Hannah laughed. "I'll settle for one that fits over my hips and doesn't cost a fortune."

Kyla hooked her arm through Hannah's. "I know the perfect place."

Peach Please was a small shop on the third floor of the mall tucked between a Godiva store and a pet boutique. The mannequins in the window were full-figured and dressed in rhinestone-covered gowns that must have weighed a ton. "Best formalwear place for women with curves like ours without having to go to Boston. This is where I bought most of my dresses for *Once Upon a Town*," Kyla said, referring to the reality TV show where she and her husband had gotten together.

"And those were stunning gowns," Tessa said.

They were immediately met by a saleswoman who was uncharacteristically disinterested in them. She pointed out the rack of new arrivals before retreating to her magazine behind the sales counter. Within a few minutes, they had more dresses for Hannah to try than she could have dreamed of—strapless gowns with gathered skirts, sweetheart necklines on A-line masterpieces crafted from heavy satin, a short lace number with a one-shoulder asymmetrical top.

She ruled out the short lace dress first, not particularly

wanting to worry about making sure her legs had an even application of self-tanner before the premiere. There was a red Grecian-style gown with off-the-shoulder straps that made her waist look super tiny but she worried the red would clash with the carpet. Rhinestones chafed under her arms, and silk showed every lump and bump when she walked.

"I think I found it," Kyla said, appearing at the dressing room with a royal purple confection of a dress. Hannah eyed the corseted back skeptically. "Just try it. I'll help you lace it up."

"Okay, but no laughing if I look ridiculous."

"You will not look ridiculous," Sabrina said to the closed door of the dressing room as Hannah put on the gown.

The gown was unlike anything Hannah had seen before. The strapless bodice featured a plunging V at the center of the sweetheart neckline, the dress hugging her curves through her waist. A deep slit ran up the side of the dress from the floor-length hem to her upper thigh, the scandalous cut tempered only by the gauzy panels falling from her hips, adding movement and shimmer when she walked.

When Hannah was ready, Kyla slipped in to pull the laces tight. Before she even touched the first lace, though, Kyla gasped, clapping her hands over her mouth. "You look *amazing!*" she squealed.

"It's not too costume-y?" Hannah asked, tugging on the skirt.

"It's just costume-y enough. Trust me. This will pop on camera."

"Hurry up! We want to see!" Tessa called through the door.

A few moments later, Hannah was cinched and laced into the dress. Kyla opened the dressing room door and Hannah stepped into the store to the sound of her new friends' gasps. "That's the one," Sabrina said. "It's perfect."

Hannah ran her hands over her hips, twisting to look at herself from every angle. She didn't love the way the fabric clung to her belly, how wide her hips appeared, the way her arms looked pressed to her side. If she had a cape, something to cover her arms and—

No. Hannah looked away from the mirror. She couldn't trust her own evaluation of how she looked, but that didn't change the fact she needed a dress. And Sabrina, Tessa, and Kyla seemed to like it...

Find one thing. That's what her therapist had said. When it was hard to love every part of herself, she should find one thing she could love, and one thing would be enough.

She made herself look back in the mirror, scanning her reflection. The color looked great with her eyes and skin tone, and the corset was doing amazing things for her breasts.

"Yes?" Hannah asked, turning away from the mirror and back towards her new friends.

"Yes!" they chorused back at her.

"It will for sure make Jackson Hayes lose his mind," Tessa said.

Kyla shot a smirk Tessa's way. "It might make your dad lose his mind too."

Comment section of Encores.com post with caption "Jackson Hayes spotted with Victoria's Secret model at an LA nightclub"

StrmChsr92: So glad to see our boy Jackson THRIVING since he dropped that Broadway chick.

XOJxsnsGurlXO: Same! Hannah Matthews was weighing him down—literally!

User182734: @XOJxsnsGurlXO That's a shitty thing to say about someone. She is a beautiful woman. How would you like it if someone went on the internet and made jokes about your body?

Here4theDrama: I took a class on body language in college and if you look at their pictures together it's super obvious he was never into her.

User182734: @Here4theDrama One college psych course does not make you an expert in body language.

StrmChsr92: She probably paid him to date her.

User182734: @StrmChsr92 How does that make sense? Jackson Hayes doesn't need any more money.

Here4theDrama: Who the hell is @User182734?

StrmChsr92: Oh my God, what if it's her DAD?

User182734: I'm not her dad.

XOJxsnsGurlXO: That's what her dad would say.

RealGirl6969: Live! Hot girls in your area are waiting to chat. Click here to connect with real, local, h0rny girls

StrmChsr92: I bet those "hot girls" are hotter than Hannah Matthews

User182734: That is clearly a fake post. And you're being disrespectful. I should report your comments to the moderator.

Here4theDrama: It's definitely her dad.

Chapter Thirteen

Ethan closed the lid of his laptop on his kitchen island and pressed the heels of his hands against his eyes. He had better things to do than argue with anonymous jerks on the internet, but he couldn't help himself. Ever since he'd discovered the steady stream of vitriol directed at Hannah online, he hadn't been able to stop himself from responding, from letting these trolls, as Tessa had called them, know how wrong they were about her. But it seemed like the more he responded, the more they doubled down on their schoolyard taunts, turning the same on him until he wasn't sure if he was helping or just making everything worse.

Hannah had been gone all day, shopping with Tessa and their friends. He hoped that meant she'd been too busy to see the latest batch of vicious commentary online. They only had a week left before she'd leave for New York again, but he intended to make the most of every moment, to prove to her she deserved better than a fake relationship with a self-centered former pop star.

Those people didn't know her, not like he did.

You hardly know her.

But he *would* know her. He just had to convince her to try.

The front door of his house opened and Hannah entered,

weighed down with shopping bags. "Hey." She flashed him a timid smile as she tried to step out of her shoes, wobbling unsteadily. Ethan rushed to take the bags from her and did his best not to notice the bag from the lingerie shop downtown. "I thought you'd still be at work," she said.

"It's after five."

"No!" she gasped, spinning around in search of the clock hanging on the far wall. "I didn't realize it was so late. I wanted to cook you dinner tonight." She held up one of the bags, the logo for the local mom and pop grocery store emblazoned on the brown paper.

"That's okay. We can order in," Ethan said, setting her other bags down.

Hannah blew out a breath. "Are you starving? We could eat a little later than usual and I could cook it anyway."

"Han, you don't have to cook for me." He took the grocery bag from her, but she snatched it back.

"I want to. To apologize for yesterday."

He startled. "There's nothing to apologize for."

"We were having a great day and then that thing happened with the woman and the camera—"

"Tisha."

"Yeah, her. And I shut down and shut you out. That wasn't fair."

"You don't need to apologize for protecting yourself," he said, reaching for her hand. The anxious itch in his chest settled when she allowed him to lace their fingers together.

Let me know you.

Hannah stared at their interlocked hands for a moment. "I'd like to make you dinner, if that's alright."

"As long as it's because you want to, and not because you think you have to."

"I want to."

Ethan nodded, taking all but the grocery bag from Hannah and carrying them to her room. "It was a successful shopping trip, I take it?" he called over his shoulder.

"Very."

When Ethan returned to the kitchen, Hannah had gathered her hair into a loose bun, leaving the long line of her neck exposed as she unpacked her groceries. He wanted to track that line with his lips and bite the tender curve where her neck met her shoulder. But if this was going to work, if he was going to remind her how good they could be together, how good he could make her feel, he needed to choose his moment carefully. He suspected that the first time she'd spoken to him in twenty-four hours was not the time.

He unbuttoned the cuffs of his flannel shirt and began rolling up the sleeves. "Put me to work."

She turned to look at him, her eyes snagging on his forearms as he rolled his sleeves to the elbow. Her pupils dilated and the corner of her bottom lip caught between her teeth. Ethan fought back a grin. Maybe he wouldn't have to wait too long after all.

"What?" she asked, blinking away.

He crowded her against the counter. "Put me to work, Hannah. Tell me what you want me to do."

She blinked again, her eyes heavy as they roamed over his face. He reached past her and snagged a sugar snap pea from the counter, biting into it as he took a step away, the crunch breaking her from his spell.

This is going to be fun.

"I'm no chef, but I can follow directions," he said.

"Right." She turned towards the counter, her hand hovering over the assembled ingredients. At last, she grabbed a small container of multicolored cherry tomatoes. "You can start by cutting these in half."

When he took the tomatoes from her, he swore he could see a blush creeping up her throat. He grabbed a knife from the butcher block and settled at the island perpendicular to her so he could watch her as they worked. "Where did you learn to cook?" he asked.

"I watched a lot of cooking shows when I first moved to the City. It was more wish fulfillment than for educational purposes, but after a while, I realized I'd picked up a few things," she said as she worked her knife through a pile of fresh herbs on the cutting board.

"Wish fulfillment?"

She stilled, the barest hint of hesitation, before she began moving again, her eyes focused on her cutting board. "Mmhmm. You know, some people watch the Travel Network and dream about going to Paris. I watched cooking shows and daydreamed about eating carbs." She glanced at him, as though assessing how he had received this new information. "I didn't eat carbs back then," she explained in a quiet voice.

"Why not?"

She shrugged, moving the herbs into a little bowl at the edge of the counter and carefully removing a cod fillet from its butcher paper wrapping. Her movements were methodical, precise, as though she was pouring all her focus into them rather than answering his question. She stared at the fish, her brow wrinkled, and he got the feeling she wasn't thinking about the fish at all. "Do you have any wine? White?" she asked at last.

"I own a vineyard. Of course I have wine." He set the bowl of cut tomatoes down by her elbow. "I'll be right back."

He took his time selecting a bottle from the rack in his basement, more to give her a minute to collect herself than anything else. When he returned, he held out the bottle of Vidal Blanc to her.

"Great, thanks." She sent him a tentative smile as she dropped shallots and butter into a pan on the stove. "You never told me what *you* were doing in Boston the night we met," she said.

Ethan leaned against the counter at her side, popping a cherry tomato half in his mouth while he considered his answer. "I had a business meeting."

"Do you do a lot of business in Boston?" she asked, scraping crushed cloves of garlic from her cutting board to drop into the sizzling butter.

He ran his hand over his jaw, scratching at his beard. He'd told her about Steph and Tessa, and maybe it was because he'd had enough of sharing his secrets for the time being, but he wasn't sure why *this* felt like the more vulnerable confession. What would she think when she found out that the voice she'd been listening to on all those AK Wild novels she loved so much was his? And what did it mean that she hadn't recognized his voice? His British accent wasn't *that* good.

"Occasionally," he said, turning to retrieve a loaf of Tessa's sourdough from the breadbox at the other end of the counter. He held it up for her approval. "Bread?"

She nodded and he busied himself with slicing the loaf into even pieces and setting a fresh stick of butter in the antique milk glass butter dish. She watched him from the corner of her eye as she pushed the shallots and garlic around the pan, her lips pressed tightly together. He hated it. He wanted her soft and open.

"It's more a hobby than a business," he said at last.

She lifted her head to look at him, waiting for him to continue. *Here goes nothing.*

"I narrate audiobooks. Only for one author. She lives in Boston." He glanced up to find her staring at him, eyes narrowed and brow lowered as she tried to work through what he'd said.

"Audiobooks," she repeated.

"Romance audiobooks." He sighed, cuffing the back of his

Cara Dion

neck. "For AK Wild. I'm—"

Hannah gasped. She pressed her hands to her mouth and the spatula clattered to the floor, her eyes going wide. "You're Slade Hardcastle!"

He gave a tight nod and bent to pick up the spatula. When he stood back up, she was blushing something fierce. He rinsed the spatula in the sink and held it out to her.

She snatched it from his hands and used the wide, flat end to hit him on the bicep. "Why didn't you tell me yesterday?"

"Hey, now," he said, dodging another strike with a smirk. "I didn't want to embarrass you."

"Embarrass me? Are you kidding me? This is the coolest thing I've ever heard!"

It was Ethan's turn to look confused. "Really?"

"Yes, really! You're famous!"

"I am not famous."

"Slade Hardcastle is," she countered, turning back to the pan on the stove. "Do you know how many times—" She cut herself off with a shake of the head.

"What, Han?" He moved behind her as she worked, not quite touching her but close enough to see the goosebumps rise on the back of her neck.

"I've listened to *The Lady's Knights* at least five times." She dumped the bowl of tomatoes into the pan and glanced back at him, a smile tugging at her lips. "There are entire fan accounts dedicated to you on social media. Do you know how many women would kill to be staying at Slade Hardcastle's house?"

His hand curled around her hip. "I only really care about one woman."

She poured a healthy splash of wine into the pan, shaking the tomatoes around in it, ignoring his comment. "Do your friends know?"

"Only Baz."

146

"And now me."

If he wasn't mistaken, there was pride in her voice. He set his other hand on her hip, tugging her gently back towards him. "Are we friends, sweetheart?"

"Well, I don't usually cook dinner for people who *aren't* my friends," she said, turning off the stove and spinning in his hold to face him.

He didn't miss the way her breathing hitched when he pulled her closer. He hummed low in his throat as he considered her words. "I don't usually want to kiss my friends."

She drew her bottom lip between her teeth, as though that could hide her smile. "I don't know. Baz seems very kissable." Ethan grunted and increased the pressure of his hold on her hips, but his reaction only seemed to delight her further. Her eyes sparkled, color dancing across her irises like ripples in the bay after a spring storm. "He's got that broody, mysterious thing going for him."

"You're not kissing Baz."

"Maybe Sabrina would share—"

She broke off on a startled giggle as he pressed his lips to hers. She melted against him, opening to his kiss as her hands wound into his hair. As he kissed her, the knots in his chest that had appeared when she arrived in Aster Bay slowly loosened, replaced by the restless need to hold her closer, to kiss her harder, to nip at her throat until she admitted she hated this distance between them as much as he did.

She doesn't want more. She said as much in Boston.

So much had changed in the last week. Surely now, after the last few days…

But had anything really changed at all? He knew she was afraid of clowns, what she did for a living, how it felt to kiss her on the sidewalk in his small town and not care who saw them—but she hadn't opened up to him. Not really. She was still keeping him at arm's length. He just wished he knew why.

He pressed his lips to her ear, dragging the lobe between his teeth. "Tell me something real, Han," he begged.

She tilted her head, allowing him better access to her throat, and stammered, lust drunk, "I—I don't—"

"Anything, sweetheart. Tell me anything." His hands slid under the hem of her shirt, fingertips digging into the soft skin of her lower back, as his lips moved down the long line of her neck. "Please."

Chapter Fourteen

"Tell me something real, Han."

There was a pleading in Ethan's tone that Hannah didn't recognize, a desperation, like he needed her to peel away the layers guarding her heart as much as he needed to touch her.

She tilted her head as his lips skated over her throat, her head spinning from the sudden proximity. The citrus and pine scent of him and the movement of his hands on the bare skin at her lower back muddled her senses.

She couldn't think straight with him so close, with the hard length of him pressing against her belly and his mouth on her skin. How was a person supposed to think when Ethan Hart was doing his best to make her come undone?

"I don't know if I want to be an actress anymore."

His mouth stilled in an open mouth kiss along her collarbone and her heart pounded in her chest. She hadn't intended to say that. She wasn't even sure if she meant it, except… How much easier would her life be if she never again had to worry about random people snapping her picture on sidewalk cafes? If she didn't have to constantly be torn between her recovery and her career?

One of his hands slid down and gripped her backside,

squeezing, as if he was rewarding her for the confession, urging her to continue. "What do you want?" he whispered, his lips ghosting over the tops of her breasts through her shirt.

"I don't know." The staticky feeling in her brain intensified as she tried to wade through the tumult in her mind. Was she really ready to walk away from everything she'd worked so hard for, the hard-won success she'd poured everything into? And if she didn't, if she chose to continue on the endless cycle of auditioning and performing, of offering herself up for inspection and criticism day after day, could she maintain her recovery? Did she actually have a choice at all?

Tears pressed at the back of her eyes and she squeezed them shut. She didn't want to cry *now*, for Christ's sake.

He murmured sounds of comfort as he pulled her close, his mouth at her waist, hands gripping her sides as he lowered himself in front of her. "That's alright. You don't need to know."

She pushed his hair back from his forehead, raking her nails across his scalp. "I want this time with you," she said, her voice raw and cracking. He looked up at her, his lips on her belly and hands sliding down to cup her ass again. She may not know what she wanted from her career, what came next, but she knew one thing with certainty. "I want you to know me."

His forehead rested against her and she cradled his head in her hands. When he met her eyes again, there was a determination there she hadn't seen before. "What about this, sweetheart? Do you want this?" he asked, his fingers slipping under the waistband of her jeans.

"Yes."

His nostrils flared, eyes darkening, and he held her gaze as he undid the button and zipper. He tugged her jeans and panties down in one pull, gently circling her ankle to help her step out of them. Even though they'd done this so many times before, there was something different about being there, in his kitchen, trading secrets, their half-cooked dinner cooling in the pan on the stove. It was profoundly personal in a way their hotel meetings never had been, in a way none of her previous relationships had ever been.

Ethan dragged his nose along the crease of her thigh, across her mound, and down the other side, breathing her in. "Do you trust me?"

"I trust you."

He bit the sensitive flesh at the inside of her thigh and she yelped in surprise. "Then let me see you."

She hesitated for a moment, not sure what he meant. At last, she pulled her shirt over her head, letting it fall in the pile with her jeans on the floor. Her bra followed. Ethan's hands skated up her back, curled around her sides and cupped her breasts, his thumbs teasing the hard peaks of her nipples.

"Let's play a game," he said.

An incredulous laugh burst from her lips. "Now?"

The corner of his mouth twitched as though he was trying not to smile. "Now."

"What kind of game?"

"You tell me things I don't know about you and I'll lick this pretty pussy the way you like." He pinched her nipples between his thumb and forefinger and she sucked in a breath, fascinated by the way his pupils blew wide at the sound. "But if you stop, I stop."

"What?"

"You want to come, Hannah? Then tell me all the things you couldn't for the last three years." He pressed a kiss to the crease of her thigh and hip, his tongue dragging along the line but stopping short of where she needed him. "Let's see how many times I can make you come before you run out of secrets."

"I don't have any secrets."

Liar.

And he knew it.

He tsked, twisting her nipple hard enough that she gasped at the bright burst of pleasure pain blooming beneath his touch.

"I never wanted to be famous."

As the words rushed out of her, his touch gentled, pinpricks of heat blooming across her breasts. He smiled wickedly and let one hand drift down to her ass, tilting her hips towards him as he dipped his tongue between her folds. He looked up at her, his eyebrow arched, tongue torturously close to giving her the relief she needed, and waited.

"I wanted to sing and act with my friends, but I never thought anyone would know who I was outside of the theater."

He lapped at her in slow, deliberate licks designed to drive her out of her mind with need and she knew if he stopped, she'd cry in desperation. She gripped his hair and let the words tumble out, how she hadn't known what to do with the press, the first time someone had photographed her in line at the grocery store and that picture ended up on the late-night talk show circuit. When he sucked her clit into his mouth, sparks went off behind her eyes and she told him about the time she had gone to dinner with Jackson, how it was meant to be a simple public appearance to confirm the rumors of their (fake) relationship, how the next morning *The Today Show* ran a story analyzing the contents of her dinner plate.

"It wasn't supposed to be about me," she whimpered as he slipped two fingers inside her, slowly driving her closer and closer to the precipice of her orgasm. "It was supposed to be about him."

Ethan dragged his teeth over her clit and sucked hard, shoving her off that precipice until she tumbled headfirst into a climax that hit her like a punch to her sternum. She was still quivering with the intensity of it when he began curling his fingers again, pressing on that soft spot on her front wall.

"It should have been about you," he insisted, his eyes locked on hers. "What you needed. What you wanted."

She opened her mouth to tell him that it had been, in a way—the exchange of her public self for the ability to pull herself from the depths of a disorder that had controlled her private life for over a decade. It had been an easy decision, and one she would make again, even knowing what she now knew: that she couldn't casually and quietly go about her life while the whole world thought she was dating a pop star. That the person the public saw would have very little resemblance to the person she was.

But she wasn't ready to tell him that. Even now. How could she tell him the ways she had hurt herself, the damage she had done? How could she explain the sticky shame of it that still coated her skin, that she was afraid she'd never fully shake?

"When I was a child, I wanted to be a ballet dancer," she said instead.

He hesitated for a moment, as if deciding if he would allow this change of subject. His eyes skimmed over the swollen place between her legs and his tongue darted out to swipe at his lips.

"I took my first class when I was five," she continued, her fingers gliding down the side of his face and over his beard. "Even at five I was behind. There were girls there who had started when they were two, barely old enough to walk."

His eyes darted between hers, brow drawn low as he listened. And she waited to see if this story would suffice. She watched him debate with himself, the knowledge she was avoiding telling him something wrinkling his forehead and tightening his jaw.

At last, he leaned forward again, latching his mouth onto her with a ferocity that startled her. She fell back against the counter, hands gripping his head as he worked her clit fast and hard. "Oh God," she whimpered, her climax already taking hold.

And then he stopped.

"Keep talking." The vibration of his voice thrummed through her. "You stop, I stop."

So she told him about being the only girl who had to order a size large leotard, about the other girls making fun of her wide feet, about the way her ballet teacher had poked at her belly with the end of her walking stick and recommended she try fasting. With each new confession, his pressure intensified.

She told him about the boy on the playground who called her Dumbo, the gym teacher who left copies of fitness magazines in her locker in high school, the prom date who ditched her when he saw she was wearing shapewear under her dress.

She came with a sharp cry, her knees giving way. But he caught her with an arm around her waist, his mouth latched onto her and mercilessly working her to a new, sharper peak.

"Ethan," she panted.

"You stop, I stop," he repeated. A challenge.

He pulled three more orgasms from her before she ran out of words, each moving closer to pain than pleasure and yet each so bright and clear she would have asked for more if she had the capacity to form any more thoughts.

Ethan cupped her gently between the legs, his lips skating across her over-sensitive skin as he murmured words of praise. "Such a good fucking girl to give this pussy to me," he said when his mouth at last landed on her own. "Such a beautiful, brave girl, letting me make you come so many times."

She glowed under his praise, the warmth of it slowly suffusing her limbs with a heavy, sated peace. He stood, supporting her as her knees shook, her legs unable to support her weight as the aftershocks of her last orgasm reverberated through her. When she kissed him, she tasted herself on his lips.

"Your turn." She reached for him, pressing her hand to the front of his jeans, but pulled it back, startled, when her fingertips met the sticky proof that he'd already found his own release.

Ethan breathed out in an echo of a laugh. "See what you do to me?" he asked, peppering her jaw with kisses, her cheekbones, her eyelids. "You didn't even need to touch me. Just the taste of you, and the sounds you make—" He bit her lip, tugging on it gently. "Fuck, I'm getting hard again just thinking about it." As if to prove his point, his cock jerked between them, the hardening outline of it pressing against her belly.

"You… in your pants?" she asked.

He hummed the affirmation.

"But I didn't do anything," she protested.

"You let me kiss this perfect pussy." His hand dropped between her legs again, fingertips ghosting over her swollen flesh, barely touching her yet still sending sparks across her overstimulated nerves. "You let me fuck you with my tongue. You screamed my name when I sucked on your clit. Christ, you're perfect."

She wanted to believe him. His praise was warm and soft, cocooning her from the riot of voices in her head trying to pierce the haze of this perfect moment. Instead of giving those voices room, she focused on his touch, the words he gave so freely, the look in his eyes, and realized she felt naked in a way that had nothing to do with skin.

Chapter Fifteen

"Mama! Mama!" Julie squirmed in Jo's arms, finally succeeding in wiggling enough that Jo set her on her feet. She toddled over to where Ethan and Hannah stood in the doorway of Jamie's restaurant, Lemon and Thyme.

"Hey, Jujube." Ethan scooped his granddaughter up and pressed a kiss to her pudgy cheek, sending her into a fit of giggles.

"Mama," she said with a toothy grin, tugging on his beard.

"Mama?" Hannah's lips twitched as though she were trying very hard not to laugh.

"Everyone's mama. It's her only word."

"No!" Julie shouted. At Ethan's startled expression she giggled again, and repeated "No!"

"Not her *only* word after all," Hannah said.

"Jujube, this is my friend, Hannah," Ethan said. The little girl's face scrunched up to match the seriousness of Ethan's tone. "Hannah, this is my granddaughter, Julie."

"Hannah!" Kyla waved to her from across the empty restaurant. "I was just telling Jo and Molly about your dress. Come show them the picture."

Hannah glanced at Ethan, and he smiled, tilting his head

towards the gathered women. "Don't believe anything Jo tells you."

"And what would she tell me?" Hannah asked.

"She likes to joke about my being a hot grandpa."

"Oh, well, can't say I disagree with her there."

Ethan leaned close and nipped at her ear.

"No!" Julie shouted again.

Ethan and Hannah jumped at the interjection, breaking apart with a laugh before Hannah joined Kyla and the others at the bar. Ethan watched her go, following the sway of her hips in the little sundress she wore. It was too cold for a sundress, but he wasn't about to tell her that, not when it swished around her thighs and perfectly highlighted her ass and breasts. He'd had to fight the urge to protest when she layered on a cardigan before they left the house, but then he reminded himself he'd get to peel it off her later and his objections died in his throat.

Julie tugged on his beard—hard—and he shook himself from his thoughts. "Let's go find your daddy," he said, bouncing her in his arms as he pushed through the double doors into the kitchen where he knew Jamie, Gavin, and Baz would be congregating.

"Hey, Dad." Tessa left the circle of Jamie's arms to greet her father. "Is Hannah here?"

"With Kyla and the others."

Julie swan dove out of his arms towards her mother, but Ethan was used to his granddaughter's antics. He held her firmly around the waist until Tessa gathered her in her arms. "Let's go, baby. We'll leave the boys to talk." Tessa placed a kiss on Ethan's cheek as she went past, the double doors swinging closed behind her.

Jamie stood in the center of the kitchen, chopping herbs at one of the stainless steel counters and swatting Gavin's hand away every time he tried to steal slivers of shredded cheese from the pile at the edge of his cutting board. Baz stood off to the side, always just far enough away from the food to ensure nothing could splatter on his suit.

"What're we having?" Ethan asked, swiping some cheese.

"Chicken parm." Jamie glanced at Ethan. "Your mom's recipe."

Ever since Jamie and Tessa had gotten together, they'd revived Ethan's mother's tradition of a regular 'family dinner.' While his mom had hosted those dinners every week, Ethan and his friends had settled into a rhythm of once a month dinners, and Jamie always cooked something from the family recipe box Ethan's mom had gifted to Jamie when he started the restaurant.

"I hear Hannah made you dinner the other night," Gavin said, grinning.

"You and your wife gossip too much," Ethan said.

"It's not gossip when it's between a married couple."

"Keep me out of your pillow talk," Ethan said.

"Are you having your *own* pillow talk?" Gavin teased.

When he didn't answer immediately, Baz chuckled, shaking his head. "That didn't take long."

Jamie glanced up from his cutting board, grabbing a large heirloom tomato and began slicing it. "So you talked it out? The Jackson Hayes of it all?"

Ethan cleared this throat, unsure how much he could tell the guys without betraying Hannah's confidence. "Yeah. I didn't have all the information before."

"See? I knew you two could work it out," Gavin said. "About time you had a real relationship."

"I wouldn't go so far as to say we're in a relationship."

"Why not?" Jamie asked.

Ethan scrubbed his hand over his face as the ease of the last twenty-four hours disappeared beneath the onslaught of his friends' interrogation. "We haven't put a label on anything."

"What, are we fifteen?" Baz asked. "You're either together or you're not."

"I mean, we're more together than not...I think," Ethan said.

"You think?" Jamie asked.

"But you're sleeping together," Gavin said, his forehead furrowed.

"We're... I'm not talking about this at family dinner," Ethan said, grabbing another small handful of cheese.

Jamie swatted at his hand. "There won't be a dinner if you don't stop stealing my cheese."

"I don't understand," Gavin said. "I thought you wanted something real with Hannah."

"I did. I do. But I don't know what she wants. I don't think she even knows."

"I heard you were spotted kissing outside of Plot Twist," Jamie said between layering slices of tomato and cheese on top of perfectly fried chicken breasts.

"I heard it was outside The Silver Spoon," Baz said.

"From who?" Ethan demanded.

"Mrs. Blumenthal told my mom when they saw each other in the grocery store," Gavin said with a shrug.

"Mrs. Greene asked Tessa about it when she stopped by the bakery to pick up the pastries for tomorrow's church coffee hour." Jamie slid the sheet pan of prepared chicken into the oven.

"I heard about it from Mac when he came to confession."

Ethan turned at the sound of the newcomer as Gavin's brother, Caleb entered the kitchen, his pristine white priest's collar in stark contrast to the black shirt and pants he always wore. Ever since Caleb had returned to Aster Bay to take over as the priest at St. Anthony's, he'd become a fixture at their monthly family dinners, falling right back into his role as the big brother who teased all of Gavin's friends.

"I thought you weren't supposed to tell anyone what

someone says in confession," Gavin said.

"He didn't say it *in* confession. He was talking about it with Mrs. Greene in the narthex." Caleb held his hand out to Ethan, pulling him in for a quick handshake and hug. "How's your dad doing?"

"Are we going to skip over the fact my love life is apparently fodder for the St. Anthony's gossip mill?" Ethan groaned.

"Don't you know by now that any PDA is fair game for the grandma gang's gossiping?" Baz asked.

"So, who's the girl?" Caleb asked.

"No one," Ethan grumbled.

"Not no one," Gavin protested. "Her name's Hannah. She's staying with Ethan for a little while."

"Living with a woman out of wedlock?" Caleb shook his head in a mock admonishment. "That'll be five Hail Marys."

"Fuck off." Ethan shoved Caleb's shoulder. The priest laughed.

"Catch me up. She your girlfriend?" Caleb asked.

"She might as well be," Baz said.

"They're sleeping together," Gavin told his brother.

"Shut up. We're not talking about this while you're wearing that." Ethan waved a finger in the direction of Caleb's priest collar.

"I'm still a priest, even if I take the collar off, you know," he said.

"Why don't you just talk to her?" Jamie asked as he finished wiping down his prep station.

"I tried."

"Did you, though? Or did you just kiss her and expect her to figure out what it meant on her own?" Caleb asked.

"Oooh, you're good at this," Gavin said.

Caleb shrugged, reaching for some of the leftover cheese. "Part of the job."

Ethan scowled. As much as he hated to admit it, Caleb had a point. He hadn't actually told Hannah he was interested in something more serious with her—at least, not since their last weekend in Boston, and even then he hadn't exactly been clear about how he felt about her.

The swinging doors opened again. This time Jo poked her head through. "Are you guys done gossiping or what?" Her eyes fell on Caleb and she grinned like she knew a secret. "Hey, Father West. It might as well be a silver fox convention in here." Caleb rolled his eyes as Jo swung her gaze around the room.

"We'll be right out," Jamie said. Jo winked and disappeared back into the dining room as Jamie skewered Ethan with a serious look. "Talk to Hannah."

Simple. Talk to her. He could do that.

"And if she's not interested?"

Jamie clapped him on the shoulder, guiding him towards the doors. "Then at least you'll know. And when she goes home next week, you can move on."

"No, I never officially met any of the other guys," Hannah said as she reached for another slice of bread from the basket in the center of the table. "Though Beckett and Nico did come to opening night."

"Can we stop talking about Midnight Storm like we're a bunch of teenage girls?" Ethan grumbled. He dropped his arm over the back of Hannah's chair, not quite touching her, but close enough that she could feel him.

"I assure you, teenage girls have no idea who Midnight Storm is," Molly, Jo's roommate, said. "They haven't had a hit in almost a decade."

"I loved Midnight Storm," Jo said. "I was a Beckett girlie."

"Of course you were." Kyla rolled her eyes.

"What? Tall, dark, and tatted. What's not to like?" Jo said with a shimmy of her shoulders.

"You guys suck at not talking about things," Ethan said.

"How long are you in town for, Hannah?" Caleb asked.

"Just another week. I need to be back in New York for the premiere of the pro shot."

"What's a pro shot?" Gavin asked.

"It's a film of a stage production. In our case, they filmed the closing week of *Bridget Jones' Musical* and it'll have a limited release in movie theaters across the country."

"That means you're not just a Broadway star. You're a movie star," Sabrina said.

"Hardly," Hannah demurred.

"When's the premiere?" Jamie asked.

"Next Friday." Ethan stiffened beside her.

"Oh. You'll miss Dad's birthday." Tessa glanced between the two of them as she absent-mindedly bounced Julie on her lap.

"It's your birthday next week?" Hannah turned towards him, their knees brushing. He leaned into the contact.

"Next Saturday," he answered tightly.

"He's turning forty-five," Gavin offered.

"Oh, it's a big birthday," Hannah said. She felt like she should have known somehow.

"No birthday's a big birthday after twenty-one," Ethan said.

"You should come with me to New York." The words were out of her mouth before she could think better of it, but now that she'd said them, they felt right. Hannah twisted to face him fully, setting her hand on his knee. "You could be my date to the premiere, and we can spend your birthday celebrating in the City."

"I don't know."

"I'll take you to all the best spots," she continued, suddenly feeling it was incredibly important that she convince him to go with her. "Central Park and the Met and the Highline."

"What about the paparazzi?" Sabrina asked gently.

Hannah's cheeks heated. For a minute there, she'd forgotten all about the paparazzi. "I'm sure it'll be fine," she bluffed. "After the premiere, they'll have no more interest in little ol' me."

"You should go, Dad. I'll help you find a suit if you want," Tessa offered.

"I have suits." Ethan's eyes darted between Hannah's and she held her breath as he considered her proposal. "You really want me to come?"

"Yeah. I really want you to come."

He nodded slowly, sliding his hand over hers where it rested on his knee and lacing their fingers together. When he smiled, his eyes crinkled at the corners and her heart fluttered. "Alright, city girl. Let's go to New York."

Warmth gathered in Hannah's chest, a glowing ball of heat that felt an awful lot like happiness. She squeezed his hand and tried to memorize the moment, the way his hand felt in hers, the soft denim of his jeans, the pleasantly full feeling of having thoroughly enjoyed a meal without concern for how many calories were in each bite, the laughter of new friends around the table as the conversation moved on without them. She wanted to remember it all, to freeze it in amber and keep it forever.

To keep him.

The thought rioted through her, sweeping cobwebs off the corners of her heart, shining a light on places she'd kept closed down for so many years, the parts that hadn't felt safe to share. Suddenly she wanted nothing more than to share them with Ethan.

"I bet Hannah could help." Kyla's voice interrupted Hannah's revelations.

"Help with what?" Hannah asked, reluctantly turning her

attention away from the man at her side and towards the women across the table.

"I teach at St. Anthony's High School and the theatre teacher left right before Christmas break. Military spouse," Molly said. "They won't rehire until the next school year—"

"Not won't. Can't," Caleb said as though they'd had this argument a thousand times before.

"—and somehow I wound up directing the spring musical."

"It's because you're an English teacher," Caleb said. "The principal assumed that since you can teach Shakespeare, you must be able to run a theater program."

"He assumed incorrectly," Molly said.

"You're underestimating yourself." Caleb's voice was sterner than Hannah had heard it before, and color rose in the apples of Molly's cheeks.

"I'm sure you're doing fine," Sabrina said.

"What show are you working on?" Hannah asked.

"*Little Shop of Horrors.*"

"Oh, I love *Little Shop!* I always loved the role of Audrey," Hannah said.

"Did you ever play her?" Ethan asked.

"No. I never really looked the part," Hannah said, brushing it aside.

"If you're not busy this week, maybe you could come to a few of our rehearsals? I know the kids would love having a real Broadway actress coaching them for a bit instead of their English teacher," Molly said with a self-deprecating laugh.

"Sure, I could do that. I don't exactly have a packed schedule while I'm in town," Hannah said.

"You better watch out or Molly'll try to get you to apply for the position," Sabrina said. "I did one play in high school and she tried to talk *me* into applying."

"Hey, one play is more than I did," Molly said.

"If she doesn't try to convince you, I will," Caleb said, breaking off another piece of bread and dragging it through the sauce on his plate.

"Too bad you're not in town long term," Jamie said, glancing at Ethan.

"Please, I bet she can't wait to get back to the City." Jo turned towards Hannah, oblivious to the way Ethan had tensed, his hold on Hannah's hand tightening. "Manhattan has to beat Aster Bay. The Thai food alone."

"Thai-d Up has some very decent Tom Yum soup," Jamie said.

"Very decent by Aster Bay standards might as well be cafeteria food compared to New York City," Jo scoffed. "I walked in a fashion show in the City once a few years back and I never wanted to leave."

"And yet, here you are," Gavin teased.

"It's not always all that amazing," Hannah hedged.

"Manhattan on its worst day is still ten times more exciting than Aster Bay," Jo said as she refilled her wine glass. She held out the bottle to ask if anyone else needed a top up, leaning over to fill Gavin's glass when he lifted it towards her.

"Exciting isn't always better," Hannah said. "The City is wonderful and alive. The food and the people and the theater."

"The museums," Sabrina offered.

Hannah nodded. "All of it. But it's also loud and crowded and it's easy to go days on end without ever seeing someone you know. Times Square smells like urine and it's too hot in the summer and you can never get a taxi when you want one—"

"Then why stay?" Ethan asked. "If it's so awful, why stay?"

"It's not *awful*. It's different. There are as many good things as there are bad. And my friends are there. My work."

Ethan's eyes narrowed, the muscle in his jaw ticking. "The same work that judges you by the way you look and sends hoards of photographers to stalk you?"

"It's part of the job," Hannah said. Was he honestly upset with her for liking the City?

"It's a shitty job."

She pulled her hand out of his, his words landing like a papercut across her heart. "I *like* my job."

"Do you?" he challenged.

"Who's ready for dessert?" Tessa asked, handing Julie off to Jamie as she got to her feet.

Around them, the conversation moved on—to the new exhibit at the university art museum and the teenager who fell asleep in the middle of Caleb's homily last week—but Hannah felt frozen, rooted to the spot by Ethan's glower. She wanted to rewind, go back to only a few moments before when she'd felt warm and fizzy with happiness. How had they gone from that, from Ethan accepting her invitation to join her at the premiere and celebrate his birthday in New York, to this coldness? How had the City she called home been an asset one moment and a strike against her the next?

And why did she care so much? They hadn't discussed the future, but with each passing day, this was feeling less and less like a fling and more like something *real*. The thought should terrify her but, she was startled to find, the thing that scared her the most was the idea of leaving Aster Bay and never again feeling the way she felt when she was with him.

But if he really thought so little of her home, of her career, how could they possibly work?

Chapter Sixteen

The drive back to Ethan's house was quiet and cold. Hannah curled in on herself and leaned against the passenger side door, as far away from him as possible. He didn't understand it. One minute they were talking about a trip to New York—a *temporary* trip—and the next she was practically dying to go back to the job she'd claimed she wasn't sure she wanted anymore. Not that he'd expected her to uproot her entire life for him after a few days, but he was having an awfully hard time not seeing her eagerness to return to Manhattan as willingness to leave him behind.

What did you expect? She already told you she didn't want a relationship.

And even if she did? Could he really expect her to give up her career, her life, for him?

A nasty voice niggled at the back of Ethan's brain, reminding him he hadn't even been able to convince the mother of his child to stay with him in Aster Bay. What chance did he have of Hannah—bold, beautiful, celebrity Hannah—wanting him enough to stay?

He pulled his truck into his driveway, gravel crunching beneath the tires, and turned it off, scraping his hand over his jaw. It wasn't her fault he wanted more than she did, that he'd foolishly thought he might be able to convince her to try with him. The things he had to offer, this small town life, could hardly compare with her world in New York. He knew that. And yet…

"I'm sorry," he said, his voice gruff as though he hadn't spoken in ages. "I was an asshole back there."

She eyed him warily. "Why?"

He dropped his head back against the head rest, closing his eyes. "I don't like thinking about you leaving."

He heard her shifting in her seat next to him. "I'm not leaving yet."

"But you will eventually."

"You'll come with me. Unless you've changed your mind about going to the premiere."

He turned to look at her. "Of course I'll go with you. But that's a weekend. That's not real life."

"Neither is this," she said.

"To me it is."

She searched his face, brow crinkled in thought, and then she was climbing into his lap, swinging her leg over his hip and straddling him. He slid his hands up her thighs, the loose fabric of her sundress bunching beneath his hands.

"I like your life," she whispered as she ghosted her lips along his jaw.

His heart pounded in his chest, naïve, reckless hope unfurling itself behind his sternum. He chased her lips with his own, catching them in a soft kiss that only made him want more.

"I like *you*," he said back.

"Yeah?" Her smile knocked the air from his lungs, the way it lit up her face from within, the sparkle in her eyes. She rocked her hips against him in a slow roll designed to make him lose his mind and his fingers dug into the soft flesh of her thighs through the flimsy material separating his hands from her skin. "I like you."

He kissed her again, this time in earnest, holding her hips snug against his own with one hand as the other snaked up her back and into her hair. He kissed her as though he could make her want to stay, as though this kiss could be enough.

Her hands slid down his chest, tugging at his shirt, fumbling with his belt buckle. He dragged his lips down her throat, sinking his teeth into the place where her neck met her shoulder. Her hand slid inside the placket of his jeans, curling around the length of him, already hard and desperate for her. She pumped her hand over him slowly, squeezing from root to tip as she stroked him.

"This what you want, city girl? You want me to fuck you in my truck?"

Her eyes flared wide before darkening. Goddamn she was beautiful like this, lust-drunk and needy.

"You need my cock so badly you can't even wait until we get in the house," he purred, skating his hands up her hips, over her waist.

He hooked one strap of her sundress with his finger and dragged it down her arm, revealing the cup of her bra, the creamy swell of her breast in the moonlight slanting through the window beside them. He held her gaze as he pulled the cup down, her breast tumbling free, then dropped his mouth to her, sucking the tight furl of her nipple between his lips as she continued to touch him. She moaned and stroked him faster.

"You wet for me, Han? That pretty pussy of yours ready for my cock?"

"Yes, Ethan," she panted.

With her free hand, she lifted the hem of her dress. He took it for the invitation it was and pressed his thumb to her seam through her cotton panties, feeling her wetness already soaking through the fabric.

"I don't have any condoms on me, sweetheart," he said softly, regret lancing through him. "If we go inside—"

"You don't need one," she said, cutting him off.

He tore his eyes away from the sight of her wet panties, holding her gaze as a new fire burned in his chest. He hadn't been with anyone without protection since the night his daughter was conceived, hadn't even wanted to, but goddamn did he want to now. The idea of sliding inside Hannah bare, of feeling the wet glide of her, of watching his cum leak out of her when they were through, knowing he'd filled her with it, that part of him was still inside her—fuck, it was too much to hope for.

Hannah's cheeks flamed bright red. "I mean, if you want..."

"I want," he said, thrusting into her fist to punctuate the point. "Jesus Christ, how I want. I just haven't done that in...a long time."

"Me either," she said. "But I have an IUD and I've been tested recently. Everything was negative."

"Me too."

He ran his eyes over her, from the wild tangle of her dark hair and the flush running from her cheeks down to her chest, the one uncovered breast bouncing gently, the tip shiny with his saliva, the bunched up fabric of her dress and the thighs spread wide over his hips, the tight grasp of her hand that he knew paled in comparison to the feeling of being inside her. He took the dress in his hands and lifted it over her head, tossing it on the passenger seat and leaving her in only her underwear and bra. She was so fucking beautiful with the moonlight painting her skin.

"Put me inside yourself, sweetheart," he grated out as he gripped the base of his cock, angling it towards her.

She hooked the gusset of her panties and pulled them to the side, lifted her hips, and lined herself up with his tip. He curled his free hand around her hips.

"Go slow. I want to watch your pussy stretch open for me,"

he commanded.

She did as he asked, lowering herself so just his crown slid inside her tight, wet heat. He hissed at the clench of her, and released his hold on himself to strum his thumb over her clit. Each pass over the swollen bundle of nerves had her sliding further down, taking him deeper, until he was fully seated. Her mouth fell open on a silent gasp as he hilted himself inside her and he caught her bottom lip between his teeth.

"Come on my cock, Hannah. Use me to make yourself feel good." He thrust up into her, their movements small and controlled in the confined space, and continued to stroke her clit as he took her nipple between his teeth.

She clutched his head to her chest, whimpering with each thrust. "God, Ethan, I'm already so close."

"That's right, sweetheart. Come for me. We're just getting started. Give me this first one, here, and I promise I'll fuck you properly when we get inside. You just have to come on my cock first." Her inner walls fluttered around him, clenching and grasping, and he pressed his forehead to hers, gritted his teeth to stave off his own orgasm. "That's right, Han. You can do it. Let me feel this pussy come for me."

She shook in his arms, her heat clamping down on him as her soft whimpers filled his ears. It took all his self-control not to come, but he wanted to watch her the first time he came inside her. She gasped and collapsed against him, her thighs tensing, and he dropped his hands to stroke over the tired muscles there.

"You're so fucking perfect, Hannah," he groaned, his cock begging for relief.

"I'm hardly perfect," she murmured, her lips against his collarbone.

He thrust up into her again and she gasped. "Time to go inside now, sweetheart, and I'll prove it to you."

Hannah reluctantly lifted herself off of Ethan's still-hard cock, and gathered her dress to hold in front of her chest. It was only a few steps from the truck to the front door and it was pitch dark out—it hardly seemed worth putting the dress back on only to have him take it off her again. Ethan tucked himself back in his pants but didn't bother doing up the zipper as he followed her up the steps to his house. He pressed himself against her back as he unlocked the door, the thick length of him against her ass.

The door had hardly closed behind them when he spun her around, pressing her against the door, and dropped to his knees. He licked her through the soaked fabric of her underwear, dragging her swollen lips between his teeth.

"Ethan," she groaned, "don't tease me."

"Can't get enough of your taste," he said, almost to himself. He pulled her underwear down, leaving it in a pool at her feet, and parted her with his thumbs. "You're going to look so pretty full of my cum."

She hardly had time to process what he'd said before he plunged his tongue inside her, licking and sucking and driving her fast towards her next orgasm. She came with a cry, her nails scraping against his scalp and her clit pulsing against his tongue.

Her thighs were still shaking when he got to his feet, his beard glistening with her release. "Need to fuck you, sweetheart. You good with that?"

Her core clenched, making her painfully aware of how empty she was. "Yes, please."

"So polite," he chuckled.

He took her hand and led her down the hall to his bedroom.

She'd never been in his bedroom before. The door was always closed, and she'd never been invited in. Until now.

She was unprepared for the starkness of the room, the sparse furniture and neutral paint, the lack of decoration on the wall. It wasn't dissimilar to the hotel rooms they'd spent so many nights in together, and her heart ached for him that his own bedroom was so impersonal.

He kissed her once, hard and fast, pulling her mind back to the moment. His hand dropped to cup her between the legs. "I want to watch this little pussy of yours milk my cock."

His dirty words in that low, gruff voice—it was so much like the audiobooks she'd listened to him narrate. But this time it wasn't Slade Hardcastle; it was Ethan. *Her* Ethan. Her heart pounded and her head spun, though whether it was at the promise of at least one more orgasm or the idea of Ethan as hers, she couldn't say for certain.

He pulled her in and spun her so her back was pressed to his front and she gasped at the reflection of herself in the floor length mirror on the inside of his open closet door, the faint red of beard burn beginning to blossom on her inner thighs. "Take off your bra, Hannah," he commanded, his breath hot on her ear.

Ethan watched her reflection as he removed his own clothing behind her, first the henley with the rolled sleeves, then his jeans, and finally his boxer briefs. His erection pressed against her as she unhooked her bra and let it fall to the floor.

"Look at how perfect you are," he said, one hand snaking up over the rounded curve of her belly to close over her breast. "So beautiful."

Her eyes danced over the silvery slashes of stretch marks on her belly, the cellulite on her thighs, the too small breasts, and landed on the look of adoration in his eyes reflected back at her. He really believed the things he said, that she was beautiful, no qualifiers needed. He didn't see the years of failed diets and self-loathing, the casting directors who seemed to get a sick sense of satisfaction out of recommending she lose twenty pounds before her next audition, the ways she's abused her body in the name of a more perfect shape. And watching the way he looked at her, the unbridled lust and something softer, a tenderness or affection she was afraid to look at too closely, she started to believe it, too.

"On the bed, sweetheart," he said.

She scrambled to comply, scooting across the soft comforter to settle on her back amongst the pillows. He lowered a knee onto the mattress and prowled over to her, his eyes taking in every inch of her, and her knees dropped open of their own accord as he drew closer. He hitched one of her legs over his hip and slid into her easily in a single smooth stroke. The fullness felt like relief, like an inevitability.

He stayed on his knees, his eyes continuing their path over her like a caress, pausing on her lips, her breasts, her hips, before finally landing on the place where they were joined. He sucked in a breath as he watched himself piston in and out of her, the stretch of her body to accommodate his.

"Can I come inside you, Han? Can I fill you up with my cum?"

The idea shouldn't have been so hot, but lord help her, it was. She wanted everything he could give her, wanted to keep some part of him inside herself even after it was over.

"Yes, do it," she cried, "I want to feel it."

He returned his thumb to her clit, pressing firmly and moving the pad of his finger in agonizingly slow circles as he fucked her. "Play with your tits, sweetheart. Get those nipples hard for me."

She did as he asked without even thinking, her hands closing over her breasts and plucking at her nipples, each squeeze sending sparks arrowing down to her core. Her thighs shook, her hips lifting off the bed to meet his thrusts, and he shifted his hand higher to press low on her belly. She gasped at the added pressure, heat flying down her spine and burning the soles of her feet as her climax gathered behind her clit and further, deeper inside her.

"That's it, Han. That's my girl. You're gonna come for me again, now, aren't you?" She thrashed on the bed, her body rebelling against the idea of another orgasm, her clit sore and swollen and yet still so desperate for relief. "That's it. This is my pussy now. You come when I want you to, and I want you to, Han. I want you to come again and again, want to watch you come so hard you forget to breathe. I fucking love it. Your orgasms are my favorite thing." He lowered his voice, a soothing croon that belied the steady press of his hand on her belly, the deep and thorough way he fucked her, the thick invasion of his cock dragging her closer and closer to another crushing climax. "It's all right, sweetheart. You can do it. I've got you. Gonna make you feel so good, Han. You just gotta come for me."

She arched off the bed as the orgasm ripped through her, tearing sinew and muscle as it seared through her with the kind of pleasure that was so much like pain. Ethan fucked her through it, roaring her name as he gave in to his own orgasm, his cock kicking inside her with each spurt of his release.

As soon as he was done, he withdrew and dropped to his forearms between her legs, holding her open for his inspection. "Good fucking girl," he groaned as he stroked a single finger through her seam. "This might be my new addiction, Hannah."

"Sex?" she asked through a punch-drunk chuckle.

"With you," he confirmed. "Your pussy dripping with my cum." He kissed her thighs, her mound, dropped a feather-light kiss to her clit as he slid his finger inside her, pushing his cum back in. "Fuck, I could get hard again just looking at you."

"You're insatiable," she said, sleep already pulling at her limbs.

"Can I slide inside you one more time, sweetheart? We can go to sleep, just let me sleep inside you. Want to feel you everywhere."

She smiled and tangled her fingers with his free hand. "I want to feel you everywhere, too."

Ethan lay down behind her, pulling her back against his chest and slowly slipping his half-hard cock back inside her. It felt right, to sleep with him as close as two people could possibly be. To be wrapped in his warmth, and to wrap him in hers.

Chapter Seventeen

"You've been holding out on me!" Hannah laughed, peering into the shoe box Ethan had retrieved from the kitchen around midnight when their third round of incredible sex had left them both feeling snackish. The box was full of every kind of fruity, chewy candy imaginable, bags of sour straws and gummy bears hidden in a box advertising work boots. "It looks like you robbed a candy store."

Ethan climbed back into bad, sliding under the covers and handing the box to Hannah. "I have a sweet tooth."

"And Tessa's regular baked goods delivery doesn't suffice?"

It had taken Hannah a few days to get used to the idea that there would always be fresh cupcakes, cookies, and scones on Ethan's counter, appearing out of nowhere. It had taken a few more days for her to decide it was a testament to her recovery that she didn't inhale the entire tray each morning, that she could instead enjoy the pastries without feeling a crippling urge to atone by skipping dipper, and that she had, in fact, gone an entire day without even thinking about the confections. Was that how the rest of the world felt?

She selected a pack of Sour Patch Kids, tearing into it and fishing out a yellow. The sugary sour goodness made her cheeks pucker. "I forgot how good these are. I haven't had a Sour Patch Kid in years."

"Why's that?" Ethan asked, shaking a few into his hand without a care for which colors he was getting. The philistine.

Hannah shrugged, chewing the last bits of the candy slowly and sifting through the bag for a green one. "It's not something I let myself have."

She glanced up at him, meeting his quizzical gaze, and knew he would wait for her to continue. Her therapist had assured her it would get easier to tell people about her struggles with food the more she practiced, but despite having told Liv and Jennifer, Jackson and Micah, her parents, it still didn't feel any easier when she said, "I am in recovery from an eating disorder."

To his credit, Ethan didn't visibly react. His movements slowed, as though he were swimming through molasses, and she got the distinct impression he was working hard not to display any emotion. It reminded her so much of her parents the night after her high school graduation when she'd stumbled home and woken them at two o'clock in the morning to announce she was drunk but had done the responsible thing by leaving her car at the party, and they'd need to drive her there to retrieve it. Her mother hadn't flinched. She'd simply said, "okay, honey," then gone back to sleep. Of course, she woke Hannah up at six for that car retrieval, so she wasn't exactly unphased by her daughter's announcement, but as time went by, Hannah could appreciate her mother's restraint.

"What are you thinking?" Hannah asked, her stomach twisting.

"I'm not sure I know what that means," Ethan said slowly.

"Which part? The eating disorder or the recovery?"

"Both?"

Hannah set the shoebox of candy aside and turned to face him, gathering the sheet around her chest. "I have had an eating disorder since I was a teenager, though I wasn't officially diagnosed until about a year ago. It means I've used food—both eating too much and not eating enough—as a coping mechanism to regulate my emotions. To feel in control. To try to change the size and shape of my body." She held up the package of Sour Patch Kids. "It means you can look at this and only see a sweet treat, but I see the number of calories and how many hours of working out it would require to counteract them, whether or not having even just one will make me crave sweets so much I can't stop myself from eating the entire package, or the entire shoebox. Whether I can eat a handful if I skip lunch, or two handfuls if I also skip dinner. Which, naturally, means I'm quite literally starving by the time I eat that handful, so then my biological need to feed myself takes over and convinces me to eat the entire contents of my kitchen cabinets until I feel so ill I have to spend the rest of the afternoon sitting on my shower floor trying not to be sick."

She clamped her mouth shut, surprised by the way the words had tumbled from her lips, as though they'd been shaken loose, these moments she'd spent the last year making sense of. More than that, she was taken aback by how *good* it felt to tell him. For the first time, the creeping shame that usually followed such a revelation didn't come.

Ethan tore his eyes away from Hannah's and stared at the candy in his hands. "All that for *this*?"

"It's not about the candy. It's hard to explain if you've never had an unhealthy relationship with food."

"And recovery...what does that mean?" he asked tentatively.

"It means I can eat these Sour Patch Kids, despite the thoughts still trying to break through, and know that food doesn't have to dictate how I feel about myself. It means I can have the candy and stop before I feel sick. It means I have a standing phone call with my therapist every two weeks and a dietitian once a month." She took a breath, blew it out slowly as she braced herself to tell him the last part. "And it means there's always a chance I'll relapse."

"Like an alcoholic?"

"Not exactly. Unlike an alcoholic, someone with an eating disorder can't abstain from food. But it's a similar idea. The thoughts will likely never go away completely, but they get quieter. A little quieter every day. And, even when they're loud, I know now that I don't have to listen to them."

Ethan squeezed her hand back. "How long have you been in recovery?"

"About six months. I was diagnosed during my run in *Bridget Jones' Musical* and I managed with therapy for a while, but I knew I needed to get away from the stage for a bit to really recover. It's hard to let yourself gain weight, and even harder when you're on stage next to *Superfan's* Sexiest Boy Band Member every night. So, when the show closed, I enrolled in an intensive outpatient treatment program."

"Six months ago was September," he said, scanning her eyes. "I saw you in Boston in September."

She nodded. "And the next day I started treatment."

"Fuck," he said, more exhale than words. She winced, and he pulled her closer, cradling her head against his chest. "I didn't know."

"How could you? I didn't tell you." She looked up at him with his big, worried, blue eyes and his scruffy beard, and her heart swelled in her chest. "I liked that you didn't see me that way."

"What way?"

"Damaged. Broken."

A low noise of disapproval sounded in his throat. "You're not either of those things."

"I liked that you didn't get your worried face every time we ordered nachos from room service."

"I don't have a worried face."

"You absolutely have a worried face." She stroked her thumb between his brows. "You're making it right now."

He caught her hand and kissed the inside of her wrist. "I wish I could have been there for you."

"You're here now."

"Did you let anyone be there for you, city girl?"

"Not at first. But eventually... Liv and my parents... and Jackson."

He smoothed his thumb between her eyes. "Now *you're* making a worried face," he said softly.

"My insurance sucks. And Jackson was—is—a good friend. He'd known other people who'd gone through eating disorder treatments. Pop stars and actresses. He got me a recommendation for the treatment center, and when I told him I couldn't afford it, he paid for the treatment."

"In exchange for you pretending to be his girlfriend?" Ethan asked, his lips pressing together and his jaw clenching.

"No. He would never ask for anything in exchange for helping someone. The fake dating was my idea. Part of the treatment plan was abstaining from new relationships for a few months. Especially physical ones. I sometimes..." She bit her lip again, looked away. "I sometimes used sex in the same way I used food. Overindulging to sort of numb out everything else. I was afraid that if I was single, I'd turn to those types of relationships to fill the void, and replace one self-destructive behavior with another. But if I was supposed to be dating Jackson, then there wasn't any risk of me slipping up. He needed to make the press believe he had settled down, and I needed to know that the next time I called you, it was because of how much I liked you, and not because I wanted to hide from my feelings."

"You used to do that with me?" He looked pained and she scrambled closer to him, cupping his face in her hands.

"No," she said vehemently. "But in the middle of treatment, I wasn't sure if the way you made me feel was an extension of my disorder or if it was real." She scratched her fingers over his beard, and he closed his eyes, sinking into her touch despite the tortured furrow of his brow. "When I called you this last time to meet me in Boston, my therapist and I had finally decided I was ready. And I hadn't been able to stop thinking about you. I knew then that what we had...what we have...has nothing to do with the disorder. I knew that my feelings for you were real."

"Then why did you say no when I asked to see you again?"

"I was afraid." Her voice wavered, but she continued. "I fought so hard for my recovery—I still fight for it every day—and I was afraid I'd mess it up by wanting you too much." She looked away, tears stinging her nose and the back of her eyes. "It's not something I'm proud of."

"Hey." He caught her chin between his thumb and forefinger, turning her to face him. "You asked for help. You did what you needed to do to take care of yourself. You should be so proud of that." She dashed away an errant tear, and his eyes softened. "Don't cry, city girl. I'll be proud enough of you for both of us."

From *The Lady's Knights* by AK Wild,
narrated by Slade Hardcastle

For three days and three nights, Lady Windtorn slept by Sir Llewellyn's side, his men taking turns keeping watch over their camp. On the morning of the fourth day, before the sun gilded the hill beyond their camp, its rays advancing like so many soldiers with blades drawn to slice apart their nighttime happiness, Sir Llewellyn woke. He brushed the hair from his lady's face and told himself to prepare for the inevitable.

"I cannot sleep while you stare," she said without opening her eyes.

He kissed her closed eyelids. "'Tis but a dream, my lady. You do not yet wake."

"I do." She opened her eyes, blue like the summer's sky.

"It is not yet morning." He lifted her hands above her head, held them fast as he moved to cover her with his body. She was soft where he was hard, smooth where he was rough, and when she parted her legs that he might settle between them, she was warm.

"The dawn has come, Sir," she said, smiling, though there was a sadness in her eyes. "My hus— The castle awaits."

She'd caught the distasteful word before it was fully formed, but he heard it still, felt the sting of it. "Do not speak of that life while I am inside you," he growled.

She had to return to Lord Havenbrook. He knew it and yet he hated it.

When the time came, he would accompany her to the edge of the keep, see her safely returned to the life he'd stolen her away from, but not yet. Their interlude had been far too brief.

He worked himself between her legs, reveled in the salt of her skin beneath his lips, and cursed the sun's ceaseless ascent.

Lady Windtorn met him movement for movement, opening herself to him, pulling him closer, deeper, with her legs around his waist. "You are correct, Sir," she said, her breathing quickening. "The sun has not yet risen. It is the moon. We still have time."

"Aye, but a little longer," he said, his fingers laced with hers, face buried in her raven-dark hair, eyes squeezed shut against the blasted sun. Then, softer, so she would not hear his heart breaking, "Would that it were enough."

Chapter Eighteen

"Thank you so much for coming. The kids are going to be so excited to meet an actual Broadway star." Molly led Hannah down the hall of the 1960s-era tan brick building that housed St. Anthony's High School, navigating with ease around the groups of teenagers gathered at their lockers.

"I don't know about *star*, but I'm happy to help in any way I can." Hannah finally succeeded in removing the backing of the adhesive nametag she'd been handed in the front office, affixing the sticker to the front of her shirt. The printing was crooked and part of the last 'h' was missing so it looked like her name was Hannan.

"And I know you're trying to keep a low profile, but you should know that there are no cell phones allowed in rehearsals, so there shouldn't be any unexpected photo shoots," Molly assured her.

It was at least the third time since Friday's family dinner that Molly had made a similar promise. Hannah was grateful for Molly's sensitivity, but she'd also already had a long conversation with Micah about what happened if one of those kids snapped a shot anyway. "You're only in that town for a few more days, so in the unlikely event a member of the AP follows a teenager from Rhode Island on social media, it should be fine," Micah had said. "Besides, if the press picked up the story that you're nursing your broken heart by volunteering with teenagers, that wouldn't be the worst thing." She'd spent the next ten minutes convincing Micah they shouldn't plant the story themselves.

"I'm hoping you'll be able to work with our Audrey, in particular," Molly continued as she led her through the double doors of a large open room with cafeteria tables folded up along one wall. "Amelia's a great kid, hard worker, very talented, but she's also incredibly self-conscious."

"What teenager isn't?" Hannah asked.

"True, but this is different. I don't know how to help her break through that barrier. I've never acted before."

"I've never coached anyone before, but I'll see what I can do."

Another set of double doors opened into the school's gym, a stage at one end, a basketball hoop raised above the proscenium. A handful of boys, lanky teenagers in the pleated khakis and starchy button-downs of their Catholic school uniforms, darted around the gym, each vying for the basketball. At the center of their group, Caleb held them off, dribbling with an ease that seemed at odds with his bright white priest's collar and pristine blacks.

Pockets of teenagers gathered in small groups throughout the room all turned their heads as Molly and Hannah entered the space. Caleb looked away from the ball, catching sight of them, and his mouth spread into a grin as gleaming white as his collar. The distraction was fleeting, but it was long enough for one of the boys to steal the ball, jumping into the air and shooting, the crash of the ball against the backboard before it dropped into the hoop echoing through the gym.

Caleb clapped the kid on the back and made his way over to Molly and Hannah. "Hannah, I'm glad you could join us."

"Are you done riling up my actors?" Molly asked, tilting her head like a confused cocker spaniel.

The priest chuckled and cuffed the back of his neck. "My apologies, Ms. Proulx. Won't happen again."

"See that it doesn't, Father West."

With a wink at Hannah, Caleb excused himself, disappearing through the doors of the gym.

"Is he your boss?" Hannah asked.

"The parish priest is in charge of the school, but he is *not* my boss." Molly turned away from Hannah towards the teenagers scattered throughout the gym and clapped her hands three times. She led Hannah towards the stage, calling, "Circle up!"

The kids made their way towards the front of the room, curiosity slowing them down as they turned to whisper to each other, their eyes trained on Hannah.

"We have a special guest with us today," Molly said when her ragtag bunch of high school actors was assembled. "My friend Miss Matthews—"

"Hannah, please," Hannah interjected.

Molly smiled indulgently. "Hannah has agreed to help us out today. She is a professional actress who comes to us straight from Broadway and we are so lucky to have her with us." Molly led the kids in an awkward round of applause.

"Thank you for letting me crash your rehearsal," Hannah said.

Molly ran through the rest of her announcements quickly (no gum on stage, she's looking at you, Tucker; don't forget to be off book by next Monday; and the candy bar fundraiser to pay for the costumes would be over in a week so get in those last-minute orders), then ushered Hannah to a seat in front of the stage as the kids took their places for the opening number. Hannah bit back her smile as she watched them shuffle about, shoving each other to the right places on stage when the music for the opening number began. She remembered those days of high school drama club, of being both proud and embarrassed to be good at something.

Then Amelia took the stage.

She wasn't at all what Hannah had expected and she found herself leaning forward in her seat to watch the shy girl move around the stage. Amelia was tall—at least a head taller than the boy playing Seymour—with a round face. It was hard to tell in the oversized sweatshirt she wore but Hannah would bet money she was also plus sized, which definitely was not the usual casting choice for Audrey.

As the cast sang louder and louder, Amelia and her Seymour leading the pack, Hannah's face split into a grin. The girl was young and probably wouldn't make a profession out of performing, but she had a pretty voice with a compelling tone. She was also clearly terrified.

The song ended and Molly leaned over to Hannah, whispering, "What did you think?"

"She's great. She just needs to get out of her own way." Molly nodded. "Do you mind if I pull her while you run the next scene?"

"Please, pull away!"

Amelia trotted down the stairs at the side of the stage, her head bowed and eyes focused on her feet, but Hannah headed her off at the pass, meeting her at the bottom of the stairs. "Amelia, right?" The girl's head snapped up, her eyes wide. "I'm Hannah. You were great up there."

"I was late on my second entrance," she said, dropping her gaze.

"Yeah, but so were half the kids up there. You'll get it. You have time." Hannah walked with Amelia towards the back of the gym where one bank of bleachers had been pulled out to allow for seating.

Hannah took a seat on the bleachers and waited for Amelia to join her. The girl eyed her cautiously. "Were you really on

Broadway?"

"I was, and I did national tours for years before that."

"Anything that came through Providence?" Amelia took a seat next to Hannah, her hands pulled into the sleeves of her sweatshirt and her shoulders hunched, like she would disappear inside the oversized clothing if she could.

"I was here with *The Little Mermaid* a few years back. I played Ursula."

Amelia's face brightened. "I saw that! You were so good!"

Hannah smiled. "Thanks. It's a fun part."

"Is that what you played on Broadway?"

"No. I was in the original cast of *Bridget Jones' Musical*."

"The one that's coming to the movie theaters next month? With Jackson Hayes?"

Hannah's smile faltered. She hadn't planned on teenagers knowing who Jackson was. His usual fan base was closer to her age. "That's the one."

"Wait." Amelia's eyes narrowed. "You're *that* Hannah? The one—" She reached inside her pocket for her cell phone, but Hannah pressed a hand to her forearm, stopping her.

"No cell phones in rehearsal," she said, her mouth suddenly dry.

Had this been a mistake? How long would it take before word spread across whatever app these kids were using that Hannah Matthews had been spotted at a high school musical rehearsal?

Amelia lowered her voice. "What they wrote about you online was fucked up."

Hannah wasn't sure which specific fucked up thing Amelia was referring to, and she wasn't sure she wanted to know. She definitely didn't want to hash it out in the middle of a high school drama club rehearsal. "Let's talk about you, Amelia. How excited are you to be playing Audrey?"

A shy smile flickered across Amelia's face before she

schooled it into submission, twisting the cuffs of the sweatshirt with fingers still hidden inside her sleeves. "I only got the part because of seniority. We were supposed to do *Hairspray* this year so I could play Tracy but Mr. Day, the principal, said we couldn't put a boy in a dress to play Edna, so Miss. Proulx picked *Little Shop* instead."

Hannah debated diving into the transphobic bullshit that was denying high schoolers the chance to do *Hairspray*, but decided it was not the time. She'd talk to Molly and Caleb about it later. Instead she asked, "Were you excited to play Tracy?"

Amelia shrugged. "It's a good part."

"It's a great part. So is Audrey."

Amelia shrugged again, focusing her attention on her cuffs. Hannah leaned back against the row of bleachers behind them, which, for the record, was much easier and more comfortable when she was seventeen than it was now at thirty-two. "You know, I always wanted to play Audrey."

"You did?"

"Mmhmm. When they did a production in New Jersey a few years back I wanted to audition, but my manager wouldn't let me. He said I didn't look the part." Amelia exhaled, her shoulders rounding even further. "Which I think was a bunch of bullshit." Amelia's eyes snapped to Hannah's. "Did you know the only description of Audrey in the script is 'honest, sweet, vulnerable, insecure. Attractive but not well educated.' Nothing specific about what she looks like."

"Attractive," Amelia repeated.

"Right, but attractive to who? Do you and your best friend find the same people attractive?"

Amelia laughed. "Not at all."

"Exactly. Attractiveness is a subjective quality. Like being tall. I've lost parts because the creative team thought I was too tall, and I've lost other parts because they thought I was too short. It's subjective. It's just that 'attractive' is a much more loaded description than 'tall.'"

Hannah let the silence settle between them as Amelia turned over her words, sentiments that had taken years of therapy and months of outpatient eating disorder treatments to ring even remotely true for Hannah, things she hoped would be easier for Amelia to believe than they had been for her.

"When everyone thought I was going to play Tracy, no one had a problem with it," Amelia said slowly, her forehead furrowing as she stared at her twisted cuffs again. "But when Ms. Proulx announced I was going to be Audrey, I could tell some of the other girls didn't think I deserved the part."

"And what did *you* think?"

"It's easier when you play the parts they expect you to."

Hannah blew out a breath. "It is. It's also easier to believe you don't deserve something than to believe you do."

"Yeah."

"But you know what? That's the character. Audrey doesn't believe she deserves the things she wants. 'Honest, sweet, vulnerable, insecure.' That's the whole point of *Somewhere That's Green*. She wants to be loved, to be happy, but she doesn't think she deserves it and she's too afraid to demand it." Hannah met Amelia's eyes, smiling softly. "Maybe you and Audrey have more in common than you think."

"The library is so thrilled to be hosting Reader Fest at Nuthatch this year." Mrs. Alcott extended a frail hand towards Ethan and he was careful to grip it lightly. Her skin was papery beneath his palms, the blue veins along the back prominent in a way that made him feel protective over the older woman.

"We're happy to have you," Ethan said.

"Well, of course, it won't be *me*, though," Mrs. Alcott said as she gathered her things.

"What do you mean?" Baz asked, a scowl beginning to form.

"Didn't you hear? I'm retiring at the end of the month. This is my last week on the job."

"Congratulations," Ethan said. "You've been the Director of the library since—"

"Since you were in diapers," Mrs. Alcott said with a smile.

"Who's running the festival then?" Baz asked, always one to cut straight to the point.

"We are." Ethan glanced up to see the grandma gang, pink jackets and all, in the doorway to his office, Mrs. White at the head of the pack. "After we stopped by last week, we told Joanie the vineyard would be the perfect place for this year's Reader Fest."

"The town will need time to find my replacement, you see," Mrs. Alcott explained, "so when Helen and the girls volunteered to step in, well, it was too good to be true."

Baz grunted in a way that somehow managed to sound sarcastic.

"Well, I'm off! I know you all will make me proud," Mrs. Alcott said, squeezing Ethan's hand one final time before sending air kisses towards the other women on her way out the door.

Mrs. Blumenthal sank into one of the seats in front of Ethan's desk and began pulling manilla folders from her rattan handbag. "We'll need to get started right away. Of course, we've asked Gavin to take a stab at revising the marketing plan for this year."

"Gavin knew about this?" Ethan asked.

"We just left him, dear. Do try to keep up," Mrs. Kemp said.

Ethan ran his thumb and forefinger over his eyes, pressing

hard enough that he saw spots. "I really don't need to be a part of the planning process. Let me know what you need from the vineyard, how many chairs, that sort of thing."

"I told you he wouldn't want to participate," Mrs. Greene grumbled, nudging Mrs. White.

"I've never read *Moby Dick*," Ethan said by way of explanation.

"No one has, dear," Mrs. Kemp said.

"That's why we're diversifying this year's festival," Mrs. Blumenthal said, opening a folder to reveal a stack of looseleaf paper covered in her neat, slanting script. "Why have an entire festival about just one book?"

"Especially a book that has such low circulation," Mrs. Greene said.

"Reader Fest always focuses on one classic," Baz said.

"Yes, and attendance has been declining for years. Joanie just didn't want to admit it," Mrs. Blumenthal offered.

"Which is where we come in," Mrs. White said, pinning Ethan with a knowing smile that made the hair on the back of his neck stand up.

"Why feature one book when we can feature multiple books, and all by local authors?" Mrs. Kemp asked.

"Does Aster Bay have any authors?" Baz asked.

"Millie DeGrey wrote that one book," Mrs. Blumenthal said. "The historical fiction about the servant at Aster Place."

"Not that anybody read it," Mrs. Greene said.

"There are plenty of authors within driving distance," Mrs. White said. "Aja Mathé is in Providence—"

"Children's books," Mrs. Blumenthal offered.

"Richard Reynolds is in Maine—" Mrs. White continued.

"Charming fiction books," Mrs. Blumenthal said.

"Philip Nathanson is on the Cape—"

"Historical fiction," Mrs. Blumenthal added.

"And AK Wild is in Boston." Mrs. White's eyes gleamed as

Ethan's stomach somersaulted.

"She writes romance books," Mrs. Blumenthal said.

"He knows, Dottie," Mrs. White said.

"That's a lot of authors," Ethan said, narrowing his eyes at Mrs. White. What the hell kind of game was she playing? "I'm not sure we can fit them all."

"Nonsense! If you can host a three-hundred-person wedding or an entire reality television production crew, you can certainly fit a handful of authors and their fans," Mrs. Kemp said.

"We can talk about the details later. We're going to be late for our lunch reservation," Mrs. Greene complained.

"AK Wild is an Aster Bay girl. Grew up here, you know," Mrs. Blumenthal said proudly.

"He knows, Dottie," Mrs. White repeated.

"He might not know," Mrs. Blumenthal insisted. "She moved away when they were all still kids. Just because he narrates her books, doesn't mean he knows her personally."

Every muscle in Ethan's body tensed as bile forced its way up his throat. His ears rang and the adrenaline coursing through his veins made him feel shaky, unsteady in a way he hadn't felt in years. It was one thing to suspect Mrs. White knew about his secret alter ego, but if the whole grandma gang knew, it was only a matter of time before everyone in Aster Bay had the information.

"Mrs. Blumenthal—" he started.

"Don't worry, dear. Your secret is safe with us. Though why you'd want to keep it a secret when you have such a lovely voice…" She shook her head and clicked her teeth.

All those years of carefully keeping his life in Aster Bay and his life in audiobooks separate and it was all about to come crashing down, thanks to his kindergarten teacher no less. He sank into his chair, stunned into silence, his gaze bouncing between the women who seemed oblivious to the grenade they'd just thrown into his life.

Baz ushered them to the door. "Let us know what you need. We'll make it happen."

While Baz and the others moved down the hall, Mrs. Greene rattling off her grievances with the new lunch specials at Lemon and Thyme, Mrs. White held back. She approached the desk, rapping her knuckles on the mahogany. "Do you remember when Mikey Greenhall broke my ceramic fox?"

Ethan blinked. "In first grade?"

"You took it home and put it back together with Elmer's glue and Scotch tape. It was on my desk, whole, if a little worse for wear, in the morning. When I asked who had fixed it, you didn't say a word. Stephanie was the one who told me it was you."

"Why are we talking about this?"

"You never did like to take credit for your accomplishments."

Ethan huffed out a laugh. "That fox was a mess."

"It was. But quite an impressive mess for a first grader, even if the tail was on upside down."

"Mrs. White, with all due respect, what's your point?"

"It's okay to own your accomplishments, Ethan. You're quite a good narrator."

He winced. "Please, stop. I would really like to pretend you've never listened to a Slade Hardcastle book."

Mrs. White sighed. "I never took you for a prude." She turned to leave, but at the last moment, turned back. "You should be proud of your work, Ethan. Your parents and friends would be proud. And secrets have a way of coming out."

Chapter Nineteen

"We have a small window to capitalize on the buzz around *Bridget Jones' Musical*," Micah said through the phone.

Hannah sat on the back steps of Ethan's house, watching a sparrow hop along the branch of a nearby tree as the sun set over the bay. She told herself that the jittery, brittle feeling beneath her skin was about the upcoming premiere and not the conversation about her next career move. Or the fact it had been a week since she'd sung a note outside of the shower and she wasn't feeling the urge to hunt down the nearest piano in Aster Bay for a practice session.

Why wasn't she dying to get back to work?

"I've had a few calls. There's some interest in seeing you for the national tour of *Les Mis*."

The false brightness in Micah's voice might as well have been a flashing neon sign: *Danger Ahead; Incoming Fatphobia.*

"What part?"

He hesitated. "Madame Thénardier."

"Of course." She pulled up a handful of grass and began methodically shredding each blade into smaller and smaller pieces. She would not think about the half-eaten pint of ice cream in the freezer in Ethan's kitchen. "What else?"

"There's an open call for Mrs. Potts, but—"

"Please at least tell me I'm too young for the Angela Lansbury roles, Micah."

"You're too young for the Angela Lansbury roles." Her manager sighed. "If only there was another Bridget on the horizon."

"No word on a tour?" she asked, but she already knew the answer.

The producers weren't going to run a tour until after they'd milked every last drop out of the pro shot's theatrical release. She switched the phone to speaker and began scrolling the take-out menu for the Pizza Stone. According to Sabrina and Kyla, the Pizza Stone had the best mozzarella sticks in town. She wondered if they'd deliver the one order by itself or if she'd need to add more to make it worth their while—maybe an order of garlic knots, too, or a slice of the turtle pie...

"There's a regional theater in Chicago prepping for *Into the Woods*—"

"So my options are a thief, a talking tea pot, and a witch."

Two orders of garlic knots. And onion rings.

"Why don't you take some time to think about it? I'll email over the songs they want on the self tapes. Just run them through, see how they feel."

She sighed, nodding.

"Hannah?"

"I'm nodding."

"Alright, good. I'll see what I can line up for when you're back in the City. We've gone almost a week without any new photos from Jackson's camp, so after the premiere, the press should lose interest and you can come home."

It should have been good news, but instead of feeling comforted by the idea that she'd soon be back in her little New York apartment, she felt like Micah had released a swarm of bees in her chest.

"We'll re-evaluate after the premiere," Micah continued. "This will be good, Hannah, you'll see. I have to go meet a client, but hang in there. I'll see you Friday."

The line went dead and Hannah set the phone on the step beside her, clasping her hands between her knees. *Garlic knots, turtle pie, mozzarella sticks, mozzarella sticks, mozzarella sticks.* She squeezed her eyes shut and focused on her breathing the way they'd taught her in therapy, focused on feeling the unsettled buzzing beneath her skin, on naming the sensations as they moved through her.

"Hey, what're you doing out here?"

Hannah looked up as Ethan sat down on the step beside her, his bare feet in the early spring grass.

"Just checking in with my manager," she said.

"Everything alright?"

"Great."

He eyed her curiously but didn't push. *Onion rings, mozzarella sticks, maybe some chicken tenders with extra honey mustard...*

"I told him we'll drive down Friday morning," she said, talking so she could drown out the litany of fried foods running through her head. "Micah arranged an early check-in and a car will meet us at the hotel to take us to the premiere when it's time."

"Are you nervous?"

"About the premiere? Not really. A little. Like the smallest amount possible. I've never been on a red carpet before."

Ethan brushed a strand of hair behind her ear. "You'll be great."

"I might trip and fall. Or say something ridiculous to the press."

"You might," he agreed, "but you might not. And either way, I'll be there."

The buzzing beneath her skin calmed to a low hum, the relentless recitation of fried foods quieting, like someone had turned down the volume. She ran her thumb over the crinkles at the corner of Ethan's eye when he smiled at her. "Thank you. I know how protective you are of your privacy."

"It's not about privacy, at least not for privacy's sake," he said, catching her forearm and pressing a kiss to the inside of her wrist. "I protect the people I care about. Sometimes that means keeping things to myself. Sometimes it means putting on a suit and holding your bag while you smile for the cameras."

"You'll hold my bag?" she asked, unable to control her smile. He'd included her amongst the list of people he cared about.

"Your bag, your shoes, your dress—"

She laughed. "My dress will be staying on at the premiere."

"After, then." He pressed a kiss to her lips. She wanted to melt into it, to melt into him, to focus on nothing but the movement of his mouth over hers, but her thoughts were still racing with the thousands of ways this premiere could go wrong. He moved down to her throat, nuzzling against the curve of her jaw, his beard rough on her skin. "You're distracted," he said, his lips skating down her neck.

"I may be more nervous than I want to admit," she said.

He chuckled. "You don't say." He sat back, taking her hand in his and squeezing. "What exactly are you nervous about, aside from the very slim possibility that you might trip on the red carpet?"

"All those cameras." She closed her eyes, seeing the bright bursts of the flashes behind her eyelids. "All those people looking at me."

His brows knit together. "Hundreds of people watched you every night on stage when the show was on Broadway."

"True, but they weren't looking at *me*. They were looking at Bridget. If the dress didn't fit right, it was because *Bridget* was wearing the wrong thing, not me. They didn't care about me at all as long as I sang well enough and made them laugh."

He nodded, understanding. "And now they're looking at you instead of the character."

"So far, when the press has looked at me as just me, they haven't liked what they've seen." A low noise rumbled in his chest, like the warning thrum of an angered predator. "Though, even then, they weren't really looking at me. They were looking at Jackson Hayes' alleged girlfriend." She winced, groaned. "And if it wasn't bad enough that they compared me to photos of the models he was caught with, now they'll be comparing us in person."

Ethan slid his hands into her hair, cupping her face and tilting it up to him, his gaze hard and hot on her skin. "There is no comparison."

She released a sound that was half laugh, half sob. "I know. How am I supposed to compete with a Victoria's Secret model?"

His grip on her tightened. "No, Han. You misunderstand. There is no competition. They are them and you are you, and you are fucking gorgeous." He kissed her forehead, her brow bone, her cheeks. "There's no comparison because there's no need to compare. Your beauty is not diminished by being in the presence of other beautiful women."

She was warm all over, like he'd shone the sun on her and her alone. Smiling, she spoke against his lips. "You have to say that because you've seen me naked."

"You should believe me more because I've seen you naked. The only thing they have that you don't is the confidence to stand on that carpet and know those photographers are damn lucky to be allowed to take their picture."

"I want to feel that way," she said, her voice small, like maybe if she spoke softly enough, she wouldn't scare away the tiny spark inside her that thought maybe, just maybe, with this man looking at her this way, maybe she could be confident enough for that.

He kissed her again, a soft, lingering kiss, then stood, pulling her up with him. "Come with me. I have an idea."

Twenty minutes and a few cryptic phone calls later, after Ethan encouraged her to change into one of her sundresses and a pair of heels—and she, of course, complied, just to see the way his eyes darkened when she came out in the curve-hugging dress—Ethan turned his truck into the parking lot of a giant stone church with large stained-glass windows. He was out of the truck and opening her car door before she'd fully registered where they were.

"You took me to church?" she asked as he helped her down from the passenger seat. "You want me to pray for confidence?"

"Not exactly."

But he didn't explain any further. Instead, he took her hand and led her up the stone steps to the medieval-looking front door. One side swung open, revealing Caleb, the scowl on his face and the wild way his hair stood up in all directions, as though he'd been tugging at it, jarring against the staid beauty of the building. "Place is all yours," he said, stepping aside to welcome them into the dim narthex. He glanced over his shoulder at a woman sitting at the far end of the sanctuary. "I'll be in my office."

Hannah watched the priest's retreating back. "What was that about?"

"I don't know." Ethan frowned, his attention focused on the woman as she stood, straightened her dress, and quietly slipped out the side door. His frown deepened as he watched her go, but from this distance, Hannah couldn't make out her face before Ethan took her hand and led her into the sanctuary. "I'll find out later. Now, we have a mission."

"We do?"

"Damn straight we do." Jo burst into the sanctuary behind them, pushing open the doors theatrically as she strode towards them. She twirled her finger in a circle. "Let me see what I'm working with."

Hannah shot a confused look Ethan's way but she did as Jo asked, her skirt flaring out around her knees. "Is someone going to tell me what's going on?"

Ethan leaned against the wall, crossing his arms over his chest, his eyes roving over her as her dress settled. "You're nervous about walking the red carpet with models. Who better to prepare you than an actual model?"

"That's me," Jo said with a little wave and a smile.

"And we're in a church because...?" Hannah asked.

"Red carpet." Ethan tilted his head towards the aisle and the plush red carpeting that ran the length of the sanctuary.

Hannah couldn't help the laugh that bubbled up in her throat and burst from her lips. It was ridiculous and wonderful and so thoughtful it made her want to wrap him up in her arms and never let him go.

Jo hooked an arm through Hannah's and began pulling her towards the front of the sanctuary. "Oh, no. I know that look. You save those horny thoughts until later. We've got work to do."

Chapter Twenty

Ethan watched from the back of the church as Jo taught Hannah how to strut the length of the aisle, moving with purpose but not rushing, like she knew exactly where she wanted to go but wasn't in any particular hurry to get there.

She was captivating—the way she slowly unfurled as Jo taught her what poses to strike on the red carpet, how her spine straightened and her shoulders relaxed, the sway of her hips and curl of her smile. She was the most beautiful woman he'd ever seen, and each laugh, each smile, hit him like a punch to the chest. He rubbed his hand over his heart, as though he could ease the ache behind his rib cage that only intensified as he watched Hannah come alive before his eyes. What he wouldn't give to be able to make her this happy every day...

"Now here's what you do if you find yourself in a group photo situation," Jo said, moving to stand beside Hannah. She slid her arm around Hannah's waist and angled herself just so. "Bend the knee, and make space. Don't smoosh yourself up against each other like this," she said, tugging Hannah closer. "You want room for the lines to breathe."

Ethan caught Hannah's eye from across the room as she followed Jo's instructions, and her smile turned shy, like she'd only just remembered she had an audience. Jo followed Hannah's line of sight and leaned close, whispering something in Hannah's ear that had her blushing and laughing breathlessly, a little flustered but still smiling.

"Don't believe a word she says, sweetheart," Ethan called. Hannah's eyes snapped to his, the laughter there like pure sunshine.

"Come on, foxy. You know you love me," Jo said with a wink.

"I'd love it if you wrapped things up here so I can take my girl out like I'd originally planned," Ethan said.

"Then you're in luck, because I've taught her all I know." Jo turned to Hannah, taking her hands. "You're gonna rock this, babe. Remember, chin up, tits out. It's all about the angles."

"Thank you." Hannah pulled Jo into a hug, squeezing her eyes shut as she embraced the younger woman.

"Alright, have fun, you two. I'm off to another thrilling shift at the Bay Breeze." Jo grabbed her purse and strutted down the aisle like it was a catwalk in Milan. When she passed Ethan, she trailed her fingers across his chest. "See you later, foxy."

"Good night, Jo," he called after her, rolling his eyes.

Hannah made her way down the aisle towards him. Her strut was less exaggerated than Jo's, perhaps a bit less confident, but her soft, knowing smile and the twinkle in her eyes were stunning and all her. He dragged his hand over his jaw as he watched her approach, his eyes dancing over the bounce of her cleavage in the low-cut sundress, the swing of her hips, the swish of the skirt around her legs, and then back to her smile. Fuck, her smile did something to him he couldn't explain.

"Thank you for this," she said when she was at last standing in front of him. She wound her arms around his neck and his hands landed on her hips, smoothing over the ruching at the dip of her waist. "I never would have thought of it, but it was exactly what I needed."

"I'm glad."

"You know what else I need?" she asked, stepping closer.

He skated his nose along the length of hers. "What's that, city girl?"

Her lips were soft when she kissed him. He wanted her closer, to slide his hand beneath her skirt and feel if she was ready for him, to kiss her everywhere—

A loud cough behind them broke through his thoughts and they pulled apart, lazily, reluctantly, as Caleb made his way up the aisle, his hands tucked in his pants pockets and his eyes downcast. "Leave room for the Holy Spirit," he muttered as he approached.

Hannah snorted a laugh and buried her head against Ethan's chest, hiding her face in his shirt. He grinned and stroked a hand over her hair as he addressed Caleb. "Thanks for letting us use the space. We appreciate it."

"Any time. You want to stay and join us for Bible study?" he asked with a knowing smirk.

"I think we'll pass," Ethan said. Before Caleb had come back to Aster Bay to take over at St. Anthony's, Ethan hadn't even set foot in a church since he was a kid, and any appearance he put in recently was more about moral support for his friend than any religious inclinations.

Caleb gave a knowing hum. "You better go while you still can then. If you're around when my mom gets here—"

"Right. We're going." Ethan's hand fell to Hannah's lower back and he guided her towards the back of the church.

"Thanks again!" Hannah called over her shoulder, blushing.

Ethan drove them home, all the while forcing himself to keep both hands on the steering wheel so he wouldn't be tempted to touch her. If he touched her while he was driving, he was likely to lose control—of himself and the vehicle. Best to wait until he'd shown her his plan for the rest of the evening.

He hoped she'd like it. That it would help her see Aster Bay the way he saw it.

By the time he shut off his truck in his driveway, it was dark, the sky a dusky blue, like velvet, patterns traced into its pile by lingering wisps of clouds moving across the star-speckled sky. Ethan climbed out of the truck and rounded the vehicle to open Hannah's door. He loved this time of year, when the air felt clean and crisp, a hint of the ocean's salt hanging in the spring mist.

It was blessedly quiet at night on the vineyard, the occasional whoosh of a car going by on the road, an owl somewhere in the trees that separated his property from Cheryl and Ricky's farm. In a few months, the cicadas would be out in full force, their din a constant white noise.

Of course, by then Hannah would be back in New York. The thought scratched beneath his skin.

He held out his hand to her. "Walk with me."

She took his hand with a coy smile and let him lead her down the path along the side of his house towards the vineyard fields that abutted his property. Her heels sank in the soft earth as he led her through an opening in the trees and onto the vineyard proper, but she didn't complain. Like she'd been walking these fields all her life. Like it was her fancy shoes that didn't belong, not her.

"Where are we going?" she asked.

"You'll see."

The first sprigs of green were beginning to burst on the vines they wandered between, but it was too dark to point out the first signs of a new season of grapes. He'd bring her back in daylight, in every season, show her the march of time measured in leaves and flowering buds and eventually heavy bunches of grapes his family had been turning into wine for decades. It might not be a Broadway stage, but it was a good life. He knew

Aster Bay didn't have the best Thai food or the bustle of the City, but it had entire fields of plants that his family had tended for generations, just waiting to bring forth another harvest. It had the Museum of Everything and the best damn caldo verde this side of the Atlantic.

And him. It had him.

They crested the small hill at the edge of the field and Hannah gasped as their destination came into view.

He'd spent the better part of the afternoon stringing fairy lights in the trees that overlooked the bay below. He'd hauled a low fire pit from the storage shed, setting it in the clearing along with two of his mother's Adirondack chairs. The heavy canvas bag he'd left behind held blankets of varying weights, a Nuthatch Vineyards sweatshirt, wine glasses, a bottle of red Tessa swore would go well with s'mores.

"You did all this?" She pressed her hands to her cheeks, her eyes darting from the chairs to the twinkle lights to the cooler beside the fire pit.

"My lady," he said with a wink, a bit of his Slade Hardcastle accent slipping into his voice as he held out his hand and ushered her towards the Adirondack chairs.

Her eyes lit up and she took the seat he indicated, accepting the soft, knit blanket Mrs. Greene and the knitting circle at the senior center had made after his father's first heart attack. She wrapped herself in the blue and white stripes and watched, delighted, as he opened the cooler, removing bowls and silverware and setting them on the wide edge of the fire pit.

"Jamie's famous vichyssoise," he said, holding up the plastic prep container he'd retrieved from Jamie earlier in the day. "There's bread, sourdough, I think, and some kind of butter with herbs in it. And a lobster corn salad thing. I think he said to spoon it on top of the soup? Or maybe on top of the bread."

Ethan paused, looking between the containers Jamie had

carefully packed into the cooler for him. Each one had its own set of instructions and he was struggling to remember them all. He swore under his breath as he held up another container, this one with some kind of green herbaceous sauce that he had no idea what to do with.

"You got enough food to feed a small army," she said.

"And s'mores with Tessa's homemade marshmallows." He gestured to another bag resting beside the fire pit, long metal poles sticking out of the top for roasting the marshmallows. "But the graham crackers are store bought because Tessa says making graham crackers from scratch is a waste." He'd worry about figuring out how to get the soft, homemade marshmallows to stay on the stick after he figured out what the hell to do with the green sauce thing and the small container of chopped herbs. "How many herbs does one dish need?" he mumbled to himself as he pried off the container of the sauce. It immediately slipped, spilling half its contents on the grass. "Fuck!"

Hannah leapt out of her seat. "It's fine."

"It has to be perfect," he said, shaking drops off green sauce off his coated fingers and setting the open container down on top of the cooler.

"Ethan, it already *is* perfect."

"It's not. I know it's not New York, but I thought if you could see…" He ran his clean hand roughly through his hair and sighed. "We have great food here, too, Hannah. Our museums don't have any Van Gogh's, but we have museums, and bookstores, and I know it's not the same, but I thought if I could give you this perfect night…"

She stepped in closer to him, wrapping her arms around his waist. He held the oil covered hand away from her. "You don't have to convince me to love Aster Bay."

He deflated, his eyes scanning the mess he'd made, the scattered plastic containers, the half-plated meal. "I wanted our first real date to be perfect."

Her warm mouth slid down over his finger before he knew she was moving. He sucked in a breath as her tongue roved over the digit, licking the sauce from his finger. She slid off his finger with a pop and looked up at him with a mischievous gleam in her eye. "Our first date, huh?" She held his gaze as she took the next finger in her mouth, sucking it clean.

A low rumble gathered in his chest and he cupped her cheek with his other hand as she drew the last finger between her lips. Each movement of her tongue went straight to his cock, and damned if she didn't know it.

"Yeah, city girl," he said, his voice gravelly. "Haven't had a girlfriend since I was a teenager. Thought maybe you'd like to help me change that."

Her eyes darkened. "Ethan Hart, are you asking me to be your girlfriend?"

He pulled her closer, his now-clean hand winding around her lower back and pressing her hips against his. "Are you saying yes?"

She smiled, the kind of bright joy on her face that made him feel like his skin was buzzing. Her lips skated over his jaw, the tip of his nose, his Adam's apple, until her mouth settled at the hollow of his throat. "I'm saying yes."

He gathered her against him, tumbling them to the ground in his rush to kiss her, to feel her. Her laughter turned to moans as he pulled down the front of her sundress and took her nipple between his teeth, worrying the peaked bud with teeth and tongue and lips as his hands roamed the dip of her waist, the plush curve of her hips, seeking the hem of the dress that had taunted him all afternoon. He rucked the dress up to her hips, hands skating over soft skin until his thumb traced her seam through the simple cotton panties she always wore.

"Yes?" he asked, looking up.

She threaded her fingers through his hair and tugged. "Yes."

He moved to the other nipple as he slid his hand down the front of her panties, fingers sliding through soft curls to the place where she was already slick and hot. He teased at her entrance, played with the little button of her clit until she whimpered, her hips rising to meet each stroke of his fingers. She came before he even put a finger inside her and he swallowed her soft cries as he continued to work her through the waves of her climax.

"Can I fuck you out there, sweetheart?"

"Yes."

The sweetest word he'd ever known, made all the sweeter coming from her.

He kneeled between her legs and pulled her panties down, tucking them into the back pocket of his jeans. Hannah sat up, her beautiful breasts with their pink, furled tips distracting him, but only momentarily. How could he be distracted when her soft, clever fingers were unbuckling his belt, undoing the button beneath, drawing down the zipper? How could he think of anything but her hands when they were slipping inside his jeans, those fingers wrapping around his shaft and drawing him out into the cool night air? She stroked him slowly, her eyes locked on his, as he pushed his jeans down over his hips, giving her better access to his body.

Her mouth was heaven, hot and wet when she slid over his erection like a dream come true. He moved the hair from her face so he could watch, traced his thumb over the hollow of her cheek as she took him deeper.

"You're so goddamn pretty with my cock in your mouth," he groaned. "Love being inside you, Han."

Not that she didn't already know.

She took him further back, her throat constricting, and he pulled out with a curse.

"You're going to make me come, sweetheart."

"I thought that was the idea," she said, her tongue darting out to swipe at her lower lip.

He took her chin between his thumb and index finger and kissed her roughly as he kicked his jeans off and knelt in the grass beside her. "I want to be inside your sweet cunt when I come," he said, his other hand moving between her legs again, teasing her. She was even wetter than before, her inner thighs slick with her need. "Want this pretty pussy to take all of me, city girl. Do you want that?"

"Yes."

He tumbled her into the grass, sliding into her heat in one smooth stroke until he was fully seated. She gasped at the intrusion, her nails scrabbling at his thighs even as she tilted her hips towards him, silently asking for more. He'd give her more. He'd give her everything, all he had to give, all she was willing to take.

"You were amazing today," he said as he moved in long, slow strokes.

"When?"

"When you were practicing." He cursed and hiked her knee up over his hip, slipping in deeper. "The way you moved."

"Jo's modeling tricks," she panted.

"No. It was all you." He let his thumb wander to the place between them, pressing gently against her clit. It pulsed beneath the pad of his finger as he continued to fuck her. "You were so confident. So…you." He groaned at the memory paired with the flutter of her internal muscles. "I wanted to take you right there. Standing in a fucking house of God and all I could think about was pumping you full of my cum."

"Yes," she gasped, arching her back as her thighs began to shake, the telltale signs of her orgasm rising to the surface.

"You like that idea," he marveled, his own release gathering at the base of his spine.

"Yes."

He'd never tire of hearing her say it, of the little cry at the start of the word, the burst of air at the end.

"Come for me, city girl. Come for me now."

She threw her head back and gasped his name as she came, her body clamping down on him in rhythmic pulls that pushed him over the edge after her. His climax raced down his spine, electricity searing through his thighs and groin as he came in long, endless spurts that stole his breath, his vision going white at the edges with the pleasure of it.

As soon as he was done, he fell on his forearms between her spread thighs and parting her with his thumbs to see his own release pooled at her opening. Some primal, feral thing hummed through his blood at the sight, the overwhelming need to claim her spurring him on. Using two fingers, he pushed the errant drops back inside her, latching his lips to her clit. His own taste mixed with hers as he urged her towards another orgasm, this one fast and hard. She came with a cry, her hands fisted in his hair, and he knew he'd never tire of this, of her.

Crawling back up her body, he gathered her against him, her limbs loose, her lips turned up in a lazy kind of smile. The knit blanket from the Adirondack chair was the perfect barrier from the growing chill in the air and he held her against him as he murmured in her ear how beautiful she was, how perfect she was for him. She wiggled her ass against his groin and parted her knees to make room for him to slide his half-hard erection inside her again, to rest in her heat as they had done so many times since she'd come to Aster Bay.

"I think I'm going to like being your girlfriend," she said sleepily. He smiled into her hair, holding her impossibly closer. "Can we stay out here a little while longer? I want to stay like this, with you, and watch the stars."

He kissed her shoulder. "Yeah, sweetheart. We can stay like this as long as you want."

Chapter Twenty-One

Gavin: Ethan, why are you dodging your mom's phone calls?

Ethan: What are you talking about?

Gavin: My mom said your mom said you haven't called her back in over a week.

Jamie: This wouldn't have anything to do with not wanting to tell her about a certain someone staying in your guest room, would it?

Baz: Like she's really staying in his guest room.

Ethan: I've been busy.

Gavin: Too busy to call your own mother?

Jamie: You better call her soon. Tessa's been stalling when she talks to her but at some point she's going to forget and say something about Hannah.

Ethan: I'll call her while Hannah's getting ready for the premiere tomorrow.

Gavin: Speaking of the premiere, what are you wearing?

Ethan: A suit.

Gavin: What kind of suit?

Ethan: There are different kinds of suits?

Baz: Amateur.

Ethan: A nice suit.
Ethan: My usual suit.
Ethan: Was I supposed to get a special kind of suit for this?

Jamie: Do you need me to ask Tessa to come help you pick out a suit?

Gavin: Maybe you could borrow one from Baz.

Ethan: No one's going to be looking at me. They're all going to be looking at Hannah.

Gavin: You are her date to her first public appearance since her very public break up from a bona fide celebrity. Everyone's going to be looking at you.

Jamie: Tessa says she's happy to come take a look at your suit and let you know if it will work.

Ethan: I don't need my daughter to dress me. My suit is fine.

Baz: Don't underestimate the importance of a good suit.

Gavin: Is suit starting to look like a fake word to anyone else?
Gavin: Suit
Gavin: SUIT
Gavin: Suit suit suit

Ethan: Would you knock it off?

Jamie: Tessa says your pocket square should match Hannah's dress.

Ethan: What pocket square? Who the fuck wears a pocket square?

Baz: Everyone who wears a decent suit.

"What about these?" Ethan appeared in the doorway to the living room holding up two ties: one a pale blue with some kind of swirling pattern in a darker shade, and the other solid black.

Hannah looked up from her book and considered the ties. "The black one."

He nodded and disappeared back into his bedroom where he'd been busy packing for the better part of the afternoon. They should have left for New York an hour ago at least, but neither of them seemed in a particular rush to leave Aster Bay. She turned her attention back to the book, a 1980s bodice ripper Ethan swore he only had as "research," and tried not to think about the uneasy prickle at the back of her neck at the idea of returning to the City.

Her phone buzzed on the couch beside her. Hannah stuck a finger in her book to keep her place and answered. "Hi, Mom."

"Oh, honey, I'm so glad I caught you," her mother said through the phone. "I know how busy you'll be tomorrow and I wanted to wish you luck on your big premiere."

"From me too!" her father shouted in the background.

"From both of us," her mother amended. "We're just so darn proud of you, Hannah."

"Thanks, Mom. I wish you guys could be there."

"We'll be there in spirit. And we already bought tickets to see it at the theater here for Saturday night."

"Tell her we're taking Bob Carmichael and his wife," her father shouted.

"She doesn't care about Bob Carmichael," her mother tutted to her father, before saying to Hannah, "You don't care about Bob Carmichael. But your father is very excited to show you off. And don't forget to send me pictures tomorrow. I want at least one good photo of you and your young man from the evening."

"There will be plenty of photos in the press, I'm sure," Hannah said.

"I don't want a photo everyone else gets to see. I want the photo you want to send your mother. The photo I would take if I was there to see you off." Hannah could hear the tears gathering in her mother's voice. "Just like when you went to prom."

Hannah groaned. "This is nothing like prom."

"Maybe I should bring both ties in case something happens," Ethan said, reappearing in the living room doorway with the same two ties still in his hands.

"Is that him?" her mother asked into the phone. "Let me say hello!"

"Mom, I don't think—"

"Hannah Matthews, you put that young man on the phone right now."

Hannah sighed and covered the microphone on her phone with her palm. "My mom wants to say hi to you." She grimaced. "You don't have to."

Ethan dropped the ties on the arm of the couch and held out his hand. "Give me the phone."

"I can tell her no."

He arched an eyebrow. "Hand it over, city girl."

Hannah lifted the phone to her ear again. "Be nice," she said, before handing it over to Ethan, just as her mother said, "I'm always nice."

"Hi, Mrs. Matthews. This is Ethan Hart." He held the phone to his ear, his other hand resting on his hip and his eyes glued to Hannah's, a playfulness dancing across his face as he listened to her mother on the other end. "Mmhmm, I agree."

"What's she saying?"

Ethan pressed his lips together like he was holding back a smile. Ethan chuckled. "You have a very nice voice yourself."

If she only knew how nice of a voice he has...

Another pause.

"I'll be forty-five this Saturday, ma'am."

Oh, not the 'ma'am.' Her mother would eat that shit up with a spoon.

He laughed again, his eyes sparkling as they skated over her, like he was cataloging the exact way she looked sitting on his couch. "It's been my pleasure."

Hannah's face was hot. Listening to him talk to her mother should *not* be a turn on.

"I promise I'll take good care of her, Mrs. Matthews."

Hannah groaned and flopped back on the couch, draping an arm over her eyes. This couldn't be happening. Her mother was not giving Ethan a "be good to her" speech. Hannah was thirty-two years old, for God's sake. And yet, there was something about the gravel in his voice that made his promise feel like it was meant just for her.

"I'd like that," he said, his lips quirking up in a grin as he watched Hannah, like he knew exactly how goddamn sexy he was. "Take care now."

He hung up the phone and tossed it on the couch beside her as he crawled over her, the weight of him pressing her down into the soft cushions.

"You talked to my mom," she whispered, scratching her fingers through his beard.

"She seems nice," he said, pressing a soft kiss to her lips.

"And she clearly liked you."

"I'm nice too," he said, nuzzling into her hair. "I can be very nice."

She lifted his face to hers and kissed him, dissolving under the solid weight of him, the pressure of his thighs bracketing her hips, the scratch of his beard. She dug her hands into his hair and tugged the way she knew he liked, a giddy giggle bubbling up behind her lips when he groaned in response and moved a thigh between her legs, kissing her deeper. He dragged his teeth over her lower lip and pulled away, shooting her a sheepish grin.

"We should get on the road before it's dark."

"Just five more minutes," she said, sliding her hands down his back.

"Five minutes isn't enough." He captured her hands and pressed kisses to each palm as he sat up, pulling her with him. She missed his weight instantly. "And we'll have all night in that fancy hotel."

Suddenly, the idea of being in a hotel with Ethan felt wrong, like taking a step backwards. She didn't want more time with hotel-Ethan; she wanted more time with Aster Bay-Ethan.

"What if I don't want to spend the night in a fancy hotel? What if I want another night here?"

He scratched his hand over the back of his neck, his eyes narrowing. "Your premiere is tomorrow."

"I know," she said, suddenly feeling like a petulant child. "I guess I'm not ready to say goodbye to this place."

"Then don't."

"What?"

He took her hand between both of his, his thumbs skating over her wrist as he spoke. His eyes were soft and earnest in a way that tugged at her heart. "Come back with me after the premiere. You can film your audition tapes from here as easily as you can from New York."

It wasn't entirely true. In New York she had a favorite practice studio and she knew the exact right place to stand in her apartment to get the best lighting. But in Aster Bay she had a gorgeous man who loved nothing more than driving her crazy with his tongue between her legs, so it seemed like a fair trade off.

"I guess I don't have anything I *need* to be in the City for right away," she hedged. "And who knows how aggressive the press will be after the premiere."

"Give them some more time to move on and stay here for a little longer."

Hannah searched his eyes, the open, hopeful gleam making her wish she could stay forever. But that would be crazy. She had a career in New York, friends, a whole life. This time in Aster Bay was a beautiful intermission but, at some point, she'd have to return to her real life.

"Doesn't that just prolong the inevitable?" she asked.

His lips pressed into a flat line, some of the hope fading in his eyes. "I'll take every day I can get, Han."

Her chest squeezed and for a moment she let herself imagine what it would be like if they had endless days. To wake each morning and fall asleep each night in his arms knowing there was no clock ticking down the hours until they'd have to admit their lives were not compatible. She didn't need to ask him to know he'd never leave Aster Bay—his family was here—and since Rhode Island wasn't exactly a commutable distance to Broadway, she would eventually have no choice but to leave.

But that was future-Hannah's problem.

"Okay. I'll come back with you, as long as you promise to tell me the second you get sick of me and want me out of your hair."

A smile split across his face and he kissed her, hard and fast. "Won't be a problem, sweetheart, because I won't be getting sick of you."

Ethan climbed off the couch and disappeared around the corner into his bedroom again. Hannah flopped back and focused on the irregular pattern in the popcorn ceiling. "We should probably talk about how we're going to introduce you," she called.

"To who?" he shouted back from the other room.

"To the press."

His head popped back into the living room. "Why would I need to be introduced?"

"When we walk the carpet, they're going to ask who you are. Your name. Who we are to each other."

"Oh." He scrubbed a hand through his hair.

"Do you want to go by Ethan, or by Slade?"

His brows knitted together. "Why would I want to go by Slade?"

"I don't know. Some people like to use a stage name with the press. I wasn't sure if you wanted—"

"But these people will be seeing my face. People I know might see these pictures. People who don't know about Slade."

"Ethan," she said gently, "even if we give the press your real name, they might still figure out about Slade."

He reeled back as though she'd punched him. "How? How would they do that unless someone told them?"

"I don't know. I don't know how much they're going to care or how hard they're going to dig, but some of these reporters..." She thought about that photo through her living room window, the one taken from her fire escape, and a shiver flitted over her skin. "They can be ruthless when they want to be. If there's any chance they could find a trail that connects you to Slade, you might want to tell your friends and family anyway, so they hear it from you first."

"That is not an option," he said, slashing his hand through the air like he could wipe away the suggestion, his vehemence catching her off guard. "And there's nothing connecting us. The only other people who know I'm Slade Hardcastle are Baz and the author. And the grandma gang."

"You're sure?"

He nodded tightly. "No one else knows. No one else needs to know."

"Okay. Then we'll introduce you by your real name. I'm sure it will be fine." She should leave well enough alone, but she couldn't help herself. "Can I ask you something? Why not just tell your friends? Wouldn't that be easier than trying to keep it a secret?"

An emotion flickered across his face before he hardened his features again, a glimpse at something he kept hidden away from her, a part of him she'd never been invited to access before.

"I've put my family through enough," he said at last.

"What does that mean?"

He sighed and sank into the armchair opposite her. She

wished he'd sat beside her, that she could touch him, reassure him while he spoke.

"You don't know what it's like in a small town. When I got Steph pregnant, it was all anyone could talk about. My choices defined my entire family for over a decade. There are still people in this town who judge me and my daughter because of a choice I made when I was sixteen."

"And you think if people in town knew about Slade, they'd judge you for that too."

"Not just me, but Tessa. My parents. My granddaughter. Those assholes who made Steph feel so unwelcome she had to leave town—what would they do to my business? My family's legacy?" Pain slashed across his face. "All my parents worked for, my grandparents, building the vineyard. I will not bring another scandal to their doorstep."

Hannah moved across the room, kneeling at his feet and taking his hands in hers. "That was decades ago. Don't you think attitudes have evolved even a little since then?"

"I won't put my daughter through that again. What kind of father would I be? What kind of grandfather?"

"Tessa doesn't strike me as the kind of person that's particularly afraid of some narrow-minded gossip. She did marry your best friend, after all. That must have sparked some rumors around town."

"It's different."

"How?"

"It just is." He stroked a hand through her hair, pushing the loose strands behind her ear, but there was a sadness in his voice that made her want to wrap him up in her arms and never let go.

"For what it's worth, I think your friends and family would want to support you. To celebrate with you. I think they'd want to know this part of you, since it's obviously important enough to you to pursue, despite the risk of being found out."

"There's no risk. I love them too much to hurt them."

"What makes you think they love you any less?"

He still cradled her cheek in his hand, but his eyes were far off, lost in thought. Hannah turned her face into his palm, pressing a kiss to the center of his hand. "I'm going to go unpack a few things, now that I'll be coming back. Then we can get on the road."

She got to her feet and was already halfway down the hall when he called after her, "Don't leave behind the red lace thing you wore the other night."

She chuckled. "Don't worry. I have plenty of lace things packed."

"But not the red one?" he hollered.

She smiled to herself. "Many red ones."

From *The Lady's Knights* by AK Wild,
narrated by Slade Hardcastle

Sir Llewellyn held his post by the dais and watched as Lady Windtorn and Lord Havenbrook twirled about the ballroom floor. Each smile the woman he loved gave to her husband, each laugh that floated on the air towards him, was a lance through his heart. Yet he couldn't look away.

It was his duty, after all, to be vigilant and never let them leave his sight.

Because he was so watchful he knew her smiles were strained, her laughter brittle. He knew she performed for the assembled lords, the ones who had come to broker a peace that had been bought with her sham of a marriage. All they had worked for, the sacrifice of her freedom, of their love, would be for naught if she was not convincing.

And, oh, how convincing she was.

Convincing enough that, had he not woken her with his mouth between her legs that very morning, he would have believed her. But Sir Llewellyn knew the woman behind the title, the one so few had dared to find, and this was not her.

"Sir Llewellyn." He stood straighter as Lord Havenbrook and Lady Windtorn approached. "Dance with my wife."

His jaw tightened, spine stiffened, as his gaze passed between the pair. "My lord?"

Her husband placed Lady Windtorn's hand in Sir Llewellyn's, clasping them together and spoke louder for the benefit of their visitors' curiosity. "I am weary, yet my wife does not tire." He laughed, but his eyes held the world-weariness of a man also playing a role. "Be my feet and give her a turn around the room."

It was a kindness, one that sent shame simmering through Sir Llewellyn's blood. That this man, the lord he had pledged his loyalty to, should offer him this moment to which he had no right, should allow them to pretend for a moment they could be the kind of lovers who danced in a crowded room...

The two men locked eyes, an understanding passing between them, and, with a creaky voice, Sir Llewellyn replied, "Yes, my lord."

He led her back onto the dance floor beneath the curious looks of the assembled guests. At the center of the floor, he bowed as she dipped into a curtsy, then he swept her into his arms and they danced. This time, when she smiled, it was with an unrestrained joy that pulled his own answering smile to the surface, and when she laughed, the sound washed over him like a balm. Her skirts swirled around their legs as he spun her across the floor, ever aware of the eyes turned in their direction.

"They all stare," she said, trembling.

He held her gaze with his own. "It is hard to look away from perfection."

Her smile faltered. "I fear this is a miscalculation. They will wonder who you are that you look at me this way."

"How do I look at you, my lady?"

"As though you..." Her voice faded away, the words unsaid hanging in the space carefully kept between them.

"As though I love you?" She drew in a breath, her feet losing their rhythm for a moment, but he swept her along. He would not let her fall. "How could anyone look upon you tonight and *not love you?" His chest ached to hold her closer, to press his lips to her temple and breathe in the rosewater scent of her hair, but he maintained their posture. "It is long past time for all to acknowledge the truth. You, my lady, are infinitely lovable."*

Chapter Twenty-Two

Hannah was trying to kill him.

That was the only explanation Ethan could find for the way his heart stopped beating when she stepped out of the hotel bathroom wearing that dress.

The deep purple color made her blue eyes seem almost indigo. A plunging neckline revealed a tantalizing strip of creamy skin rivaled only by the equally tempting glimpse of her bare thigh through the slit running up one side of the dress. It was cinched tightly at her waist, sheer fabric flowing out from her hips, and a line of laces ran up the back of the bodice. It made him think of a scene in one of AK Wild's books where the heroine was laced too tightly in a corset and the hero used his knife to cut her free.

"Do you like it?" she asked, smoothing her hands over her hips self-consciously.

He was on her in two strides, gathering her in his arms and kissing her as though they had all the time in the world. Her startled laugh turned to a deep sigh as she draped her arms around his neck and kissed him back, the sensation of it making him feel like he was floating. When they finally pulled apart, she pressed a hand to her lips. "It's a good thing I didn't put on my lipstick yet."

"I like smearing your lipstick." He kissed her again, softly. "You look stunning."

She smoothed the lapels of his suit jacket. "You don't look half bad yourself."

He watched as she flitted about the room in her last minute preparations—applying her lipstick and adding the tube to the small clutch she would carry with her to the premiere, fluffing her hair in the mirror, checking her cell phone for the arrival notification from the car they'd ordered—and with each smile she shot his way, each offhand remark about something she wanted to remember to tell Tessa or a movie she wanted to show him when they went back to Aster Bay, his chest expanded. Like a balloon overfilled, any more affection for her and he knew his heart would burst.

Not just affection.

No, affection was too mild of a word. But it was too soon for the alternative. Wasn't it?

"Ethan." He blinked back to the present moment at the sound of his name on her lips. "Are you ready?"

"I am."

Hannah filled the brief minutes of the car ride to the theater with chatter about the people he'd meet at the premiere, which reporters were friendly and which ones were always hunting for a scandal, and he did his best to listen. But all he could think about was the overfull balloon feeling, the pressure against his sternum as the words he was holding back pressed forward, threatening to crack apart his ribs.

Tomorrow. You'll tell her tomorrow.

This was her night, after all. She deserved to revel in her achievement, to be showered with the adoration she'd worked so hard for.

The car slowed and came to a stop and, even through the

tinted windows, the flash of cameras pulled Ethan from his thoughts. Hannah took his hand in hers. "Stay close, okay?"

"Always."

Then the door was open, and a harried-looking man stuck his head inside. "You two ready?"

"Ethan, this is Micah, my manager," Hannah said. "Micah, this is—"

"Ethan, you'll go first. Then help Hannah out and she'll take the lead." He turned back to Hannah. "Jackson is two cars behind you. We'll do a reunion photo on the carpet, then head inside. Watch out for Johnny Blue on the left. He's hunting for a scandal."

Hannah rolled her eyes. "What else is new?"

"You remember what to say?"

"I'm so excited for everyone to finally see our little show on the big screen," she recited.

Micah nodded, then stood back. "It's go time."

Ethan squeezed Hannah's hand one more time, before exiting the car. He was immediately blinded by the flashes. It was disorienting, like stepping outside on a sunny day after having your eyes dilated, and combined with the noise of the city streets and the shouts of the assembled press, he wanted to retreat back into the car as quickly as he'd exited. But he was there to support Hannah, and he'd be damned if he let her down.

He turned his back on the press and focused on Hannah. She took the hand he offered her and climbed out of the car. As he helped her to her feet, the noise around them swelled, people shouting her name from every direction. He felt dizzy. Trapped. His heart raced as the faces in front of him blurred together and his first few steps were stilted, unnatural.

"Stay close," she whispered through a smile.

He nodded, swallowing hard. So long as he remained focused on her, he hoped the rest of it would fade away. It was only a few yards to the door. He could make it a few yards.

He dropped his hand to the small of her back and let her lead the way, pausing when she paused, his eyes focused solely on her. She was a revelation, sparkling and effervescent as she turned for the cameras, charming and so at ease while inside he was barely holding it together.

"Hannah Banana!"

Ethan barely saw the man moving before he had barreled into Hannah, wrapping her up in a hug that lifted her off her feet.

"Jackson! Put me down!" she laughed.

He set her down, beaming, and held out a hand to Ethan. "Nice to meet you."

Flashes burst in a flurry around them as Ethan accepted the handshake, wincing with each new burst of light aimed in their direction. Hannah wrapped her hands around Ethan's arm, grounding him. "Jackson Hayes, this is Ethan Hart. Ethan, this is Jackson."

Ethan tried to remember that Jackson wasn't actually Hannah's ex, just her friend, but when Jackson turned his stupid-wide, gleaming white grin in her direction, it was hard for Ethan not to imagine punching him in his chiseled jaw.

"Babe!" Jackson called, waving to a statuesque blonde woman who was still posing by the car. "Come meet Hannah!"

The woman took her time making her way to them, or maybe the floor length red dress she wore was too fitted through her legs for her to take larger steps. Either way, the cameras ate up every moment of her walk down the carpet. Hannah's smile turned wooden as she watched the willowy blonde approach.

Jackson slung an arm over the woman's shoulder. "Yvette, meet Hannah Banana. Oh, and her date, Ethan. This is Yvette."

Yvette smiled widely, the bright flash of it a perfect match for Jackson's, and Ethan wondered what kind of heavy duty chemical whiteners were in Hollywood toothpaste.

"It's so nice to meet you, Hannah. Jax has told me so much about you, I feel like I know you," Yvette gushed, clasping Hannah's free hand in hers.

"That's so kind. You were wonderful in the Twiggy biopic," Hannah said.

Yvette touched her long blonde hair with a self-deprecating chuckle. "You're too sweet."

Jackson slid his free arm around Hannah's back, placing himself between the two women, and tilted his jaw towards a bank of photographers calling for a picture. Ethan stood firm on her other side, blinking against the bright lights. "You look good, Banana." Something in Jackson's tone shifted when he asked, "Are you? Good?"

"Really good. I promise," she said.

Jackson exhaled happily, like he was relieved. "Good. Good." He guided them down the carpet to the next cluster of photographers who snapped away.

"Jackson! Over here!" someone shouted. "How about one of you and Hannah alone?"

Jackson turned his megawatt grin towards Hannah. "What do you say?"

Ethan waited for the moment he'd be cast aside. This wasn't his world. He didn't belong on a red carpet.

Hannah's hold on him tightened and she called back to the crowd, grinning, "I made him promise he wouldn't leave my side tonight, so you'll have to crop him out if you don't want him in your shot."

Ethan felt the moment the cameras' attention swung his way, intrigue rolling through the crowd as they tried to puzzle out who he was that she would decline their request.

But he didn't care about the cameras. He was only paying attention to Hannah, to the bright glow of joy on her face and the warmth in her eyes and the heat of her hand wrapped around his arm.

He dipped his head and pressed a kiss to her bare shoulder before he could think better of it, so lost in the balloon feeling he hardly noticed the frenzy the small gesture set off around them.

"Hannah! Has Jackson apologized for Bora Bora?" another voice called from the crowd.

Ethan felt Hannah stiffen at his side. "There was nothing to apologize for," she replied through a wooden smile. He hated that smile and the way it replaced the genuine happiness he'd seen on her face mere moments before.

"We're all friends here," Jackson added.

"Hannah, what do you have to say about the reports you've been hiding out at an eating disorder clinic in the Berkshires?"

The color drained from Hannah's face. "I—I—"

Ethan took a step towards the jackass with the snide smile who'd asked the question, but Hannah's hold on him was firm. *Stay close.*

"You're out of line, Johnny," Jackson said, pinning the reporter with a glare that would have sent lesser men running. Maybe Jackson Hayes wasn't so bad after all.

"But you *were* at an eating disorder clinic in the Berkshires, no?" the jerk—Johnny, apparently—insisted.

"No," Ethan said, whipping his head in the reporter's direction. He wanted to memorize his face so the next time he saw the asshole, he could pummel him for embarrassing Hannah on her big night. "She was with me."

"That's enough, folks. We'll see you inside," Micah said, appearing from nowhere. He ushered Ethan and Hannah past the remaining reporters into the lobby of the theater. "Stay here," he said. "Don't move until the screening is about to start."

"Where's Lana?" Jackson shouted across the lobby. "I want Johnny Blue's credentials revoked. Someone find me Lana!"

"Don't," Hannah said. "It'll only provoke him."

"He can't just say shit like that," Ethan said. "It's none of his goddamn business."

"I'm gonna go find Lana," Jackson said, excusing himself and leading Yvette away, leaving Ethan and Hannah alone at the edge of the lobby.

"Baz has a great lawyer," Ethan continued, adrenaline making him feel like his skin was on fire. "We'll sue the shit out of Johnny Fuckface. He doesn't get to put your personal business out there."

"That's exactly what he does."

Micah appeared at their side. "What do you want to do?"

"What are my options?" she asked.

"We can ignore it, though I suspect he's already got some kind of source confirming your treatment or he wouldn't have brought it up. His information is too specific."

"So ignoring it's out. What else?" she asked.

"We can ask for privacy and for the press to respect your right to keep your medical information out of the public eye."

Hannah scoffed. "Like that's ever worked."

Micah nodded gravely. "We make a statement. Confirm Johnny's speculation on your own terms."

"It's nobody's goddamn business," Ethan snapped. His muscles screamed for him to get them out of there, to take her away from this insanity where any jackass on the street could shout out the most private details of their lives for all the world to hear.

"You're right, but maybe it's time I stopped trying to hide this part of myself. Maybe if more people talked about it, it would have been easier for me to ask for help sooner." She turned back to Micah. "But I'm not giving the story to Johnny Blue. Get me anybody else."

Micah nodded. "On it," he said, before disappearing back into the crowd.

"Are you sure?" Ethan asked, drawing her into his arms, focusing on the feel of her, solid and strong, beneath his hands as some of the tension left him.

"No," she said with a laugh, reaching up to smooth her palm over his beard. "But I'm done being afraid."

Hannah's skin buzzed as she looked into Ethan's eyes. There was so much she wanted to tell him, about the way he made her feel like she could be someone new, about how she never wanted to be apart, but this didn't seem like the time.

He had kissed her on the red carpet.

Well, her shoulder. But still. It counted. Lips had made contact with skin.

He'd kissed her in front of all the photographers.

"Ms. Matthews?"

She tore her eyes away from Ethan and refocused on the older woman seated across from her in the tiny theater office. Elizabeth? Ellen? She couldn't remember. Micah had ushered her into the cramped space and made introductions so quickly, she'd hardly had a chance to thank him before he was gone. But not Ethan. He'd insisted on staying—with her permission, of course—and had taken up a position leaning against the corner, though he hardly fit in the space, like some kind of bodyguard. The idea made a giggle bubble up her throat, but she covered it with a cough.

"I'm sorry. You were saying?" she asked.

Elizabeth-Ellen smiled indulgently. "You wanted to make a statement about the accusations made by Johnny Blue on the red carpet," she prompted.

Hannah clasped her hands in her lap, the distant staticky

hum in the back of her mind reciting Ben & Jerry's flavors, but she pushed the sound away. She didn't need a pint of New York Super Fudge Chunk. Her eyes flashed to Ethan again, to the careful way he watched her, the worry line between his brows.

"Yes," Hannah said, turning her attention back to the reporter. She inclined her head towards the small recording device the woman had placed on the desk. "Are you ready?"

"Ready when you are," Elizabeth-Ellen said. "Hannah, did you receive treatment for an eating disorder at an outpatient clinic in Massachusetts?"

"I did." As soon as she said the words, she felt lighter, the noise in her head quieting. "About a year ago, I was diagnosed with an eating disorder. The official diagnosis was 'eating disorder not otherwise specified,' which basically means it didn't fit easily into the current available classifications. My disorder presented as a mix of behaviors usually associated with anorexia, exercise bulimia, and binge eating disorder. While I wasn't diagnosed until a year ago, I have lived with some form of an eating disorder since I was a teenager, but back then, according to the wisdom of women's magazines, I was just 'dieting.'"

Elizabeth-Ellen smiled kindly. "And when did you enter treatment?"

"I began seeing a therapist and a dietitian pretty much right away. I was actively performing in *Bridget Jones' Musical* at the time, so more intensive treatment was difficult to fit in the schedule and I did not want to take time off from the production. But by the time the show closed, it was clear to me I needed more help. Jackson had friends who sought treatment in the Berkshires—"

"Your co-star, Jackson Hayes?" the reporter clarified.

"That's right."

The more she talked, the easier it became. She carefully

sidestepped the details of her relationship with Jackson, playing coy, but made sure he was given credit for coming to her rescue financially. If she was going to tell them about her disorder, at least her friend could get some good publicity out of it, and she could shine a light on the financial inaccessibility of quality mental health care.

By the time she was through, there was a short knock on the door and Micah poked his head inside. "It's time for the showing. Are we all set here?"

"I have what I need," Elizabeth-Ellen said.

"I'd like to say one more thing," Hannah said. "Please tell your readers... I spent years, decades really, being ashamed. At first, I deluded myself into thinking my behavior was normal dieting, but I knew something was wrong for a long time before I got help."

"Why's that?" Elizabeth-Ellen asked.

Hannah glanced at Ethan, the familiar shame slithering beneath her skin. He tipped his head in the barest of nods, his eyes fixed on her with an intensity that felt like the sun— warm and cleansing, because he saw her, *all* of her, and was still standing by her side. She filled herself with the heat of his gaze, allowed it to banish the shame back to the recesses of her mind, and turned back to the reporter patiently waiting for her answer.

"I was embarrassed. I thought people would look at me and decide I wasn't thin enough to have an eating disorder, or there must be something really wrong with me to be incapable of properly feeding myself. There's an immense amount of shame that comes with mental illness. But I was also afraid of giving it up. Who would I be if I wasn't always on a diet? What would happen to me if I let myself eat the way other people did? My eating disorder was the thing that terrorized me, but it also comforted me. It made me feel in control. But I wasn't, and I couldn't see it until I got help. So, I don't know, tell your readers I've been there, and I've seen how incredibly freeing recovery can be. If I can do it, so can they."

Hannah glanced around the room, taking in this surreal moment where she'd spilled her guts to a complete stranger, signed releases so the details of her most private struggles could be published for the whole world to read. She had expected to feel nervous, unsure, but she just felt...right. Ethan winked at her from across the room, his worry face transformed into the picture of beaming pride, and she wanted nothing more than to leave the theatre right then and go home with him.

As they got to their feet, Elizabeth-Ellen held her hand out for Hannah to shake. "Thank you, Ms. Matthews, for your honesty and for trusting me with your story."

"Thank you for listening."

Elizabeth-Ellen gathered her recording device and notebook. "What's next for you, after the premiere? I imagine your phone must be ringing off the hook."

"Hannah is in very high demand," Micah confirmed.

Hannah looked between Micah and Ethan, then settled her gaze on Elizabeth-Ellen. "I don't know what comes next," she said honestly, "but I can't wait to find out."

Chapter Twenty-Three

Ethan woke in the morning to the heat of Hannah's mouth as she took his already hard cock between her lips. He swam up through the remnants of sleep towards the pleasure already gathering at the base of his spine.

"Good morning," she said, when she noticed he was awake, before dragging her tongue from his base to his tip. "Happy birthday."

In all the excitement and emotion of the night before, he'd nearly forgotten it was his birthday, but clearly Hannah had not. She lowered her mouth over him again and he slid a hand into her hair, groaning as he hit the back of her throat.

"Good morning," he said, his voice hoarse with disuse and an impending orgasm.

"How did you sleep?" she asked innocently.

He chuckled at the absurdity of the question, the sound breaking off on a hiss when she flicked her tongue over the ridge at his crown, pressing her tongue into the slit at the top before taking him between her lips again.

"I always sleep well when I fall asleep inside you." He strained to hold back the wave of his climax. "You're gonna make me come," he groaned.

Her eyes sparkled and she moved faster, hollowing her cheeks and urging him closer to the edge.

"You want me to come in your mouth, sweetheart?" he asked, his thumb tracing the corner of her lips where they stretched around him. "What if I want to come in your pussy instead?"

She slowed her movements, considering, and he bit back a grin.

"What if we stay in bed all day and I fill all your pretty holes with my cum? What if the thing I want for my birthday is to taste myself on your lips while you come on my cock, over and over and over?"

She replaced her mouth with her hand, stroking him slow and tight, his tip pressed to her cheek. "What about seeing the City?"

"The City's overrated," he said. "I want to spend the day with you, inside you." He ran his thumb over her bottom lip. "But if you want to spend the day outside this bed, we can do that too. Just know, if you make me come in your mouth right now, we're not leaving this room until you come for me at least three times. We're not going anywhere until I'm dripping down your thighs."

She smiled and her tongue darted out, lapping up the precum beading at his tip. "Is it your birthday or mine?" she teased before taking him all the way to the back of her throat again.

He was a man of his word. No sooner had he thrown his head back, roaring his release as she swallowed him down, than he flipped her over on her back and buried his face between her legs. He licked her to orgasm over and over, until she was shivering and gasping each time his tongue approached her clit, until he was so hard he thought he might pass out from lack of blood flow to his brain. She welcomed him inside her with a soft moan and a smile, her limbs loose with pleasure.

It felt like coming home, like knitting together the pieces

of himself he hadn't realized had been fractured for so many years. He twined his hands with hers, pressing them into the mattress above her head as he worked himself into her, slow and deep, and peppered her face with kisses.

"One more, sweetheart," he whispered against the underside of her jaw.

"I can't," she said.

"One more." He took both of her wrists in one hand and dropped the other between them, pressing gently low on her belly. She shuddered beneath him, her thighs shaking. "See, sweetheart? You have one more in you. Your body knows what to do. You just have to let go for me."

He could see her debating with herself as her orgasm gathered with each stroke, could see the tinge of fear as her body barreled towards yet another climax.

"I've got you, Han. I'll never give you more than you can take," he promised, maintaining his slow rhythm, building the inexorable tide of pleasure within her. His thumb slid lower, skating over her swollen clit and she inhaled sharply, her upper body arching off the bed. "One more, and then I promise, I'll fill you up, sweet girl, just the way you like."

Her hips lifted off the bed, angling into his touch. "I'm so close. Don't stop," she moaned.

"No danger of that," he said. Beneath his thumb, her clit throbbed, so he pressed harder, his palm against her belly.

She shattered beneath him with a strangled sob, her body going taut before shaking wildly as she soaked his hand, his cock. He emptied himself inside her, chanting her name over and over until he fell forward against her, hoarse and exhausted. Her inner muscles clenched around him again and again, each one sending an aftershock through him.

"That was more than three," she whispered when he slid from inside her and gathered her against his chest.

He hummed in agreement.

She snuggled against him, burying her face against his chest as he ran his fingers through her hair. "Give me a minute to get feeling back in my legs and then we can go out."

"There's no rush, sweetheart. We have time."

Within minutes, Hannah's breath slowed to the deep, rhythmic cadence of sleep. Ethan brushed the hair back from her face, and studied the upturned end of her nose, her kiss-swollen lips, the line of her throat, and he knew he would happily spend the rest of his life watching her sleep.

On the bedside table, his phone buzzed to life and he lunged to answer it before it woke Hannah. "Hello?" he whispered without checking the caller ID first.

"Ethan Henry Hart, are you avoiding your own mother on your birthday?"

"Hi, Mom. I was going to call," he whispered.

"When? On your next go round the sun? I labored for sixteen hours for you, Ethan, the least you can do is return your mother's calls."

"I'm sorry."

"Why are you whispering? Oh! Does this have anything to do with the young woman staying with you?"

Ethan glanced over to where Hannah had snuggled into the pillows, the sheet barely covering her round backside. "I take it my daughter ratted me out."

His mother tsked. "No, she kept your secret. Dot Blumenthal, however…"

He should have known the grandma gang couldn't be trusted.

"So, who is she?"

"She's…" He skated his free hand over the dip of Hannah's waist, settling it on the curve of her hip. "…someone very special."

His mother squealed so loudly he had to pull the phone away from her ear. "Well, happy birthday, indeed! What's her name?"

"Hannah," he said, and even he could hear the way his voice softened.

His mother prattled on about answered prayers and birthday miracles as Hannah stirred beside him. Her eyes were hooded and liquid when she opened them, her lips curved into the most kissable smile. He tilted the phone away and mouthed, "Sorry. It's my mom."

"Is she with you now?" his mother demanded, her voice trumpeting through the phone.

Hannah smirked and held her hand out for the phone. He shook his head, but she arched an eyebrow at him and dammit, he couldn't say no to her.

"Hi, Mrs. Hart," she said, flopping onto her back. The movement exposed her breasts and, though Ethan was certain he shouldn't be staring at her breasts while she was on the phone with his mother, he couldn't help it.

As his mother chattered through the phone, Hannah's smile grew. "Don't be too hard on him. It is his birthday, after all," she said. Then a laugh, followed by, "I'm looking forward to meeting you too."

Ethan hardly heard the rest of Hannah's conversation with his mother. He was too busy picturing the rest of their lives—they'd get married at St. Anthony's with Caleb officiating and Julie as their flower girl. They'd go for milkshakes at the Dockside Diner on Saturdays and play trivia on Mondays with their friends. They could get a dog, have a baby, build that picket fence he'd heard so much about. The point was, they'd figure it out together.

When Hannah handed the phone back to him, grinning from ear to ear, his insides had gone all buzzy and tight, like a coiled spring vibrating with the restrained need to make his vision a reality.

"Now we've both met each other's mom," she said.

"Then I guess we're official now," he teased as he crawled on top of her, bracing himself on his hands planted on either side of her head.

"Oh, is that what makes us official? The multiple orgasms weren't enough?" she asked, wiggling beneath him.

"There are never enough orgasms." He kissed her, slow and lingering, his tongue sliding against hers.

When they pulled apart, she ran her nails down his chest, lightly scraping at his skin. "I'm glad I got to talk to her."

"Me too, sweetheart. I wouldn't be surprised if she was booking a plane ticket to come meet you in person as we speak."

"Better watch out. If my mom catches wind of that, she'll get the same idea."

"I want to meet your parents," he said, gathering her close and sweeping her hair behind her ear.

"My mom will probably grill you about whether or not you want kids," she said with a nervous half laugh.

He hummed to himself as he studied her eyes, the hint of anxiety creeping in, dimming her sparkle. "Do you want kids?"

She shrugged one shoulder, focusing her eyes on his chest like she did when she was afraid of letting him see too much. "It's hard to have kids when you work in the theater. Taking time off to be pregnant and have a child is enough to stall most careers, and then even if you do manage to get work again, you miss so much. I don't know how Liv and Daemon do it."

He slipped a knuckle beneath her chin, tilting her face up to him. "But do you want kids?"

She bit her lip, eyes wide and vulnerable. "I do. Do you...do you want more kids?"

He smiled, kissing the tip of her nose as that overfull balloon feeling took over again. "I do. I missed so much when Tessa was young, and for so long I've thought maybe it wasn't in the cards for me. Maybe I had my shot at fatherhood and I blew it."

"You didn't blow it. Tessa adores you."

His heart wrenched at the words, and how much he hoped they were true. "She didn't always."

"I think you'll be an amazing father."

He studied her eyes as the image of Hannah round with his child flashed behind his eyes. Christ, he wanted that. He wanted her and the family they could have together. When she kissed him again, soft and sweet, he filled the kiss with all his hopes, all the deepest desires of his heart. It was too soon for these huge feelings bubbling out of him, too soon to be getting hard at the mere thought of Hannah pregnant with his child—but was it? They'd been dancing around each other for years.

Hannah broke the kiss with a smile that made her glow from within. "I was thinking, why don't we head back to Aster Bay?"

"Now?" he asked. "I thought you wanted to spend some time in the City."

"I want to spend time with you. If you want to see the City, then I'm happy to show you around, but it's your birthday. We should spend it where you're happiest."

He nipped at her ear. "I thought we already established we weren't spending the day in bed?"

She laughed. "I'm serious." She took his face in her hands and looked deep in his eyes, inviting him into the liquid blue of her own. "Let's go home."

Home.

He felt tingly all over, like a bottle of champagne bursting from the cork, like she'd lit every one of his nerves on fire. He kissed her again—would he ever get tired of kissing her?—then pressed his forehead to hers. "I love you."

The words tumbled out of him on that tingly popped-champagne filling. He was helpless to stop it and, even if he could, he wasn't sure he would have. He loved her. He was in love with her and he wanted her to know it, to feel it.

"I love you too."

His heart cracked open, organs rearranging to make room for her inside his chest in the little nest he'd build for her. He met her eyes, so full of hope and tenderness, and he'd never felt like this before, like all the mistakes, all the wrong paths, had somehow untangled themselves and led him here, exactly where he was always supposed to be.

"Let's go home."

Chapter Twenty-Four

"Dad!"

The front door slammed and Tessa's voice rang out through the small house. Ethan rolled away from Hannah in bed, tilting his alarm clock towards him. It was eight o'clock in the morning. What in the world could possibly be so important at eight o'clock in the morning on a Sunday?

"Dad!"

He sat bolt upright and climbed out of bed, fumbling for his boxer briefs. "Just a minute!" he called back as he searched for the jeans Hannah had peeled off of him the night before when they'd gotten back to Aster Bay.

"What's going on?" Hannah asked sleepily.

"I don't know yet."

He tugged on his jeans and pulled a t-shirt over his head as he slipped out of his bedroom, making sure the door closed behind him. "Tessa?" he called back. She appeared around the corner to the kitchen. "What's wrong? Is Julie alright?"

"Julie's fine," she said, shaking off the question. "Are you alright?"

"Of course I am. Why wouldn't I be?"

"Where's Hannah?" Tessa peered around him towards the

closed bedroom door.

"She's sleeping. T, what's going on?"

"You better wake her up. I think she's going to want to see this."

The bedroom door opened. "I'm here." Hannah stood in the open door in a pair of his sweatpants and one of his old Nuthatch t-shirts, her hair a mess of tangles. If Tessa wasn't making him so nervous, he'd have paused to appreciate the sight of Hannah in his clothing, or at least, he'd have paused longer.

Tessa led them into the living room, typing on her phone, then thrust the device at him. "It's all over the internet."

"What is?" Hannah asked, coming up beside Ethan.

He wrapped an arm around her shoulder as they read together, headline after headline.

Hannah's new man not so new after all.

Who cheated on who? What we know about the Jackson Hayes / Hannah Matthews timeline.

Infidelity and secret identities.

"The first story came out around midnight on Encores. com." Tessa crossed her arms over her chest and watched as Ethan and Hannah continued scrolling.

"Johnny Blue," Hannah said, wincing. "He was probably pissed he didn't get his eating disorder story so he dug something else up."

"What is there to dig up?" Ethan asked. "What does this mean?"

"Daemon called this morning. He said Liv and Micah have been trying to call Hannah. You weren't answering your phone," Tessa said.

"I left my phone out here on the charger last night," Hannah said, lurching towards the device on the side table. As she reached it, it lit up with another incoming call, which she immediately declined. "I don't understand."

"They have photos of you two. From six months ago," Tessa said, taking the phone back from Ethan and scrolling to the image. "They're saying you've been together this whole time. That Jackson's not the one who cheated—Hannah is."

The photos were poorly lit and grainy, like someone had zoomed in on a low-quality cell phone in the dim bar lighting, but it was undeniably the hotel bar in Boston where Hannah and Ethan had so often met. The first photo showed Ethan and Angie in their usual booth, a stack of *Her Lady's Knights* on the table between them, Ethan signing his name inside the front cover. He remembered that day, how he'd signed a dozen copies of the book as a favor for Angie for her to give away to her newsletter subscribers who pre-ordered the next book in the series. The next was of Ethan and Hannah side by side waiting for the elevator, Hannah's hair swept up in a ponytail pulled through the back of a baseball cap, Ethan's hand resting on her lower back. The final photo was just a sliver caught through the elevator door of them kissing.

He wanted to love that photo, this stolen moment between them captured on film when none of their moments before this weekend had been, but how could he love it now? The happiness on her face, the adoration in his eyes had been immortalized on film and turned against them.

"How did they get these?" Ethan asked no one in particular.

"The girl who took the photos recognized the author in the first photo. That's why she started taking pictures, and she followed you, Dad, because she says you're the narrator of the audiobook."

Ethan's anger and frustration at the media intrusion paled in comparison to the alarm he felt at those words coming from his daughter. It felt like when he was kid and his mother found out he and Gavin had been skipping Sunday School in favor of playing on the playground on the Town Common across the street from the church. Like being trapped with his shame while someone he loved recalibrated their opinion of him.

Tessa continued, seemingly unaware of her father's internal crisis. "She didn't know what she'd gotten until you showed up on the red carpet together two nights ago."

Hannah, who had been scrolling through her unread messages, gasped. "They're saying I used Jackson to get ahead, that you and I were sneaking around behind his back for months. They're saying—"

"Stop reading it." Ethan stormed across the room and put his hand over hers, lowering the phone. "Don't read their lies."

"I have to call Micah. I have to call Jackson." Hannah pushed past him, disappearing back into the bedroom, the phone already pressed to her ear.

"Dad, what's going on?" Tessa asked.

She looked so young, standing there with her arms crossed, confusion written all over her face.

"Hannah didn't cheat on anyone," he said.

"I know that." Tessa waved away the comment. "Anyone who's spent two minutes with her knows that. Were they ever even together?"

Ethan's jaw clenched. This wasn't his story to tell, and yet... wasn't it? Now that the media was hellbent on making him a villain in this story, on making *Hannah* a villain, wasn't it his right to set the record straight, at least with his own family?

"No. It was all a show for the press. Something about cleaning up his image."

"That makes sense." Tessa paused, frowning. "You're an audiobook narrator?"

Heat crawled up his throat, his ears blazing with it. But he wouldn't lie to his daughter. Not anymore than he already had, anyway.

"I am."

"Why didn't you tell me?"

"I narrate under a pseudonym. It's not something I tell people."

"I'm not *people*. I'm your daughter." He hated the hurt laced in her voice, the betrayal in her eyes. "Does Jamie know?"

Ethan shook his head. "Only Baz, because he does my taxes. And Hannah." Tessa nodded, but hurt still slashed across her face. "I don't do it all the time. I only narrate for Angie—AK Wild," he corrected himself. "These books…they're not family friendly."

Tessa snorted. "No shit. Mrs. White and her friends wouldn't be reading them at book club if they were. Wait, is that why you didn't tell me?" Ethan cuffed the back of his neck and looked away. "For fuck's sake, Dad, I'm twenty-eight years old. I'm married to your best friend. I have a child. I think we're past the point of pretending I don't know about sex."

"I didn't want it to blow back on you, kid," Ethan said with a sigh. "You've already been put through enough because of my choices."

"I thought you said it didn't bother you that some people still judge you for being a teenage parent—which says more about them than it does about you, by the way."

"I don't give a shit what people judge *me* for. I don't want them to judge you! Or Julie! I don't want my choices to tarnish the legacy our family has built here any more than they already have."

"Are you ashamed of these books, Dad?"

He straightened his spine, meeting her eyes directly so she would know he meant it when he said, "I'm not."

"Then why would you think I would be? Why would you think any of us would be ashamed of your success?"

He didn't know what to say. She was right, and yet he still couldn't shake the feeling he should have protected her from the inevitable fall out. "People might say some nasty things," he said.

Tessa rolled her eyes. "Fuck them. People have said nasty things about our family for years." She wrapped him in a hug and he felt a lump rise in his throat as he wound his arms around her, accepting the absolution he hadn't realized he'd been so desperate for. "Now no more secrets."

"Why do all my clients end up with pictures of their trysts in Johnny Blue's column?" Micah sighed on the other end of the phone.

"I'm so sorry, Micah. I thought we were careful. I thought—"

"You don't need to apologize. But we do need a new strategy. Hiding out isn't going to work this time."

Hannah went cold, ice sluicing down her spine. "Why not?"

"For one, they know Ethan's name—both of them. He announced to the press that you've been staying with him. How long do you think it'll take them to figure out where his vineyard is?"

"They can't really care enough to come to Rhode Island," Hannah protested. "I'm not famous enough for that."

"No, you're not, but Jackson Hayes is, and he's left the country again. Like it or not, you and Ethan are very much people of interest to the celebrity news media right now."

"Then we'll tell them the truth—all of it." She paced the length of Ethan's bedroom, her bare feet leaving indents in the plush carpet. "We'll tell them Jackson and I were never really together. We'll tell them we lied."

"Jackson's people will never agree to that. It would be your word against his," Micah said.

"Jackson will tell the truth if I ask him to."

"Will he?"

Her stomach sank. She wanted to believe their friendship was important enough to him that he'd defend her, especially when it was as simple as telling the truth, but when the truth meant admitting to months of lying and baiting the press...

"Midnight Storm is announcing a new nationwide tour next week. Even if you could get him on the phone from whatever island he's partying on now, you'll never get his publicist to sign off on a statement that alienates the press and his fans. Not right now."

Hannah sank down on the edge of the bed. She knew Micah was right. She'd tried calling Jackson first, but the line rang and rang before clicking over to a voicemail too full to accept new messages, and her texts were still marked as unread. Jackson wasn't going to be able to save her from this.

"What do we do?" Hannah asked.

"We'll issue a short statement. Focus on our disappointment that they've doxed Ethan by connecting his photo and legal name to his pseudonym. We won't deny the pictures—there's no point. We'll say you've known Ethan for a long time and your relationships with both him and Jackson are built on trust and mutual respect."

"Will it work?"

"No." She closed her eyes as her stomach roiled, bile rising in her throat. "But we do it anyway. And if anyone asks about this, anyone at all—reporters or baristas or the little old lady who walks her dog down the street—you have only two words for them."

"No comment," she whispered.

"Let's hope someone else does something salacious soon so everyone moves on."

Salacious.

Ethan had worked so hard to keep his audiobook work separate from his life in Aster Bay, to insulate his real life from the *salaciousness* of it, and now there would be no keeping the two parts of himself from bleeding into each other. More than that, the whole world thought he was a liar at best, and an accomplice in infidelity at worst. And it was all her fault.

"I'll send over a draft of the statement when it's ready for you to review. By the time Midnight Storm announces the tour, this will all be in the past. We can't let this overshadow the momentum you have coming off of the premiere. I'll line up some auditions for you for the following week. Hang in there, Hannah. This too shall pass."

She let the phone drop from her hand onto the comforter, still rumpled from the night before, and stared at her hands. Everything was a mess and there was nothing she could do to fix it.

"Are you alright?"

She lifted her head to see Ethan leaning in the doorway, his hands tucked in his jeans pocket. Tears stung her nose and eyes. "Are you?"

"It's not the way I would have wanted Tessa to find out about my audiobook work, but we're okay. I'm more worried about you right now, sweetheart."

"I don't know why," she sobbed, hiding her face in her hands. He was across the room and kneeling at her feet before her fingers even touched her face. He gathered her against himself, murmuring words of comfort, soft, low barely intelligible sounds deep in his chest that were soothing all the same. "I'm sorry."

"You have nothing to be sorry for."

"If it weren't for me, no one would know you're Slade Hardcastle."

He pushed her hair behind her ear, tutting. "I'm the one who should be apologizing. If that girl hadn't wanted photos of me, she never would have gotten ones of you."

"But If I hadn't—"

"We could go back and forth all day. I'm not letting you beat yourself up over this, Han." His tone brooked no argument.

"Micah thinks some reporters might come here."

She thought of the photo taken from her fire escape, the feeling that nowhere was safe or private anymore. She hated imagining the vineyard swarmed by paparazzi, yet another safe place turned upside down because she'd gotten herself in over her head. Why had she thought she could lie to the press in the first place? Why had she thought any of this was a good idea?

"Then we'll deal with them together," he said.

"If I left, they'd leave you alone."

His eyes hardened, his features turning harsh. "Do you want to leave?"

"No, but I—"

"I'm not letting some assholes with nothing better to do than spread gossip all day take you away from me. We'll figure it out."

She swallowed back a sob. "How?"

"I don't know, but we will. I'll fix it."

"Ethan—"

"I'm sure I can find a way to fix it."

"Ethan, stop." His eyes darted between hers, worry making them sharp and bright. "I'm scared."

His breath gusted out of him, his eyes narrowing. "Of me?"

"No. Well, maybe a little." He looked stunned and she hastened to add, "Of losing you. This is a lot for anyone to deal with and… You could break me, Ethan. You could devastate me in ways nobody ever has before."

"You think I'd hurt you?" he asked, his voice lanced with pain.

"Not intentionally… I'm not afraid of the press, even though they keep finding new ways to blow up my life. But I am terrified of losing you."

He kissed her, his lips slanting over hers with such urgency it nearly knocked her back, but she clung to him as she opened for him, kissing him back. She'd never tire of this, of his fingers tangling in her hair and his tongue sliding against hers, of the hum low in his throat when she pressed her hips against him and the feeling that, if she could keep kissing him, keep holding him, everything else would work itself out.

They parted on a gasp and he pressed his forehead to hers. "You'll never lose me, Han."

"I hope not," she whispered.

"All I want is to make you happy, sweetheart," he said in between kisses.

"We'll make each other happy."

He caught her behind the thighs and tumbled her backwards onto the bed where they landed with a startled laugh. "I'm gonna marry you, city girl. One day, when we're both ready, I'm gonna put a ring on your finger." He drew the finger in question between his lips, dragging his tongue over the digit.

"I've always wanted to be Mrs. Slade Hardcastle," she teased, already feeling lighter.

Ethan threw his head back and laughed, the sparkle of his joy mixed with relief. He hooked his fingers in the waistband of her sweatpants and tugged, shimmying them over her hips and down her legs. "You can call yourself whatever you want, as long as you're mine."

She didn't have time to respond before his tongue hit her core, sliding between her lower lips. She dug a hand into his hair, lifting her hips towards his mouth and he hooked his hands around her thighs, holding her open as he lapped at her clit.

"Ethan," she groaned, giving herself over to the heat gathering low in her belly.

"Christ, you taste so good," he rumbled before diving back

in, teeth and tongue and fingers driving her closer and closer to orgasm. "Tell me you love me, Han," he demanded.

"I love you."

He sucked her clit into his mouth, working her in long pulls that made her cry out with the intensity of it.

Her thighs shook, her stomach contracting as her climax gathered, and she wasn't sure if her hand in his hair was tugging him closer or pulling him away when the first wave of her orgasm broke over her, like drowning in sensation. Ethan only gripped her thighs tighter, holding her against his face as he worked her with single-minded focus. One orgasm morphed into another under his relentless attention and she squirmed in his hold, chanting his name in a mindless refrain with each new crest of pleasure.

When, at last, he pulled away, his beard glistening with her release, and tore at his zipper, shoving his jeans down his hips, she watched with lust-drunk eyes as he notched himself at her opening.

"Tell me you're mine," he said.

"I'm yours."

He slid inside in one brutal stroke, filling her so completely it knocked the air from her lungs and sent heat zinging down her spine.

"You want to be my wife, Hannah?" he asked with a cocky grin as he fucked her slow and deep.

"You asking me to be?" she replied, smiling.

"Not yet. But someday."

"Someday," she agreed, rocking against him, her inner muscles clenching around the thick intrusion of his cock.

He grunted. "Gonna make you mine, so I can spend all day every day playing with this perfect pussy."

She laughed, the sound breaking off on a moan when he dropped his thumb to strum at her over-sensitive clit. "And what am I supposed to do all day?"

"Lay back and take it," he said, his eyes crinkling with his smile before her inner muscles fluttered around him again and they both groaned. "Christ, sweetheart. I'm gonna marry you and then I'm gonna put a baby in your belly."

"Oh, God!"

"You like that, Han? You want me to get you pregnant?"

"Someday."

He grinned. "Someday. Gonna pump you full of my cum day after day until I do. Keep you so full it drips down your thighs when you walk."

"Ethan," she whimpered, bracing her hands on the wall behind herself as she met his thrusts, "I need more."

"Let me take my time, city girl."

He slid his hands under her shirt and tugged it over her head, casting it aside, covering her bare breasts with his hands. He squeezed gently, and she gasped, locking her heels behind his back.

Ethan pinched her nipples, rolling the hard peaks between his fingers, his eyes glued to her face as though he were memorizing her reactions. "More?"

"More."

Goosebumps rose on her skin as he trailed his hands down her sides, over the soft swell of her belly with its pale pattern of stretch marks, around her hips, until he cupped her ass and squeezed, pulling her closer. He somehow slid deeper, his cock pressing against the most hidden parts of her, and they both hissed at the new sensation.

"More?"

She nodded, her fingernails digging into one corded forearm. "More."

His finger ghosted over her back entrance and she gasped, her body going taut with need. "Can I touch you here, sweetheart?" he asked.

"Yes. Please, Ethan," she begged.

He growled, sliding his finger up around the place where they were joined to coat himself in her wetness, before moving back down to play at her pleated rim. "Fuck, I like when you say please."

"Please," she repeated, canting her hips towards him.

He worked his finger inside her little by little, a slow pressure that made his cock feel impossibly larger, her body clamping down around him. "Jesus, sweetheart, you're so tight here," he said as he fucked her with his finger. The sound of their coupling was obscene, the wet press of flesh and her breathy moans. "Look at how wet you are, city girl. Look at how much your pussy likes it when I play with your ass."

Electricity shot down her spine, burning the soles of her feet, dragging her closer and closer to the abyss of another orgasm.

"You're so goddamn beautiful, sweetheart. I wish you could see how beautiful you are like this." He thrust harder, faster, his eyes hazy with lust, and she lifted her hips to meet each movement. "Atta girl. So gorgeous. And you're even prettier when you come." She groaned, shivered, her orgasm right there… "Come for me, Hannah. Come with me. Want to feel this pussy strangle my cock."

She broke apart with a sharp cry punched from her chest as he buried himself inside her once, twice, three more times, before he came with a roar, his cock pulsing within her. He collapsed forward against her, covering her chest, her throat with kisses.

When at last their breathing had evened out, he pressed his forehead to hers, his softening cock still inside her, holding her as close as two people could be.

"You're mine," he said, the words like a prayer.

She smiled, pushing the hair back from his eyes. "I'm yours."

From *The Lady's Knights* by AK Wild,
narrated by Slade Hardcastle

The sun had not yet risen and Lady Windtorn had already stolen from Sir Llewellyn's bed. He heard the rustling of her robes as she hurriedly dressed by the still-glowing embers in the fireplace. The sound ushered in a melancholy that visited him more frequently in recent days, a discontent he feared would break them.

The bedclothes fell to his waist as he sat up in bed. "You leave so soon."

She did not pause in her hunt for something amongst the pile of their discarded clothing. "The maids will be in to light the fire. I must return to my chambers before they mark my absence."

"Surely the maids already know the truth of your marriage." He spat the last word, hating the feel of it in his mouth.

She turned a look of horror his way. "Pray they do not. For if the maids know, then the whole kingdom will know, and none of us are safe."

He threw back the sheets and climbed from his bed, stalking towards her heedless of his nakedness. She held her ground—yet another thing he loved about her—merely tilting her face up to his when he stood beside her, toe to toe.

"Let them know."

"*Bold words spoken under cover of darkness, Sir. And if my lord were to peel back the curtain on this façade, we would all be damned.*"

She spoke the truth and he knew it, but he hated it all the more. Since returning from the woods, since Lord Havenbrook had returned home, their meetings were hurried. There was never enough time when half of it was spent dreading its end.

Lady Windtorn slid her hands over his bare chest, her nails scratching lightly through the hair there, and gentled her tone. "You are a bird, Sir, and I am a fish. Neither can stay in the other's world for long."

He captured her hand, holding it tight against his breast that she might feel the pounding of his heart. "I would. For you, my lady, there is nothing I would not do."

"And yet, you are still a bird, and I am still a fish."

Chapter Twenty-Five

Ethan shut off his computer screen and tried to forget the insane comments he'd just read on yet another post claiming to have insider knowledge of his and Hannah's relationship. None of them knew shit, though each one intensified the headache building behind his eyes. But he couldn't think about that now, or the troubling ways these strangers on the internet were speculating about his sex life.

On the other side of his desk, Baz and Gavin looked grim.

"Three cancellations?" Ethan dragged his thumbs over his closed eyes, as though that could make the last vestiges of the comment section leave his mind. He knew he should stop reading them, but somehow he always ended up right back there, doom scrolling as Tessa called it. "There are three couples who are offended enough by my audiobooks they've cancelled their weddings?"

"I'm sure they'll get married somewhere, but it won't be at Nuthatch Vineyards," Baz answered calmly.

"They'll forfeit their deposits."

"They don't seem to care. Margo tried talking each of them out of it. Even with retaining the forfeited deposits, it puts you down five figures in revenue for the year."

"And that's if no one else cancels." Ethan sighed and pushed the papers aside.

"We'll find new couples or other kinds of events altogether," Gavin said. "I'm already working with Margo on a new marketing campaign to reach romance readers and let them know Nuthatch is happy to welcome the romance community. Reader Fest could be just the beginning."

"You want to replace our wedding income with events catering to romance readers?" Ethan wasn't sure whether his friend was brilliant or insane.

"Mrs. White and her book club think it's a great idea," Gavin said defensively.

"I'm sure they do," Ethan grumbled.

"What's a great idea?" Jo asked, appearing in the open door to Ethan's office with Julie in her arms.

"Holding romance events at the vineyards. Author signings and book launch parties. Did you know there are entire romance conventions?" Gavin asked.

"Sounds fun." Jo set Julie on the floor and watched fondly as she toddled across the room to Ethan.

"Might be fun but there's no way they pay as well as weddings," Baz pointed out.

Ethan swept his granddaughter up in his arms. "Hi, Jujube."

Julie giggled, reaching her hands up to tug on his beard.

"If you're all done talking business, I've been sent to fetch you," Jo said.

Baz scowled. "Fetch us?"

"Your game night awaits," Jo said with a wink before turning and marching down the hall, clearly expecting them all to follow.

Which, of course, they did, despite Baz's grumbling.

When they arrived back at Ethan's house, Sabrina and Tessa had hauled out what looked like every board game from the closet in the hall. Ethan set Julie down in front of her toybox in the corner of the room and headed back to the kitchen, leaving Baz and Gavin to help with board game selection. He hadn't seen Hannah since she'd left for St. Anthony's High after lunch to help with play rehearsal. It might have only been a few hours, but with each new cancellation and each new prickle of dread creeping up his spine, the need to see her increased.

Unfortunately, Caleb and Jamie were the only ones in the kitchen. Jamie had already set out a full spread of tapas on Ethan's kitchen counter and Caleb eyed it hungrily.

"Did you make mini pizzas?" Caleb asked Jamie.

Jamie gestured to a small tray of miniature pizzas, each topped with a single pepperoni slice, chopped herbs, and a drizzle of sticky honey. "Down there, you heathen."

"I am a man of God, sir," Caleb said with mock offense. He took a bite of the pizza and groaned before gesturing for Ethan to join them. "Ethan, you have to try one of these."

"In a minute. Has anyone seen Hannah?"

"Out back with Kyla and Molly," Jamie said, barely looking up as he removed another sheet pan of empanada-looking appetizers from Ethan's oven.

Ethan moved through the kitchen and out the back door to where the women stood talking. His steps slowed as he approached, clocking the pained look on Hannah's face.

"What's going on out here?" he asked.

"Rehearsal didn't go as planned," Kyla said.

"What does that mean?"

"Some kids did a deep dive on social media and dug up some pretty nasty opinion pieces about the whole you-her-Jackson thing," Molly explained.

"And you let them?" Ethan snapped, stepping closer to Hannah, as though he could retroactively shield her from adolescent fuckery.

"They're kids, Ethan. Kids who are addicted to their phones," Molly said.

"They didn't do anything wrong," Hannah added. "They had questions, that's all."

"What kind of questions?"

"Mostly the 'is it true' kind. It's fine."

"It's not fine," he snapped.

Her eyes darted to his and she looked so tired he wanted nothing more than to gather her in his arms and tell everyone else to fuck right off. But it wouldn't fix anything.

Christ, he just wanted to fix it.

"No, but it's…whatever. I'm going to stay away from the school," Hannah said, turning to Molly.

"You don't need to do that," Molly protested.

"I'm a distraction. My being there isn't helping anyone."

"I'm sure that's not true," Kyla said. "Those kids are learning so much from you."

Hannah barked out a bitter laugh. "Sure. How to be the center of a celebrity scandal without even being a celebrity 101." She rolled her head on her shoulders, like she was trying to physically shake off the frustration. "It's fine. I won't be here much longer anyway."

Ethan's lungs stopped working, blood whooshing past his ears. "I thought we talked about this. You don't need to go anywhere."

Kyla and Molly glanced anxiously between them, but he couldn't care that he had made the whole thing awkward. He'd only just convinced her to stay with him in Aster Bay for a while. He'd thought they'd have a little time before she started making plans to leave again. Time to sort out how to make their relationship work long term.

"I think Tessa and Sabrina need some help setting up," Kyla said, leading Molly back up the steps and into the house.

Ethan and Hannah stood alone in his backyard staring at each other. The few feet between them suddenly felt like a chasm.

"You can't deny your life would be easier if I wasn't here right now," Hannah said.

"I do. I deny it."

"Micah is lining up some auditions," she admitted softly, "for the week after next. I'll need to be back in the City at least a few days before to prepare. I haven't sung through any of my audition rep in weeks—"

"You can do that here." He crossed his arms over his chest, widening his stance.

"It's not the same."

"I thought you said you didn't want to be an actress anymore."

"I said I don't know."

"Same thing."

"It's not." She searched his face, and for a moment, he thought he saw a softening, a bending towards the idea of leaving it behind, of choosing something else.

Or someone.

She shook her head as though he was being unreasonable. "I've spent my entire life working towards being where I am now."

"Hunted by the paparazzi? Afraid to be in your own apartment?"

"You don't give up on a career because it loses its luster. Not everybody loves their job all of the time. And it's not just the job. It's the City, and my friends."

"You have friends here now too."

"I didn't realize I had to choose."

He scrubbed a hand over his jaw, his chest aching as muscle and sinew and bone twisted and cracked.

"I'm not asking you to choose," he said, his throat burning with the words.

She crossed her arms, closing herself off from him. "You

kind of are, though."

"If you want to go back to New York, go. I'm not stopping you. But don't run away."

"I'm not running away. I'm trying to keep my mess from invading your life."

"I want your mess!" He scowled, intentionally lowering his tone. "You're the one making this an either-or situation. Not me."

She scoffed. "That's not reality, Ethan. I can't hide in Aster Bay forever. I was always going to have to go back eventually."

Anger flooded his veins, his ears hot and his heart pounding. "And what was your plan? To leave me behind again? Call again in six months and see if I'll meet you for a quick fuck?"

"What was *your* plan?" she countered. "Did you really think I was going to give up *everything* after a few weeks together without taking the time to think it through?"

"It's been years, Hannah, not a few weeks. And I'm not asking you to give anything up. I'm asking you to make room for me in your life. To figure this out with me. I'm asking you not to throw what we have away."

"But you're never going to move to New York."

"Of course not."

"So when you say 'figure it out,' you mean I have to be the one to give up my life. You're asking me to choose."

He threw his arms out wide, unable to contain his frustration. "Fine, I want you to choose me, Han. Choose *us*. For fuck's sake, choose yourself."

She took a step back as though she'd been hit. "What's that supposed to mean?"

"That career is no good for you. And you said yourself you didn't even know if you wanted to do it anymore. You made yourself sick trying to fit into the box they wanted to put you in and then that world literally ran you out of town."

"What am I supposed to do, Ethan?" she demanded,

stepping toe to toe with him, her eyes blazing. "At least I've put myself out there. At least I haven't been afraid to let the world see who I really am."

Her accusation left him breathless, grasping for words, as anger simmered low in his gut. "It's not the same thing."

"I couldn't hide if I wanted to. They've literally hunted me down."

"Us. They've hunted *us* down," he said, stepping closer.

She shook it off, determined to make her point. "I've made mistakes and being an actress isn't always fun or easy, but I've never hidden who I was."

"Except when you were lying about fucking a pop star," he spat.

She sucked in a breath, and he knew he'd gone too far, could see the walls going up behind her eyes. "And what are you hiding, Ethan? I don't think you were afraid of the world finding out about Slade because he's so different from you. I think you were afraid because you're too much alike, because Slade is the parts of yourself you don't let anyone see"

He struggled for words, to find some way to refute what she'd said, prove her wrong, and yet…

Hannah blinked, her expression going blank, and took a step away from him. "I don't want to fight with you."

He huffed out a breath, reaching for her, but she moved out of reach. "Then let's not fight. Let's go inside and—"

"I need some space. I'm going to go for a walk."

"You shouldn't go out alone. What if the paparazzi find you?"

She laughed bitterly. "Then they'll get another crappy picture of me. What's one more at this point?"

She started to walk away, but Ethan caught her hand, regret clawing up his throat. "Hannah, please, don't leave like this."

"It's just a walk, Ethan." She stared at the place where his hand gripped hers, her brows drawn together in the center and her mouth set in a grim line.

He released her, though everything in him was screaming to pull her back towards him, to do *something*, anything to make her realize she belonged with him.

Instead, he watched as she walked away.

Hannah kicked a rock along the side of the road and clutched the phone to her ear, watching as it skittered across the gravel and disappeared into the grassy bank on the other side. The streetlights were starting to come on as the sun set. Terrence McFancyCock crowed in the distance and a smile tugged at her lips despite how miserable she felt.

She should head back to Ethan's soon, before it got dark out and she lost her way. She hadn't walked far, only around the block, but these small town blocks were much larger than anything she'd encountered in the City.

"What are you going to do?" Liv asked through the phone.

Hannah sighed. "I don't know. I don't want to fight with him, but I don't know how this is going to work. I love bringing a show to life. I love that feeling, like electricity, when a show is going well and can *feel* it in the air." She paused, considering a cluster of wildflowers at the edge of the pavement. "But I don't love having my personal life the subject of public debate. Or photographers thinking they're entitled to take pictures of me whenever and wherever they want." She sat on a large rock by the side of the road, suddenly feeling exhausted. "And I am really scared if I go back to performing I'm not going to be able to maintain my recovery."

"Why?"

Tears pricked at the back of her eyes, her nose stinging.

"I don't know if I can do another audition season, Liv. I don't know if I can stand in a room full of people telling me what's wrong with me again and again and again in hopes that one of them will like me enough to cast me as the funny fat friend."

"You're not the funny fat friend, Hannah. You're Bridget freaking Jones."

"That's one part. One part in an entire industry." She closed her eyes as the first tear slipped down her cheek. "I'm tired, Liv. And I'm scared. What if I give it up and it's the wrong decision? What if I wake up in a year and realize I don't love Ethan as much as I thought? Or what if I go back and I'm still in the same place I've been for years, only this time I've let the love of my life go, and for what?"

"The love of your life, huh?"

"Maybe." Hannah sighed and watched the early evening breeze ruffle the leaves on a nearby maple tree. "I've wanted to be on Broadway since I was a little girl, but I can't help feeling like I climbed to the top of the mountain and looked around and there's nothing there. What if staying on the mountain is just another way to hide?"

The line was quiet enough that Hannah wondered if maybe they'd been disconnected.

"Are you still there?"

"I'm here. I'm always here," Liv said. "Did I ever tell you about the letter my dad left for me and my brother before he died?"

Hannah dashed away a tear, confused by the subject change. "No."

"When he got sick, he wrote a letter and left it with my mom. She was supposed to read it to us when the time was right. And apparently that time was my wedding," she said with a chuckle. "Anyway, he said the things that scare us are the things most worth doing."

Hannah swallowed a sob.

"Maybe you're scared because it's important."

"Which part—going back to New York or staying here?"

"I can't answer that for you," Liv said. "Which one scares you more?"

The house was quiet when Hannah returned, only Ethan's truck still in the driveway. He was putting things away in the kitchen when she came in, his back to the front door. He spun around, his eyes wild, at the sound of the door closing. "Jesus, Han." He set aside the stack of dishes in his hand and crossed the room to her in long strides, cupping her face in his hands as his eyes roved over her. "Are you hurt?"

"No, I'm fine." She could only imagine what he must be seeing—puffy eyes, embarrassingly red cheeks. Hannah was not a cute crier.

"What happened, sweetheart?" His thumbs slid tenderly over her cheeks, soothing the phantom tracks of her tears.

"Nothing happened." She gripped one of his wrists, sliding her hand up his forearm. "I'm sorry I ran away."

He exhaled harshly through his nose. "I'm sorry I pushed you."

His hands slid into her hair as they moved closer, almost as though their bodies were magnetized, an invisible force drawing them together as her arms wound around his waist.

"This is all harder than I thought," he admitted.

Her stomach churned. "This?"

"Being in the press. Having people know about my audiobooks. Talking about us like they know us. How do you do it?"

"I didn't have a choice." His arms were strong beneath her

palms as she skated her hands up his biceps. "But you do."

He huffed out a frustrated breath. "We've been over this."

"You didn't sign up for this. It's okay if you don't want to deal with it, but if you want out, you have to tell me now."

He captured her lips in a soft kiss, so sweet it had her eyes welling up again. What was she going to do if he really didn't want to deal with her baggage? She wouldn't be able to blame him, but she wasn't sure she would survive the loss, either.

"It's late," he said. "Let's go to bed."

She hesitated, aware he'd dodged the question, but she wanted his comfort more than she wanted to press the issue. After all, if she pressed and he decided to cut bait and run, what then?

So instead they stripped their clothing slowly, eyes glued to each other the whole time, and slipped beneath the covers of Ethan's bed, a bed that smelled like her now as well. He pulled her to him, her back to his chest, and pressed a kiss to her shoulder. He held her tighter, his face buried in her hair and, within minutes, he had drifted off to sleep. But Hannah stayed awake, trying to memorize the feel of his hands on her skin, his body against her, so someday, when he decided he'd had enough, she'd at least still have the memories.

Comment section of Encores.com post with caption "Hannah Matthews spotted with spicy audio star in hotel bar. Who's the cheater now?"

StrmChsr92: I can't believe she cheated on Jackson and tried to make everyone think he was the bad guy!

Here4theDrama: I don't know, that Slade guy is hot AF. I can see the appeal.

XOJxsnsGurlXO: His name is Ethan. He's just pretending to be Slade.

PennyReadsSmut: He's not pretending. It's a stage name. Like how actors don't always use their real names.

StrmChsr92: So they're both liars.

Here4theDrama: Have you heard some of the dirty things he says in those books? *hot face emoji*

PennyReadsSmut: He could probably break your back and you'd say, 'please sir, can I have some more?'

TheSpicierTheBetter: Did you see the way he looked at her on the red carpet? Girl, no wonder she cheated.

BookstaGirliesDoItBetter: What if she wasn't cheating? What if she was with them both? Why choose, right?

StrmChsr92: There was a story about Jackson having a threesome in Cancun a few years ago.

XOJxsnsGurlXO: Jackson would never!

Here4theDrama: He 100% would.

TheSpicierTheBetter: Slade would.

BookstaGirliesDoItBetter: As long as he does that growl thing he does, Slade can do whatever he wants to me.

PennyReadsSmut: Who do you think has a bigger *eggplant emoji*?

XOJxsnsGurlXO: Jackson

TheSpicierTheBetter: Slade

Chapter Twenty-Six

Ethan bounced Julie on his hip, the overtired toddler barreling towards full-on meltdown territory. "My answer is still no," he said into the phone as he paced around his office.

"Ethan, come on. Everyone knows now. It's time to lean in," Angie said through the phone.

"I'm not fu—" He glanced at Julie, catching the swear before it left his mouth. "I'm not *leaning* in. I've got weddings canceling left and right—"

"It was *four* weddings," Angie said. He could practically hear her rolling her eyes at him.

"That's sixteen percent of my wedding business this year, Ang. That's not insignificant."

"And I'm offering you a way to gain back that business from people who don't care if you read dirty books."

"My parents wouldn't want—"

"Have you talked to Louise and Henry? Because I don't remember them being as uptight as you're making them out to be."

Julie pounded her tiny fist against his bicep. "Mama!" she wailed for the umpteenth time in the last hour.

"You have to own your choices, Ethan."

"I am. I do," he insisted. "But I still run a family business, Ang."

"You run a vineyard, not a fucking preschool," Angie said with an exhausted sigh. "Look, I won't come to the Reader Fest thing if it bothers you so much, but I think you're making a mistake. You've got some weird puritanical bullshit in your head about people knowing you're a sexual being and you have to sort that shit out."

They said their goodbyes and Ethan hung up the phone as Julie started wailing. "If you would just go to sleep," he muttered, increasing his pace.

The landline on his desk rang—again. It had been ringing nonstop for the last two days as various reporters tried to get a statement from Ethan. The ringing stopped and abruptly started again.

"Christ's sake." He reached over and flicked the receiver off the cradle, hanging up the call and leaving the phone off the hook.

"Need a hand?"

Gavin pushed into the office and held his arms out for Julie. Ethan let his friend take his granddaughter and paced back over to the phone, putting it on the hook but unplugging the cord. "I need reporters to stop calling. I need brides to stop canceling their weddings because their Catholic mothers think the whole vineyard is tainted by my scandal. I need right wing nut jobs to stop tanking our online reviews and I need Julie to take a nap and I need—"

"You need to take a breath," Gavin said as Julie tugged on his tie. "And don't worry about the brides. I had phone calls with four separate companies this morning who are interested in booking events at Nuthatch—two corporate retreats, some kind of restauranteurs conference, and a singles event. You can't see it now because you're in the eye of the storm—"

"The eye is the quiet part."

"Is it? Huh. Weird. Well, you're in whatever part of the storm is hairiest, but it will calm down. This could end up being a good thing."

Ethan stared at his friend in disbelief. "How?"

"Diversifying the vineyard's event rentals beyond weddings can only be beneficial in the long run. And I know you've been too busy hiding out on your own property to know this, but having the press in town has actually been great. One outlet wrote a whole piece about how Aster Bay is the undiscovered gem of the Northeast, and another did a profile on Aster Place as one of the most haunted houses in New England."

"It's not haunted."

"It could be haunted. You don't know."

"You don't think we'd know if Aster Place was haunted?"

Gavin shrugged. "I think you're missing the point. An article showed up online today touting Aster Bay as the ideal vacation destination for a girls' weekend, in part because you can visit the vineyard owned by romance audiobook narrator Slade Hardcastle. The only one still stressing about this is you."

"Because it's my life!" Ethan shouted.

Julie jolted in Gavin's arms, her face turning towards her grandfather and crumbling. Ethan saw it in slow motion, the way her nose scrunched up and her lip quivered moments before she let out a frightened wail. He lowered his voice, crooning apologies and words of comfort as he scooped Julie out of Gavin's arms, cradling her against his chest.

"This might be fun for the rest of you but I'm the one having his private life speculated about all over the internet. The things people are saying—" He broke off, shaking his head. "I'm a private person, Gav. I *like* my privacy. I do not like strangers on the internet speculating about the size of my..." He gestured to his crotch and Gavin's eyes widened.

"Ethan—"

"I need to get Julie to sleep. I'm going to take her for a ride and see if she'll calm down."

He hardly heard Gavin's goodbye as he bundled Julie out the backdoor of his office, the one the press hadn't yet found, and trudged across the gravel strip to his truck. The strap of her car seat clicked into place at the same time some reporter who'd snuck around the side of the building to smoke a cigarette—despite the multiple 'no smoking' signs, the asshole—caught sight of him.

"Hey, Ethan!" the reporter shouted, snuffing out his cigarette with the toe of his shoe.

"No comment," Ethan barked as he closed the door on Julie and stalked around the truck to the driver's side.

"Did you know you were the other man?" the reporter called, moving closer to the truck. "Or was it the other way around? Was Jackson the other man?"

Ethan swung into the driver's side and tore out of the driveway as he buckled his seatbelt. In the backseat, Julie continued to wail as the reporter jogged across the parking lot towards his rental car. Ethan turned off onto a small side street that wound around the edge of the vineyard property, glancing at Julie in the back seat. It would never cease to amaze him how quickly his granddaughter would start to nod off in a moving car. Her little head bobbed with sleep as he took another turn, winding past Cheryl and Ricky's farm.

Headlights flashed in his rear-view mirror, and he cursed to himself, pressing harder on the gas pedal. His eyes darted between the headlights moving ever closer and the road ahead of him as it twisted and turned along the edge of town. On the passenger seat, his cell phone rang and he reached over, blindly grabbing for it, to silence it before it could wake Julie, the truck swerving into the other lane as he did.

He over-corrected, guiding the truck past his lane and onto the rumble strip at the edge of the road before finding the balance in the middle of the lane again.

And still those headlights came closer.

These paparazzi fuckers don't give up.

With a hard turn of the steering wheel, he swung onto a narrow side street by the cemetery, his speed climbing. In the backseat, Julie snored softly, undisturbed by Ethan's erratic driving. The phone rang again, but this time, in his fumbling to silence it, he accidentally answered.

"Dad?" Tessa's voice came through the truck's speakers as the phone connected. "Where are you?"

He glanced in the rear-view. Julie scrunched up her face, but kept sleeping. "I took Julie out for a drive to get her to sleep," he whispered. "I can't talk right now."

"Why don't you bring her home? I'll meet you there. It's slow at the bakery today anyway," Tessa said.

Ethan was so focused on the advancing headlights in his rear-view, he blew through a stop sign without even seeing it, a car on the opposite side of the intersection laying on its horn as he flew past. "Shit," he muttered.

"Everything okay?" Tessa asked.

"Fine. I'll see you at your house in ten."

He hung up before she could say anything else. He needed to stay focused on the road. And those fucking headlights were riding his tail, high beams flashing erratically, blinding him.

He sped up, flying past the smaller houses of Gavin's mother's neighborhood and the Portuguese butcher shops. Finally, the street widened into the larger main road, two lanes on each side, and the car that had been following him since the vineyard pulled up alongside him. He slowed the truck as the car sped past, the sides scratched and dented, with a familiar bumper sticker on the passenger side fender: "Honk if you love a frat boy."

Ethan pulled over to the side of the road, stopping the truck, and leaning his head back against the seat.

It wasn't a reporter chasing him down.

It was the Collins kid, out for another one of his joyrides. A fucking nineteen-year-old adrenaline junkie.

With the car parked, Julie stretched and fussed in her car seat. The sound sent guilt flooding through his veins, a sinking, nauseous feeling. He'd driven like a maniac with his granddaughter in the car—and for what?

They could have been hurt.

She could have been hurt, and it would have been all his fault.

Bad enough that his business was in disarray and his personal life was being ripped apart by literal strangers, but now he was putting his family's safety at risk?

No. No more.

This has to stop.

Chapter Twenty-Seven

Later, Hannah would swear there was something off from the moment she returned to Ethan's home that afternoon. The air was thicker, or maybe thinner—either way, it had changed. The sunlight streaming through the kitchen windows seemed dimmer, the house colder.

"Ethan?"

She set her bag down on the kitchen table and made her way through the house towards the bedroom at the back. She didn't toe off her shoes like she usually would, and later she would wonder if it was a kind of premonition, like knowing she shouldn't get too comfortable. The door to the bedroom was open. Ethan stood in front of the closet, staring at the row of her sundresses hanging alongside his button-downs.

"Ethan?"

He turned to her, his jaw tense and skin ashen, and she knew. Her heart sank into her stomach, a strange tingly feeling climbing up the nape of her neck, like when she'd watch a scary movie and the music would change, her body responding to information she had yet to receive but knew was coming.

"What happened?" she asked, her mouth dry.

He didn't respond at first, his eyes skittering away from hers as though the answer to her question might be found in the bed they'd shared for the last several weeks.

"Just say it," she said.

"I don't think I can do this."

She'd known it was coming and yet the words still landed like a blow. Or maybe more like shattering glass, a priceless vase knocked off its ledge and smashing at their feet, a gulf of brittle shards forming between them.

"I thought I could handle it. Fix it. But I just keep making it worse."

Hannah held up her hand, closing her eyes. Mercifully, he stopped talking. She didn't need to hear his reasons why she wasn't worth the circus their lives had become. Hadn't she always known she wouldn't be?

"Say it," she repeated.

"I think it's better if we end things."

Another breath in and out, another moment to let those shards of glass sink into her skin before she began the awful process of extracting them—and him—from her life.

She moved to the closet, still open, her sunny yellows and purples next to his muted olives and taupes. As if she needed even more evidence that they didn't fit together.

One by one she removed the dresses from their hangers, draping them over her arm as she worked, slow and steady so her fingers wouldn't shake. Methodical. If she could keep this unemotional, just another item on the to-do list, another step and then another and another, then she'd be back in New York, back in her lonely little apartment before her brain would have time to catch up with her heart. She could be back in her real life before she had time to mourn the ending of this fantasy.

But what a fantasy it had been.

"Say something," he said, his tone pleading.

"I think I left my bag in the guest room." She glanced around the bedroom, eyes skimming over the rumpled sheets, the little pile of books on the bedside table on her side of the bed, frozen moments of a life that didn't belong to her.

"Don't you want to know why?" he asked, and there was that glass again, though this time it was fashioned into little jagged darts lining his words as they sped across the room towards her.

Why was she so tired all of a sudden?

Focus on the list. Get your clothes, don't forget your things in the bathroom, pack a bag and call a car. Or take a train? Maybe call Micah and let him sort it out, so long as he does so quickly.

"My business is falling apart. It's only a matter of time before my family is caught in the crossfire," he said. "The way I feel about you hasn't changed, but—"

"But it has, Ethan. Less than a week ago you sat on that bed," she jabbed a finger at the offending furniture, "and said we'd figure it out together. You said you wanted to marry—" The words broke off as she swallowed the sob climbing up her throat.

Taking her armful of dresses, she marched down the hall to the guest room she hadn't slept in since her first few days in Aster Bay, her mostly empty suitcase open on the bed where she'd left it.

Focus on the list.

Ethan appeared in the doorway, his face contorted in pain. *Good,* she thought. *I hope it hurts.*

"I meant everything I ever said to you," he said.

She loosed a bitter laugh as she slammed the dresses into the suitcase and pushed past him to gather her creams and lotions from the bathroom. "I'm sure you meant it in the moment."

Her hairbrush next to his comb, her shampoo on the little ledge next to his woodsy body wash. She hesitated as she reached for her mouthwash, her cool mint beside his wintergreen, then stormed back to the guest room.

Keep moving.

"In a few months when things calm down—"

She turned on him. "Don't. This is my life, Ethan. It's messy and chaotic and I—"

I would have given it all up for you.

But she hadn't. Maybe if she had, this wouldn't be happening.

Or maybe it would have happened anyway, and then you'd really have nothing.

She squeezed her eyes shut, unable to see the hurt on his face without either becoming completely enraged or falling apart herself, and neither seemed like the right choice. His words from the other night in his backyard came back to her. She couldn't choose him, not when he was clearly unwilling to choose her, but she could do one better.

Choose yourself.

"I'm standing in the middle of a storm, and I thought you wanted to stand in it with me. Storms don't last forever, Ethan. They don't. But if you can't stand in the chaos with me now, then you don't deserve to stand with me when it's calm."

When she opened her eyes, the devastation in his was more than she could bear.

"I wanted to," he said softly. "I wanted to be that guy for you."

"Be that guy for yourself." She dashed away the tear slipping down her cheek. When had she started crying? "You think no one can handle all the parts of you, but you don't even give anyone a chance to. You think you're fixing things or protecting people but you're just hiding—and, trust me, I know hiding."

"What am I hiding from?" he asked.

"I don't know, Ethan. But I hope you figure it out." She shoved the last of her things into the suitcase, zipping it closed. "I'll call a car from the vineyard. Please don't follow me."

Chapter Twenty-Eight

Hannah pulled the baseball cap low over her forehead and adjusted her sunglasses before climbing out of the taxi with a murmured 'thank you' to the driver. There were no photographers outside the diner that she could see, but she wasn't risking it. She was in no mood to have her unwashed hair and dark undereye circles splashed across the internet. The chime over the diner door announced her arrival, the tinkling sound cutting through the low buzz of early morning activity.

She'd barely taken two steps into the diner before she was blindsided by Liv and Jennifer barreling into her, wrapping her into giant hugs that made her feel both safe and completely exposed. "It's good to see you too," Hannah laughed with false brightness.

"Good to have you back, Han," Liv said, squeezing her one last time before releasing her.

Three mimosas waited for them at their usual table in the back. Hannah set aside her sunglasses, but opted to leave the baseball cap on as she took a sip, the bubbles tickling her nose.

"Before we go any further, tell us—do we hate him?" Jennifer asked.

Hannah fingered the stem of her champagne flute and shook

her head. "We don't hate him."

"You two seemed really happy at the premiere. What happened?" Liv asked.

So she told them the whole messy story—milkshakes and kissing in the bookstore, trivia matches and game nights, volunteering at the high school, dates under the stars and lazy mornings in bed. And the end, when she was ready to choose him, but he wouldn't choose her.

"It was a lot for him, you know?" she said, blinking back tears. "That kind of attention from the press would be a lot for anyone, but especially for him. I think he really loved me—" She broke off as her words caught in her throat. "But it was too much. I was asking too much."

Jennifer reached across the table, wrapping her hand around Hannah's. "You were not asking too much. You are beautiful and brilliant and fucking fantastic and if he couldn't see that you were worth fighting for, it's his loss."

"People always say that. 'It's his loss.' But it's mine too," Hannah said, shaking her head.

"It sounds like he has some things he needs to work through, and that has nothing to do with you," Liv said.

The server dropped their food at the table, three plates piled high with golden brown French toast topped with strawberries and creamy pats of butter, a dusting of powdered sugar around the rim of the plate.

"Is this our order?" Hannah asked, confused.

"We figured this called for a change to the usual routine to welcome you home," Liv said.

Jennifer cut into a slice of French toast and popped it in her mouth, moaning around the bite. "Besides, carbs are incredible. All this time, why did no one remind me carbs are incredible?"

Hannah smiled as she cut into her own French toast. "It's nice to see you eating all the food groups again."

Jennifer shook her head, shoveling another bite into her mouth. "I'm off dairy." She glanced at the plate in front of her. "Except for today."

"So, what's next?" Liv asked.

Hannah dragged a strawberry through a pool of maple syrup. "First, I need to buy thicker curtains for the living room."

"And then?" Jennifer prompted.

"I don't know. Micah has some auditions he wants me to go on, but I've been thinking…" She glanced at her friends, at their open expressions and kind eyes. Together they'd braved the open cattle calls and taken countless dance classes, cheered each other on through callbacks that went nowhere and opening nights that felt like a triumph. "I loved so much of my time in Aster Bay. Not just because of Ethan—"

"And the multiple orgasms," Jennifer offered. Liv's eyes flared, her lips pursed in a look of censure. "What?"

"Yeah, not just because of the amazing sex, either," Hannah said, a wistful melancholy creeping in. "The people were great, and there's something kind of fantastic about waking up to a rooster instead of a car horn. And I really loved working with the kids at the high school. I felt like I was making theatre *and* making a difference, you know?"

"Are you thinking about teaching?" Liv asked.

"Maybe." She shrugged, popping the strawberry into her mouth and chewing slowly to give herself time to think. "I'm not saying I'm going to give it all up and move to the suburbs and start teaching—"

"Are you sure? Because it sounds like that's what you're saying," Jennifer said.

"And if you are, that would be fine," Liv added. "We'd support you."

"Obviously," Jennifer added.

"I don't even know how I would go about doing that, but I

think maybe it's time to consider all my options."

"For what it's worth, I think you'd be an incredible teacher," Liv said.

"But, to be fair, we think you'd be pretty kick ass at whatever you decide you want to do," Jennifer said.

Hannah smiled, affection overwhelming her. "For now, I want to eat this entire plate of French toast and hear all about what you two have been up to."

"Jennifer banged her yoga instructor," Liv said with a grin over the top of her champagne flute.

"I did not!" Jennifer protested with a laugh. "We made out against the wall of mirrors once."

"And?" Liv prompted.

"And there may have been some tongue action below the belt," Jennifer hedged.

"Twice," Liv said, flashing two fingers as Hannah.

"Are you going to see him again?" Hannah asked.

Jennifer shrugged. "He's not really my type."

"He asked her out for this Friday," Liv said.

"To some kombucha bar opening." Jennifer wrinkled her nose. "I don't know if he gives good enough head to pretend I like kombucha."

Hannah laughed, settling in as Jennifer told them all about her yoga instructor and the many ways he was not her type, except, of course, when they were hooking up. With each laugh shared, each moment of playful teasing, she felt more and more at home, sinking back into the life she'd left behind when her world had imploded. It should be easy to pick up where she left off, to fall back into the familiar routine.

But something was missing.

Or someone.

A painful pang tugged at her heart, and she flagged down the server to order another round of mimosas. She loved her friends and the diner and being a part of the theatre community, but it wasn't enough anymore. Not now she was keenly aware of the things she'd left behind in Aster Bay.

Ethan swung the sledgehammer harder this time, the thwack of it colliding with drywall echoing off the walls. He brushed the sweat out of his eyes with his forearm and lifted the heavy tool, rearing back and lodging it in the wall.

"Ethan?" Jamie's voice rang out through the empty house upstairs.

"Down here," Ethan grunted as he swung again.

A few moments later, Jamie descended the stairs into Ethan's basement, ducking under the beam halfway down the stairwell. "What are you doing?"

"What does it look like?" Another swing, another thwack, and the hole widened.

"Any particular reason you're demolishing your house today?"

Ethan shot a glance at Jamie over his shoulder and set the sledgehammer down, reaching for his bottle of water. "Needed a change."

Jamie's eyebrows shot up his forehead. "Hannah moving out wasn't enough?"

Ethan scowled. "Did you need something?"

"Tessa wanted me to remind you about family dinner."

The sledgehammer dislodged a chunk of drywall, the misshapen piece falling onto the tarp Ethan had spread on the ground beneath the wall. "I haven't forgotten one yet."

He could feel Jamie standing behind him, watching him swing the hammer over and over, slowly widening the opening in the wall, his attention like a sticky syrup coating his skin.

"Did you need something else?" Ethan grunted.

"What happened?"

"I've always wanted to open it up down here."

"Not with the wall. With Hannah."

Ethan faltered in his swing, the hammer landing off center and not making as big of an impact as he'd intended. He frowned at the hole, setting the hammer down again. Raising the hem of his t-shirt to wipe the sweat from his face, he turned to his friend. "Nothing happened. It just didn't work out."

Jamie arched an eyebrow that made it clear exactly how much he believed that story. "You've been completely gone for this woman since the moment she showed up in town—"

"I have not."

"—and you're trying to tell me it *just didn't work out*?" Jamie scoffed. "What did you do?"

"Nobody did anything. Our lives are too different. It was never going to work long term anyway."

"Says who?"

Ethan shook his head, reaching for the sledgehammer again. "I did what I had to do. It's best for everybody."

"Doesn't look like it's best for you."

Ethan ignored him, putting all his energy into swinging the sledgehammer harder. Maybe if he could hit hard enough, exhaust his muscles enough, make a big enough hole in the wall, maybe then he wouldn't have time to think about all the destruction he'd caused elsewhere in his life.

Behind him, Jamie sighed. "Don't be late for dinner."

He wouldn't be. Ethan was never late. That was his whole schtick, after all, wasn't it? He did what he said he would do. He solved problems. He fixed things.

The way you're fixing this wall?

He was never disruptive or inconvenient or unreliable in

any way.

Except for Hannah. She trusted you and you were completely unreliable.

Another swing, another thwack. This time the hit reverberated up his arm. How many swings would it take to forget the look on her face when she told him not to follow her? How many swings to stop wondering if she was right about him, if he was hiding?

As he suspected, he didn't have enough swings left in him for that. When his arms felt like Jello and his chest was heaving with the exertion of it, the wall stripped down to the studs and providing a clear view all the way across the basement, he dragged himself back upstairs and took a scalding hot shower, washing away the sweat and the grime, bits of plaster dust and drywall. But not the ache making his chest feel heavy. Not the emptiness opening inside his ribcage and threatening to pull him under. No amount of hot water could ease those things.

He was seven minutes early for family dinner, but he was still the last to arrive. From the moment he stepped into Lemon and Thyme, he knew something was different. Instead of the laughter and chatter that usually greeted him at a family dinner, the room was quiet, his friends and family talking in hushed tones, already seated at the tables Jamie had pushed together to make one giant table. The hair on the back of his neck prickled as he moved into the room, all eyes turning in his direction.

"Where's Julie?" he asked, scanning the group for his granddaughter.

"With Cheryl and Ricky," Tessa said, coming around the table to greet him with a hug and a kiss on the cheek. "Adults only tonight."

"What's going on?" Uneasiness rippled over his skin, raising goosebumps as his senses kicked into overdrive, looking for the threat.

"Come sit down, Dad. Dinner will be ready in a few minutes."

Tessa led him to a seat at the table, taking the chair beside him. Gavin's eyes shone with pity and Baz wouldn't even make eye contact. "Someone needs to tell me what's going on right now," he demanded.

Caleb glanced around the table before locking eyes with Ethan, as though he'd come to some sort of decision. He wore his priest's collar—he rarely wore his collar to family dinner—and somehow that fact sent dread sinking into Ethan's gut more than anything else.

"We're all here because we care about you," Caleb began.

"And because it's family dinner," Ethan said uncertainly.

Caleb nodded. "And because families need to be honest with each other, even when it's hard."

"What, is this an intervention?" he scoffed. Jamie and Tessa exchanged a nervous glance and Ethan barked out a laugh. "You've got to be fucking kidding me? An intervention for what?"

"For you," Tessa said gently. "Because we're all worried about you."

"You're knocking down walls in your house," Caleb said.

Ethan shot Jamie an accusatory glare. "I'm renovating."

"You didn't tell us about the audiobooks," Gavin said.

"I like my privacy," he shot back.

"There's privacy, and then there's shutting people out," Jamie said. The wounded edge to his voice caught Ethan by surprise, made him hesitate.

"The fewer people that knew, the better." He huffed an incredulous laugh. "Look what's happened since people found out? I was trying to protect the vineyard." He turned to Tessa. "To protect you, and Julie, and—"

"Shutting us out isn't protecting us," Tessa said.

"I'm your father. I'm never going to stop trying to protect you."

"You're missing the point," Jamie said.

"Then what's the point?"

At the other end of the table, Baz raised his head and skewered him with a look. "Where's Hannah?"

The sound of her name here, in a room full of the people he loved, a room she belonged in where her absence was so noticeable it was a physical thing, rocked him. "She left."

"You sent her away," Kyla corrected.

He shook his head. "No. It wasn't like that."

"You didn't tell her you couldn't be with her anymore?" Molly asked, shooting him a challenging look.

"I think we're getting off track," Caleb said. "The point is, we're concerned about you, Ethan."

"Oh, are you *concerned*, Father West?" Ethan spat.

Caleb flinched, but Gavin picked up where his brother left off. "We think you should talk to someone."

"We're talking right now," Ethan said.

"What you've been through, with the press and your life coming under public scrutiny, it would be a lot for anyone. Having someone to help you process it could be helpful," Caleb continued.

Ethan shook his head in disbelief. "I'm being ambushed."

Tessa scooted closer to him. "You were so happy these last few weeks. I don't think I've ever seen you like that. It was nice."

He swallowed down the lump forming in his throat, wrapping an arm around her shoulder and tugging her into his side. He pressed a kiss to the top of her head. "I'm fine, T."

"You could be better than fine. You *were* better than fine." She didn't say the last part, but she didn't need to. He heard it anyway.

With Hannah.

You were happy with Hannah.

And you fucked it up.

"Now you're so..." Tessa trailed off.

"What?"

"Angry."

The word knocked the wind out of him, all his bluster and indignation dying. She was right. He was angry. He was fucking furious. But only with himself.

"I was protecting you," he repeated lamely.

"I'd rather you were happy," Tessa said.

"We all would," Gavin added.

Tessa squeezed his arm. "Just think about it, okay?"

He nodded, the crushing weight of exhaustion making his limbs heavy and slow. "Sure, kid. I'll think about it."

From *The Lady's Knights* by AK Wild,
narrated by Slade Hardcastle

The night air was cold as it whipped around Sir Llewellyn, the ends of his black cloak flying out around him on the ramparts. In the distance, his men had lit a bonfire, their raucous laughter carrying on the wind through the trees circling their camp.

Peace.

Sir Llewellyn had not known a time of peace in all his many years as a knight of the realm. He should have been celebrating with his men, toasting to their victory and a future without war. The treaty signed that morning would ensure a generation of prosperity. Serenity.

But Sir Llewellyn felt anything but serene. His insides were twisted and knotted, tormented. Peace meant Lord Havenbrook would have no need to travel quite so often, to entrust his wife to his faithful knight's care. But she could be safe, now, the threat of the warring families neutralized, not through Sir Llewellyn's care and military might, but with a stroke of her husband's pen. He wanted to rejoice in a peace brokered without any more bloodshed, but when peace came at such a great personal cost… Instead, he mourned.

"Do you know what I have often wished?"

Sir Llewellyn spun around to find he was no longer alone.

"My lord," he said, dipping his head in deference.

"Nights when I could not sleep, I would climb these ramparts and look out into the darkness. And I would pray."

"We have all prayed for peace," Sir Llewellyn said.

"Not for peace." Lord Havenbrook shot him a sidelong glance before turning his attention back to the distant glow of the bonfire flickering through the trees. "I would pray that when I woke, you would be gone."

"My lord?"

"Both of you."

Sir Llewellyn's breath burned in his lungs, shock stealing his words. "My lord—"

"What is it that has kept you here, Sir?"

"Duty," the knight answered instantly.

"What of your duty to her?"

"My lord, we would never be free of the stain of having betrayed you."

"And so instead you shall live with the stain of betraying your love for each other."

Chapter Twenty-Nine

"He'll be here." Micah tilted his head meaningfully towards the cell phone clutched in Hannah's hands.

"Sure," she said, setting the phone down.

Though the 'he' she was hoping to hear from was not the 'he' she and Micah were waiting for.

The night before, during her third re-listen of *The Lady's Knights* in as many weeks, Hannah had received a message from Ethan. The first message since their terse exchange confirming she'd arrived home in New York safely three weeks before. He'd sent a photo of a milkshake with three little words that had tilted her world on its axis and had her stomach in knots: *Thinking of you.*

She wanted to be furious. The absolute gall on this man to send her *that* message after the way they'd left things.

And yet…

Instead she'd sent back a screenshot of her audiobook app. *You too*, she'd written.

And then nothing. Crickets.

Thinking of you. What was she supposed to do with that? And what did he *want* her to do with it? And did she even care what he wanted anymore?

Of course, you do, you glutton for punishment.

"Howard's always at least ten minutes late," Micah said, pulling her thoughts back to the 'he' she should be focused on. "It's a power move."

Hannah rolled her eyes. "Because being an old white dude isn't enough of a power move."

"Hannah, darling!" Howard King's booming voice thundered through the quiet café at the edge of the theater district. Half the eyes in the room turned to take in the eccentric director where he stood in the doorway, his arms spread wide and head cocked to the side in an affectation of warmth. "There's my little star," he announced as he made his way towards them.

Hannah greeted Howard with a kiss on each cheek. "Always good to see you, Howard."

"And Micah, it's been too long." Howard clapped Micah in a handshake-hug hybrid that looked uncomfortable at best. "Sit, sit. Mustn't draw too much attention to ourselves. I'm sure you've already had plenty of that," he said to Hannah with a wink and a smarmy grin.

Her smile was more like a grimace, but she couldn't summon the desire to play the part of the fawning ingenue. Not anymore. Not when Ethan hadn't texted her back in eighteen hours and thirteen minutes.

"We were so glad to get your call," Micah said, nudging Hannah. "Word on the street is you've been tapped for another limited run revival at Lincoln Center this fall."

"Oh, that," Howard said with a dismissive wave of his hand. "What are we drinking? I could kill for a matcha latte."

Hannah dug her fingernails into her palm as Howard flagged down the harried waitress and placed his order, including specific instructions about the exact temperature the cup should be before his latte was poured. To her credit, the waitress' smile never faltered, though Hannah had the distinct impression she'd be spitting in Howard's drink.

"Now, where were we?" Howard asked, turning back to Hannah and Micah. "That's right, your recent popularity. Or was it notoriety?" He laughed. "I do always get those two confused."

"Press interest has died down now Hannah's back in the City where she belongs," Micah said.

"You know how I hate a media scandal." Howard shot Micah a pointed look. "Whoever said 'there's no such thing as bad press' never worked in the theater. Not that your little film debut seems to have been hurt too badly, though I suppose that has more to do with Jackson Hayes and his devotees."

"Hannah's performance in *Bridget Jones' Musical* has been very well received. There have been rumors of a Drama Desk nomination," Micah added.

"There have?" That was news to her.

Micah's eyes widened, a silent signal to sit there and be silent—exactly the way Howard liked all his actresses.

"No one ever accused you of failing to capitalize on press interest," Howard said. "Ah, there you are, darling, at last." He took the latte from the waitress and set it on the table, not bothering to take a sip.

"So, the revival. I've heard *Chicago* is in the mix?" Micah asked, trying valiantly to steer the conversation back to the matter at hand.

"Why are you droning on about the revival?" Howard asked, his brows furrowing in an approximation of confusion. "We're not here to discuss Lincoln Center."

"We're not?"

Howard laughed. "Oh, I've missed your sense of humor. No, we're here to talk about Boston. The fall musical in concert at Symphony Hall, of course."

The mere mention of Boston had Hannah itching to check her phone again. How long had it been now? Eighteen hours and twenty-three minutes?

"We're doing *Little Women*," Howard continued. "Those New Englanders are so sentimental about the source material, though if you ask me, it's a complete waste of paper."

Micah glanced at Hannah. He knew Jo March was one of her dream roles—challenging and triumphant, a full range vocally and emotionally. Hell, to play Jo March she might even be willing to put up with Howard again and brave another visit to Boston.

Or at least she might have been before. Now, when she tried to picture taking the stage in Boston, all she could think about was the person who wouldn't be meeting her at the hotel after.

Eighteen hours and twenty-four minutes.

"We could be interested in *Little Women*," Micah answered for her.

The long rehearsals, the costume fittings where she was never quite small enough, the backhanded compliments from the choreographers about her "stamina"—was all that worth it? Her mind wandered to Amelia and the other kids at St. Anthony's High. Their rehearsal would be starting right about then. She wondered if Amelia had tried the new blocking they'd gone over before she left, and felt a pang of regret at missing their rehearsal that was far greater than her fear of missing out on any role.

"Of course you are! I don't see any other directors fighting for my seat at this table." Howard chortled as he lifted his latte. Before the drink had even passed his lips, he scoffed and set it back down. "That is not the right temperature at all. Where is our waitress?"

"Howard," Micah said, drawing Howard's gaze back to the table. "*Little Women*?"

The director turned to Hannah in a flutter of hands. "Yes, right. You, my darling, will make a perfect Marmee."

"Marmee?" Hannah asked, an incredulous laugh bursting forth.

"Hannah's too young to play Marmee," Micah protested.

"The wonders of stage makeup. And you'll need to drop at least ten pounds, of course."

Everything in Hannah's body tightened, readying itself for the inevitable internal spiral those words would usually set off…but she felt nothing. No panic at the idea of trying—and failing—to lose weight again, no sudden urge to purge all the carbs from her apartment and subsist on carrots and non-fat yogurt for the next week, no mental shopping list of every type of sour gummy candy compiling itself in her brain. Only the smallest flicker of embarrassment, a recoiling from this awful man and his casual cruelty as, for perhaps the first time, she realized his issues with her body said so much more about him than they ever had about her.

Howard took a sip of his latte, then grimaced, as though he'd forgotten about the unacceptable temperature at the same time as he'd discarded his sense of common decency. "The usual terms. Though, of course, we'll need to add a behavior clause to ensure there's no more unpleasantness with the press. Rehearsals begin in September." He stood with a flourish.

"That's it?" Hannah sputtered.

"Darling, I've done you a tremendous favor," he said, pressing his hand to his chest, his face twisted to show how affronted he was by her displeasure. "There's no need to formally audition for the part. It's yours. A few signatures and we'll be off to the races."

"Marmee," Hannah repeated. "The mother."

"Mothers and best friends are exactly in your wheelhouse," Howard said, as though it were some kind of grand compliment. "I'll have the paperwork sent over, but really, I must have your answer quickly. We have at least three other actresses interested in the part."

Doubtful.

This time, when Howard leaned in for his cheek kisses, Hannah didn't bother getting to her feet. She half listened as Micah said goodbye, discussed the timeline for making a decision and assured Howard they would give his offer its due consideration, but she didn't need to consider anything. If she'd needed confirmation it was time to move on, she'd just received it in the form of one of Broadway's most legendary assholes. She was no longer willing to make herself smaller—literally or figuratively—to fit someone else's ideal, not now that she knew what it was like to have people love her exactly the way she was.

"What do you think?" Micah asked when they were alone.

"I think I'm done." The words hung between them, but the longer she sat with it, the more she knew it was true.

"We'll tell Howard 'thanks, but no thanks,' and get you back on the audition circuit," Micah said, typing something into his phone. "I hear there are some interesting things slated for Papermill this year and I know you were hesitant about playing another witch, but there's a rumor *Into the Woods* is—"

"No, Micah. I'm done," she repeated. He looked up from his phone, confusion pressing his lips into a thin line. "Not only with Howard. With all of it."

"You can't let him get to you, Hannah."

"I'm not. I'm just…done. I've been thinking about it for a while, and I think—no, I know, this is it. It's time for me to close this chapter."

"You're a Broadway actress," Micah said, shaking his head. "You don't give all that up."

"I *was* a Broadway actress. And I've been miserable. Now I think I'd like to like to try just being Hannah for a while."

Chapter Thirty

Angie crossed the gravel parking lot and wrapped Ethan in a hug. "You're sure you can be seen with me? It won't sully your family name?"

"I deserved that," Ethan said as he gestured for her to go ahead of him into the vineyard.

"You deserve worse, but I suppose if I can forgive you for the time you threw a snowball at me and it was made entirely of ice, then I can forgive you for this."

"I was seven."

"And I forgave you." Angie stepped into the large open lobby and sighed deeply, her shoulders relaxing as her eyes scanned the space. "I haven't been here since we were kids."

"It hasn't changed much."

"By design, I'm sure."

Ethan invited her to take a seat in one of the oversized leather armchairs. "I owe you an apology."

She leaned back in the chair and crossed her legs, studying him with an amused expression. "Finally, we get to the good stuff. I love a good grovel."

"I've never been great at trusting people. At opening up. And after everything that happened when Stephanie got pregnant…

My therapist says I put too high of a value on other people's approval because I learned acceptance was conditional on my not fucking up, and when I did fuck up, it cost me my family."

"Your therapist, huh?" Angie smiled. "Glad to see you're finally exorcising those demons you've been carrying around."

Heat rose in Ethan's ears, but he shook it off. "The point is, all that stuff about you not coming to Reader Fest, about not letting this part of my life be associated with that part of my life, it had nothing to do with you or your books. That was all me and my shit."

"Oh, Ethan, please, I'm well aware," she chuckled.

"You should come to Reader Fest. I don't know if I'm ready to be there as Slade yet, but that shouldn't stop you from attending."

"Thank you. And don't think I won't be writing extra spicy dragon shifter scenes for you to narrate just to see you blush as pay back," she said, waggling a finger at the lingering redness in his cheeks. "But I know you didn't drag me all the way down to Rhode Island to apologize, so spit it out. What's on your mind?"

This time he couldn't shake off the embarrassment coloring his skin. "Another thing I've never been good at is asking for help."

She leaned forward, bracing her elbows on the knees of her tailored linen pants. "Now I'm intrigued."

Six weeks, three days, five hours, and twenty-seven minutes.

That's how long it had been since Ethan had last seen Hannah. Within minutes of letting her go, he'd known it was a mistake, that he would regret it for the rest of his life if he didn't fight like hell to get her back.

That the fight had begun without her knowledge in weekly therapy appointments and long, uncomfortable conversations with his parents and Tessa, well, that was something he hadn't anticipated.

He just hoped he hadn't waited too long.

Six weeks, three days, five hours, and twenty-eight minutes.

Hold on, city girl. I'm coming.

"Dad, are you listening?" Tessa asked.

"I heard you the first time. Who's the parent here, me or you?" he said, taking the pastry box she offered to him and setting it on the kitchen counter.

"Sorry we're late!" Gavin called as he and Kyla pushed through Ethan's front door.

Jamie swung Julie up onto his shoulders, the little girl's giggles floating through the kitchen. "You're fine. We're still waiting on Baz and Sabrina."

Ethan watched his friend and daughter dote on their child and his heart clenched in his chest for the millionth time since Hannah left, thinking of all the things he wanted with her, things he hoped she still wanted as well.

"We're here!" Sabrina appeared in the doorway followed by Baz. "Sorry, there was traffic getting back from my parents' house."

"I didn't know you were going to be at your parents' today. You didn't need to rush back for this," Ethan said.

"As if we were going to miss game night, or the chance to wish you good luck," Sabrina said.

"Best if our visits with the Pages are kept short anyway," Baz added.

"Are Jo and Molly coming?" Tessa asked.

Kyla shook her head. "Molly's got a bunch of papers to grade and Jo couldn't switch her shift at the bar. But," she turned to Ethan, "she said to tell you to 'go get your girl, foxy.'"

Ethan rolled his eyes.

"Still don't love that nickname," Tessa said with an exaggerated grimace.

"Caleb's got some church thing but he sends his best," Gavin said.

"Caleb's always got some church thing," Jamie added.

Gavin shrugged, reaching for one of the cupcakes Tessa brought. "That's what happens when you're a priest."

The house filled with laughter, everyone talking over each other, as they filled plates in the kitchen and took them into the living room to kick off board game night. It wasn't their usual night to gather, but Ethan wouldn't be there for their usual night this week, and the guys had insisted they not skip it altogether.

"What are we playing?" Ethan asked as he took his seat at the table in the corner of the living room.

"Trivial pursuit," Baz said reaching for the box.

"We have too many players," Ethan said.

"No, we don't." Kyla took Julie from Jamie's arms, tickling her under her chin. "I'm going to sit this one out. Julie and I have a date to take some pictures in the yard now that the flowers are blooming. The light right now is perfect."

Ethan watched as they left through the back door, Kyla's camera bag slung over one shoulder and Julie balanced on her hip, giggling all the way out the door. He had a good life, a house full of people who loved him, a thriving business. And he had never felt more alone.

"She looks good with a baby," Gavin mused. All eyes snapped to him. "What?"

"Are you two...trying?" Jamie asked.

"No, not exactly *trying*," Gavin hedged, lifting the lid off the game box. "Not exactly *not* trying."

Jamie whooped. Tessa squealed. Sabrina pressed her hands

to her lips. Ethan's stomach dipped, happiness and something a lot like envy swirling together.

"You two will have the cutest kid," Sabrina said.

"You can't tell her I said anything." Gavin set a stack of game cards down in front of Sabrina with a pointed look. "We haven't told Brodie yet."

Baz leaned back in his chair, slinging his arm around Sabrina's shoulders. "Brodie won't care."

"He might. It could be kind of weird for him to have a little brother or sister young enough to be his own kid," Gavin said.

"If he says anything, I'm sure your mother will knock some sense into him," Jamie said.

"He won't," Tessa insisted. "If Dad had another kid, I'd be happy he was happy."

Ethan's stomach somersaulted. "You would?"

"Yes, of course! Why is that so hard to believe?"

He could picture it—a little girl with big blue eyes and an upturned nose, a baby asleep on his chest, Hannah singing a lullaby, all the little moments he'd missed the first time around.

"Julie would be older than her uncle or aunt," Gavin said.

"Just one more way our family would be unique," Tessa said.

"For someone who married his son's ex, you're way too concerned about age," Baz said to Gavin.

Six weeks, three days, five hours, and forty-three minutes.

Ethan pushed back from the table. "I need some air."

He stumbled from the house onto the front porch, drawing in huge lungfuls of crisp spring air. He could see it all so clearly, the way things could be, the holes in his life even the best friends couldn't fill. His chest ached with longing, and he braced himself against the railing.

"Dad?"

"I'm okay," he said, forcing himself to breathe.

Tessa's hand fell on his forearm, squeezing lightly. "She's going to be so glad to see you, I know it."

"I hope you're right."

Chapter Thirty-One

Hannah scrolled past another lackluster job posting. It turned out finding a decent-paying theater teacher job was harder than she'd thought, especially since she was limited to private and parochial schools until she completed an alternative teacher certification program. Apparently her Broadway credits didn't override the minimum qualifications.

Of course, the posting for the perfect position had been forwarded to her two weeks ago. A decent salary, a beautiful location close enough to the City she could visit on weekends, and a friend already on the staff. But she couldn't apply for the job at St. Anthony's High School, not when Ethan hadn't even texted her in days…could she?

Ever since his first message, he'd taken to sending her photos every few days of things that reminded him of her—Terrence McFancyCock, the sunset over the vineyard, a tattered copy of an old school romance novel. She wanted to believe it meant something, but days at a time would pass without a new message and they still hadn't talked about what happened, or where they went from here.

As much as she missed him—and she did, so much that she felt like an actual part of her had been severed and left behind in Aster Bay—and as much as she loved him, she couldn't sit around and wait for him to decide to pull his head out of his ass.

And if he never gets his shit together?

She should give that part time job on Long Island another look. Or she could take her parents up on their offer to move back to Philadelphia, even if the idea of moving home at thirty-two made her sick to her stomach.

Her phone dinged with a new email and Hannah thumbed it open. The familiar header of AK Wild's newsletter filled her screen and she skimmed the email quickly. A surprise sneak peek at AK Wild's upcoming dragon shifter's romance audiobook available to newsletter subscribers only. Hannah's finger hovered over the download link, the name Slade Hardcastle seeming to dare her to do it.

As if there was ever a chance she wasn't going to listen.

She watched impatiently as the story downloaded, shoving her earbuds into her ears. She could go back to doomscrolling the job postings after she listened. The audio was only a few minutes long anyway.

"*The Dragon Duke* by AK Wild, narrated by Slade Hardcastle."

Ethan's voice filled her ears and she leaned back, sinking into the deep timbre of it. This was the only time she felt close to him lately, when she listened to one of his books. Someday, she told herself, she wouldn't need to listen to them anymore, wouldn't keep torturing herself with the reminder of the way his chest vibrated when he talked low like that or the memory of the heat in his eyes when he got all growly. Someday she'd move on.

But not today.

"*You will submit to me, mea dulcis, on your knees, on your back. Any way I desire you. Every way,*" Ethan rumbled through her earbuds. *"You will know what it is to be mated to the dragon duke, to surrender your body and heart to my keeping. And when you have done that, little one, oh how I shall reward you."*

There was a crackling in the audio, an almost imperceptible shift in the white noise, and then—

"Hi, city girl."

She sat bolt upright, looking around her apartment, but the words—in Ethan's own voice and not the British accent of Slade Hardcastle—had come from her earbuds.

"Two months ago, I recorded those words, and I had an idea. What if, like the dragon duke, I could convince you to surrender your body and heart to my keeping? How I would reward you," he groaned, the sound conjuring memories of his lips and hands on her skin.

Her breath caught in her chest, lungs burning, her nose stinging.

"But, like the dragon duke, I miscalculated. I didn't realize I would also be surrendering my heart to you. I have lent my voice to some of the greatest love stories, but I didn't know how to love you the way you deserved, how to stand in the storm without trying to stop it. For so long that is what I've been good at—putting up barriers, being in control. And this storm…it made me feel out of control like I never have before."

A tear slid down Hannah's cheek and she dashed it away, focused on the ragged exhale on the recording.

"It's no excuse for hurting you. You once said you wanted to know all the parts of me, even the messy, sordid parts. This is the messiest part, sweetheart, but it's a part of me you never should have had to know.

"Six weeks, two days, seven hours, and ten minutes ago I made the worst mistake of my life when I let you go. You gave me your heart and I didn't protect it, and I will regret it every day for as long as I live. I regretted it before the door even closed behind you. But I was so deep in the mess, I couldn't see a way out.

"I'm sorry, Hannah. I am so sorry for all the ways I've hurt you. For all the ways I let you down. I have spent the last six weeks cleaning up the mess and building a stronger foundation so the next time we are caught in a storm, I will know how to stand in it with you. If you'll let me."

Hannah got to her feet and ran to her bedroom, still listening as she tugged the suitcase out of her closet and began throwing things in. She had to go back. Her throat burned with all the things she needed to say to him, things she wanted to say in person.

In the living room, someone knocked on her door, but she didn't have time to tell another delivery driver he had the wrong apartment, not when she had a life to start.

The recording continued playing. "I promise, this time, I'll keep your heart safe. I'm sure I will make mistakes, but I promise I will never again run or give up or hide from you. Or from myself. I surrender my heart to your keeping, Hannah. I love you."

"I love you too," she said, as though he could hear her.

Another knock. "Hannah?"

She ripped the earbuds from her ears and then froze, listening.

Was that...?

"Hannah, please."

It was.

She tore through her apartment and flung open her front door. Ethan stood in her hallway, his hair a mess and his clothing rumpled. One corner of his mouth quirked up despite the sadness in his eyes. "Hey, city girl."

She flung herself at him, wrapping her arms around his neck and burying her face in his shoulder, breathing in the familiar scent of him as tears streamed down her cheeks.

"Hey, now, don't cry," he murmured, cradling her against him and pressing his lips to her hair. "Fuck, Hannah, I've missed you."

"I missed you," she choked out.

"I'm so sorry, sweetheart."

"I know. I got your message."

He slid a knuckle beneath her chin and tilted her face up towards him so she could see the brief happiness flash across his face before it was replaced by the tortured look in his eyes. "I meant every word. Please give me another chance. I know I don't deserve it but—"

She kissed him, her hands tangling in his shirt, as she pulled him closer. A groan rumbled in his throat as she deepened the kiss, licking into his mouth. When they broke apart, he dragged his lips over her cheekbones, settling on her temple.

"I love you," he said, the words deep and jagged, roughened by everything that came before.

"I love you." Some of the pain melted from his eyes, replaced by a fragile hope. She smoothed her thumb over the crease between his brows. "You're making your worried face."

He caught her wrist and pressed his lips to the sensitive skin on the inside. "How can you forgive me so easily?"

"Did you not want me to?"

He huffed out a laugh. "It's not that."

"Then what?"

He trailed his lips higher on her forearm. "I want to earn you."

She ran her fingers through his hair, her heart so full it hardly felt like she could keep it in her chest. "Haven't you learned yet? Love isn't something you earn—it's something you receive, something you do. Something you choose."

"I choose you. I should have chosen you every day before now, but I will choose you every day from now on."

"Even when things are chaotic?"

He snaked an arm around her waist, pulling her closer, hip to hip. "Even then. Always." He pressed his forehead to hers, their noses sliding against each other. "I choose you. I choose us."

"There's something I should tell you."

His shoulders tensed, and his eyes fell closed, but he nodded. "Tell me."

"I'm done with Broadway." His eyes flew open and he pulled back to look at her. "You told me I should choose myself. You were right."

"Are you okay?" he asked, his fingers stroking her spine.

Her whole body glowed with the possibilities in front of her. "I am. It was like I was wearing a weighted vest and didn't realize it, and when the vest finally came off, I felt…free."

"What will you do now?"

"I think I'd like to teach. And figure out what life looks like when my job doesn't dictate every part of it."

His lips grazed hers. "I'm so damn proud of you."

She grinned against his kiss. "I was thinking, maybe this new life looks a little less like Manhattan and a little more like Aster Bay."

"Oh, yeah?" He slid a hand into her hair, his mouth spreading into a grin that made his eyes crinkle at the corners. "You want to come home with me, sweetheart?"

From *The Lady's Knights* by AK Wild,
narrated by Slade Hardcastle

Their horse's hooves raced over the baked earth in the early morning mist, dirt kicking up behind them as they took their flight. Sir Llewellyn snapped the reins, urging the horse faster towards the horizon, his lady at his back, her arms around his waist and thighs bracketing his. The court would be scandalized to see Lady Windtorn riding astride, and with a knight of her husband's guard no less, but for once, Sir Llewellyn cared nothing of the scandal.

Beyond the horizon, the wide world waited for them, a ship in the harbor ready to take them overseas where she would not be lady of the keep and he would not be required to maintain his distance.

With one hand, he gripped her thigh, tugging her more snugly against him. Let there be no more distance between them.

"Almost there, my lady," he said, his gloved fingertips digging into the soft flesh beneath her layers of skirts.

"I am not a lady any longer, Sir. But I am yours."

Chapter Thirty-Two

Ethan steered his truck into the parking lot at the Rookery with one hand, his other clasped in Hannah's. "You ready for me to kick your butt again?" Hannah asked with a grin.

"It was one time," Ethan said, but he was too happy to even pretend to be annoyed.

"You don't think I can do it again?"

He put the truck in park and gripped Hannah's thigh, sliding her across the bench seat towards him. "I think you can do anything you want to."

She bit her lower lip to hide her grin, but his eyes tracked the movement, a hunger rising in him that should have been sated after the last day of holing up in her Manhattan apartment. In between packing, they'd made love in every room. They'd have to go back at some point to finish cleaning out her things before her lease was up in a few months, but for now, everything important to her had been stowed in suitcases and brought back to Aster Bay, her dresses hung back in his closet, her clothing beside his in the dresser, lotions and shampoos in the bathroom. Hannah was home. There was nothing that could ruin his mood, not even losing trivia.

She dragged her fingers up his forearm, over his bicep.

"Anything?"

A noise rumbled low in his chest and he caught her chin with his thumb and index finger, tipping her lips up to his. "Anything."

Their lips met in a heated kiss, her mouth parting for him. He twisted to pull her closer and his elbow collided with the steering wheel, the loud honk startling them both. She laughed and kissed him again, softer this time.

"Screw trivia," he purred. "Let's go home."

A loud banging on the side of the truck pulled them apart and Ethan turned to see Gavin through the driver's side window. "You're back!" Gavin exclaimed, throwing his hands in the air.

"Go away. We're busy," Ethan shouted through the closed window.

Hannah laughed. "Come on. It's time for me to defend my win."

"Hannah, good to see you again," Gavin said with a grin when they climbed out of the truck.

Tessa slammed into Hannah's side, nearly knocking her over as she wrapped her in a hug. "I knew it! I knew you two would work things out!"

Ethan caught Hannah's eye over Tessa's shoulder as the two women hugged. His whole body felt warm, his blood fizzy.

"You're back!" Kyla leapt at the tangle of limbs, joining in on the group hug. "Does this mean what I think it means?"

"That depends," Hannah said with a laugh. "What do you think it means?"

"That we get to keep you," Kyla said.

"Excuse me, I'm the one who gets to keep her," Ethan said.

"Nope. Sorry. She belongs to all of us now, just like we all belong to her," Kyla said.

"Lost your girl already? I thought you just got her back,"

Baz said, coming up behind Ethan, his arm wrapped around Sabrina's waist.

Tessa hooked her arm through Hannah's and the women began making their way towards the front door, Ethan and his friends following behind. "This is great. I'm so tired of losing every week to the grandma gang," Tessa said.

Inside the bar, they ordered their drinks and grabbed their usual table, crowding chairs around it so they could all fit. Sabrina settled on Baz's lap and reached for the specials menu. "I hope they have something deep fried and cheesy on special this week. I'm starving."

"Queso dip," Tessa said, stabbing the menu with her index finger.

"Don't eat that crap. They don't use real cheese," Jamie said. "I'll make you real queso dip."

"Sometimes you need the artificial stuff," Tessa said, giving him a peck on the cheek as he rolled his eyes.

"What do you think, Hannah?" Sabrina asked. "Queso or avocado eggrolls?"

Hannah snuggled closer to Ethan as he draped an arm over her shoulder and laced their fingers together. "I say we get both."

Jamie sighed. "Heathens."

"I've got a good feeling about tonight," Gavin said. "I think we're going to win this time."

"Correction, *we're* going to win," Tessa said, gesturing to the other women.

"Where's Caleb?" Jamie asked.

"He's been recruited to the dark side," Baz said, tilting his chin towards the table at the front of the room where the priest sat flanked by the grandma gang.

"Traitor," Gavin sputtered.

A woman in her early twenties approached their table, fishing a notepad out of the apron she wore tied around her waist. "What'll you have tonight, folks?"

"Queso," Tessa said.

"And avocado eggrolls," Hannah added.

"Oh, and some of those little buffalo chicken wonton things," Gavin added.

"You've got it." When the waitress looked up, she froze, almost as though she were seeing them for the first time. Her eyes locked on Ethan and widened, her eyebrows shooting up. "Oh my God, it's you."

Ethan glanced over his shoulder and looked around the table in confusion. "Me?"

"You're Slade Hardcastle," she breathed. Beside him, Hannah stiffened and turned slowly to look at him. He could feel his friends' eyes all swing in his direction, a tense hush falling over the table. His stomach flipped, but the waitress didn't notice the change her announcement had wrought. "I am such a fan. I've listened to all of your audiobooks."

"Thank you," he said slowly, as though testing the words. With the hand that wasn't wrapped around Hannah, he reached out to shake the waitress' hand. "I'm glad you've enjoyed the books."

"So much!" she squealed. She glanced around the table, as though suddenly realizing how still everyone else had become, and paled. "I'm sorry, I shouldn't have bothered you."

"No bother," Ethan said with a reassuring smile.

Hannah glanced between Ethan and the waitress. "Would you like an autograph?" she asked, gesturing towards the notepad still clutched in the woman's hands.

"That would be amazing!" she said, a look of relief washing over her.

Ethan accepted the notepad, but he paused with the pen hovering over the paper.

"You okay?" Hannah asked.

"Yeah. I'm great." A smile stole over his face as he scribbled a signature somewhat resembling his pseudonym and handed the notepad back to the waitress, feeling lighter.

"Thank you!" she said, clutching the notepad to her chest. "Your food will be right out." Then she scampered off into the kitchen.

Baz took a sip of his Scotch. "That was fucking weird."

"Dad, you're a celebrity," Tessa laughed.

"I see your lady friend has returned," Mrs. White said, appearing at the side of their table. "Welcome back, dear."

"Thanks, Mrs. White," Hannah said.

"It will be nice to have a challenge at these trivia nights again," Mrs. Kemp said as she joined them.

"Jesus Christ, they travel in packs," Baz muttered.

"What's that, Sebastian?" Mrs. Blumenthal asked.

"Nothing, Mrs. B," Baz intoned.

"Judy, did you leave Father West alone with Ruth?" Mrs. Blumenthal asked, an admonishment in her tone.

"I'm sure Caleb can handle himself," Mrs. Kemp said. "I wanted to say hello to Hannah." Then, turning to Hannah. "Hello!"

"Hello," Hannah laughed.

Ethan's heart was so full he thought his chest might burst, all those holes that had haunted him for years filling themselves in. He leaned over and pressed a kiss to Hannah's cheek.

"Hello to you too," she said, turning to him with a glimmer in her eyes.

Mrs. White smiled, shooting a knowing look at Ethan before turning back to Hannah. "I hope we'll see you at next month's book club. We'll be reading AK Wild's latest release."

Hannah grinned. "I wouldn't miss it."

After the grandma gang had left for their own table and the rest of the group had returned to bickering about whether or not avocados belonged in eggrolls, Hannah turned in Ethan's arms, sliding a hand onto his thigh, her fingernails scratching lightly over the denim. "Maybe you'll give me a private performance before it comes out," she said.

"I thought I already did." He caught her lips with his own, his fingers sliding into her hair and tipping her face up to his. Everything else fell away—the bar, his friends' bickering, all the complications and detours they'd taken along the way. All that mattered, all that was left, was Hannah and the endless possibilities in front of them.

"Get a room!" Jamie teased.

They pulled apart when Jamie lobbed a wadded up napkin at them and it hit the side of Ethan's head. Hannah smiled and Ethan couldn't help but kiss her again to taste her joy. "Welcome home, city girl."

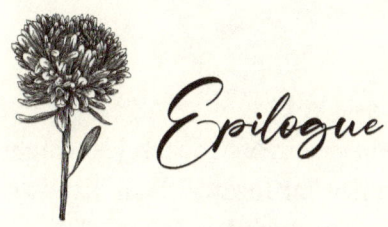

Epilogue

Seven months later, Christmas Eve

His tie was crooked.

Ethan frowned at the mirror and undid the knot for the third time.

"Do I look okay?" He turned to find Hannah in the hallway wearing an emerald green velvet dress that nipped in at the waist and swirled out below her knees. "I haven't been to a church service in years. I wasn't really sure what was appropriate."

"You look fucking incredible, like always," Ethan said, abandoning his efforts with his tie and stalking towards her.

"It's not too tight?" she asked, frowning and tugging at the skirt.

"It's perfect." He slid his hands over her waist and pulled her to him. "How long until we have to leave?"

"Twenty minutes or so. Why?"

He bent at the knees and lifted her over his shoulder before striding towards their bedroom. One heel slipped from her foot and clattered to the hardwood floor. "Ethan!" she squealed. "Put me down! You'll wrinkle it!"

"Then I guess we'll have to take it off," he said, pushing open their bedroom door.

"Everyone is waiting for us."

He set her down on the edge of their bed and dragged the zipper of her dress down. "We'll sneak in the back. No one will even notice we're missing."

"I don't think that's true."

"Used to do it all the time as a kid."

Then his hands were on the bare skin of her back. Her laughter turned breathless and his brain went fuzzy. Ethan's hands slid over the expanse of exposed skin unimpeded. "No bra?"

"I can't wear one with this dress."

"This is my new favorite dress," he said, sliding the sleeves off her shoulders and down her arms.

"You say that about all my dresses."

The dress fell away, leaving her in the cotton panties she favored. Her nipples were already pulled into tight furls and he cupped her breasts, running his thumbs over the stiff peaks. "How am I supposed to behave in church knowing you're bare under that dress?"

Her hand slid down his chest and she palmed his erection through the placket of his dress pants. "Maybe we can be a little late."

Ethan dropped to his knees at her feet and tugged the cotton panties down her legs as her hands ran through his hair. He dragged his hands up the back of her calves, over her knees, and pressed her thighs apart to make room for him between them. "What do you think, city girl? You want to go to Christmas Eve Mass with my cum inside you?"

He didn't wait for her to answer. Instead, he leaned forward and pressed his tongue to her core. She moaned and rocked against him, urging him on. If they had more time, he'd make her come a half dozen times before he gave her his cock, but she was right—everyone would be waiting for them. Still, he'd be damned if he didn't make her come at least once on his tongue before he fucked her.

It didn't take long for her to come apart for him, shivering and gasping his name. Christ, he'd never get used to the sound of his name on her lips when she was like this, soft and needy and so ready for him. He pulled back from her reluctantly, nipping at the sensitive skin on the inside of her thighs as he undid his belt.

"Later, we'll do this right," he promised as he stepped out of his pants.

"That wasn't doing it right?" she asked with a pleasure-drunk laugh.

Ethan strummed his thumb over her clit just to see her squirm and moan in response. He slid his free hand over her hip and across the soft round of her belly where she tangled her fingers with his. The sight of their joined hands over the place where she'd someday grow round and full with his child made his heart ache and his cock kick, eager to be inside her.

"Fuck, Hannah, look at you."

He lined the tip of his cock up with her entrance and filled her with one smooth stroke. They both groaned, the heat of her closing tightly around him. With their joined hands, he pressed on her belly as he pistoned in and out of her, and she moaned at the added pressure, arching her back and driving her hips up to meet him.

"You're so beautiful, sweetheart," he groaned, moving faster. "You take me so well."

He caught her knee with his free hand and lifted it higher, spreading her open wider so he could watch the slide of his thick cock in and out, the stretch of her around him, the way her body molded itself to his.

"I can't wait to marry you," he whispered, the words like a prayer as he stretched out his thumb to play with her clit. The way she whimpered in response nearly drove him out of his mind with need.

"You have to ask me first," she teased, her hips rising up to meet his thrusts.

He bit his lip to keep from saying more, and heat raced down his spine, urgent and unstoppable. "Where do you want my cum, sweetheart?"

She groaned. "Someone promised me I could go to church tonight with a pussy full."

"Fuck, you're perfect," he groaned. "You be a good girl and keep every drop inside, Han, and I'll fill you up again when we get home."

"Do it," she gasped.

He came with a roar, driving into her in an effort to get closer, deeper, as he came in endless ropes that stole his breath. When at last he was done, he dropped to his knees between her legs, using two fingers to shove his release back inside her. He flicked her clit with his tongue. "Give me one more, city girl. One more and then you can put back on your pretty dress and I'll take you to church."

She groaned, her pussy fluttering around his fingers as he worked her. He loved this part, watching her greedy pussy pull his release deeper, the contractions of her inner walls making sure she kept it all inside.

"Gonna put a baby in you one of these days, Hannah," he said, his voice ragged, wrecked by the idea of it.

"Then we better keep practicing," she panted, breaking off on a groan when he locked his lips around her clit and sucked in the long, rough pulls he knew never failed to make her orgasm.

This time, when she came, she arched off the bed, pressing her pussy against his mouth, covering his lips and beard with their mingled release. He worked her through it, not letting up until she collapsed back against the pillows, her moans turning to satisfied giggles.

"I love you," she said, dragging her fingers through his damp beard.

"I love you." He extended a hand to her. "Let's get cleaned up. We're already late."

The service was well underway by the time Ethan and Hannah arrived, but he had been right; no one noticed when they snuck in the back and took a seat in the last pew. Their friends were all seated towards the front with Caleb and Gavin's mom and Sabrina's aunt, but Ethan was grateful for another few minutes alone with Hannah. The ring his friends had helped him pick out was heavy in his jacket pocket. Waiting.

When the service ended and the congregation began filing out of the sanctuary, he and Hannah hung back. She was distracted, her eyes snagging somewhere off behind his shoulder.

"Everything alright?" he asked.

"Yeah, I just thought I saw..." She shook her head, moving her attention back to him. "Sorry, I think I'm imagining things."

"What is it?" he asked, turning in the direction she'd been looking, but all he saw was Caleb greeting the grandma gang, though he seemed distracted, too.

"No way," Hannah said. Then, waving a hand over her head, "Jackson!"

"Jackson?" Ethan pulled his focus away from Caleb, searching the crowd.

"Hannah Banana!" A moment later, Jackson barreled towards them, the parishioners parting for him as though he were Moses himself. He swept Hannah into a hug, twirling her around. "What are you doing here?"

"What are *you* doing here?" she asked when he set her down. "*I* live here."

"I know!" He clapped Ethan on the shoulder. "This place is fucking amazing."

"The church?" she asked, her brows knitting together in amused confusion.

"No, Aster Bay. We saw all the coverage of this place when the press was following you guys a while back and I told Becks we had to check it out."

"Beckett's here?" Hannah turned, searching for Jackson's twin brother.

"The whole band is here!" Jackson said, flinging his arms out to the side. "Well, not *here* here. It's only me and Becks and Mom *here* here. But the whole band's moving to AB, man. We bought out a whole cul de sac and everything. The houses will be ready when we get back from the first leg of the tour."

"You're the one building the new development by the beach?" Ethan asked.

"Midnight Storm," Jackson confirmed. "We needed a new place to settle down and write the next album. Can't reinvent yourself if you stay in the same old place."

"Jackson, we have to go." A tall man who looked strikingly similar to Jackson save for the abundance of colorful ink peeking out of the collar of his suit jacket appeared behind them.

"Becks, you remember Hannah Banana," Jackson said, "and this is her guy, Ethan."

"Merry Christmas," Beckett said with a tight smile, then, all business again, "Jackson, now."

Jackson rolled his eyes as his twin brother left. "Always so serious. But it was good to see you!" He pulled Hannah into another hug. "You guys should come to the show on New Year's Eve! We're kicking off the tour in Providence. I'll put your name on the list. Bring your friends!"

"Jackson!" Beckett barked.

And then they were alone again. "Midnight Storm is moving to Aster Bay," Hannah said, shaking her head and laughing in disbelief.

"Do you think the town's ready for them?" Ethan asked.

"I don't think they're ready for this town."

"There you guys are! We thought you didn't make it," Gavin said as he and Kyla made their way through the crowd.

"Was that Jackson Hayes?" Kyla asked.

"Yeah, it was," Hannah said.

"Hey, forget about him for a minute. What's up with your brother?" Ethan asked, tipping his chin towards Caleb.

The priest looked like he'd seen a ghost, his eyes dark and haunted and his hair disheveled as he distractedly made small talk with his congregants.

"I don't know. He's been weird all week," Gavin said.

"Leading a church during Christmas can't be easy," Kyla said. "I'm sure he's just tired."

"Come on. Everyone's heading to Lemon and Thyme. They'll be wondering where we are." Gavin gestured for them to put on their coats and follow him out the back of the church.

On the front steps of the church, the hum of parishioners wishing each other a merry Christmas behind them and the faint sound of Christmas carols on the winter air ahead of them, Ethan paused, pulling Hannah to the side. In the distance, the bay sparkled in the moonlight. "Let's walk for a bit," he said.

"You heard Gavin," Hannah said. "Everyone's waiting."

"They can wait a little longer."

He linked his hand with hers and led her down the stone steps of the imposing church and across the street to the Town Common. The streetlamps cast halos of light and illuminated the first few flakes of snow as they fell from the sky. At the center of the Common, the white gazebo was strung with Christmas lights and swags of greenery, red velvet bows dotting the railing in a festive display. Ethan led her to the small bench beneath the gazebo's shelter. She nestled against his side, hooking her arm through his and resting her head on his shoulder.

He wasn't sure why he was so nervous. They'd been living together for months, and they'd known each other for years. After so much public attention on their relationship in the beginning, he'd thought he'd never be happier than when they settled into the calmer routine of every day. But as the months had gone by, he realized he loved it all—not only the quiet nights at home and waking up with her each morning, but the book signings with Angie and the occasional red carpet in New York when her friends opened a new Broadway show. Every day was magic, because every day was with her.

"You're happy here, right?" he asked.

"Of course, I am. Why would you ask me that?"

"I want you to love it here as much as I do," he said. "This town is so much a part of me, of my family…"

"I know," she said. Her smile was like a lasso around his heart, tugging him towards her. "That's exactly why I love it here. Well, that and the milkshakes are amazing."

He chuckled, pressing a kiss to her temple. "And you don't regret leaving New York?"

"Not for a second." She paused, thoughtful. "Sometimes I miss performing, being part of a cast and putting on a show, but I never miss the business of it, and I love teaching at St. Anthony's. It was time for a new start."

"I used to think I was too old to start again. That I'd missed my shot at all this years ago. But with you…" He struggled to put into words the enormity of his feelings. "I want everything with you, Hannah. The good days and the hard ones."

"Every messy, sordid part," she said softly, the words they'd repeated to each other over the last few months like a mantra, a reminder of all they'd been through, that they were still in it together, always.

Ethan took in a shaky breath and got down on one knee at her feet. Her eyes widened and her lips parted as he reached inside his jacket pocket and produced the small velvet box.

"I want to marry you, Hannah, and have a family with you and build a life with you. I didn't know I could love someone the way I love you, or that someone could love me…" He opened the box to show the simple engagement ring he'd chosen, a thin gold band with an emerald cut diamond solitaire. "Marry me, city girl. Be my wife. Please."

Her eyes brimmed with tears and a small sob fell from her lips. "Yes, Ethan. Yes."

He gathered her into his arms, kissing her until neither of them could breathe. Ethan ran his thumb over the ring on her finger. He wasn't sure how people survived this much happiness, but there, on a bench in the center of town on Christmas Eve with the woman he loved, he made himself a promise to never take it for granted.

The End

Also by Cara Dion

Love Song Series
Irreplaceable

Indiscreet

Undeniable

Aster Bay Series
Whisking It All

Just For Show

First Comes Marriage

Claim to Fame

Visit my website to learn more and download free bonus content:

Author's Note

I have tried—and failed—to write a character like Hannah at least three times before to *Claim to Fame*: a woman in an average-sized body who has struggled with an eating disorder. (Fun fact: according to a study from the International Journal of Fashion Design, Technology and Education[1], the average size of an American woman is between a 16 and an 18.)

And each time before now, I have failed. My own struggles with eating disorder recovery have gotten in the way. It felt too vulnerable to put a character like Hannah on page, too revealing, and yet I still felt driven to do so. That Hannah ultimately ended up being a Broadway actress (my one-time dream job) who had to face the realities of living in a "larger" body in the entertainment industry was unplanned, but ultimately felt right.

Here's why[2]:

- Every 52 minutes, someone dies as a direct result of an eating disorder, making them the second most deadly psychiatric illness (the first most deadly is opiate addiction).
- 30 million Americans will have an eating disorder in their lifetime, but less than a third of them will ever receive treatment.

---

[1]   https://www.tandfonline.com/doi/abs/10.1080/17543266.2016.1214291
[2]   All statistics from the National Alliance for Eating Disorders and the National Eating Disorder Association as of the time of the writing of this book in May 2025

- Despite the fact that people with higher body weights are more than twice as likely to engage in disordered eating than those with a "normal" body weight (which, I'm sorry, can we just pause for the absurdity of the concept of a "normal" body weight for a moment?), these individuals are diagnosed with an eating disorder half as frequently. Only 6% of those with a diagnosed eating disorder are medically underweight.

I have struggled with an eating disorder for almost two decades. My official diagnosis, like Hannah's, was Eating Disorder Not Otherwise Specified (EDNOS). My research taught me that the EDNOS diagnosis was replaced by OSFED (Other Specified Feeding and Eating Disorder) with the DSM-5, but I chose to leave Hannah's diagnosis as EDNOS. I don't have any particularly compelling reason for this choice.

I wanted to put a character on page who struggled with their eating disorder, despite not fitting the typical image in people's mind of what that might look like. I wanted to show a woman who could find recovery, who prioritized her recovery, but who understood that recovery is not a linear or time-limited process. I wanted to show that a happily ever after is possible, no matter your struggles. I hope her journey will resonate for you.

This book is dedicated to Emily, the amazing dietitian behind my own recovery. While it truly takes a team to support someone recovering from this illness, and I am immensely thankful for each and every doctor, therapist, and other professional who has been a part of my team, Emily has always gone above and beyond. She was there for me when I wasn't ready for recovery, and she's been there for me every step of the way since. We all need an Emily in our corner, and I am forever grateful to have her in mine.

As I say in every book, I also need to thank my parents—mom and John, there are no words for all the ways I love and appreciate you. And to my husband and son, thank you for supporting me on this crazy journey.

I'm not sure I know how to write a book with Ginny Moore's insight and feedback, and I know for sure I never want to have to try. Thank you for being my first reader, for the constant insane text conversations, and for being my bookish bestie.

And to you, my amazing reader, thank you for going on this journey with me. I appreciate you more than you can know.

About the Author

Cara Dion writes steamy, contemporary romance, often with a forbidden or age gap relationship.

Cara has always had an overactive imagination and spent much of her teenage years watching 80s and 90s romcoms with her aunt. She read her first romance when a friend snuck one of their mother's Harlequins into their Catholic school and passed it around like contraband, but she didn't return to romancelandia until the pandemic.

She has been an English teacher, professional musician, and nonprofit administrator. When she's not reading or writing romance, Cara loves cooking, Broadway musicals, and all things Disney.

Cara lives in a small town in New England with her husband, son, and two very demanding cats.

Follow Cara on Instagram at caradion.author and contact her at cara@caradion.com. Visit the website and join Cara's newsletter to get insider information on upcoming books and exclusive content.

www.ingramcontent.com/pod-product-compliance
Lightning Source LLC
Chambersburg PA
CBHW020551120726
47903CB00001B/217